&

BLOOD

BOOK 2, DRAKKON KIN TRILOGY

NEW YORK TIMES BESTSELLING AUTHOR

KERI ARTHUR

Published by KA Publishing PTY LTD, PO Box 415, Shop 11/47-49 Sydney St Kilmore Vic Australia 3764

keriarthurauthor@gmail.com

Printed and bound by IngramSpark.

Australia: Ingram Content Group AU Pty Ltd, Melbourne, Victoria. US: Lightning Source LLC, La Vergne, Tennessee / Allentown, Pennsylvania / Jackson, Tennessee, United States. UK: Lightning Source UK Ltd, Milton Keynes, United Kingdom. Europe: Lightning Source UK Ltd, with facilities in Germany, France, and Spain.

The authorized representative in the European Economic Area is Lightning Source France, 1 Av. Johannes Gutenberg, 78310 Maurepas, France. compliance@lightningsource.fr

Cover Art by The Book Brander Boutique

Interior Art by Etheric Designs

Map by Sarah from Illustrated Page Design

Print ISBN: 978-1-923169-31-9

❀ Created with Vellum

With thanks to:

The Lulus
Indigo Chick Designs
The lovely ladies at Hot Tree Editing
Jason Nuhrung Editing Services
The ladies from Central Vic Writers
The Book Brander Boutique for the gorgeous cover
Interior Art in the paperback by Etheric Designs
Sarah from Illustrated Page Design for the exquisite map of
Arleeon and Mareritten in the paperback & hardcover

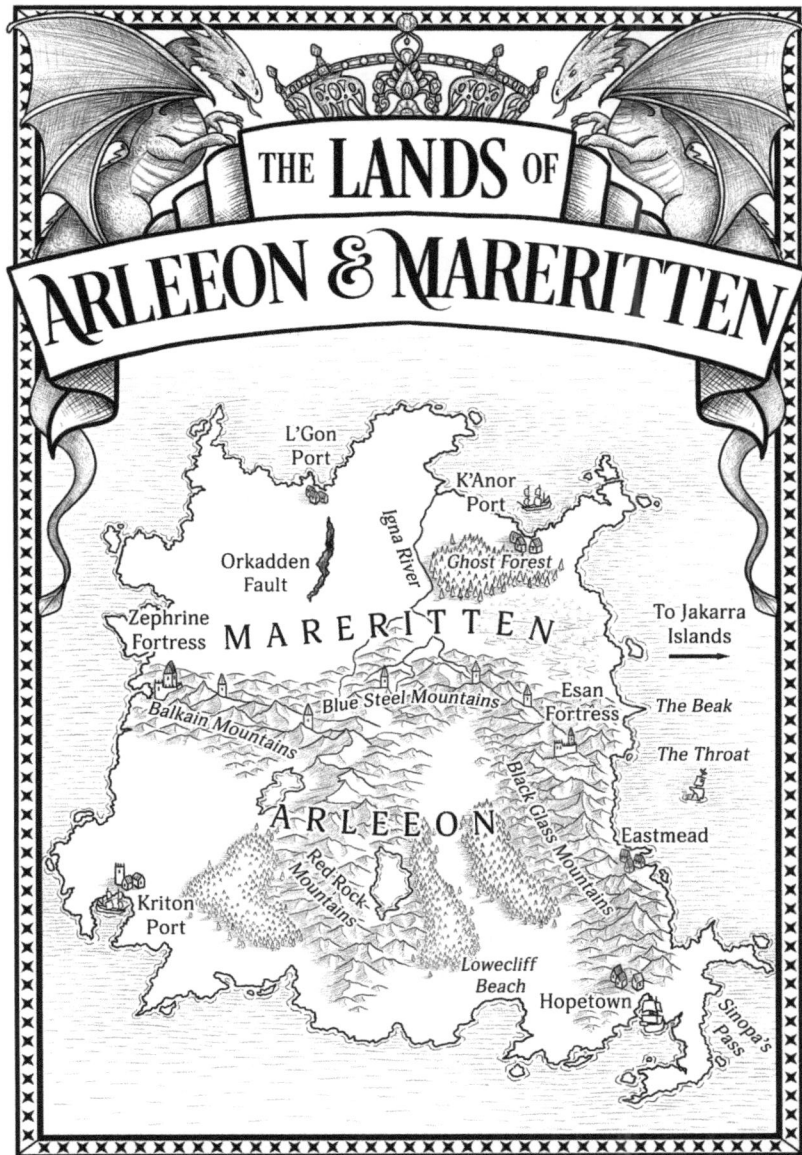

THE LANDS OF
ARLEEON & MARERITTEN

L'Gon Port

K'Anor Port

Igna River

Orkadden Fault

Ghost Forest

Zephrine Fortress

MARERITTEN

To Jakarra Islands

Balkain Mountains

Blue Steel Mountains

Esan Fortress

The Beak

The Throat

ARLEEON

Black Glass Mountains

Eastmead

Kriton Port

Red Rock Mountains

Lowecliff Beach

Hopetown

Sinopa's Pass

Riders & their drakkons

Bryn – Kaia (burnished gold drakkon. Queen.)

Kele – Yara (burnished gold drakkon. Queen)

Hannity – Rua (Red drakkon)

Miri – Lura (Red drakkon)

Halka – Kiko (Red drakkon)

Rayka – Aarvi (Red drakkon)

Jassy – Tartia (Bronzy gold drakkon)

Beth – Cansu (Red drakkon)

CHAPTER 1

WHEN I WAS A CHILD, I used to dream of riding Arleeon's mighty drakkons. Dreamed of soaring over her vast mountain ranges and golden plains upon drakkon back, the wind streaming my long hair behind me, the sun in my face and joy in my heart.

The reality was colder, wetter, and far more dangerous, especially on days when storms crowded the peaks, the wind was high, and any abrupt shift in direction by the drakkon underneath me could launch me from her back.

But there was no denying the joy and exhilaration that filled my heart, and it far exceeded those childish dreams.

Of course, the only reason they'd come true at all was through tragedy. As a nation, Arleeon had hunted the drakkons to near extinction and, even now, centuries after the ballistas had fallen silent, they remained wary of humans and rarely flew over highly populated areas. While I'd spent the last fifteen years doing all that I could do to learn about them, I'd done so from the dangerous heights of the Black Glass Mountains—the rugged and often deadly range that lined the far reaches of East Arleeon, and whose foothills were a three-hour ride from Esan, my home city and the fortresses that guarded the eastern gateway into Arleeon. Zephrine, our sister fortress, guarded the western gateway.

Kaia had, of course, featured prominently over those fifteen years, but it had taken a long time to gain her trust. It helped that I was a strega witch—a rather derogative term given to those of us gifted with magics of the mind rather than the more highly prized mastery over earth, air, or even healing. While the term had once umbrellaed abilities such as the creation or manipulation of fire, the movement of objects, and mind reading, these days it was generally only directed at those of us who could understand the thoughts of animals and control their actions.

I'd inherited the gift from my mother, but it remained something of a mystery where my ability to call forth fire had come from. There was nothing on my father's side of the family that suggested any sort of magical skill, be it strega or not, but then, he'd come from a long line of kings who'd valued practical skills and human ingenuity over magical abilities that were often limited by the strength of the practitioner. I wouldn't have been at all surprised if they'd actively worked on erasing any sort of magic or mind skill *out* of the line—it would certainly explain why a number of "spares" had inherited the throne over the heir in centuries past.

Kaia and I hadn't really conversed all that much over the decade and a half I'd watched her, but the few times we *had* allowed her to see I meant no harm to either her or her two drakklings.

That was the only reason she'd come to me in Esan, seeking help for her young, both of whom had been attacked by those we now referred to as the gilded riders—

armor-wearing warriors of unknown origin who rode huge birds with beaks of bronze, sharp metallic feathers they could launch with deadly force at their foe, and acidic dung that could burn through flesh, wood, and rock with equal ease.

They'd attacked the three drakkons with little warning, in what we now knew was one of several "minor" skirmishes meant to test what forces Arleeon could bring to bear against them. The little male had died by the time we'd gotten back to him, but I'd managed to patch up the larger female—in the drakkon world, females were always larger than the males—enough to allow her to fly again. Gria, along with Rua and Tane—the mated pair of red drakkons who'd come to our rescue when Kaia and I had been attacked by gilded riders on our way back from Jakarra—now resided in the abandoned aerie high above Esan.

In the three days that had passed since our dramatic return to Esan, Damon—the man tradition and treaty had forced me to marry—had raised barriers via blood magic to prevent anyone—aside from a few necessary exceptions—using the two external entry points into the aerie. The gilded mages were probably capable of breaking those protective spells, but it would take time and effort, and that would give *us* the time to retaliate.

Kaia banked right and swept over the grasslands. This area was sparse, skimming the foothills of the Black Glass Mountains for hundreds of miles before sweeping down to the sea and the port of Hopetown. It was mainly inhabited by herders, their semi-domesticated bovine, and wild long-horns, the latter being large, hairy ruminants with horns that stretched at least three feet on either side of their blunt heads. While they were by nature intractable, farmers had for centuries crossbred them with the much smaller bovine to produce an animal that could be used for multiple purposes—neutered bulls to pull carts and plowing equipment, and cows for their fat-rich milk.

The sheeting rain made it impossible to really see anything other than faint shadows on the ground below, and, even then, it was the flick of hunger that burned through Kaia's mind that told me those shadows were indeed longhorns rather than bovine.

Hairy ones sweet, came her thought. *Good to eat.*

Their meat is way too tough for me, I replied, amused.

My teeth sharper.

Sharp enough to bite a human in two with ease, in fact. Thankfully, drakkons apparently considered us poor eating, which was why, on the few occasions they *had* attacked human settlements, they generally just spat us back out. *How much farther have we got to go?*

Twenty sweeps past Ebrus's ashes.

Given I had no idea where the ashes of her young male currently were in relation to the grasslands I really couldn't see below us, that wasn't much help.

She arced to the left and began a descent, the four main phalanges on each wing shimmering like flame in the wet shadows of the day. At well over eighty feet long with a wingspan more than double that, she was big for a drakkon, and I doubted I would ever escape the awe that rose every time I sat astride her neck. Of course, part of that came from the fact she wasn't *just* a drakkon. She was a queen. *The* queen, the one they all obeyed, if you believed what she said —and, having witnessed the deference the two younger drakkons had given her, I certainly did.

The sharpness of our descent increased, and I instinctively tightened my grip on the spine directly in front of me even though a slip wouldn't actually send me falling to my death. When Kaia had consented to me riding on her back, I'd made a makeshift harness to help keep me attached. It was little more than a series of courser breast plates looped around her neck and simple U-shaped harness to anchor it —and me via the climber's harness I was wearing over my oilskin jacket—to one of her spines, meaning if I did slip, I'd at worst end up dangling via the ropes from her neck.

I'd asked the saddlers to come up with a better solution and given them both Kaia's and Rua's measurements, but I was well aware it was going to take time to construct something more serviceable.

Overhead, thunder rumbled, an ominous sign the storm was getting worse rather than better. Anyone with any sense would not have come out on a day such as this, but in many respects, its ferocity gave us the perfect cover, as the gilded birds appeared to avoid full daylight or indeed inclement weather. Of course, given how little we still knew about them, we had no real idea whether it was actually a restriction or a choice on their part.

Needing to find at least *some* answers was one of the reasons we'd come out here today. Kaia had torn a rider free from his bird when they'd attacked her and her drakklings and cast him to the ground. While we had no use for his body—we now knew what they looked like even if we had no idea where they came from—we desperately needed to know what common weapons could pierce the armor they wore. Hot enough flames could certainly melt both it and the feathers that protected the birds they rode, but fire-capable stregas were not plentiful here in Esan, and our effectiveness was restricted by just how long our physical strength held out. Weapons made of Ithican glass also worked, but then, there were very few substances in this world that it *couldn't* pierce. It, however, came with two major problems: one, only those of us tasked with scouting Mareritten for any sign of activity or armed build-up possessed such weapons and, even then, their scarcity meant they were shared between detachments. And two, it was impossible to use a sword or knife on drakkon back or indeed on foot against a winged foe simply because their use, by necessity, meant getting too close.

I did own both an Ithican knife and sword—my father had gifted them to me when I'd first gained my captain's pips—and Mom, who'd been weapons master on Jakarra before she'd married my father, had recently given me her bow and a quiver. Though it was far more useful against winged foe, of the dozen or so arrows she'd brought over, only nine now remained. And Jakarra, the one place we could have easily gotten more from, had all but been destroyed by the gilded riders and its people made refugees in their own lands.

My parents *had* reached out to Ithica with a request to purchase more of the "waste" shards the arrowheads were made of, but as yet, we'd had no reply. But even if they did come back with an affirmative tomorrow, the supplies would still take time to get here.

And I very much suspected time was the one thing we didn't have much of.

Kaia's flight straightened again, the very tips of her wings lightly brushing the tops of the wind-flattened grass stalks. Though we were flying low, we weren't intending to land. We simply wanted to know if the rider's body remained where she'd flung it, and more importantly, if the armor was intact or had been scavenged by one of the herders who called this place home.

If the armor *did* remain, then we'd swing back here and pick it up on our return to Esan.

Nearing, Kaia said.

I leaned sideways to get a view past her spines, and the wind hit me full force, the hail hiding within the rain slamming into my face and drawing blood. I swore and tugged the collar of an undershirt farther up in an effort to gain more protection.

Not bright move, Kaia said, her mental tones dry.

No, I agreed with a smile. *It was not.*

Perhaps need sleep not mating.

My smile grew. *But mating is fun.*

And however much I might not have wanted to marry Damon, the man was certainly made for fun. Our compatibility in the bedroom was the one bright spark in the sea of desolation and sadness that hit whenever I thought of my impending move to his home city, Zephrine. It wasn't only the fact that I would no longer be the captain of a scouting team—a position I loved—but also leaving my family, my friends, and, perhaps worst of all, the drakkons.

But I'd married Zephrine's heir. There was no other choice for me.

Body two sweeps away, she said.

I leaned out again, this time a little more prepared for the wind blast. Though we were close to the ground—or as close as a drakkon her size could be without actually landing—I wasn't seeing much.

Is the armor intact?

Instead of answering, she dipped slightly to one side, then tucked her wing back to give me a better view of the ground and the body that had obviously become a meal for the scavengers that roamed these plains. The armor was nowhere to be seen.

I swore softly, though in truth its absence was unsurprising. Gold was rare in our part of Arleeon, and though the armor wasn't actually made of that valuable metal, it certainly *appeared* to be. It would have been handy to have a full suit rather than the bits and pieces we'd managed to retrieve from the remains of the riders that had chased us into Esan, but it appeared the goddess of good fortune was not favoring us today.

Fly on? came Kaia's thought.

Yes. We still needed to check the rest of the coastline for new sentry points and then sweep past Hopetown to ensure our main fishing port was making the necessary preparations. My father had sent orders to anchor the fleet well out to sea and to prepare for attack, but there'd been obvious incredulousness in the initial missives we'd received back from them. That had definitely changed once the port's governing body had received the news of Jakarra's destruction, but I suspected they'd have a hard task convincing those within the city to evacuate. Especially given we had no idea if moving inland would be any safer.

Kaia did a lazy turn and then rose, heading once again for the forbidding sweep of mountains that were visible even in conditions such as this. The higher we got, the more intense the storm became, until it was constantly buffeting us sideways. She didn't seem to care—in fact, the happiness rumbling through her thoughts suggested she rather enjoyed the wind's fierce play across her wings and was making something of a game out of keeping us in the air and on track—but I was getting colder and wetter by the hour. I could of course ramp up the inner fires to keep the chill from my skin and dry out the increasing dampness of my clothes, but I was wary of doing too much in case we were once again spotted and chased. No matter how unlikely that might be in these conditions, Túxn did like throwing out challenges to those wishing good fortune rather than bad, and she'd certainly seemed intent on sending more than a few such challenges our way recently.

We followed the mountain's spine for who knew how many hours, but given the unhappy rumbling in my stomach, it had to be well after midday when we got the first inkling of trouble. It was little more than a flicker of red and gold in the dark heart of the expansive if barely visible sea far to our left, but it nevertheless had my pulse rate leaping.

In weather this bad, that fire had to be pretty fierce to be seen from this height.

Go check? Kaia asked.

I hesitated, my gaze scanning the sharp mountain shadows that pierced the swirling gray of the storm surrounding us, and caught site of a landmark the fleet—be they from Esan or Hopetown—used as a navigation marker in better weather. We were near the Sinopa Pass, the valley that split these far reaches, and whose long right "leg" ran down to the very edges of the sea, providing a sheltered harbor for Hopetown while protecting it from the worst of the winter storms that crossed the eastern seas. Which meant these boats were roughly at the midway point between Hopetown and Kinara, the only island on *this* side of Jakarra. We'd lost contact with all five islands when the gilded riders had swept in, and so far had only been able to reestablish it with Jakarra and Zergon—the latter being the smallest, and the closest to Jakarra—and only then because they were within easy reach of our cutters. Sending out galleons was pointless, because they did not have the speed to reach the islands within daylight hours, and that made them an ideal target for the riders who'd set up camp within the ruins of Illistin, Jakarra's capital. We were currently in the process of evacuating both those islands during the day, but with the cutters being the only practical option, it was a painfully slow process. Survivors on four of the five islands did at least have shelter in the form of volcanic caves that riddled their mountainous regions, though as far as I knew, this was the first time they'd ever been used as refuge against an attack rather than a tropical storm and tsunami.

If what burned out there in the sea *were* boats from Kinara, then either something truly bad had happened on the island to drive them out of the caverns, or they'd simply decided help wasn't going to get to them soon enough to ensure survival.

Yes, I replied eventually, *but keep high, in case it's a trap. No see gilded ones.*

Yeah, but would you, in this weather?

Not old, sight good. She sounded more than a little put out that I would think anything else.

A laugh escaped, though it was seriously muffled by the wet undershirt collar protecting the bulk of my face. I really needed a better solution to keeping my face warm and dry. *I never meant to imply you're an ancient one.*

Though in truth, she wasn't exactly young either and had at best only one breeding cycle left. Which still meant she'd likely be around long after I was dead, given how long drakkons lived.

She harrumphed, though amusement ran through the sound. *Flicker is fire. Smell.*

In this weather?

Nose good. Smell bad.

Any idea what burns?

Watercraft. Flesh. She paused. *Three.*

Three boats?

Yes.

I couldn't help hoping they belong to the gilded riders rather than the islanders, even if I knew that hope would turn out false. Which begged the question, why only three boats? Even with overcrowding, three boats would not have carried all those who'd lived on Kinara.

Unless, of course, they were simply carrying all that had survived....

But again, would they really risk their lives leaving in such a storm?

Similarly, it couldn't be a fishing fleet—aside from the fact the sheer height of the white caps dominating the seas below made casting nets impractical, the ferocity of the storm deepened the risk of waves swamping the boats.

But perhaps they had air mages aboard. Just because Jakarra had been bereft of their services didn't mean the other islands were.

Are all three on fire? I asked.

Two. One stands apart. She paused. *People in water.*

Túxn help them, I thought, though if they were in the water, then it was likely that Vahree—the god of death, and taker of souls—had already claimed them for his own.

Any sign of the gilded ones?

No.

Which didn't mean they weren't out here, of course, just that they were currently out of Kaia's sensory range. Something must have attacked these boats, though, and it wasn't likely to be pirates. Aside from the fact Esan's patrols normally kept them away, it made no practical sense for them to burn their prize.

So why were two of the boats on fire? When the gilded riders attacked us near the Throat of Huskain—the nigh on impassible mountain that dominated the northeastern edge of Arleeon—they'd used both the gilded birds' feathers to kill our mage and their acidic droppings to sink the boat. Fire had never been a feature of their attack.

Did that mean this was yet another weapon in their arsenal?

We'd find out soon enough.

Kaia tipped low enough for me to see without our presence being obvious and glided over the one boat that wasn't on fire. The tattered remains of the flag fluttering lightly from its mast told me these boats *were* from Kinara.

They'd hung thick nets over the starboard side of the boat and the people in the water—men, women, and, Túxn help us, children—were clambering up them, more than a few of them injured and burned. A thin strip of calm water connected that boat with the other two, while the storm's fierceness and the worst of the seas was being deflected away from them. Somewhere down in that chaos, there was at least one air witch, if not two, alive, giving those still aboard the burning vessels and those already in the sea a better chance of survival.

Of course, for many down there, it was already too late.

We had to help the survivors. Had to do something to get them and the remaining boat to safety. We couldn't simply leave their fate in the hands of a fickle goddess.

As the boats disappeared in our wake, Kaia swept around, the wind's ferocity easing as we flew with, rather than against, it. As we drew near once again, the mast on the closest boat gave way, falling with slow grace into the sea, shattering what remained of the port side in the process and dangerously tilting the entire boat. People ran to the starboard side in a futile effort to balance it, but most were washed away by the waves that swept in through the breach. The small bubble of calm that had surrounded that boat burst, and the sea surrounding claimed its prize, sinking the boat so swiftly it was there one minute, gone the next.

Nothing remained. Not debris, not survivors, not even steam rising from the now extinguished fires.

The bubble remained around the other two boats, but for how long? An air mage, however strong, could not battle the elements for hours on end, and these mages had obviously been doing so for at least five hours now, given where they currently were. It would take another four, if not more, for the remaining boat to reach Hopetown, especially given how overcrowded it was and how low it was now sitting in the water.

Which meant they would not reach safety before the gilded riders were aloft once more.

We swept past the burning boat and circled around again.

What do? Kaia asked.

That is a damn good question.

Help?

Yes, but how? It's not like you can carry them all, and towing isn't exactly practical, given the sheer weight of that boat and the fierceness of the storm.

What towing?

I sent a mental picture of her skimming the waves, ropes in her claws, hauling the vessel through the rough seas.

How far tow?

Hopetown. There's no safe port between here and there. Eastmead might once have been a possibility, but Eastmead had been erased.

She continued to circle as she contemplated my reply. *Could do, if air master helps.*

My heart began to race. *Are you sure?*

She did the mental equivalent of a shrug. *Can try. May fail.*

Then I need to get onto that first boat and arrange for

several ropes to be cast forward. It'd probably be easier for her to grab multiple ropes rather than just one, and if the saker sitting at the bow of the boat could haul in a pod of white fins—the largest fish to call these seas home—then it'd surely have the strength to withstand the forces a drakkon could bring to bear. Or at least it should for the few hours we needed it to hang on.

I fly low. You drop.

It was said in a blasé manner, as if leaping off her back and landing on the pitching, crowded deck would be the easiest thing in the world to do rather than one of the riskier things we'd tried in the short time we'd united against our common foe.

It's far too crowded for me to jump safely onto the deck of that boat. It's better if I aim for the water and swim to the nets everyone else is using. It also means you don't have to worry about clipping the mast with your wings or tail.

Not that careless.

Mistakes happen, I said, amused.

My mistakes meant.

I laughed and tugged the bow and sword from my shoulders. If I was going in the water, it was better to do so without anything that could hamper my movements. I clipped them to the rope leashed around her front spine, on the opposite side to the hooded quiver—a suggestion Mom had made, and one designed to keep the arrows in place if Kaia banked sharply or turned upside down—and my back-pack, which contained not only food and medical supplies, but also a scribe quill and tablet. Scribes—which used magic to pair one quill with another, meaning what one wrote on one tablet, the other copied onto its pair—were a recent development, but now used widely throughout the main-land and the islands simply because they weren't restricted by distance, though being deep underground *did* hamper effectiveness. Mom had started insisting I carry one whenever I went aloft with Kaia, and given the number of times misfortune had chased our tails over recent days, it certainly made sense.

Fly straight up once I jump, I said to Kaia. *There's an old harpoon saker aboard that boat and one of the men down there might be fast enough to fire it at you.*

What saker?

I hesitated. *It's similar to a ballista, but the bolts are smaller and have a multi-pronged head designed to lodge into flesh.*

Of course, drakkon scale was far tougher to penetrate than white fin, but that didn't mean it couldn't cause her harm.

They fire, you burn. There was a hint of anger in that snapped command. She might have been very young when the ballistas had been in action, but she obviously hadn't forgotten the damage they'd done.

I'll try.

Not try, do.

And that, right there, was my queen speaking. With another grin, I unlocked my harness from the front ropes and kicked my feet out of the stirrups. *Let's get this done.*

She didn't reply. She simply tucked in her wings and dropped. The force of our descent flung me back, and a gasp escaped my lips, the sound torn away by the rain and the wind whipping past.

Her chuckle ran through the back of my thoughts but before I could say anything, she banked sharply and said, *Jump.*

I scrambled to my feet and leapt high, not forward but back, over her wing and past her hind legs and tail as she shifted position and rose vertically. Then I was dropping fast toward the unnaturally calm sea. After checking I was in no danger of landing on anyone, I crossed my legs at the ankles and held them tightly together in an effort to avoid them being forced apart by the impact. Then, after clutching my right elbow tightly with my left hand and holding it close to my chest, I used my right hand to cover my mouth and pinch my nose tightly closed—all the things the yearly evacuation drills Esan's sailors were taught as a matter of course, and everything I'd forgotten to do the one time I *had* been caught in a sinking boat. Of course, I also hadn't really had time to think about protocols—I'd been too busy trying to free myself from the chunk of wood dragging me ever deeper into the black depths.

But *that* experience had taught me just how damn cold the water would be, and the last thing I needed was to be instinctively sucking in a breath that was nothing but sea.

Shouts filled the air, drawing my gaze to the boat. They'd seen me. What they thought about my sudden appearance I'd uncover soon enough.

I hit the water feet first and plunged deep. Shock rippled through me, and a gasp rolled up my throat, but I fought the urge to release it or suck in air and started kicking toward the surface I really couldn't see, guided by instinct and the occasional bubble that drifted past my face.

When I broke the surface, I quickly spun around, looking for the boat. Saw the now listing remains of the second boat and the half dozen people in the water between it and the sole remaining one. It was a good one hundred feet away from where I was bobbing, and while I was no swimmer, even I could make that distance easily enough.

I kicked toward it and then reached out to Kaia. *You there?*

Where else be? No sweet water beasts here to tempt.

And thank goodness for that. While white fins didn't actively hunt humans, there was a lot of blood and plenty of bodies in the water, and even if it didn't attract their attention, it would eventually attract other predators.

I reached the net hanging over the side of the boat about the same time as the last of the six refugees from the burning boat and clambered up, my wet gloves protecting my hands from the rope's salty harshness. Two people helped me over the gunwale then stepped back, letting me flop in an untidy, shivering heap to the deck. I ramped up my inner fires to chase away the chill then pushed upright. The soft murmur that ran around me was filled with suspicion and confusion, but none of them moved or even spoke to me.

Behind us, the second boat made a sound not unlike that of a dying beast, then split in two and sank beneath the waves.

The sea between us became rougher, but the bubble protecting this boat from the worst of the storm remained, meaning the air witch was on here somewhere.

"Out of my way, all of you," came a gruff voice from the back of the crowd surrounding me. They obeyed as well as they could, given the overcrowding, and a big, bald man with a wiry red beard long enough to be plaited appeared. Though I didn't recognize him, the ink decorating his bare arms said he was the captain of this vessel. "Who are you, and why the fuck are you dropping out the sky and the storm like that?"

"I'm Captain Bryn Silva, and I'm here to offer assistance getting your boat back to Hopetown."

He scanned me for a second, his expression wary—and really, who could blame him for that? "How? It's not like you came on another boat—we would have seen it if you had. We've barrelmen in the nest."

My gaze shot upwards. There were two men stationed in the crow's nest with long viewers held to their eyes. These were longer than ones we sometimes used on scouting missions, so didn't have such a limited range but did take longer to actually focus—the one factor that made them a little dangerous for us to rely on in tight situations needing a fast response. For watercraft, however, they were ideal. The two men also stood back to back—a clever means of covering the entire three-sixty-degree spectrum while avoiding the need to move or turn too far.

"I'll explain later, Captain, but right now, I need to speak to your air witch, and I need you to attach the strongest net you have to that old harpoon and ensure the brakes on your saker are in good working order."

"I'll not be doing anything—"

"Captain, we haven't got time to debate this." My tone was cold and authoritative—one I rarely used but had definitely learned from all the years of watching my father deal with those who procrastinated on decisions. "We need to get underway now, before the things that attacked you come back. And they *will* come back, probably at dusk."

He scowled but nevertheless made a quick motion for me to follow him. The crowd surrounding us parted again, though with the vessel so crowded it was hard to move with any sort of speed. The air was thick with the scent of burned flesh and despair, and filled with the sound of crying, both children and not, and the soft murmurings of those trying to comfort them all.

We reached the forecastle and quickly moved up the steps. There were perhaps a dozen people up here, and one man stood out—he was tall, thin, with silvery-gray hair that streamed behind him, caught in the stream of power that whirled lightly around his body.

The air mage.

The captain stopped to one side of him. I stopped just behind the captain, my gaze scanning the mage. His skin was pale, almost gray, his cheeks sunken, and his lips held a faint hint of blue—all telltale signs he was pushing his limits.

"What is it, Captain? I'm a little too busy for chitchat."

The mage's voice was at odds with the brusqueness of his words, his tone whispery and gentle. A summer breeze rather than a raging storm, I thought.

"We've a woman here insisting on talking to you—"

"Yeah, well, tell her to—"

I stepped forward with a quick, "Ah, no, I won't, because we both know your strength will give out within an hour—at best two—now that you stand alone, and you're not going to get this ship and these people anywhere near Hopetown in that time."

He glanced at me. His eyes were silver and shone like the stars. "And you have a plan to fix this matter?"

"I do. In fact, I have a drakkon, and she will, with your help calming the seas directly in front of us, tow this boat to safety."

"A *drakkon*?" the captain and the mage said in unison, and then the captain added, "Has the drop into the sea addled your brains, woman?"

I mentally reached out to Kaia and then pointed a finger upward. Kaia skimmed past us, her burnished gold scales gleaming like fire in the storm's hazy light. "The queen has decided to aid us against a common foe. And I will remind you, Captain, that I am the daughter of your king, and you *will* treat me with the deference that deserves."

His gaze widened. He honestly hadn't realized who I was. "I'm sorry—"

"Captain," I cut in, "please arrange for two of your strongest ropes to be attached to that harpoon and then use multiple others to anchor the saker down so it's not torn out of the deck the minute she starts towing us."

"It's not going to be torn free—it handles white fin, so it can handle a drakkon."

He obviously hadn't taken in her full size. Or maybe he'd simply never seen a drakkon in flight and had never witnessed the sheer power and speed their wings could generate.

"Humor me, Captain, and just do it anyway. We'll shoot the harpoon directly in front of us, and Kaia will swoop down, catch the ropes, and tow us."

"With me easing the weight of the boat by calming the seas and the force of the wind around us," the mage said.

I nodded.

He glanced up as Kaia disappeared back into the clouds. "And you can really control that drakkon?"

"I don't control her. I ask her to do things, and she may or may not oblige. She *has* consented to doing this."

"Why?"

"Because the gilded riders—the people who destroyed Jakarra and, I presume, Kinara, given your presence here—killed one of her drakklings. She wants revenge, she wants them all dead, and helping us is one way to achieve that."

He studied me for a minute, then his gaze shifted to the captain. "We'd better try this, Grant. At the very least, it saves me the effort of pushing the boat forward while maintaining the bubble."

The captain sniffed, a sound that suggested deep disagreement, but he nevertheless turned and began shouting orders. In very little time, two heavy ropes were attached to the harpoon—which was as thick as my fist—while several others lashed the saker to gunwale cleats on either side of the boat.

"What next?" the captain said. "We just shoot the harpoon out across the sea and hope your drakkon has good enough timing to catch the thing?"

"Timing won't be a problem if your men do their job properly."

Him annoying, Kaia said. *Should toss in water.*

He's just lost two boats and escaped Túxn only knows what catastrophe on the island. We can cut him a little slack.

No cut slack. No like.

Neither did I, to be honest, although on the scale of unpleasantness, he was a lightweight—especially compared to my father-in-law. *Stay up until the harpoon shoots past, just in case their aim is off, and then grab the ropes.*

Will.

I returned my attention to the air mage. "When Kaia has the ropes, flow all your protections forward. The calmer the seas and the air, the easier it'll be for her to tow."

When he nodded, I said to the captain, "Do it."

The captain turned and made a sharp downward motion. The winches were immediately employed to draw back the firing mechanism's twisted cords. Once they were locked into position, the harpoon was added and the saker aimed. The man at the release point glanced at the captain, who gave the final go-ahead.

The harpoon was released and shot like an arrow over the prow, the two ropes unspooling behind it. It travelled straight and true for several hundred yards before it began to lose speed and trajectory, and it was at that point Kaia swept in and caught the ropes.

"Everyone hang on," I shouted and grabbed at one of the ropes lashing the saker to a gunwale cleat.

The ropes between us and Kaia snapped taut, and her grunt of effort ran through our link a heartbeat before the boat lurched after her. The sudden shift forward sent me stumbling, and I would have fallen had I not been holding on. At least six or more people on this upper deck hadn't been quick enough to heed my warning and were now lying in an ungainly heap on the deck. The captain wasn't one of them, and there was a part of me that was rather sad about that. I daresay there'd been falls on the main deck, too, but they were so tightly packed together that, from where I was standing, it was hard to see anything more than a mass of confused and frightened faces.

The air streamed past my back, catching my long wet plait and tossing it forward. The air mage—who hadn't fallen, despite the fact he wasn't holding on to anything—had redefined the limits of his air bubble and was now casting it forward to form a large expanse of calm out the front of the boat. It was also far out enough to encase Kaia, allowing her to fly in air unaffected by the weight and fierceness of the storm that chased the boat's stern.

The boat lurched again as the rope slipped between her claws. A grumbly sound of annoyance filled our link, then she removed one clawed foot from the ropes and grabbed the dangling harpoon. It was long enough to hold crossways in both claws, so she released her grip on the ropes and used the harpoon instead.

The boat lurched forward a third time as she snapped her wings down hard to get the boat moving again, then, as she found her rhythm, it began to cut through the glassy seas more evenly.

"Is that harpoon going to hold up against the stresses being put on it?" I asked.

The captain's expression was an interesting mix of disbelief and awe. "It should. Like the saker, it was designed to hold double the weight of any white fin we caught."

I'd have thought this boat, with all the people aboard, would have weighed far more than a couple of white fins, but the captain obviously knew his boat and the fish he hunted far better than me.

I watched Kaia for a couple of minutes, marveling at her sheer beauty and grace, then said, "Tell me, Captain, what happened in the caves? What forced the decision to evacuate everyone except fighting-age males?"

He grimaced. "We could see the smoke coming from Illistin and knew she'd come under some kind of attack. We immediately shifted the boats to a concealed harbor on the far side of the island and stocked the caves as best we could, but those winged bastards still caught us before the full retreat could be completed."

Meaning, no doubt, that just like at Illistin—Jakarra's main settlement—her fighting force had held the line as best they could while the retreat continued. And, just like at Illistin, they'd most likely paid the ultimate price. I frowned. "Didn't you receive the missive from my father warning of the attack on Eastmead and the possibility of an ongoing threat to all five islands?"

"Not as far as I'm aware, but then, I am but a sea captain and not privy to security information."

"But you've scribe quills on this boat, have you not?"

They might not have been able to use scribes in the mountain caverns, but if they'd docked these boats in a safe harbor, they should have been able to contact Esan about their plight when they were boarding everyone. We might not have been able to send help, but we could have at least warned Hopetown to get ready for evacuees.

"No," he said. "What point are they in a fishing vessel such as this?"

"But if you sink—"

"If sea or storm sinks us, despite the service of our mages, there is little point in scribing for help. Rescue would never reach us in time."

All of which was likely true, but it never stopped us sending our fleet out with tracking stones *and* scribe pens. "But surely given you were evacuating the young and the old—"

"I don't question my orders, Captain Silva. I just do."

Amusement teased my lips. Questioning orders was something I wasn't afraid to do, especially when I could see no sense in them. But that was my father's blood coming out in me. "What of Jacklyn's fate? She's the new governor there, is she not?"

"She's the one who ordered the evac. A stock take revealed we simply didn't have the necessary supplies for a long stay, and when the winged bastards attacked the entrance, we thought it best to get the noncombatants out of there."

"Then Jacklyn's here somewhere?"

"Of course not. She stayed with those who are fight capable." He glanced at me. "Why didn't Esan send boats our way? Given you obviously knew about the attack on Jakarra, why were we forced to risk evacuation without the help of the galleons?"

"The galleons, even when fully manned by air mages, would be too slow to reach any form of safety by the time the winged riders come back out. Until we find a means of countering their weapons, it's too risky using them for longer sea journeys." I paused. "Why were those two other ships on fire?"

He grimaced. "The riders sent some sort of brown fiery liquid streaming our way. It hit the wooden decks and spread like wildfire. This boat survived because we were the farthest away, and that gave Sam here time to create a wind shield and blast both them and their streams of fire away from us."

We were well aware that the liquified form of their gilded birds' shit was not only acidic but also explosive—Damon and I had barely escaped such an explosion in one of the caverns that littered the blue vein tunnels above Esan—but the news that they could deliberately use it as what amounted to a fire stream definitely wasn't good news.

"Is that why your sails were down? As a precaution?"

"Yes. As I said, we were far enough away from the other two to react proactively."

Someone shouted his name; he turned, then gave me a nod and left to attend whatever problem had arisen. I ducked under the rope anchoring the saker and stood beside Sam. I didn't say anything. I simply crossed my arms and watched Kaia pull us through the still seas for the next few hours.

By the time we neared the heads—which were basically the "foot and toes" section of the Sinopa Pass's longer leg—the storm beyond our bubble had eased dramatically, and the seas had calmed. We weren't all that far away from Hopetown now, which was a damn good thing given the weariness that filled the link between me and Kaia. Sam was almost skeletal, and I suspected the only reason he was still standing was the constant supply of greenish goop he was drinking every half hour or so. It reminded me somewhat of the stamina potion Maree—Esan's chief sickness "diviner," and an herbalist who was second to none—had given to both me and Damon to not only stave off sleep but to ensure we had the strength to finally consummate our marriage in a satisfactory manner—satisfactory, in her terms, meaning over many hours.

The potion had definitely worked as advertised.

As the shadows of the night closed in, faint wisps of pink stained the distant horizon, lending a warm glow to otherwise stark foothills that lined the shores. In the sky above, I caught the faintest glimmer of red and wondered if drakkons hunted high.

Are, came Kaia's weary thought.

Maybe you should join them, I said.

Will. You?

Can hunker down the night in Hopetown.

Safe?

As long as the gilded riders don't attack, it should be.

From behind us came a sharp tearing sound. I spun and saw one of the ropes Kaia was using to pull the boat snap past the prow on the starboard side, taking out the saker's right arm and two men on the way through. But it wasn't only the rope that had snapped—the planks around the saker's base were now cracking and lifting. The ropes leashing it to the gunwale cleats continued to hold it in place, but if the strengthened planks under the saker's base were beginning to give, the gunwale surely couldn't be far behind.

The captain shouted orders for more ropes but even as men ran to obey, the cleats on both sides shattered and the ropes tore free; the saker catapulted forward, past the prow and into the water, bouncing across the glassy smoothness like a rock being skipped.

Release? came Kaia's thought.

Yes. Go grab something to eat, but be careful, and remember to find somewhere to roost before the night truly sets in.

Need no more help?

If Sam can get us past the heads, we can signal for help from the port if necessary.

Call if need.

I sent an affirmative, and she released the harpoon and spun away from the boat, flying toward the ominous foothills and the drakkons who flew there. It almost felt like a vital part of myself was leaving with her.

I shook the thought away and turned. The captain was ordering the sails to be raised, a hard task when the deck was so crowded. Unlike many of Esan's fleet, these smaller fishing boats didn't have the option of oarsmen for the few times the air mage's strength gave out. I watched as the thick canvas was slowly hauled up the mast; if Sam's energy held, then he could release the overall bubble and simply push the wind into the sails and guide us forward. If it failed, there was enough of the storm left to catch them. Either way, we wouldn't end up on the rocks, which might have been a possibility had the saker given out earlier. Neither Kaia's nor Sam's strength would have held out had we been forced to battle the storm's full force earlier.

Once the sails were set, Sam did release the bubble protecting the boat and pushed the wind into the sails instead. As they bloomed, the helmsman spun the boat away from the shore, and we tacked with speed around the remains of Sinopa's toes and into the wider, calmer waters of the bay.

The minute we docked, Sam collapsed.

What followed was several long and tedious hours of officialdom—ensuring all those on the boat were taken to either appropriate accommodation or for medical attention, then meeting with Hopetown's council of six, not only reporting to them but getting updates on their preparations for the eventual attack. The latter had not progressed as far as they'd claimed in their missives to us, but I think the captain's story and the horror of seeing so many refugees in such a bad state finally made them understand the true gravity of their situation.

"Are you staying in Hopetown until your escort arrives from Esan, Princess Silva, or do you wish a mount?" Veretti Ghan asked. She was one of two women on the council and had obviously spent many a year at sea. Her skin had that weatherbeaten, heavily tanned look of an old sea salt.

"I'm here as a Captain of the Guard, not a princess, so there will be no one coming to fetch me." Though there was definitely a part of me wishing Damon was, if only because I missed his touch. Missed *him*. And who'd have thought I'd even be thinking such a thing only a few days ago. "If you could arrange for a mount to be ready at five in the morn, that would be appreciated. And a bed for the night, of course, and perhaps the loan of a scribe pen so I can contact my father."

Mine remained lashed onto Kaia, along with all my weapons and spare clothing. The pack also held my tracking stone, which no doubt was sending some confusing signals home while Kaia hunted.

"Of course." She made a flicking motion with her fingers, and the man stationed at the door nodded and slipped away, no doubt to make all the necessary arrangements. "And your drakkon?"

"Hunting in the hills far away from here."

She nodded but I could see the curiosity in her—and indeed, all of their—expression. A drakkon helping humankind was not something any of us had thought we'd see. But they didn't ask any more questions about her or my relationship with her. Perhaps they were afraid to. Or perhaps they simply thought both I and the captain were caught in some sort of joint delusion and were merely humoring us until a healer was free to examine our mental facilities.

I rose. "And my room is where?"

"Regus?" she said. "Please escort our royal captain to her room."

A stout bald man stepped forward and, with a brisk, "This way, please," opened the door and walked out.

I started to follow, then paused and half turned. "Councilor Ghan, could you also arrange a light breakfast to be brought in for four-thirty?"

She nodded. I thanked her and continued after Regus. The hubbub of raised voices that immediately started once the door closed behind us suggested there was some serious debate happening about me, and perhaps more importantly, Kaia, in that room now that I was no longer present.

Which was good. The more people saw drakkons as a help rather than a hindrance, the more likely it was that people would stop trying to kill them.

We moved at a good clip through the myriad of corridors lined with windows that faced the harbor. Lights danced across the water below us, the reflections coming from the multiple buildings lining the port as well as the hazard lights flickering at the ends of the five docks. I'd suggested a blackout starting immediately, but obviously the word was taking time to get out. Perhaps said order needed to come from my father before they'd put any haste into it. Or perhaps the slow reaction was simply a result of my insistence I be treated as a regular captain rather than the only child of Esan's king.

Still, I couldn't help but wonder what sort of fire needed to be set under their butts to get them moving. If this port came under attack and suffered the same disaster as the islands, then those same councilors would be held responsible. I knew my father well enough to be sure of that.

If said councilors survived, that was. Hopetown did not have the option of volcanic caves to retreat to. None that were close, anyway.

My insistence that I be treated as a captain wasn't reflected in the nature of my accommodations, and I really couldn't be sad about that. The room was housed within a curving wing of the main administration building rather than the military section, and it was generously sized, with a sleeping platform covered with an extra-thick mattress and several warm blankets, and a large bath—the latter of which I desperately needed.

I could smell me, and it wasn't pleasant.

There was also a seating area near the tall windows that faced the harbor, consisting of two well-padded sofas and a small table, the latter holding a generous tray of meats, cheeses, and breads. My stomach rumbled a loud reminder that it hadn't eaten since breakfast, but it was the steaming pot of shamoke—a bitter brown bean that was mixed with cane crystals to make a pleasant hot beverage—that caught my interest. I not only loved the stuff, I was addicted to it—as anyone who'd seen me in a shamoke-deprived state would readily testify.

Beside it was a scribe pen and its tablet. The council obviously could work with some speed when they wanted to.

I hurried over and poured myself a cup of shamoke,

inhaling its strong and earthy scent for several seconds before taking a drink. And sighed in sheer and utter pleasure. After a few more sips, I picked up the quill and began to write. While I had no doubt the council would make a report to my father, he'd be wanting a direct report from me; he'd also want an explanation as to why the tracking stone still showed me aloft when I clearly wasn't.

I scribed everything that had happened, from the armor's disappearance to the wonderful news that the liquid shit could be set alight and used as a flaming spray. Then, munching on the meat, cheese, and bread, I waited for a reply, watching the blinking dot sitting in the middle of the screen that indicated its pair remained active.

It came through after what seemed an agonizingly long time, though in truth was probably little more than a few minutes. He'd no doubt first relayed my comments to my mother and whoever else was in the war room with him.

I'll task Hopetown's council with sending cutters out to Kinara with supplies and scribe pens. With the aid of air mages, they have a far better chance of reaching that sheltered harbor before we could, and certainly before the gilded riders become a threat. What of Hopetown itself? Are the preparations coming along satisfactorily?

No, though they may well hasten after the influx of refugees. You need to order a blackout. I suggested it but everything remains lit up. I paused. *How goes things there?*

No change. If you actually mean, how goes the husband, I believe he's currently assisting Kele and your mother haul several freshly killed boars up to your young drakkon. She is a hungry one.

Kele wasn't only my friend, but also a strega witch whose fire ability was even stronger than mine. Damon had recently modified his blood-produced magical shield guarding the internal entrance into the aerie to allow Mom through, simply because she was the only other person beside me who could mind speak to all the other drakkons.

I frowned. *Are Rua and Tane not hunting for her?*

Yes, but according to your mother, there is no filling a hungry teenager.

I smiled. She'd said that same phrase about me when I'd suggested Gria couldn't still be hungry after the boars we'd already fed her. *Tell Kele I expect a jug of mead to be ready and waiting when I get back, as per usual.*

I might want to see—and bed—my husband with a surprising degree of desperation, but there were some traditions that needed to be maintained, especially when I'd lose them—and Kele—when I moved to Zephrine. I *had* offered her the position of personal guard, which would have meant a serious step up in pay and position, but her mom and her lovers lived in Esan, and even as I'd made the offer I'd known she'd refuse it.

Will do. There was a slight pause. *Be careful.*

Always.

He didn't reply, but it wasn't hard to imagine his responding snort. I was, after all, his daughter and had inherited his innate need to explore, no matter what the danger. It was one of the reasons he'd never stopped me heading out to watch the drakkons—he'd understood the inner urge I just couldn't ignore. It was for that same reason Mom had insisted I learn to use a sword and bow, though neither of them had thought it would end up with me enlisting.

But then, what was a girl to do when the prince she's supposed to marry continually dragged his heels when it came to anything related to our marriage and the treaty negotiations that had started when we were both barely teenagers?

I poured myself another hot drink then finished the rest of the platter. Feeling much better with a full belly and two cups of shamoke under my belt, I ran the bath, gathered some soap weed and drying towels, then stripped off and stepped into the steaming water.

I stayed there an indecently long time, soaking away the grime and the aches that came with drakkon riding. It was only when the water began to cool that I climbed out to dry myself and then wash my undergarments. This room—like most of the buildings in Hopetown and towns like her—had a form of underfloor heating. Unlike the volcanic steam vents that both Esan and Zephrine used, here the air was heated by a furnace and forced into a series of hollow chambers between the ground and the floor, and then up into either exposed pipes in the wall or through floor vents to heat rooms. A hanging rack had been placed over the vent here, so I hung out my things, then climbed naked into bed. Like any good soldier well used to grabbing sleep when and where they could, I was asleep almost as soon as my head hit the pillow.

A sharp knocking on the door woke me hours later. "Yes?" I mumbled.

"I have the breakfast you ordered, Captain," came a softly feminine voice.

"Please, bring it in and place it on the table."

As she did so, I yawned and stretched, then glanced at the window above my head. It was pitch black outside, but at least the wind no longer howled, and the distant glimmer of stars said the clouds had cleared. I waited until the woman had left and then tossed off the blankets and padded across to the hanging rack to check if my underclothing had dried. I could've dried it myself by applying a little inner heat once it was on, of course, but there was nothing worse than trying to pull on damp clothes.

I quickly dressed, very aware of the strong, musky, and very drakkon scent the leathers were emitting. I didn't find it offensive, but I daresay others might.

I took my fill of pottage—a thick soup made from various grains boiled in milk and sweetened with honey—and finished the shamoke, then slipped on my coat and harness and headed out the door.

A guard was waiting for me in the hall beyond. "This way, Captain."

"Thank you."

As I followed him through a mindless number of corridors —this place was a damn maze—I reached for Kaia. *You awake?*

Hunting.

You didn't hunt last night?

Did. Still hungry. You on way?

About to collect my mount and head out now.

Where meet?

I don't want to spook the city's inhabitants, so I'll ride about an hour out and meet you on this hill.

I sent her an image of one of the many foothills that surrounded Hopetown—one that stood out thanks to the rather large round boulders that encircled its crest—and she came back with an affirmative. Then a rush of hunger filled the link, suggesting she'd spotted her next meal. I quickly shut the link down, leaving her to enjoy her hunt in peace.

The guard led me out into a yard, then up a series of stairs that led us past the wide but flat grassy area behind the admin buildings. It had once housed the port's poorer folk, but a past administrator had decided she wanted a better view out of her windows and had relocated all the old tenants to "newer" accommodation at the far edges of the town before demolishing the centuries-old buildings and regreening the entire area. Subsequent councils had not reversed the decision, suggesting they all considered their view remained a higher priority than the need for additional housing in the increasingly crowded town.

We continued on up the steps, heading for the military section situated against the curtain wall. It housed the mounted force as well as the infantry, while the other, smaller military zone positioned next to the harbor housed the sailors who manned the war galleons—none of which were here, suggesting the council had at least moved the main fleet out. Hopetown might primarily be a fishing port, but in times past, it had come under plenty of attacks, both internally and externally. Arleeon hadn't always been a peaceful continent.

We walked into a long range of stables that hunkered in the shadows of the city's wall, directly opposite what I presumed was the barracks. Coursers stomped and snorted, but most were dozing, dreaming of the long grasses and longer fields they very rarely saw aside from the times they were under saddle.

The courser I was given was a lovely dappled gray mare who'd already been saddled up. I ordered the removal of the tack, which earned me a dour look even as the stable hand obeyed, and lightly connected with the mare's mind. She snorted, tossing her head uneasily over both the light caress of my thoughts through hers and my musky scent—she'd smelled the drakkons once before when a yearling when they'd attacked the city's breeding herd—but, like most animals I communicated with, she calmed down after a few gentle words. Animals were, in my opinion, far easier to deal with than most humans.

I leapt onto her back, gathered enough of her mane to hold me steady until I'd adjusted to her gait, then glanced at the guard. "The gates will be open, I take it?"

He nodded. "Safe journey, Captain."

As he stepped back, I nudged the mare forward, moving at a trot through the stable's exit and down the road to the gate. The guards stationed there saluted and, once we were through, the gates were closed and locked behind us—the latter something I heard more than saw.

I urged the mare onto the softer grass crowding the sides of the road, then into a canter, moving easily with her as the miles went by and the sunrise slowly began to paint the sky with a pastel palette.

Arrive, Kaia said. *Fly high.*

Remain there until I dismount and send the mare back.

No eat?

No, I said dryly. *No eat.*

Shame. They tasty.

Didn't you just feast on a longhorn?

Yes. Point?

I laughed, the sound echoing across the still morning. Somewhere off in the distance, in the shadows of the Black Glass Mountains, something stirred.

Something that had the small hairs across the back of my neck rising.

I narrowed my gaze and scanned the distant blots of black, but couldn't see anything untoward. My long viewer, like practically everything else, was in the pack tied onto Kaia. *You seeing anything over near the mountains?*

She didn't answer immediately, but I had a sense of her

lightly circling as she studied the area. *A male flying. Aerie there.*

There is? I asked in surprise.

New. A young queen, two females, and their mates there. Why?

No room in others.

Which was becoming a major problem as drakkon numbers grew and the vast breeding areas above Esan and Zephrine, which had once held hundreds of drakkons, remained beyond the use of most.

Is it not a risk for them to be this close to Hopetown?

No choice. Safe breeding places few.

Which was basically what I'd thought. I studied the distant mountains and the drakkon I couldn't see for a few seconds, the inner niggle continuing to strike. *Keep an eye on him, Kaia, just in case.*

Her full attention snapped back to me, the weight of it briefly buckling my knees. *You sense winged ones?*

I hesitated. *No. It's just a bad feeling.*

No like bad feelings.

Me neither.

We fly along wildlands not mountains. Safer.

Agreed. And at the very least, we'd have a good long time to spot any of the gilded riders before they ever got into attacking range.

I stopped the mare near the top of the hill, then slid off her back and gave her a good ear scratch. She snorted in soft appreciation and lowered her head to graze, but I caught her thoughts again and impressed the need for her to return to the city. She rather reluctantly did so, and only after I'd pointed out the presence of a drakkon.

Once she was a good distance away, Kaia swooped in, extending her rear legs so that she could land before lowering a front leg, providing a scaly ramp for me to climb. I scrambled up and across her shoulder, using the decidedly wicked-looking spur that jutted out from the wing's thumb to steady myself before settling on her neck. After clipping my harness onto the ropes, I slung the bow back over my shoulders, then dragged the long viewer from my pack and focused it on that distant drakkon.

There was something about the way he was flying—an odd sort of desperation—that had that inner unease ramping up some more.

I tucked the long viewer back into the pack and tied it down again. "I think we need to fly over that way and see if he's okay."

Maybe hunting. Good eating there.

"He doesn't look to be cruising for his next meal to me, Kaia."

She studied him for a second and then hunkered down and launched hard into the air. *We check.*

She arced gracefully around, then flew upward at such a sharp angle that the ropes snapped taut. I couldn't see the drakkon past her spines and head, but there was an odd sort of cloud now forming around one of the Black Glass Mountains' ragged peaks.

Aerie, Kaia said. *Roosted there last night.*

And now it was surrounded by a strange cloud, and one of their males was winging his way toward us at a speed drakkons rarely use except when fleeing... *Was there any sign of the gilded riders when you went in or left?*

No. Checked.

Which was something, but still... I flexed my fingers, trying to ease the spiraling tension, sending tiny sparks of fire spinning into the air that were quickly caught by the sheer force of our speed and extinguished.

Kaia bugled, a long and demanding sound that was almost deafening. The male replied with a strange mix of bugles, growls, and whistles, and the anger that surged through Kaia just about fried my mind.

What? I immediately said.

Aerie attacked, she growled. *Three gilded riders. Others melt rock and close entry. We help?*

We help, I replied. And hoped like hell Túxn felt like throwing luck our way.

Because two against five were not at all good odds.

We'd already learned *that* the hard way.

CHAPTER 2

KAIA, *can you ask the male where the gilded riders and their mages were positioned when he left?*

She didn't bugle this time, simply reached out and connected to his mind, probably because, with the speed she was now going, the distance between them had greatly decreased. Though I wasn't part of their conversation, a backwash of images floated through my link with Kaia; the riders seemed to be using that odd cloud to hide their presence. One rider circled just below it, obviously acting as lookout, while two more had landed on the end of the cavern's long tongue—a thick protrusion of rock that allowed the drakkons to land before entering the aerie proper. The mages were standing either side of the cavernous entrance, slowly melting the black volcanic rock and refashioning it into a wall, while the riders stood at the tongue's end, spraying their birds' acidic shit at any drakkon who tried to leave. *That* was why the young male was flying strangely—he'd been leaving to hunt when the riders had arrived, and the riders had sprayed at him. Only the end of one wing had been hit, but the acid was slowly eating away at the rest of it.

What do? Kaia asked.

We need to take out those mages, first and foremost.

How?

Good damn question. I studied that ominous cloud for a second. *Can you fly higher than that?*

Yes. Her tone said it was a totally stupid question. And in some respects, it was, because we'd certainly flown much higher over the last few days.

I meant without being seen.

Should. Rise now though.

Do it. She flicked her wing and rose sharply, causing the harness ropes to snap taut again. *Is the male willing to help us?*

Dree. Yes.

Then tell Dree to fly back toward the aerie and, when you give the word, do a quick fly past the two grounded riders. Make sure you emphasize the need to fly fast to avoid getting hit by more of that spray. It should distract them long enough for us to swoop in and kill those mages.

They too close to wall.

Not for fire, Kaia.

Good. Burn all. It was viciously said. The queen was in a fighting mood; she was not going to let these bastards take any more drakkons, young or old.

The male banked and chased after us, flying hard to catch up. Kaia rumbled approval as she reached out and gave him his orders. And they *definitely* were orders.

As he banked again and flew toward the mountain, Kaia kept climbing. The air grew colder, the ground more distant, the mountains sharper, more dangerous. Then we were above even them and swinging around once more, flying back along the Black Glass's mountainous spine toward that swirling, yellowish cloud.

Have you any sense of them? I asked, uneasily studying the unnatural-looking phenomenon below us. *Or is that thing blocking your senses?*

Not changed position.

Then once the patrolling rider has flown past us, we dive hard and fast. You take out the two riders on the tongue, and I'll kill the mages.

Like this plan.

It still leaves one rider to deal with.

One better than three.

It certainly was. I glanced down at the ominous cloud and couldn't escape the notion it was something more than mere cloud. But going through it was our only means of approaching without being seen.

Is Dree ready?

Yes.

I took a deep breath, released it slowly, then said, *Go.*

Kaia flicked her wings and then tucked them close, diving hard and fast. I held my breath as we hit the fog and felt her do the same. Perhaps, like me, she felt the wrongness in this cloud and didn't want to risk breathing in the thick and gelatinous muck that moved sluggishly around us, taking the edge off our speed even if it didn't stop us.

Then we were through and almost immediately, the stinging started. The strange cloud was acidic—maybe not as much as the sprays they used, but probably still enough to damage in deeper concentration. Whether our speed through the cloud would mitigate the effects or not was something we'd soon find out.

And there wasn't much we could do about it right now anyway, because we were approaching the tongue at breakneck speed, and I needed to be ready. Below us, a drakkon bellowed, the sound echoing loudly in the thick hush underneath the cloud. Dree appeared, swooping not only low but close enough to flick his tail at the first rider, hitting his bird hard enough to send it staggering sideways several steps. He didn't attack the second, instead swooping away and flying on fast. The second rider yelled something that sounded like a guttural curse, then raised his weapon and fired on Dree. Kaia flicked him a warning and he banked hard; the brown liquid skimmed underneath his belly, barely missing his tucked-up claws and left wing.

Then, with a roar that echoed so loudly it hurt my ears, she shifted her feet forward and swept up the unbalanced rider and his bird, crushing them both in her murderous claws. The second rider immediately spun around, and his bird fluffed up its feathers.

It's about to fling its feathers at us, I yelled mentally and unleashed the fires pressing at my fingertips, spearing them along the tongue's length before sweeping it left and right across the cavern's maw-like entrance. The two cloaked mages went up in a whoosh and Kaia roared her satisfaction.

A heartbeat later, she was banking hard and fast, almost unseating me. I caught the leash with one hand and hung on grimly, waiting for her to turn enough for me to see the rider and his mount. As the deadly rain of golden feathers flew past us, the bird rose, its wings pumping hard, still glittering gold despite the barrage it had sent at us. The rider twisted around in his saddle and aimed his weapon at us, but I hit the thing with a fierce fist of fire. It exploded, taking out not only the rider but a good chunk of the creature's spine. It collapsed but wasn't dead, so I turned the lance of heat toward it and speared it through its brain, killing it instantly.

Then I burned its body, forcing so much heat into my fire that the creature's deadly feathers became a river of gold that splashed down onto the tongue even as the flesh underneath burned.

Pain ripped through my brain, and the mote in my eye—something all fire witches had—burst. It was a warning that I'd put too much oomph into that last attack, but I didn't for one moment regret it.

Kaia bellowed a warning to the drakkons caught in the cavern to remain there, then swooped upward sharply. The last rider was barreling toward us, a metal spear raised over his head, though how he was maintaining its position given the speed they were going, I had no idea.

It was the same sort of spear that had killed Ebrus.

He released the spear; it shot with unnatural speed toward us, forcing Kaia to bank sharply away. As she swung back around, the rider raised a tube.

Kaia bellowed again, this time in fury, and with a fast flick of her wings, her body rolled up and over the stream and the rider. It happened so fast I barely even left her back. The brown liquid shot past us, splashing lightly across my arm and the spine directly in front of me. As the shit began to eat into clothes and bone, I swore and spun more fire at the banking rider. It wasn't as fierce as my previous lance but didn't need to be—human flesh was far easier to burn than metal-feathered bird. The latter spun away from us as its rider was crisped, but Kaia used her tail as a whip and flicked the bird hard into the black surface just above the cavern's entrance.

It fell, broken but not dead, to the tongue. A burnished gold drakkon appeared and, with a snarl that was filled with fury, ripped out the bird's exposed underbelly then kicked its remains off the tongue.

It was then I saw the raw and smoking wound across her chest. She'd been hit by the liquid shit.

Kaia, you need to tell that female—

Queen. Yara.

Are all queens a burnished gold color?

No. Just special ones.

Fair enough, I thought with a smile. *Tell Yara, Dree, and any other drakkon who has been hit to follow us into the sea to neutralize the acid.*

Kaia roared in response—I think more to catch everyone's attention—then passed on my message. As Yara lumbered out onto the tongue, we swung around and arrowed toward the sea. The ominous cloud was now dissipating, and while I didn't know a lot about spell craft, I suspected it was happening because the men who'd formed it were now dead. Still, enough of it remained to be problematic, so Kaia flew well under it and told the other drakkons to do the same.

I twisted around to check them. There were five behind us—six when Dree tucked in behind a youngish-looking red female—and my inner kid who'd dreamed of drakkons for so damn long couldn't help grinning widely. If Khuld's eternal garden—the realm where those souls not claimed by Vahree went to await rebirth—really did exist, then this would probably be my perfect version of it.

Not that I wanted those drakkons or indeed anyone else I knew to find themselves in such a place. Not for many, many decades yet, anyway.

By the time we reached the rocky shoreline lining Sinopa's calf, the exposed part of my face was beginning to sting, and small holes were appearing in my clothes as well as in the external sections of Kaia's wing membrane that hadn't been tucked close to her body when she'd dived—all the confirmation we needed that the cloud was indeed acidic. These bastards certainly had a wide range of dangerous magics at their disposal.

Kaia banked and extended her rear claws, landing gracefully but nevertheless sending rocks scattering. As the six younger drakkons flew over our heads and landed on the beach farther down, Kaia extended a leg so I could clamber down. I unclipped myself, grabbed my backpack, quiver, and sword, and then slid down to the beach. She immediately lumbered into the water, having learned from past encounters with the riders and their liquid weapon that it was the best way to stop the acid burning further. Three of the six other drakkons followed her somewhat reluctantly in, while those who hadn't been hit regarded me from a safe distance, curiosity and wariness evident.

They no touch, Kaia said. *Warned them. You kin.*

Did you explain what that actually meant? I asked, amused. She'd started referring to me as kin after I'd explained that I didn't need her to carry me back to Esan that fatal day she and her drakklings had been attacked because my kin were coming to get me. After discovering it meant family, she'd decided I now was.

Yes. They curious. Answered many questions.

I dropped my pack up the shoreline, well out of the reach of the incoming tide, then walked fully clothed into the sea. My flame might be reduced but it would still be strong enough to dry my silk undergarments and the leathers, although the latter would take much longer. *No doubt most of them being "why the hell are you allowing a human on your back?"*

They saw flame. Know reason.

You told them about the attack on Gria and Ebrus?

Yes. They fly to our aerie. Safer.

Meaning you're now in charge of a second aerie, but what of your own flight?

A flight was what we called a grace, and it basically meant there were twenty breeding drakkons in each aerie, consisting of a queen—the grace's main protector—five to eight younger, breeding females, a gaggle of males who vied for the attention of the smaller females, and the elders who helped tend and protect the eggs and the drakklings. Kaia's grace was one of the largest within the Red Ochre Range—as benefitting *the* queen, I guess—and had close to twenty-five adults and fourteen drakklings in various stages of growth.

Too many young to move.

Then let's hope we can stop these bastards before they ever reach those mountains.

Will. Trust.

I sucked in a breath that was as much to do with the sheer weight of the trust she was now placing on me as much as the icy water reaching my nether regions. I hoped, *really* hoped, that none of my actions ever betrayed that trust.

I continued on into the sea, stopping only when the depth reached my chin, allowing the gentle waves to wash over my head and hair. The salt stung like blazes when it hit the multitude of pin-prick wounds that littered my face, but that was better than allowing that acidic cloud muck to burrow ever deeper.

The longer I stayed, the more the water's chill began to invade my bones; when the shivering got bad enough, I ramped up the inner flames and stayed in for as long as I could. It took another twenty minutes or so before the stinging stopped and I was able to climb out. After squeezing the worst of the water from my plaited hair, I dripped over to my backpack and tugged out a meal sack. It was little more than dried meats, nuts, and fruit-encrusted bread, but right now it felt like a feast.

Kaia climbed out of the water just as I'd finished and, after shaking the worst of the water from her long body, extended her leg. I hastily tucked the meal sack away then slung the bow back over my shoulder, gathered everything else, and ran over. After scrambling up her leg and edging past her wing spine, I clipped on once again.

Yara stepped toward us, her gaze—and thoughts—inquisitive. *How you flame?*

I blinked. The last thing I'd expected was her directly speaking to me. Usually, it was the other way around, and often came with an instinctive surge of surprise that had them lashing out before they realized I meant no harm. Rua had certainly tried to stomp on me when I'd initially met her, although that was long before she'd come to our rescue or moved to Esan's aerie. It was my flames that had stopped her—not because she was afraid, but because she was curious. *Kaia, did you tell her I can mind speak?*

Yes. She queen. Should know.

Which was an interesting statement, if only because it suggested not all drakkons would be—or deserved to be —told.

Queens defend, Kaia said. *Is duty to know.*

I broadened my mental touch to include Yara and said, *It's partially magic, partially a mind gift.*

You teach magic?

Wish I could. It would be far easier to burn the winged ones if drakkons had that power.

You find way? she insisted.

I'm not sure—

Mate magic, Kaia cut in. *Ask.*

It wasn't a suggestion, it was an order, and I couldn't help smiling again. *I will.*

Good. We go now.

And with that, she launched into the air. The six other drakkons followed, forming a V-shape behind us. It gave us a lot more sky coverage and a far bigger chance of spotting the riders before they ever got close enough to cause any of us damage.

The remnants of morning gave way to a long afternoon, and as the evening closed in, ominous-looking storm clouds once again crowded the horizon. We were going to get wet before we got home, of that I was sure.

We were probably half an hour away from Esan's aerie when I dragged out the scribe quill and tablet. After hunkering fully down behind Kaia's spine to protect me from the worst of the air flowing past, I sent a quick message to my father, letting him know we were coming in with six new drakkons. I doubted Mom, Kele, or Damon would be in the aerie with night closing in, but it was better to be safe than sorry.

The tablet blinked for a few seconds before his reply came through. *You collect drakkons the way I used to collect boats.*

I could practically hear his dry amusement in that comment and couldn't help but laugh. My father had been an avid mariner in his younger years and, much to his own father's horror—who'd disliked the sea almost as much as I did—had collected over a dozen of them, of all shapes and sizes, that he alternated between depending on whim and destination.

I'm not collecting them; Kaia is. I'll report when I get down from the aerie.

No need to immediately do so. The morning will do.

No, I replied, *it won't.*

That sounds ominous.

Because it is. I paused. *Tell Kele I'll have to take a raincheck on the flagon of mead but request she meets me after first light in the stables.*

Will do. Fly safe.

I smiled, tucked the quill and the tablet away, then straightened again.

Teach Kele to ride? Kaia asked.

Yes.

Good. Rua wants own flamer. Wants to come on flights.

I gathered that. She certainly hadn't been happy yesterday morning when I insisted she stay behind until Tane had fully recovered and was able to take over hunting duties for Gria.

Another flamer? came Yara's thought.

Obviously, listening in on other peoples' conversation was something all drakkons did.

No, Kaia said, amusement obvious. *Just queens.*

I rolled my eyes. It was bad enough that one queen was listening in, but two? Túxn help me... *There are, but some are males—*

No males, Kaia cut in firmly. *They killed. No control us ever.*

I don't control you, Kaia. They wouldn't either.

No ride, she repeated, even more firmly.

Which did cut down our already slim options. *I think there's three or four fire witches in Esan, but only two in the military.*

What mean military? Yara asked.

Trained fighters, I said.

Use small throwing sticks to kill birds, Kaia added helpfully.

Take Kele, Yara said.

She queen, came Kaia's thought. *Should take second strongest.*

Rua won't be happy.

She get military flamer. Same.

Except that Rua already knew Kele, and that would have made their transition to being a team that much easier. Still, it wasn't like Rua really had any choice. Kaia's word was law.

Lightning flickered across the ominous-looking clouds ahead and, a few seconds later, the storm hit us. None of the drakkons seemed to care, but we were flying straight into the driving rain, and it basically made it impossible for me to see. We definitely needed to develop some sort of eye protection, especially given the long months of winter would be here quicker than any of us wanted.

Although in truth, we needed to stop the winged riders long before summer found its end, let alone autumn.

Kaia sent a mental order for the drakkons to form up single file behind us, then swooped down, landing smoothly on the tongue before strutting quickly into the main aerie. Rua and Tane bellowed in greeting, but Gria waddled over, looking well satisfied with herself.

Flew in aerie, she said. *Want hunt now.*

Good, Kaia said, shooing her to one side. *Hunt tomorrow. Dark now.*

The others came in one by one, each bugling a greeting introduction to Rua and Tane.

Yara strutted in last, her expression and thoughts pleased as she looked around. *Nesting grounds big. Hold several flights.*

This isn't the only cavern, I told her. *There are more above us, though their exit lies above Esan fortress.*

What Esan fortress?

Where flamers live, Kaia said. *My flight claim above nesting when come.*

Meaning she had no intention of going back to her old grounds. And while I was happy she'd not only decided to claim this place as her own but fill it with drakkons, just as the child in me had always dreamed, it also meant the only time I'd be able to see her was when we were on official visits back to Esan.

And that once again had grief rising, even though the move hadn't happened yet. In fact, we were still a *long* way from it happening, given my father had already stated I wouldn't be going anywhere until the threat of the gilded riders had been dealt with. His publicly stated reason was the fact he didn't want to lose one of his best captains, but I rather suspected it was due more to my mother and her knowing I didn't want to leave Esan or the drakkons. Of course, the delay also meant Damon and I had more of a chance of knowing and understanding each other in an environment *I* was at ease in—especially given the likelihood I would never be at ease in Zephrine while his father remained in control. Aric had barely managed to conceal his contempt of me—with my soldier skills and strega abilities—while he'd been here. It would be open slather when he was back on home ground. And...

...and I really needed to stop feeling sorry for myself. It wasn't as if this fate had been dropped on me only weeks ago. I'd known about it since puberty, and it was beyond time I simply accepted it.

I firmly pushed the grief back into its hole, then quickly undid all the ropes and the neck plate, letting the latter fall to the ground as I slung all my various bits and pieces over my shoulders. Once Kaia had extended her leg, I slid down to the warm sands. This cavern was situated close to a volcanic steam vent that not only heated what had once been an ancient seafloor, but also the caverns themselves. As Yara had noted, this main chamber was vast and could easily have held more than a grace of full-sized drakkons, while the eight smaller, C-shaped chambers running off it provided easily defended, much warmer areas for eggs to be laid and newly hatched drakklings to be safely reared in. But this chamber was small compared to the size of the upper one, which was undoubtedly why Kaia had claimed it as her own.

Gria pushed her head underneath her mother's neck, her dark eyes shining in the sand's subtle glow. *Scratch?*

I grinned and willingly scratched the ridge above her eye. She closed her eyes, bliss rumbling through her thoughts. After I'd repeated the process for Kaia, I carefully made my way through all the new drakkons—who were all very careful not to move while I was doing so to prevent an accidental squashing—then headed through to one of two internal entrances that led deeper into the mountain. After hanging the makeshift harness over a fingerlike outcrop of rock to save the effort of carrying it back up with me again, I strapped on my sword, then headed on through Damon's blood-created shield. Its magic danced lightly across my skin, a tingling sensation that, when compared to the acid cloud, was positively pleasant.

I hitched the pack and quiver into a more comfortable position on my shoulders, then heard a soft click. As light spun around me, I turned sharply, my hand raised and fire burning across my fingertips—and almost immediately lowered it. The man standing in front of me was neither a threat nor a stranger.

He was my husband.

Damon rose and walked toward me, and I couldn't help but be reminded once again of the elusive high-forest wildcat I'd once been lucky enough to see when I was kid. He, like that cat, moved in a manner that was sheer grace and restrained power combined.

He was also a magnificent-looking man.

The gentle glow of the light tube he carried made his closely shaven head gleam like newly oiled blackwood while highlighting the sharp but very pleasing planes of his face. His leather jacket was undone, and his undershirt loose at the neck, and while it wasn't open enough to provide anything more than teasing glimpses of his muscular chest and stomach, my imagination was well up to the task. No imagination was necessary when it came to the impressive mound of his crotch, however. His leather pants almost lovingly emphasized its size while also highlighting the lean strength of his legs. I knew well enough the power of those legs. Knew they were more than capable of holding my weight against a wall as he sheathed himself within me again and again....

Desire stirred through me, a heat that was echoed in his lovely blue eyes. No matter what else happened in this marriage of ours, physical attraction was never going to be a problem.

"What brings you to this tunnel, husband?" I asked, amusement teasing my lips.

"The conclusion that if my wife will not come to me, I should come to her."

His voice reminded me of a good mead—deep, rich, and so very... stimulating? Arousing?—and the inner trembling deepened. "To be honest, I'd rather my husband come *in* me than to me, but to each their own."

He laughed and caught my hand, his fingers warm and

strong against my own as he dragged me into his arms. Our kiss was long and deep, an exploration of desire and a heady declaration of what was to come. Of what we both wanted.

"Wife," he said eventually, "you stink of drakkon."

I grinned and pulled away from him. His erection, I couldn't help but notice, was positively fierce. "Then perhaps we need to hasten our journey back to Esan so I can bathe and present myself to my husband in a more suitable manner."

"I suspect the husband doesn't really care which way you come, as long as you do come." He made a "give me" motion at my pack and the quiver.

"Ah, such thoughtfulness will be the end of me." I slipped them off and handed them to him, then started down the tunnel. "Anything interesting happen while I was gone?"

He fell in to step beside me. "There's been sightings of renewed Mareritten activity. A patrol was attacked yesterday morning."

The Mareritt were a warrior race who lived in the vast subarctic wilderness beyond the Blue Steel Mountains, the long range that unevenly divided our shared continent. Mareritten itself was a land so harsh that for nine months of the year its people lived in expansive underground cities that drew on volcanic heat to survive their long winters. In years past, they'd used the short, three-month window of summer to attack both us and Zephrine in an effort to gain control over our mineral and pastorally rich lands, but this year had seen a strange absence of them. While there were some who believed they'd finally accepted the futility of attacking either fortress, I feared they were building up to something big—an opinion shared by both my father and mother.

"Any injuries?" I asked, managing to keep my voice even. I'd seen the roster and knew it had been Kele's team out yesterday. Though if she had been injured, my father would surely have said something when I'd scribed him.

"A broken leg—the result of a fall off a small cliff—but other than that, no. And before you ask, Kele is fine. But the patrols out today apparently saw further signs of movement."

"But not the Mareritt themselves?"

"No." He glanced at me, a hint of... anticipation?... in his blue eyes. It suggested he'd welcome the resumption of hostilities between us and Mareritten and that, for some reason, sat oddly on the man I knew. Of course, it could also be said that I really didn't know him in any real way beyond the physical. "I believe the lull we've experienced might well be over."

I hoped he was wrong—even if I didn't think he was—more because the last thing we needed was being attacked on two fronts. "Was it a full host that attacked yesterday?"

He shook his head. "Only six rather than the usual thirteen, from all accounts."

That in itself was an oddity, given the Mareritt didn't, from what we knew of them, like even numbers. They considered them bad luck. "And the tracks they discovered?"

"Suggested several hosts had moved through."

"To where? Do we know?"

"They skimmed the edges of the marshlands, then followed the Igna River inland."

The scouts would have stopped at the river, because crossing it meant getting too deep into Mareritten territory. "Have they just been sighted near Esan? Or has Zephrine seen an increase in their patrols as well?"

"My father still sails toward Kriton. I doubt an update will be sent to your father until he reaches Zephrine."

Kriton was the closest port to Zephrine, but a good day's ride from the fortress itself. I glanced briefly at him, eyebrow raised at the slight edge in his voice. "And yet he obviously sent you one?"

Damon smiled, though there was very little mirth in it. "Only to remind me that my duty lay with him and Zephrine."

"That's an odd thing to say, given you're his heir, isn't it?"

"My father is nothing if not odd."

I couldn't disagree with that, but there was more to the situation than what he was saying—especially given my mother's intuition that Aric was lying. While her seeress abilities could be somewhat reticent, and nowhere near as strong as her ability to mind-speak to animals, they weren't often wrong.

"Yes, and one of these days you'll trust me enough to tell me why that is."

"When it is safe to do so, I will."

I frowned. "Why would you, of all people, have to worry about safety when it comes to your father?"

"It's a long story, and not one I have any desire to detail without several flagons of ale within reach."

A statement that made me wish I hadn't cancelled my drinking session with Kele, just so we could mull over the enigma that was my husband.

We continued on in companionable silence, working our way through the feeder tubes and then the rough-cut black stone tunnel that led to the vent situated midway between Esan and the second aerie entrance. It was a long walk down the mountain from there and, by the time we reached the external gate, I was wretchedly tired. It had been a *long* day.

The guards saluted as we approached, then the older one said, "The commander awaits your report in the long room, Captain."

I returned the salute and moved through the gate once the second guard had opened it, then glanced at Damon. "You should come with me. Your father will no doubt get a report from mine, but given the amount of distrust he exudes, he might also appreciate a personal report from you."

"I think the correct wording there is 'expect' rather than 'appreciate.'"

"What on earth has happened to cause such a rift—" I stopped and held up a hand. "Yeah, I know, you'll tell me when you can."

"This whole situation is not what it seems." His reply was grim, his expression dark. "And there are lives depending on my silence. Which is more than I should ever share right now, and I would appreciate it if you kept that information to yourself. And if you see Gayl, avoid her."

Gayl was his aunt and mentor—of what I had no idea—and a rather strange woman who barely even looked my way, let alone talked to me. And despite the fact she'd been his ring bearer at our marriage ceremony, they didn't seem to be very close. I was also under the impression she'd returned home with his father, but obviously, I was wrong.

And what lives were on the line? Hers? It didn't sound like it from what he'd said, but it was still a worrying admission. What in Vahree's name was happening in Zephrine? What, exactly, hadn't they told us? Whatever it was, I could only hope it was sorted out long before I ever moved to the wretched place.

We came out of the dark tunnel and moved into the large courtyard. It was ringed on three sides by the palace, the administrative and military center that sat atop the wall, and the palace stables and tack area, with the fourth wall being the high soaring mountain. By day this whole area was a mass of noise, color, and a multitude of aromas as men and women went about the daily business of keeping the place running. But with the onset of night, most had obviously returned to their homes if not their beds. It was really only the night patrol that remained. I saluted those who crossed our path and clattered up the metal stairs leading into the administrative building's main corridor before heading right toward the military section. Our footsteps echoed softly in the shadowed silence, announcing our presence long before we approached the heavily fortified war room. The guards saluted and opened the thick metal door as we neared; I once again returned their salute and stepped inside.

The room beyond was a long but gently sweeping space that spanned the full width of the wall, with thickened windows that swept its length on both sides; one provided a view across the courtyard while the other looked over Esan's great outer wall. Eight long-viewing scopes lined its sweeping curve and, from this height, the soldiers manning the outer wall looked minute. Beyond it, Mareritten lay stretched out like a map, enabling us to see any attack long before they reached us. It was a huge advantage the Mareritt had yet to find a way around.

Although maybe they now had, given the attack on the patrol last night. If they'd been sighted along the edges of the marshlands, we really should have seen them with the long viewers, at the very least.

One long table dominated the center of the room,

while multiple smaller ones were dotted about, holding strategic maps and troop placement boards amongst other things.

My father sat at the far end of the table. Mom wasn't here, which surprised me a little, but Vaya and Jarin—the day- and night-shift generals—sat either side of their commander and king, Rion Silva, who was also my father. He was a tall man and broad of shoulder, with weatherworn brown features, golden eyes, and a thick plait of gray hair that hung halfway down his back. That plait was a conceit I followed, even if it really wasn't practical when it came to war. But then, skirmishes with the Mareritt aside, it wasn't as if any of us had truly seen war.

My father gave me a quick, warm smile before stating briskly, "Captain Silva, please make your report."

I stopped at the end of the table and stood at ease with my hands behind my back. Damon continued on and claimed the chair to my left. I quickly and without emotion detailed everything that had happened with the attack on the aerie above Hopetown, and the odd cloud that had turned out to be acidic.

My father scrubbed a hand across his unshaven features wearily. "This all just gets better and better, doesn't it?"

"I don't get why they would attack the drakkons," Jarin said. "They've already proven to be basically ineffectual against the birds."

"Perhaps the riders believe that, given the effectiveness of Bryn's attacks on them so far, that our drakkons are very much the same as their birds," Damon said. "That is, a flighted force we can use at will."

"That's more than possible," my father said. "Vaya, get word out to Hopetown immediately—tell them we think an attack is imminent."

Vaya rose and hastened down the room to the table holding multiple quill tablets.

"If there's one bit of good news to be gleaned from that report," Jarin said, "it's that the effects of the cloud—and possibly their acidic shit weapons—can be neutralized by water."

"The latter we were already aware of, but we need to develop a means of firing the water with far greater accuracy *and* distance than our current hoses are capable of," I said. "We could certainly pump water onto the walls to protect the stone, but that doesn't help anyone manning them if those things attack en masse."

"Using air mages to create a shield of wind and rain should certainly take care of both their riders *and* any acid cloud their mages send our way," Damon said.

"Yes," I said, glancing at him. "But these bastards are brutal enough to sacrifice one attack force to ensure a secondary assault from a different direction is successful."

"Air mages are a finite resource," Vaya added. "And let's face it, it's not like Zephrine will send us some of theirs."

"Indeed," Damon said, in somewhat dark amusement. "Sharing is not a word that often enters my father's vocabulary or indeed his thoughts."

"Which is why I've set the engineers the task of designing a safe means of flooding the walls while protecting our soldiers," my father said. "It's also why we're re-establishing watch stations on the peaks."

My gaze snapped toward his. "I hope you placed them well away from the drakkons."

"I thought you said they don't eat humans?" Jarin said.

"They don't. But if they feel threatened, they'll certainly sweep you up and spit you out."

"Charming."

"It's a more humane fate than we probably deserve, considering what we've done to them over the centuries," Damon commented mildly. "Remember, it wasn't only the so-called threat to human population that saw their near eradication, but also the value we placed on the ivory of their horns and claws."

And in some of the wilder parts of Arleeon, that ivory was *still* a greatly sought after commodity for both medicine *and* jewelry.

Jarin grunted, though I wasn't sure if it meant agreement or not. His expression was more annoyed than contrite, though I think its cause was more Damon's gentle chastisement than any real disagreement with what was said.

"We've only reestablished two so far," Rion said. "One at Brimstone's Pass, and the other at Crooked Thumb."

I nodded. Both were situated well away from the aerie's entrances and the drakkons' usual hunting grounds, and the Thumb also had an additional advantage—it overlooked the Eastern Sea and the sweep of mountains past the Beak, where the riders were establishing a series of look-out points. Keeping an eye on their movements was vital.

Of course, it'd be even better to get rid of the bastards, but to do that might well prompt a full-on assault we weren't yet prepared for. We needed as much time as we could get for our earth and air mages to find a way of countering their weapons without draining so much of their own energy that they killed themselves.

"Anything else, Captain?" my father added.

I hesitated. "What news of Jakarra?"

What news of Garran, my cousin, and his heir? is what I really wanted to ask. And the flicker in his eyes suggested he was well aware of that.

"Nothing more than what is known to date. We've begun evacuating women and children from the Helvede caverns, using a newly created tunnel that exits at the closest point to Zergon."

If Rudy—who was the only earth mage left on Jakarra— had created that tunnel in the short space of time since I'd seen him, he was far more powerful than he'd let on.

"Your mother," he continued, "is helping to register and settle the first intake."

No doubt hoping to get news of her sister, Glenda, who was Garran's mother. "Was Hanna in the first intake?"

"No. She wished to remain on the island until news is had of Garran."

While that was understandable, it was also very risky given she now had their infant son to worry about.

I stepped back, then hesitated yet again. "Could a message be sent to Hannity Gordan this evening, asking if she's interested in becoming a drakkon rider? If she is, can you order her to meet Kele and me at the stables an hour after sunrise? Our new queen has decided Kele is to be her fire weapon, so Rua will need another rider."

"New queen?" Vaya said as she returned. "We've more drakkons?"

"Kaia brought the Hopetown aerie back here for safety reasons," my father replied before I could. "What response from Hopetown?"

"They've begun evacuations. Their earth mages spent the day hollowing out the hills surrounding the city and will continue to do so during the night. They should have multiple shelters done within two days."

And if they'd started the shelters when they should have, they would have been ready to be used by now. "The earth mounds won't stop the acid."

"No," my father replied. "But it should conceal their presence and, for the moment at least, the riders seem more intent on wiping out supply chains and any means we might have of a sea response than erasing entire populations."

Tell that to the people of Eastmead, I wanted to say, but held it back. He was in truth partially right as, aside from the initial attack on the refugees in the Helvede caverns, they'd basically left them alone. And besides, he was my commander rather than my father right now, so I could not backchat.

"If there's nothing else," he added, "you're dismissed. Go rest, Captain, before the morning's tribulations begin anew."

I nodded, saluted, and left.

Damon rose and followed me. Once we were back in the hall, I said, "I take it you'll make the report to your father while I bathe?"

He nodded. "Gayl took the tablet so she could have a message relayed to her sons, so I'll have to head across to her room."

"We can just send someone around to grab it from—"

"A move that would not be successful. Gayl can be... difficult."

"You're a prince of Zephrine and your father's heir—relation or not, surely she could not ignore a direct order?"

He raised his eyebrow, amusement dancing through his lovely eyes. "And how often does my wife follow her own advice and order people about?"

I couldn't help smiling. "Well, rarely, but I'm not the heir, am I? For Túxn's sake, husband, there is sex to be had, and time is a-wasting."

He laughed, caught my cheeks lightly between his

hands, and kissed me hard, in full sight of the guards standing at the door. I should have objected to the breach of protocol but didn't. I wanted this man with a ferocity I'd never experienced with anyone else, and this kiss at least went some way to blunting its force.

And if I ignored the blooming ache deep within, I might actually believe that.

"Shall I order us a meal and a pot of shamoke on the way back?" he asked.

"Does the sun set in the sky every evening?"

He laughed again, then released me and motioned me forward again. Once we left the building, we clattered down the metal steps and ran through the rain to the palace. It, like most others within this main keep, was a squat and rather sinister-looking building, thanks mainly to the fact it was made of the same black stone as the mountain that soared above us.

The two vast and rather ornate metal doors that stood atop the stone steps were closed, but the right side opened as we approached, the guard obviously spotting us through the spy hole. I thanked him and continued on, footsteps echoing in the small but lofty entrance foyer. By day it was filled with light thanks to the heavily fortified light wells cut into the ceiling and the multitude of bright tapestries that adorned the stone walls, but at night, it was all shadows and flickering torchlight. I'd always loved nights here in the palace—loved the atmosphere and warmth the black stone seemed to exude once the sun went down. A grand stone staircase dominated the central space, sweeping up to the accommodation section—our private quarters to the right and guests to the left—but the ground floor held the grand hall, and to the left, the kitchens, buttery, and stores.

Tucked behind the staircase was the private chapel where we'd been officially married.

Damon lightly touched my arm then, when I glanced at him, said, "I'll head into the kitchens first, then go see my aunt and contact my father. That'll give you privacy for a bath."

I raised my eyebrows. "And what if I don't want privacy?"

Heat and amusement rolled through his eyes, and a wave of desire hit me, thick and needy. "The little understanding I have gained of my wife tells me her need for shamoke will take precedence over any other need, no matter how fierce."

I laughed, kissed him, then grabbed my pack and quiver from him and ran up the stairs. My suite was at the opposite end of the hall to my parents', close to the thermae bathing facilities generally reserved for guests. It was large and bright, consisting of a bathing and dressing area, a sleeping platform big enough to party in, and a seating/eating area. Having spent well over ten years in military accommodation, many of them shared with five other soldiers, I'd certainly gained a new appreciation for the luxury of space *and* privacy in which I'd been raised.

Once I'd secured my sword, bow, and quiver, I hung the pack on the nearby coat hook, then ran a bath and stripped off, tossing my leathers and undergarments into the laundry chute to be washed. While the tub was filling, I grabbed a scented soapweed—the verum, because I knew Damon loved its intense, spicy aroma—and a couple of towels, placing them near the bath in readiness, then undid my plait and ran my fingers across my scalp. Small bits of grime fell around me like rain, though I wasn't sure where a lot of it had come from, given I'd been on drakkon back a good percentage of the day.

I turned off the tap, stepped into the hot water, and began the long process of washing the grime and drakkon scent from my skin and hair. Once done, I dried myself, then donned a pretty robe—one that was basically sheer aside from a few discreetly placed panels. Something else Damon loved.

The food arrived before he did, so I poured myself a cup of shamoke and sat down, crossing my legs, then tugging the gown over them—a brief nod to the decorum I generally ignored.

He appeared ten minutes later, his expression less than pleased—which was something of a common occurrence whenever he'd been speaking to his father, I'd discovered.

"Problem?" I asked.

He stripped off his jacket and slung it over the top of the sofa, then poured himself a shamoke and sat down opposite.

"Not really." His gaze scanned me appreciatively. "I do love what you're almost wearing, but you didn't have to make such an effort. Nakedness would have been fine."

"Ah, but imagine the fun to be had slowly peeling away the silken layer to expose the goodness underneath."

"Wife, I want you so bad I doubt I have the restraint to peel."

"Then perhaps, husband, I should first peel away *your* layers before you get to mine."

"Because that isn't going to increase the intensity of my need at all, is it now?"

"Probably not, but it'll nevertheless be fun." I paused. While I was well aware of how little he wanted to talk about his father and their relationship, I also knew how important it was for *ours* that he did. Still, it was dangerous territory, given I might well destroy whatever harmony we'd developed if I kept pressing. Of course, it wasn't part of my nature to just ignore it, either. "If your relationship with the man is so fraught, why not just walk away? You've already said he prefers Tayte over you, so why not step aside and let your brother take the throne? Or do you actually want the role?"

"I do not and, given the choice, would certainly walk from all of this. But as I have said, things are complicated." He motioned to the food. "Let's eat, before my appetites are spoiled by such a discussion."

Annoyance slithered through me, but as my father was wont to say when confronted by seemingly insurmountable problems, Esan wasn't built in a day. I *would* uncover the mystery Damon was hiding, no matter how long it took.

When the last of the shamoke had been drunk, I unfurled my legs and rose. His gaze skimmed my length and came up heated, but he didn't move, and he didn't say anything.

He didn't need to. His desire was a force that echoed through every bit of me.

I hitched up my gown and sat astride his legs, my knees either side of his thighs. A tremor ran through him, and he caught my hips, holding me still against him.

"I wouldn't be moving too much over that particular area right now, because I might well lose it."

I tsked. "And where is the man of legendary control and stamina I heard so much about before our wedding?"

"He never had a hope against the nubile force that is his wife."

"I've been called many things over the years, but a nubile force is definitely a new one." I caught the laces on his undershirt and started to undo them. "And not one many past lovers would agree with."

"I, for one, am mighty glad for their lack of appreciation, because it has ensured you are and forever will be mine."

The final lace came undone; I caught the bottom of his shirt and, motioning him to raise his arms, pulled it up and over his head. "That would suggest my lack of womanly assets wasn't behind your resistance to meet me at the altar."

"I do believe it was mentioned, but the man who decried the lack is a fool." He slowly ran a finger down the outside of my thigh then back up the inside. "*I* am not a fool."

My breath hitched when his fingers brushed the top of my mound. A knowing smile touched his lips, but he didn't say anything. He simply continued his agonizingly slow journey down the inside of my other thigh.

Two could play *that* game.

I slowly ran my hands down from his shoulder to his chest, paused briefly to play with his nipples. "Then why such a long delay?"

"Reasons I cannot explain right now."

"That appears to be your go-to answer to every question right now."

"It is also nothing but the truth."

"And an incredibly frustrating truth it is too."

I slowly slid my fingers down the sculpted magnificence of his abdomen until I reached the sharply defined V that led down to his groin.

"You're playing with fire if you go any further," he murmured lazily.

I undid the first fastening on his pants. "In case you haven't noticed, husband, I enjoy playing with fire."

"Then you will be aware that there are varying degrees of fire, some more satisfying than others."

The second fastening came undone. The force of his erection was threatening to pop the third, but I didn't immediately release it, instead running my fingers down his long, encased length.

"I, dearest husband, am of the opinion that all fires can be satisfying, whether they flame hard and fast or long and slow."

His fingers moved up my left thigh again, but this time, he brushed past hair and found my clit. I shuddered, a deep moan of delight escaping my lips.

"And I," he said, in that same lazily heated tone, "believe that for any fire to burn satisfactorily, the fuel must be fully primed."

I laughed softly and popped the final fastening. His erection sprang free, gloriously thick and glistening with precum. The man really did want me so *very* badly. "Fires burn best when the fuel is dry, and I'm thinking that's not the best analogy to be using here."

"Ah, but is the fuel dry? I rather suspect it is not."

And with that, he slipped down through my wetness and thrust inside. I gasped in pleasure, then leaned forward, claiming his lips, kissing him hard even as I rocked against his fingers, wanting his touch and yet needing far more.

He slid his free hand through my hair and deepened our kiss, all the while continuing his gentle stroking, causing all sorts of havoc to my breathing and heart rate. His thumb grazed my clit, and another gasp tore past my lips. I reared back, my hands on his shoulders, bracing myself as his stroking intensified. Then he caught one aching nipple between his lips and sucked hard; it was almost my undoing. Almost. As the low-down tremors began to take hold, I pulled away from his fingers, rose onto my knees to position myself above his erection, then thrust down on him, taking him in, all the way in. He was hung like a stallion, and it felt like he was spearing through the very heart of me. But it also felt so very perfect. Like I'd been specifically designed to sheathe this man, and *only* this man.

In the sheer and utter perfection of that fragile moment, neither of us moved. I stared into the glorious blue of his eyes, seeing the heat, the hunger, and perhaps even caring. But there was also power in those deeper depths, and shadows, and secrets, and it was the latter two that scared me.

They had the ability to destroy this perfection.

Something flickered through the blue—an emotion too fast to pin down—then he lightly ran a finger down my cheek and across my lips. I caught it, drawing it gently into my mouth, and he sucked in a sharp breath. The heat and hunger surged, erasing the shadows and the danger, and he began to move, not slowly, not gently, but fierce and hard, all control gone.

I moved with him, just as needy, just as desperate.

When release came, it was explosive, wrenching a cry from my lips as his body went rigid against mine and his seed exploded into me. I shuddered and shook, riding that wave until the very end, then slumped against him with a sigh.

"You must admit," I said softly, trailing my fingers down his muscular right arm, "that there is something to be said about a fire that burns hard and fast."

"Which is not to say long and slow is without its merits. I believe it is only fair that we test both statements before any real conclusion is made."

"I would not be against such an exploration." Especially when the man inside of me was already thickening for another round. Those who'd whispered of his legendary stamina and resilience had definitely *understated* fact, in my experience.

I rose and moved into the bathroom, quickly cleaning up while he fully stripped off and moved over to the sleeping platform. I joined him under the covers and, for the next couple of hours, we explored, touched, teased, ultimately proving that not only were slow fires as equally satisfying as fast but also that Damon wasn't the only one with legendary stamina.

———

I woke just as the first strains of pre-dawn color were beginning to paint the bit of sky visible through the light tube above the bed. There was little sound to be heard, either within the palace or without, though the latter wasn't really surprising given the thickness of the walls. Still, something had woken me, something that had unease stirring, and I wasn't entirely sure what.

I carefully slid out of bed, then padded naked into the bathroom to use the facilities.

"Problem?" Damon said, voice rumbly and deep with sleep.

"Right now, only a full bladder."

"Suggesting something other than a full bladder is worrying you."

"It's a niggle, nothing more."

"Then I had better order us shamoke and breakfast, just in case that niggle becomes a full-blown problem."

"It probably won't, but it never hurts to be prepared."

"So says my drakkon-riding, sword-wielding wife."

There remained a small part of me that still wanted to

rage against the unfairness of our marriage even if it was becoming more and more obvious that we were not only compatible sexually but emotionally as well. "Neither of which she'll be doing once she moves to Zephrine."

Blankets rustled as he climbed out of bed. "What if she could?"

I frowned. "Could what?"

"Still wield a sword."

Confusion stirred. "I can't see your father allowing that, especially given he no doubt wants his bloodline secured and grandsons born."

"Right now, I'm not worried about what he wants when it comes to our marriage. Honest answer—given the choice, what would you do?"

I finished my business, then moved over to the washing sink, quickly rinsing my hands before switching over to the hot water so I could clean up. "Aside from stay here? Continue scouting for as long as is feasible."

"Then perhaps we could make that happen, given I, too, have no desire to vegetate within the red halls of Zephrine."

"I can't see your father allowing that, either."

"Oh, you would be surprised what my father would and wouldn't allow when it comes to me."

It was once again said with an edge of bitterness and only served to sharpen my determination to uncover what the hell was going on. Maybe I needed to talk to Mom again. While her seeress abilities might be hit-and-miss, it was possible that if she used something personal of Damon's, she might be able to more accurately pin down what was going on between father and son.

I walked into the dressing area to don clean undergarments, leathers, and boots, then strapped on my knife. It, like my sword and the arrowheads, was made of Ithican glass, but I tended not to wear it when I was astride Kaia, simply because its length made it decidedly ineffectual against the riders or their mounts.

Damon's gaze scanned me as I came back out, and his eyebrows rose. "That niggling is obviously strengthening if you've come out dressed for war."

"I do have several new riders to introduce to their drakkons, remember." I sat on the sofa and slathered butter over a piece of fruit-and-nut bread from last night's meal.

"You never don the knife when you patrol on Kaia. Besides, you're not meeting Kele and the new rider until an hour after dawn."

He walked past the sofa and headed for the bathroom. My gaze lingered a little longer than necessary on his taut butt, and a soft sigh escaped. The man really was magnificent.

"Yes, but by the time I have a good breakfast, it'll be time to go. What are your plans for the day?"

"A not-so-subtle attempt to shift the conversation, but I shall play along for the moment." He ran water into the washer basin and then moved across to grab soapweed and a towel. "I'll be accompanying the cutters out to the Helvede caverns to help secure the evacuation there."

Alarm cut through me. "That's dangerous—"

"No more so than you going out on drakkon back. Besides, my ability to shield others is a more useful gift in this circumstance than your fire."

He speak truth, came Kaia's thought. *You ask about flame share?*

No. Did you just wake up?

No. Ask.

You are a seriously bossy drakkon.

Am queen.

I snorted softly. "Kaia wishes me to ask you something."

"Ask? Not demand?" He grabbed a fresh undershirt and pulled it on, the blue somehow deepening the color of his eyes. "Should I be worried?"

"No, although technically, it *is* a demand. She wants to know if there is any sort of spell that will allow the sharing of my witch fire abilities with her."

He came out of the bathing area, tucking his undershirt into the waist of his pants. "Theoretically, yes. I believe they're called competency transfers, and while they were done in the past, it's a spell that's not been performed for a very long time. I suspect there's a very good reason for that. Why?"

A gentle knock on the door stopped me from answering. Damon walked over to unlock it, then ushered in the small woman carrying a large tray of food. She was followed by a man carrying a pot of steaming shamoke and fresh cups.

I thanked them both and, once they'd collected the remnants of last night's meal and had left, said, "My flames have proven capable of bringing down the gilded riders and their mounts, but it's restricted by my strength. If we could find a way to give fire to the drakkons, their size, bulk, and strength will prove a far more formidable weapon."

He sat down opposite and poured us both a cup of shamoke. "Any sort of spell involving the transfer of powers—"

"I don't want to transfer. I want to share. We need both drakkon and rider to be flame armed. It's the best defense against them swarming us."

He slid the cup over to me, then grimaced. "Again, that's theoretically possible, but any such merging might have greater consequences than the mere sharing of your fire skills."

I lifted the lid on the pottage, filled a bowl with it, and handed it to him. "Like what?"

He nodded his thanks. "The sort of spell you're talking about is basically a merging of beings. Of souls, almost. It could bind you to each other in ways we simply can't understand."

"If we can't find a means of combating the gilded riders, that may well be a cost we will have to pay."

"It's not one I'm willing to pay. The risk to life is too great and I—"

Don't want to lose you. He didn't add that. He didn't even look at me, in fact. But it nevertheless skimmed through my mind, clear and fierce.

Dhrukita, an inner voice whispered.

That inner voice was obviously shamoke starved. Dhrukita was a tale told to little girls growing up and a belief that while not everyone would achieve happiness in their lifetimes, everyone *did* have a perfect partner. A destiny of heart and soul, if you will, that echoed down through every life, every rebirth. It was also a belief I'd never really subscribed to. My mother and father were perfectly matched in almost every way and loved each other dearly, but there was nothing magical about their match. Nothing that suggested a meeting or merging of minds, or even the ability to catch one another's thoughts.

Although even if they *could*, it was probably nothing more than a bleed over from her strega abilities. It wasn't unknown for those of us who could connect with animals to sometimes have it bleed over onto people. It might not have happened to me before this man, but that didn't erase it from being a possibility.

I served up another bowl of pottage, then leaned back in the chair. "If war comes to this land, I will not hide in this palace and watch others fight, Damon. I'll be in the thick of it. It's what I was trained to do, and I *will* do it."

"I'm well aware of that, and I will be by your side every step of the way." He paused, a wry smile teasing his lips. "Well, at least when you're on the ground rather than astride your drakkon."

"We have a far better chance of winning if those drakkons have a means of protecting themselves."

He studied me for a second, then nodded. "I'll scribe Angola and see what can be found in the old libraries. No promises."

Angola was the largest of the floating islands in the Black Claw Sea near Zephrine, and the place where he'd been taught to use his blood magic. "But you will tell me if they do find a spell?"

Something flickered through his bright eyes. Annoyance, and something else, something that seemed akin to regret. Which was a very odd emotion in the circumstances.

"Yes, I will tell you."

"Thank you."

The words barely left my lips when a siren rang out—two short blasts.

My pulse rate stuttered briefly, then leapt into overdrive.

Esan was under attack.

CHAPTER 3

I SHOVED my bowl back onto the table, then ran over to the cabinet to grab my sword, bow, and quiver of regular arrows. The Ithican glass would be a better choice if the gilded birds were the source of the alarm, but I simply didn't have enough of them.

Damon was shoving his feet into his boots, so I grabbed his sword and tossed it over once he was ready, then strode out, walking fast but calmly through the halls and down the stairs.

The guards had already sealed the main palace door, but they opened the smaller, hidden side entry for us. I slipped through, then paused, gaze scanning the orange-kissed skies, looking for but not seeing the gilded riders. Which might not mean anything if they were attacking the curtain wall rather than this upper one.

I ran through the courtyard, dodging both soldiers heading for their stations and the non-military personnel running for the underground shelters located in the deep caverns that ran under Esan, and took the metal steps two at a time.

"You don't have to head to the wall?" Damon asked, obviously shortening his longer strides to keep beside me.

"Scouting teams are generally kept in reserve unless the attacking force is massive. If it was all hands to the wall, the two short blasts would have been accompanied by a longer blast." I glanced at him. "I take it Zephrine doesn't do that?"

"No, but we don't have scouting teams as such, just regular military units with a specialist scout attached."

Which made me wonder how he realistically intended to implement us becoming a part of those units. I couldn't imagine him being a welcome addition to any fighting regiment, let alone me, given his death would probably bring their king's wrath down on them. No matter what Damon thought of his father or how tenuous their relationship seemed to be, he *was* still heir.

The heavy metal mesh yetts—which were basically a metal gate—had already been swung into place over the building's windows and half deployed over the entrance itself. The guards swung the remaining door open as we approached, then locked it fully down once we were through. We hurried on, our footsteps barely even registering against the babble of voices and the noise of lockdown procedures being implemented.

The war room's shield—which was basically a solid piece of metal that rose at an angle from the floor and locked into place above the war room's entrance, providing not only an additional barrier, but shelter for the guards and arrow slits through which they could fire—hadn't yet been deployed but would be the minute any attack swept this way.

The war room itself was a hive of activity but surprisingly calm. Soldiers manned the various scribe stations and the long-viewing glasses, while others were at the troop movements table, making minor adjustments to match what those at the long-viewing stations were calling out. None of the other scouting captains were here, but that was not unexpected, given none of them lived in this upper level but rather the military section. They'd be gathered in the secondary operations center, which would now be under Vaya's command. Jarin, as night watch commander, was here, standing beside my father in the middle of the front-facing windows.

Both glanced around as we approached. I saluted and said, "Who attacks?"

"The Mareritt."

Jarin's tone was abnormally calm—almost monotone—under attack conditions, so the fact it held just the slightest edge suggested this attack was anything but normal.

"How great a force?" I asked.

"Five hosts."

"Sixty-five warriors is not what I would call a true threat to either Esan or her wall," Damon said with a touch of surprise. "Why the full alarm?"

My father's expression was grim. "Because they tested a device we've not seen before, and it partially destabilized a section of the wall."

"What sort of device?" I said in alarm. "Magic or mechanical?"

"A mix of both is our best guess at this point," Jarin said. "The five hosts attacked immediately after the destabilization and managed to partially climb the wall before we could beat them back."

"They also," my father added flatly, "had some sort of protective spell shielding the destabilized area, protecting their warriors from our regular weaponry. It was only when our mages started healing the breach that they fell away and retreated."

"How far did they retreat, though?" Damon asked. "It's generally not in their nature to do so."

"They've set up a forward encampment several miles out," Jarin said. "Hard to see what is going on at the moment, though, because there's a heavy fog currently sitting over the bogs."

I automatically looked out over the wall, even though several miles out would have put them well beyond the range of normal sight. Nothing moved in the areas I could see, which in itself was bad news. As Damon had said, they were not a race inclined to retreat until most of their forces had been spent.

"The air mages haven't been able to move the fog?" Damon asked.

"No."

"Which suggests magic is being employed, however natural that fog looks."

"Indeed." Jarin studied him for a moment. "Would you be able to destroy the pin they're using to anchor that fog spell?"

"My magic is protective in nature rather than destructive, but I should be able to find its location. Once found, it's easy enough to destroy the pin using a sword." He paused. "May I use one of the viewers to check the area out?"

Jarin immediately ordered the soldier at the nearest viewer to step aside. Damon walked over and bent to peer through the eye piece. After a few minutes, he straightened and stepped away. "Given the very slight current eddying through the fog, I would guess that there's three pins—one at each end of the concealment fog and the third centrally located, probably within the barrier itself."

"Would destroying one erase enough of the spell for the fog to dissipate and allow us to see what lies hidden?" my father asked.

"In theory, yes."

"Then let's go out and check," I said.

My father glanced at me, eyebrows raised. "You've new riders to break in. We've other squads who are more than capable."

"I'm aware of that, Commander, but we can't fly out for a few hours yet, and I—"

"Have your father's curiosity and need to uncover first-hand what is happening out there."

My lips twitched. "Indeed, Commander, I do. But it also gives the drakkons extra time to hunt."

"Which is no doubt a good thing," Jarin commented somewhat wryly. "I can't imagine it would be fun riding a hungry drakkon."

"They'd only ever eat us under dire circumstances; we're far too gristly for their liking," I replied and somehow kept my amusement in check at his expression, which was now a mix of disbelief and horror.

Truth, Kaia said. *Rua and Yara take Gria to hunt. I fly with you.*

You should be with Gria, not me.

You fight. I fight.

The Mareritt aren't your fight, Kaia.

Your enemy mine. Kin.

"Bryn?" my father was saying, "Everything okay?"

I started slightly. "Sorry, yes. I was talking to Kaia. If we go out to investigate, she'll come with us and act as forward scout."

Jarin glanced at my father. "That's an advantage we should definitely make use of."

My father hesitated for the briefest of moments, then nodded. "Go mount up. Your squad will meet you at the outer gate."

I nodded, saluted, then headed out. With most nonessential personnel now having retreated to cavern shelters, the building was unnaturally quiet. Shadows danced thickly through the corridor, the lights having been extinguished and the tubes shuttered over in readiness. Anticipation and fear surged through me in equal amounts. I might have trained most of my life for battle, but to date I'd really only experienced what amounted to little more than minor skirmishes. Often fierce ones, granted, and sometimes against far greater numbers than our own, but still... Mom had once said that doubts before any major battle were natural and should, in fact, be welcome. With nerves came caution, and a cautious soldier was far less inclined to throw him or herself into the thick of it without thought, and therefore more likely to survive.

That, of course, led to one vital question—why did I think we would be riding into a major battle?

I didn't know, but we'd find out soon enough whether it was based in foresight or simple fear.

We clattered down the steps and ran over to the stables. Though they weren't normally guarded, with the sounding of the alarm, a squad would have been deployed to man the half dozen archer slots in the roof. While they weren't obvious to a casual glance, if you scanned the roofline carefully enough, you'd see a curious number of gaps in the roofing where the tiles had been retracted. Coursers were a necessary and valuable part of our military and had to be protected.

I shoved the door open, grabbed some carrots from the tub near the door, then handed a couple to Damon and strode down the center aisle. A figure appeared high above and said, "What news, Captain?"

I glanced up, vaguely recognizing the woman's face but not knowing her name. "At this point, it seems nothing more than a minor assault, but keep alert. We believe there's a major force hunkered beyond our immediate line of sight."

"Will do, Captain."

As the woman disappeared back into the shadows, Desta stuck her head over the door and nickered softly. I gave her a carrot and rubbed her velvety nose, then motioned to the big chestnut in the stall opposite. "Damon, meet Red. He's a good war mount—strong, fast, and reliable."

"Unimaginative name for such a stunning-looking courser." He offered the gelding a carrot before scratching behind his ears. "Where's his gear?"

"This way."

We continued on to the tack room. The smell of well-oiled leather hit the minute we walked in, and I breathed deep then sighed in contentment. There was no nicer smell in the world—except, perhaps, that of freshly brewed shamoke. Or the warm, spicy scent of the man walking beside me.

I found Red's gear for Damon, then moved on to collect Desta's. When I was riding for pleasure—or going to visit the drakkons' hunting grounds—I usually went bareback, but that practice was far too dangerous when scouting. Desta and I could and did move as one, but I still needed the security of a saddle in the midst of a battle.

She moved about skittishly when I returned with her gear, anxious for a run after too many days spent cooped up in the stall. Once I'd placed the saddle on and cinched it up,

I tied the saddle bags onto back loops, then slipped the halter on and threw the reins over her neck.

"Ready?" I asked Damon as I led her out.

He nodded and motioned me to continue. I hurried down to the doors, Desta all but dancing behind me. Once out, I hooked my foot into the stirrup and swung onto her back, quickly finding the other one before loosely gathering the reins. She half-reared, her thoughts filled with the need to fly over fields.

I patted her neck, promising her we'd run when it was safe, then bid her into a trot toward the gates. Damon swung his mount in beside us, the chestnut making Desta seem small by comparison, although she was in truth a standard height for courser.

"I seem overly large on this mount," Damon commented, as two men came out of guard houses and began to raise the upper gate's portcullis. "This wouldn't be some evil plan to get rid of the unwanted husband by making me a target, would it?"

I laughed, and some of the tension in me shattered. Perhaps that's what he'd intended. "You've proven your worth in the bedroom, dear husband, so there is no current plan to be rid of you."

"Suggesting if I fail to meet said standards further down the line, said plan might well be introduced."

"I do like to keep my options open." I cast him an amused glance. "Especially considering said husband has a reputation for going through lovers with the voracity I consume shamoke."

He laughed, a warm sound that caressed my senses but jarred uneasily against the tense air that held the fortress in its grip. "Not even I could keep up that sort of pace. Besides, I'm now a married man, and my playing days are over."

I snorted softly. Time would certainly tell the truth of *that* statement. And yet, there was a glint in his eyes that suggested he was serious, and as much as I knew I was a fool for believing it, part of me did.

I just had to hope that part wasn't headed for heartbreak.

We clattered on, following the winding stone road through the various levels. Though it hadn't been evident from the war room, a thin stream of whitish smoke drifted past the top of the curtain wall. There was a cluster of men and women nearby, some peering over the edge, others talking and gesturing animatedly, no doubt discussing the damage and means of preventing it in the future. Of course, until we were sure the area beyond the gates was clear, no one would be going out to make a real assessment.

The rest of my team—seven men and four women— were waiting near the portcullis covering this end of the tunnel that ran under the main wall, their mounts stomping and tossing their heads in anticipation. With Damon and me, that made thirteen, a number that some considered unlucky. I didn't, but tension nevertheless slithered through me. Túxn, I suspected, would not ignore the unintended challenge.

Kerryn Vertale—my second, and one of the best trackers in the squad—nudged his mount forward slightly and saluted. "What's our target, Captain?"

"An unidentified fog shield a couple of miles into the Barrain Ghost Forest. Damon is a mage and will accompany us to advise the best means of its disposal."

His gaze scanned Damon curiously, though he was aware of my marriage and knew well enough Damon was heir to Zephrine. But all he said was, "Usual formation once beyond the wall?"

"Until we near the forest, yes."

He nodded, and the team swept in behind us as we clattered through the now open portcullis and into the long dark tunnel that had further portcullis slots every twenty feet and regular murder slits in the ceiling. If the Mareritt ever managed to break through into the tunnel, they'd be greeted by boiling liquid.

Perhaps the awareness of that possibility was why they were now attempting to break the main wall itself.

The tunnel led out into the mountain pass known as the Eastern Slit—a deep, angular crevice created by a long-ago eruption that sliced right through the mountain's heart. I twisted around once we were beyond the entrance, but even though I could see the tiny figures atop the wall, I really couldn't see the damaged section, thanks in part to the still rising layer of smoke, and in part due to the heavy spray coming from the nearby waterfall. Once we made our way past its lake without seeing any sign of the Mareritt or their magic, I raised a fist to let those watching know the area was clear, then pushed Desta into a canter, leading the way through the valley's twists and turns then out into the wasteland.

Am here, Kaia said.

I glanced up and spotted her high above, her wings outstretched as she soared on the breeze. *Any movement visible across the plains?*

No white hairs. No horned ones.

According to the accompanying image, the horned ones were what we called moosu, a large deer-like creature that was almost six feet tall, with multi-pronged horns and shaggy brown hair. They tended to live in Mareritten's higher elevations, but came down to the plains to mate and raise their young in the milder spring and summer months.

Their meat was gamey, but good eating when on a long line sweep and surviving on little more than trail rations.

Can you see the fog from up there?

Is fog false cloud?

Yes.

See. Looks like stinging cloud.

I hoped not, and not just because there were no handy seas or large expanses of water anywhere near this part of Mareritten but because it would be yet another sign that they might be working with our foe.

We fanned out and formed a V-shape, with me and Damon at the head, three riders either side of us, and the rest in a well-spaced line behind us. It was a formation that made it harder for the Mareritt to take everyone out in the one attack, and was so successful that we maintained a tighter version of it in the marshlands and forests. Kaia kept high, so as not to spook our mounts or draw unwanted attention from any sentries the Mareritt might have placed.

It took a couple of hours to reach the outskirts of the marshlands, and another half hour to reach the foothills of the Barrain Ghost Forest, which had gained its name because of the cloak of silver fronds that covered its twisted trees in summer and the soft, ghostlike moans they emitted whenever touched by the wind.

I called a halt and ordered everyone to take a mounted break, then nudged Desta closer to Damon's mount. "Are you sensing anything untoward as yet?"

"I can feel magic thrumming ahead." His gaze met mine, bright depths troubled. "But it's more like the magic we found in the blue vein caverns than anything the Mareritten mages have ever produced."

I frowned. "The Mareritt are surely too territorial for any sort of alliance."

"I guess it would depend on how desperate they are to destroy Esan and claim at least one part of Arleeon."

"I can't imagine the gilded riders will be the type to share the spoils of victory. Besides, for an alliance to exist, that would mean they revealed themselves to the Mareritt long before they attacked Eastmead, and I just can't see how that timeline is feasible."

"Feasible or not, it's a possibility we have to consider. You want me to take the lead?"

I nodded. He might not be familiar with this area, but he had been well trained militarily and was well used to riding out on investigative forays. He also had the extra benefit of being able to spot magical traps.

He nudged his mount into the lead, and we moved on, our formation by necessity tighter than it was out on the plains. The forest itself was hushed aside from the soft moan of trees teased to life by the wind and the occasional rustle of small creatures running through the soft undergrowth. But as we moved deeper into the forest, other sounds began to intrude—the sharp thwack of axes biting wood, the metallic song of metal against wood, the occasional wisp of guttural conversation. It very much sounded like the Mareritt were digging themselves in.

We continued on, weaving through the trees and around the increasingly large mounds of rock. This entire area had once been a flood plain for the multitude of volcanos that still existed along the Blue Steel Mountains, and eons of eruptions and lava flows had forever pockmarked this landscape.

The deeper we moved into the forest, the sharper the noise became. I glanced upward, but couldn't see Kaia through the gently whispering fronds above us.

Am here. Bored.

Then you should have gone hunting with Gria.

You need more.

And I appreciate your help, but your drakkling should be your first priority.

She didn't reply, but wisps of her thought suggested revenge remained her main priority and keeping me alive was a means of gaining that. Drakkons were nothing if not practical, it seemed.

Is the cloud still there?

Thicker. Hear movement, not see.

I urged Desta closer to Red, then repeated what Kaia had said. "Is the magic getting stronger or remaining the same?"

"It remains steady, but that's not unexpected if it is nothing more than a shield."

A lark call came from the right. I raised a fist to signal a halt, then replied with a low whistle with a slight uptick at the end—code for, *what have you seen?*

Kerryn, who we couldn't see from our position but was in the trees to our immediate right, replied with a soft, staccato series of whistles—*two sentries, one hundred yards, above.*

I sent a hold signal, then knotted Desta's mane around the reins to ensure they didn't get in her way if she decided to eat—she was too well trained to run, even if startled—and dismounted. "We've a sentry to our right. Mac and I will take care of them."

Damon looked set to argue but nodded instead. I undid the nearest saddlebag and pulled out the long viewer, then motioned Mac to follow me and headed into the trees, sweeping around to the right so we could come in from a northerly direction, directly toward Kerryn's position. The Mareritt weren't dumb—our whistles, however like the birds we imitated they were, would have put them on alert for any movement coming from that direction.

The necessity of avoiding the whispering fronds slowed our progress, but we were closing in when I heard it—the faintest creak of wood followed by a sniff. They were in a tree somewhere up ahead. I motioned Mac to stop, then knelt then raised the long viewer, briefly adjusting the focus before scanning the trees—and saw them. Two Mareritten soldiers wearing leather armor the same ghostly gray as the foliage in which they hid. One had a crossbow nocked and ready, while the other used a flatter version of our long viewer to scan the general area where Kerryn was.

I handed Mac the viewer so he'd know their exact position, then, once he'd returned it, I motioned him to the right and raised five fingers. He nodded and slipped silently away. I retracted the viewer and tucked it inside my jacket, then went left, internally counting down. At two I stopped, unhooked my bow from my back, and nocked an arrow. At one, I drew back and sighted. At zero, I released. The arrow cut silently through the fronds and thudded straight into the Mareritt's body, piercing his flesh deeply enough that only the fletching could be seen. He straightened in shock, a gargled cry escaping his lips, then dropped. A second later, his companion also stiffened, then raised his hands, as if intending to remove the arrowhead now sticking out of the side of the neck. Blood bubbled from his lips, and he dropped to his knees, his breathing harsh rasps that rose above the whispering fronds. I slung the bow over my shoulders, drew the knife, and ran forward, reaching the ladder—which was nothing more than notches in the tree's trunk—a few steps ahead of Mac. I quickly climbed, saw the surviving warrior crawling toward the far edge of the platform and the weird-looking mechanical device stationed there. Some sort of alarm, no doubt.

As he reached for it with bloody fingers, I lunged at him, grabbing his boot and dragging him well away from the device. I killed him, then swung around, bloody knife at the ready. The other warrior was obviously dead, given he wasn't breathing and there was a chunk of arrowhead sticking out of his chest, right where his heart would have been, but Mac nevertheless knelt beside him and checked.

"As dead as a winter's evening," he said and pushed back to his feet. "If this setup is any indication, they've been here for a while."

"Yes." And that was alarming, given our regular patrols through the area. How had we missed all this? I motioned to the dead Mareritt at his feet. "Pat him down and see if he's holding anything useful."

I cleaned my knife on the other Mareritt's jacket, then checked his various pockets, finding little more than a few tokens dedicated to their god of war that supposedly brought holders luck and fortune. Obviously, said god hadn't been overly fussed with these two.

I whistled the all-clear, then we climbed down from the platform and walked back to Kerryn's position, softly calling out once we were close enough.

He lowered his weapon when we appeared through the fronds. "How many, Captain?"

"Only two, but there may well be more guard posts positioned closer to that barrier."

"How far away is it from our position now, do you think?"

Two wingspans, came Kaia's thought.

"About one hundred and sixty feet, according to Kaia."

Kerryn's gaze darted upward, though he wouldn't see her through all the foliage. "She's with us?"

I nodded. "Consider her an advance scout and a Mareritt murder machine if they dare attack us in the open."

He grinned. "I'm liking the sound of that."

If the rumble of approval running through my background thoughts was anything to go by, so did she. "Let's head back. Now that we've taken out their guard post, you and the squad can safely hold here while Damon and I head in on foot to investigate the shield and the lay of the land around it."

"And if you're attacked?"

"I'll call Desta in. Follow her lead and cause a little havoc."

"Good plan, Captain," he said, with an anticipatory grin.

Once I'd called in the two other riders, Kerryn offered me a hand so I could mount up behind him. When Mac was similarly mounted, we made our way back to the rest of the squad, signaling ahead so that they knew it was us coming in.

"Guard post?" Damon asked.

I nodded and slid over the rump of Kerryn's mount, dropping lightly to the ground. "Given the likelihood of there being others, we've more chance of getting close to that shield unseen on foot. The squad will hold here while you and I see what we can do about that shield." I glanced up at Kerryn. "Call in the rest of the team and stay wary."

"Aye, Captain."

Damon dismounted, then handed his mount's reins to Sora. "Shall I take lead?"

I nodded, and we moved out quickly. The odd sense of

wrongness up ahead sharpened abruptly, and unease crawled across my skin. "Something's happening."

He nodded. "Feels like they're refreshing their barrier spell, which suggests they haven't linked it to the energy within the earth."

"Why wouldn't they do that? It would conserve the strength of their mages, wouldn't it?"

"Yes, but Esan's earth mages would be able to detect the unusual flow of energy through the ground."

Fog stirs, came Kaia's thought. *See white ones.*

Doing what?

Make small throwers.

The images accompanying the comment showed what initially looked like our ballistas, but where the arrow should have sat was some sort of metal tube—one that looked a little too much like a larger version of the ones the gilded riders used.

"According to Kaia, the fog dissipated briefly during the renewal; the Mareritt are making mobile weapons."

"Which explains the construction sounds we're hearing, though it's a strange place to make any sort of siege weapon. It won't be easy to haul them through this forest." He motioned to the left. "The nearest pin lies that way."

We cut to the left, moving quickly and silently through the trees. It was another dozen or so yards before the fog came into sight, and it was utterly solid. Sound might creep past but there was no seeing through it.

We followed its length until we came to an unnaturally sharp junction of two walls. Even someone with absolutely no knowledge of magic would have guessed this wasn't a natural phenomenon.

Damon squatted a few feet away from its sharp point and brushed his fingers across the ground, his expression distracted yet intense. After several minutes, he glanced up at me. "There's no taint of the gilded riders in this wall, no matter how it might seem from above or how foul it feels."

"Which doesn't discount the possibility of them working together."

"The Mareritt are no more the type to share the spoils of victory than the gilded riders appear to be."

"Perhaps not, but what if they have a trading relationship? I did find a golden feather on that Mareritten youth, remember, so they've obviously been here."

"I suspect when we get past this wall, we'll uncover the answer." He drew his sword. "I'm going to slide the sword into the ground and under the pinning stone to push it slightly out of alignment. That should briefly alter the viscosity of the spell without rupturing it and give us a small window in which to slip through."

"We can't just destroy it, like we did the one in the blue vein?"

"Aside from the fact I have no idea what else is woven through the spell aside from the barrier threading, we also have no idea of their numbers or indeed what else lies inside."

If fog break, Kaia said, *I attack. No like white ones.*

I passed the comment on to Damon, and he laughed softly. "Her chance will come, and sooner than any of us might want."

Not soon enough, she grumbled in response.

"Ready?" he added.

I nodded and drew my sword, tension running through my limbs and flames briefly flickering across my free hand.

He thrust the sword at an angle into the soil, under the fog, then twisted the blade sideways a fraction. There was a soft clunk as metal met stone, then the wall shimmered, shifting in and out of existence. Damon grabbed my hand and pulled me into it. Tiny particles of moisture slid across my face, the sensation oddly unpleasant, feeling more like oil than water. I shuddered but resisted the temptation to raise the inner heat and burn the droplets from my skin. As Damon had said, we had no idea who or what lay beyond this barrier, and I was better off conserving every scrap of flame strength I had.

We came out a few steps later. The small valley that lay before us was pitted with rocks and covered in long, yellowish grass. It had also been partially deforested, the trunks of the old ghost trees now piled beside several forges, ready to fuel the fires that burned within. Thick columns of smoke rose, staining the underside of the fog wall, which was undoubtedly the reason for its yellowish color when viewed from above. Hammers clanged as smiths worked metal into long rounded forms that looked far too similar to the tubes the gilded riders used to fire their liquid shit, while in other sections of the valley, a good dozen smallish catapults mounted on wheels sat in various stages of production. Beyond that were a series of temporary shelters and kitchen facilities.

We ran low and fast down to the nearest outcrop of rock and hunkered down behind it.

"They've been here for a while by the look of things," I whispered. "So why haven't any of our patrols ever noticed the fog or come to investigate the noise?"

"There's probably some sort of redirect woven through the magic creating the fog."

"And yet we heard hammering on approach and weren't redirected."

"No, because they're still in the process of revitalization." He pointed to three red-robed gaze men standing, hands linked, on a wooden platform that had been constructed midway up the other side of the slope. "You might not be able to see it, but there's a triangular vortex of power flowing from those three."

"Then they need to be the first thing we attack the minute we get that barrier down."

"Agreed." His gaze met mine. "Though the odds are greatly against us, no matter how capable your squad is."

"Then we don't use the squad. We use our ace."

What ace? came Kaia's thought.

I hesitated, then simply said, *The reason we win.*

Am queen. We always win.

Not always, and certainly not against better armed foes, but she knew that as much as I did, even if she wasn't admitting it.

"That is a dangerous ploy for us all," he said grimly. "We have no idea what weapons they have here, and if they *have* gained the cylinder construction details from the gilded riders, that's more than capable of bringing Kaia down."

"Only if they get the chance to deploy it. We need to make sure they don't." I met his gaze. "Will destroying the pin behind us result in the same sort of explosion that happened in the blue vein tunnel?"

"Unlikely, given the scale of the barrier. It'd take out a good chunk of their own encampment."

"So it'd simply retract?"

He nodded. "But given its triangular nature, it's likely only two sides will fall, not the three."

"Two sides is more than enough."

I quickly explained what I had in mind, and his expression darkened. "You'll end up trapped."

"No, because I'll call in the team the minute those

ballistas are ash. And if I can't get back here, then Kaia can grab me on the fly." I placed a hand on his arm. His muscles tensed under my fingers, making it feel as if I was gripping warm steel. "I can't throw flame from here, Damon—it's simply too far away."

He took a deep breath and released it slowly. The man definitely wasn't happy with the plan but all he said was, "Keep low and as close to the fog wall for as long as you can."

I studied the sweeping line of the barrier for a second, seeing plenty of areas that provided good cover, and plenty of areas that didn't. But a good portion of the smoke coming from the smithy fires drifted over this half of the valley, and that at least gave me a little extra cover. I drew my sword and exchanged it for his. It had been carved from stone of the Blue Steel Mountains, and while it was prized for its strength and imperviousness to weather, it simply didn't have the capacity to cut through steel and stone that the Ithican blade did. "I'll head for the privy block—once I'm in position, take out the stone."

He nodded. "Best give me your bow and arrows. I can take out anyone who gets close and give you time to run if you flame out."

If I got to the point of flaming out, I wouldn't have the strength to run, but I wasn't about to mention that. I handed him the weapons. "If they charge you, you run. Don't wait for me—Kaia can get me out."

His expression suggested him running was not going to be an option. Not until I was safe, anyway. "Don't get dead."

I grinned. "I can't get dead because I haven't finished playing with you yet."

He scowled, though amusement danced briefly through

his eyes. "Begone, woman, before I do something I might regret."

My eyebrows rose. "Like what?"

"Like kiss you senseless and run the risk of discovery."

"There's a part of me definitely wanting to run that risk."

"An insane part, I suspect."

I grinned and didn't bother denying it. I squeezed his arm, then rose and padded away, following the line of rocks and using them as cover. Damon's gaze was a heated weight that pressed against my spine long after I'd left.

The ground sloped downward toward the small stream that meandered through the center of the shallow valley, and was littered with not only stone but the shattered remnants of the old trees, making caution even more necessary. The last thing I needed right now was to be tripping over and gutting myself on one of the thick splinters rising from the stumps.

The closer I got to my target, the thicker the smoke became and the more difficult it was to breathe without coughing. I continued on warily, fighting the growing tickle in my throat, my gaze constantly scanning the area, keeping an eye on the few Mareritt that were close enough to see me.

I was near to the stream, about a dozen yards away from the privy sitting on the other side, when it happened—the tickle in my throat overran my control, and I coughed.

Just as a fucking Mareritten warrior came out of the damn building.

CHAPTER 4

WITH A ROAR that echoed across the valley, he charged. He wasn't huge—as a race, the Mareritt tended to be short, squat, and powerful—but he was damn fast. He reached the stream before I'd even reached for my flames and was within sword-striking distance when they hit him. My flames were so damn hot they rendered him ash in an instant.

But the damage had been done.

A klaxon bell sounded, a piercing noise that echoed across the valley. As guttural shouts rose in response, I continued on, keeping low, jumping the stream and scrambling up the slope. A short, sharp explosion briefly overran the noise of the klaxon, but it came from the area behind me. Damon, destroying the pin stone.

Kaia? Get ready.

Am.

I reached the flat area and ran as hard as I could toward the privy. Felt the air brush a warning across the back of my neck; dropped low and whirled around, lashing out with a booted foot. The blow hit the Mareritten warrior coming at me in the knee, sending him staggering back but not down. I drew my weapons and lunged at him. Flames would have been quicker and easier, but I had no idea how much strength it would take to cinder their ballistas, and I had to conserve it where I could.

I swept his blade to one side with my knife, then thrust forward with my sword, sweeping it across his body, slicing through leather, then into flesh, gutting him from hip to hip

He didn't drop, even if his innards now were.

He roared, swung his sword above his head, and brought it down hard and fast, forcing me to throw myself sideways to avoid being split asunder. His blade skimmed my bootheels and thudded deep into the ground, but he didn't try to free it; he simply lunged—practically fell—at me. I swore, raised a hand, and cindered him.

As his ashes fell around me, I scrambled upright, sheathed my knife, then ran on toward the long privy building.

But there were now multiple Mareritt heading my way. Time was running out, and the damn shield still hadn't fully dissipated.

Another man appeared, this time to my right. I slashed wildly with my sword—an uncontrolled blow designed to do nothing more than force him to jump back. As he did, there was a soft "thwack," and he fell backward, the end of an arrow jutting out from his right eye. Damon, protecting my back as promised.

I sheathed the sword and sprinted on, my gaze on the edge of the privy's roof. Like them, their buildings tended to be squat and square, so with a bit of speed, I should be able to leap up, grab the edge, and clamber up.

Another Mareritt appeared and was shot down.

I lengthened my stride and leapt. My fingers caught the

joint between roof and wall, the roughhewn rock tearing at my skin as my body thumped into the side of the building. Pain spun through me, but I ignored it, digging my fingers deeper into the small gap before swinging my right leg up and hooking it over the edge. From there, I was able to drag myself up. My breath was now a harsh rasp, and my heart galloped, but it was the awareness that time was running out, that I would be dead if I didn't get my butt into gear, that had me scrambling toward the front edge when all I wanted to do was rest a minute or two.

Fog clearing, came Kaia's thought. *Can sweep through.*

Wait until I burn their weapons. It's safer for you, and I can use your attack to get back to Damon.

Me no carry?

You can't fight with me in your claw.

Truth. Want to fight.

I'll tell you when.

Hurry.

I gathered every ounce of inner strength I had, then raised a hand and cast a thick stream of fire toward the long line of semiconstructed catapults. My flames were so damn hot, their color was violet blue rather than my normal yellow red, and they instantly crisped any Mareritt foolish enough to not dive out of their way. They hit the first machine, spread across its frame, and, with a satisfying whoosh, the whole thing went up. I directed the flames on, leaping them from one machine to the next, feeding more and more energy into my fire to ensure it remained at its hottest, and the machines went up the instant flame caressed their wooden bones.

Pain pulsed through my brain, and the mote in my eye popped, pouring blood over my lashes. I ignored it, pushing on, until every single machine was burning beyond repair.

Now, Kaia. Now.

With a mighty roar, she dropped through the remnants of the fog, her murderous claws stretched out in front of her as she soared only yards above my head. The Mareritt shouted and pointed; some aimed crossbows while others raised heavy throwing spears. I flicked my flames toward the latter, and though they no longer held the heat to cinder in an instant, they still set hair and skin alight, and, more importantly, destroyed their weapons.

Kaia dropped lower, the force of each wing sweep sending dirt, ash, and men flying. Her claws raked everything before her, scooping up man and machine as one; she swiftly squashed then released the shattered remnants before scooping up the next lot. As she reached the end of the valley and swung around for her next run, I called for Desta, then scrambled to the side of the building and jumped down. My fingers briefly brushed the ground as I steadied myself, then I thrust up and on. Heard footsteps coming in fast from the back of the building. I drew my sword but didn't stop or attack. If I got too bogged down with fighting, I would die. There were simply too many of them, even if Kaia was killing them off by the dozens.

An arrow shot past me—a blur of air I felt more than saw—followed by a soft thump. Damon, once again proving how skilled an archer he was.

I continued on, down the slope and over the stream. Two Mareritt appeared out of the smoke to my right, one far closer than the other. I drew my knife and flung it hard at the nearest warrior. As he batted it away with a sneer, I lunged in low and swung at his thigh, the sword slicing through muscle, bone, and veins with equal ease. It didn't completely sever it as my Ithican blade would have, but there couldn't have been much holding it on, either. He didn't seem to care; he simply roared and swung his weapon. I countered, the heavy clash of steel against stone ringing out across the haze of noise surrounding us, my arms quivering with the sheer damn weight of his blow. I swore at him, and he laughed, an anticipatory sound if ever I'd heard one.

Laugh at this, you freak, I thought, and flicked a thin lance of fire at his face. He instinctively jerked back, and I swept my sword around and down, completely severing his wrist. His hand and sword fell, but he somehow caught the latter with his left hand. He didn't attack. He was mortally wounded, and we both knew it. Instead, he raised the bloody blade to his forehead, an acknowledgement of my successful ploy, then cut his own throat. For the Mareritt, there was no shame in taking one's own life. They believed it to be a far more honorable death than allowing an enemy to claim victory over them.

I scooped up my knife and ran on, but the second warrior was closing in, his gaze a weight I could feel on my back. I tried to increase my speed, but I was running on empty, strength wise, even if I wasn't yet totally flamed out. Something sharp hit the bottom half of my leg and I staggered for several steps before catching my balance and running on.

But I was hobbling now, and there was warmth spilling into my boot and weakness washing through me.

Movement, directly ahead. Damon, standing tall, bow nocked and aimed. Heard, internally rather than physically, his order to dart left and immediately complied. An arrow shot past me and thwacked into the warrior behind me. He dropped. I hobbled on up the rock-strewn slope, following the line of the barrier that no longer existed.

Behind me, chaos ensued. Kaia continued her sweeping

runs, destroying everything she could get her claws on. Another arrow shot past me, but this time, there was no sound of it thudding into flesh, but rather the soft clang of metal against stone. A miss. I swung around, sword raised. Saw two Mareritt coming in at speed, heard Damon's internal shout to go right, and again obeyed without thought. The nearest warrior followed my movement and attacked, swinging his heavy blade at my head. I raised mine, catching and deflecting the blow, the force of it shuddering through my entire being. Even if I had been at full strength, the likelihood of me beating this particular warrior would have been low. He was too big, too strong, too damn fast. I sucked in a breath and unleashed what remained of my fire. It wasn't hot enough to melt his blade or even ignite his leathers, but it certainly consumed the exposed parts of his flesh, burning through his eyes and into his brain. The man was dead before he even hit the ground.

Pain exploded through me, and I dropped to my knees, somehow managing to sheathe my weapons before cradling my head in my hands and rocking lightly back and forth. Fresh blood ran down my cheek, and consciousness faded in and out. But I couldn't let go. Not here. Not now. Not until we were back behind the safety of Esan's black walls.

Somewhere ahead of me, Kaia bellowed, a furious sound of intent. *I come, I save.*

Somehow, I forced my head up. Saw, through a bloody veil, a full host of Mareritt racing toward us. Felt the ground under my knees begin to shake, heard the sharp retort of hooves striking stone. Then my squad swept past me and thundered down the hill toward the Mareritt. Desta stopped beside me, snorting softly, the scent of her sweat lightly stinging the air.

I patted her velvety nose, then asked her to move

forward and grabbed the stirrup, using it to help drag myself upright. The white-hot heat that shot through my body had nothing to with flame, but rather the agony now radiating from my leg. Warmth continued to flood down the inside of my trousers and fill my boot, and sweat broke out across my brow. As the world briefly spun, my knees threatened to give way and I wobbled, but a hand caught my arm, holding me, steadying me.

"How badly are you hurt?" Damon asked curtly.

"It's just a cut. Nothing to—"

"Of course there's not," he cut in angrily. "Nothing aside from the fact your face is as white as the ghost fronds, and you can barely even stand."

"I'm fine, really." I glanced past him; my vision briefly faded in and out before focusing. The squad were wheeling back toward us, the Mareritt in brief retreat. It wouldn't last. It never lasted. "And you can berate me later. Right now, we need to mount up and get out of here."

"You'll bleed out long before we reach Esan, Bryn. Call in Kaia and let her fly you out of here."

"*Damon*, it can be bandaged—"

"*Bryn*, I can see bone. How the fuck you were even walking, let alone running, I'll never know."

Listen, Kaia growled. *No bleed out.*

I ignored her. "I'm the captain of this squad—I can't just up and leave in the midst of a battle."

"Kerryn's a capable second, is he not?"

"Yes, but—"

"Look, I admire your determination to stay and lead, but remember, you promised not to get dead. I'm going to hold you to that damn promise, even if it means I have to tie you up so Kaia can sweep in and grab you."

Like this plan.

Obviously, I was never going to win this particular battle. And in truth, they were both right, even if I didn't want to admit it. "Fine. We'll do this your way."

"A sensible woman. My wife is a rare jewel indeed."

"You, sir, are an idiot."

"And you, ma'am, are stuck with me."

I rolled my eyes and glanced around as Kerryn pulled his mount to a steaming, stomping halt in front of us. The rest of the team swept in a semicircle around us, ready to respond to another attack. Jax had a bloody cut across one eyebrow, and Nico's mount a shallow wound across his flank, but for the most part, the squad had escaped this first rally unscathed.

It was something that wasn't likely to hold if we didn't get out of here fast.

"Kerryn, lead the team back to Esan. Damon will ride with you and provide any necessary magical assistance."

"And you, Captain?"

"Will fly ahead with Kaia."

His gaze dropped briefly to my leg. He might not be able to see the wound from that height, but he'd certainly see the blood soaking through my leathers. There was enough of it. "The prince will have to ride on Desta, as we left Red tied up in the forest. We'll collect him on the way through."

I nodded, patted Desta's nose, and informed her of our plans. She wasn't happy about having a new rider, but the promise of extra carrots secured an agreement not to buck him off. Though I suspected Damon had a good enough seat not to be dislodged by her antics. I unknotted her reins and handed them to Damon. "Take care of her."

His gaze dropped briefly to my lips, and warmth briefly flooded the chill beginning to seize my body. He didn't step toward me, didn't kiss me, as much as I wanted him to. He simply mounted and nodded his readiness.

"You want us to wait until your drakkon snares you?" Kerryn asked.

"No. Go. Kaia can't approach with all of you here."

"Good luck, Captain."

And with that, he pushed his mount past me, into a gallop. The squad wheeled around and followed. Desta half reared, eager to be with them, but Damon held her in check, then leaned down and kissed me fiercely.

"See you in Esan," he said, then spun Desta around and raced after the squad.

Leaving me standing on the hill alone with the Mareritt racing toward me, their battle cries filling the air and their swords and axes raised high. Behind them, a line of archers was forming. We really *were* running out of time.

Am above, came Kaia's thought. *Move not.*

I glanced up sharply. She filled my sight, her scales glowing like fire in the hazy light of the day. *Won't.*

She dropped slowly, carefully, toward me, one leg outstretched, the others tucked up out of the way. But the Mareritt were now far too close, and the archers were nocking their crossbows. We had to get out of here, and fast.

Kaia...

Know.

Hurry.

Am.

But she continued her slow descent, inching toward me, then, when she was finally close enough, opened her claws and, with surprising gentleness, wrapped them around me.

Just as the Mareritt crested the hill and charged.

CHAPTER 5

"GET US OUT OF HERE, KAIA." I raised my arms as her claws snapped closed around me, holding me tightly but securely. The beat of her wings increased, and a cloud of dust and stone particles rose with us, filling the air and making it difficult to breathe. An arrow cut across my cheek, drawing blood but thankfully not doing greater damage. I swore and cast what little fire strength I had left at the long, tinder-dry grass that dotted the slope between them and us, hoping it would make them hesitate and give us the few vital seconds we needed to get away.

They didn't hesitate, but we were above the treetops now and rising ever higher.

Then I saw it—the long cylindrical weapon being held steady by two Mareritt while a third stood at the back, seemingly arming it.

Fuck. *Kaia...*

See.

She swooped around to the right and flew hard toward the tree line. A long stream of liquid streamed after us—it wasn't brown, but rather this odd greenish color, meaning it wasn't the same substance the gilded riders used—but lost speed and fell away inches from Kaia's tail. Still, the cylinders could throw liquid farther than anything else they'd hit the walls with over the decades, and that was not a welcome revelation. Not given the destruction they'd already caused.

The Mareritt scrambled to reload their weapon, but we were now over the trees and beyond their immediate line of sight.

Safe, at least for the moment.

I relaxed just a fraction, and that's when the pain hit. It washed over me, thick and fast, and darkness loomed, threatening to sweep me into the deep well of unconsciousness. I fought it with every remaining scrap of strength I had left. I would collapse once we were home, not before.

It was a vow I kept right until the moment Kaia placed me gently in the palace's courtyard and I all but fell into my mother's waiting arms.

———

I woke to the sound of my childhood—a melodic song as bright and airy as the scent in the air. Mom, sitting near my bedding platform, softly singing while she waited for me to wake.

While the inner child smiled, the inner woman was disappointed it wasn't Damon.

Rather than immediately acknowledging her presence, however, I reached for Kaia. *You safe?*

Am. Hunted earlier. Gria caught large runner.

What Kaia called a runner was what we knew as capras. She sounded so very proud, and I smiled. *She's very clever.*

Is. Train new riders now?

Next task on the list. I paused. *Any sighting of the gilded ones?*

No. Is dark. We in aerie.

If it was now dark, then I'd been out for a couple of hours, at the very least. So why wasn't Damon here? Were he and the squad even back yet? The sharp stab of concern had my eyes snapping open. Mom sat on a comfortable old chair that again harked back to my younger years, her booted feet propped on the platform, her wiry red-brown hair tied back in a ponytail, and a colorfully woven blanket draped around her shoulders.

"What time is it?" I asked softly, somehow managing to keep the anxiousness from my voice.

Her gaze met mine, and she smiled widely, then put down the cotte she was embroidering for my father. It was something she'd been doing for as long as I could remember, and a task I seriously doubted she'd ever finish, given she only ever worked on it when sitting by either my bedside or his, waiting for us to recover and wake.

"It's just on seven."

She shucked off the blanket, then stepped onto the platform and walked to my end, dropping a kiss on my cheek before lightly brushing the hair away from my eyes. It was another thing she'd always done, and I couldn't help but feel safe and loved. It was a feeling I had the sudden urge to hang on to, because its memory might be the only comfort I'd have in the long, cold years that awaited in Zephrine. I had Damon, but one man, however wonderful he might be, however strong our relationship might yet grow to be, would never be able to replace the joy, love, and memories that echoed through the very foundations of this place.

"The healers," she added somewhat wryly, "wanted to keep you unconscious until the morning to give your wound time to properly seal, but given the seriousness of the situation and the impatience of our queen, we reached a much shorter compromise."

I couldn't help but chuckle. Patience definitely *wasn't* one of Kaia's virtues. Nor, in truth, was it mine—except when it came to watching the drakkons, anyway. Patience had never been an issue when it came to *that*.

"Are Damon and the squad back yet?"

"Not yet, although they scribed your father half an hour ago and said they should be here around eight."

I relaxed a little, though I wouldn't be entirely happy until I saw the man myself. "Why has it taken them so long to return? Were they attacked?"

"They encountered a few patrols, but there was no major battle and, aside from a broken arm, no major injuries."

"Any day there are no major injuries is a good damn day." I pushed upright, then tossed the blankets back to study the wound on my leg. A thick line of red and rather puckered flesh ran down the outside of my calf from just below my knee to the top of my ankle. It was definitely going to be an impressive scar, and I was okay with that. The healers could, of course, smooth the skin and make the scarring far less noticeable, but like many in the military, I considered them badges of pride—visible memories of close calls and survivals. That said, if I ever received a scar to my face, I'd definitely get it fixed. My womanly assets weren't all that many, and my facial features one of my few "good" points.

I carefully prodded the scar; it felt tender, but that was to be expected given how recently it had been healed. I returned my gaze to Mom. "I take it I am allowed to move about?"

"Yes, but there will be no major hikes until tomorrow morning. They were quite insistent on that."

They usually were, and, for the most part, I generally obeyed. In this case, there was actually no reason for me to be going on any sort of hike, let alone a long one. Not at this hour of the evening.

"Do you know if Hannity Gordan—a junior scout from Dale's group—has indicated whether she's willing to become a drakkon rider?"

Mom laughed. "I'm told her exact words were 'In Vahree's fucking name, are you serious?' followed by a quick, 'Yes.' Your two rather dramatic entrances have fueled more than a little excitement amongst the ranks, and it makes me believe if we made a broad appeal for riders, we'd have more volunteers than we could handle."

"Which is rather odd, don't you think, given the fear the drakkons have generated for hundreds and hundreds of years?"

"Man has always feared what he cannot leash and control. Your actions have proven they can be controlled."

"But I don't—"

"No, but the general population do not know that." She grimaced. "Which is not to say there aren't those who believe we should not be trusting the drakkons."

"Who, specifically? Dad's advisors? Or the general population?"

"A bit of both, and nothing we can't handle." She patted my hand. "Your father should be here soon. Go bathe while I order us something small to eat."

My stomach rumbled a reminder that it hadn't eaten anything aside from some meager trail rations, so I climbed out of bed and warily put my weight on my leg. There was several twinges, but otherwise, the leg held up fine—even if

I limped a little as I moved into the bathroom. After using the privy, I ran a quick, shallow bath and felt better for being clean.

I pulled on a robe and tied it closed as I walked out. "Mom, can I ask you an odd question?"

"Odd questions are your forte, my dear child. Always have been."

I smiled. "This is about you and Dad."

She raised her eyebrows, amusement and curiosity glimmering in her blue eyes. "What is it you wish to know?"

"Do you and he communicate? Mentally, I mean."

"No, though I lived with the man long enough that I know the way his mind works and can pretty much guess what he is about to say at any given moment. Why? Can you and Damon?"

I hesitated. "No, not really."

"Then why the question?"

"It's just... sometimes I *think* I can sense his emotions and hear a word or two." I hesitated again and half shrugged. "It's probably nothing, but—"

"But you're wondering if it means there's a deeper connection?" When I nodded, she grabbed my hand and squeezed it. "I think it's probably something you should discuss with him."

I dare say I should, but the thought rather weirdly had my stomach churning. What if he denied the connection? What if the link I perceived growing between us was nothing more than a desperate need on my part to have at least one deep and emotional connection before I left everything and everyone I knew for Zephrine?

Logic said *that* was more than likely. And yet the deeper, more irrational part of my soul was having none of it. Of course, that irrational part also whispered the possibility of *Dhrukita*—a belief that everyone *did* have a perfect partner, a soul that was the other half of their own—even if it was something I'd always thought to be nothing more than a tale told to amuse little girls growing up.

A soft knock at the door dragged me from my thoughts. "Yes?"

"Your meal, your ladyships," a soft voice said.

"Enter, please."

Mom's "something small" to eat consisted of a big pot of stewed meat and vegetables, various breads and sweet pastries, a jug of shamoke, and a dusty bottle of wine—it was something of a tradition to bring out the "good" red from my parents' personal cellar when one of us survived a close call—and was followed into the room by my father. I walked over and gave him a hug. "Have the mages discovered what substance the Mareritt used on—?"

"There will be no war room talk during the meal," Mom cut in briskly. "You, my dear daughter, are every bit as bad as him."

I grinned. "And *he* would solemnly declare that I am too much like you for any man to have a peaceful life."

She laughed. "As if Rion would ever want a peaceful life. Neither, I wager, does Damon."

I wrinkled my nose. "I'm not entirely sure what that man wants, but he's definitely keeping more than a few secrets from me. Us."

"Indeed," she replied calmly, "but until we uncover just what those secrets are, we have to play along."

"I detest playing along and I hate secrets." I grabbed a bowl and filled it with the hearty stew. "But I take it you *do* have a plan to uncover said secrets? Or have your seeress skills suddenly decided to work on demand?"

My father laughed. "While *that* would be majorly

handy right now, we're doing it the old-fashioned way—via spies in Aric's court."

I scooped up some stew with my spoon, but it was so damn hot I burned my tongue. I gulped down the wine Mom handed me, then said, "Why was I never told we had spies in his court?"

"Not even Vaya and Jarin know. There's less risk of them being caught that way." He accepted the stew Mom handed him with a nod of thanks. "Aric has several here. In fact, you're now related to one of them via marriage."

"*Gayl?* I thought she was his aunt rather than a spy."

"Oh, she's definitely his aunt, though she's Aric's half-sister rather than full. He has ten half-siblings, apparently."

"*Ten?* In Vahree's name, the men in the Velez line certainly like spreading their damn seed about, don't they?"

"Yes," Mom said. "Though I do believe it's a tradition that will stop with Damon."

I snorted. "According to the military rumor mill, he flaunts his wares about just as much as his father and brother."

"The rumor mill has some decidedly conflicting things to say about Zephrine's heir. If one did not know better, it would not be hard to believe we were dealing with two separate men."

"Aric does have something of a split personality—ruthless one moment, charming the next, depending on who he is dealing with," Rion commented. "I suspect that might well be what we're seeing when it comes to his firstborn—rumor wise, at least."

"Then maybe I should ask Damon about his aunt and her real purpose here."

"No, you should not," Mom said, with surprising force. "I have no idea why they are lying or why Gayl continues to be a presence here, but I am certain of one thing—whatever is happening, Damon is an unwilling participant."

"And given Aric's... shall we say, volatility?" my father added, "even voicing your knowledge about Gayl could have dire consequences."

"Damon did say recently that he'd answer my questions when lives were no longer on the line, but that really makes no sense. He's the heir, for goodness' sake." I stabbed my spoon in the air to emphasize the point. "The trade contracts are signed, and our marriage consummated, so why continue the farce? What else could they be up to?"

"Well, there hasn't been an assassination attempt for a few centuries now," Rion said, with a half-serious laugh. "Perhaps they plan to install Damon on our throne."

"Except for the fact Mom becomes regent if anything happens to you or your nominated heir until either Garran's son is old enough or I produce a son. Which, in this case, would be a second son, as any firstborn would ascend the Zephrine throne. Damon *can't* rule in your stead, no matter what."

"Which is why I'm sure Gayl is here to do nothing more than report on, rather than murder, me."

Mom put a hand on my knee, her gaze solemn as it caught and held mine. "You must believe one thing—I would never have allowed this marriage to proceed had I in any way believed Damon was a bad man or that you would not have a happy life with him."

"A fact I can confirm," my father said in a dry sort of tone. "We had multiple... rather heated... discussions about the relevance of treaties and their necessity to avoid war. It was only when your mother met Damon that she agreed not to tear up the contracts. And we all know that while it might have taken the threat of war to drag my Zephrine counterpart to the negotiation table, if we *had* then torn up the hard-won contract, he would have reacted negatively."

An understatement if ever I'd heard one. I smiled and placed my hand over Mom's. "Thank you for being in my corner."

"*Never* doubt the fact that I'm also in your corner, Bryn," Rion said, with just the touch of an edge. "But I have the weight of a kingdom on my shoulders and sometimes I must consider the safety and happiness of the many over that of the one, even if that one is more precious to me than life itself."

And yet, he would have allowed Mom to tear up those contracts and gone to war on my behalf if her doubts had intensified on meeting Damon. Of that, I had absolutely no doubt.

Mom withdrew her hand from under mine and elegantly motioned to the food. "Our meal grows cold. Enough talking until all this is consumed."

"Dear heart, there is enough here to feed an army."

My father's voice was dry. Her response was a somewhat prim, "But only a very *small* army, and I'd wager you have not eaten all day."

He grumbled softly but amusement danced around his lips as he lifted his bowl and began to eat. Once the bulk of the meal had been consumed to Mom's satisfaction, I picked up my shamoke and one of the remaining sweet pastries and asked, "So what news on Jakarra?"

Mom blinked and looked away, but not before I saw the brief shimmer of grief.

"Nothing new on Garran or Glenda," my father said, "but hope lingers."

Not for Mom, though, obviously. She was nothing if not practical and would know that had either survived, they'd have found a way into the caverns or at least found a means of contacting Esan. "The evacuation continues unhindered, though?"

Rion nodded. "We've now sent several squadrons over to both Jakarra and Zergon to help protect the caverns and those who refuse to leave."

Katter Reed, Garran's uncle on his father's side and the acting administrator, would undoubtedly be one of them. "What of Kinara? Have Hopetown's ships made it ashore there with supplies?"

"Aye. A message came in from Jacklyn just before I left the war room. They're fifty strong in the caverns, with two mages and enough weaponry to last several assaults—which, aside from the first and most destructive one, have not been forthcoming."

"Which is rather an odd way of going about business, isn't it?" I asked.

"Not really." He shrugged. "There are few other cultures so bloody-minded and determined to win no matter what the cost as the Mareritt. It makes more sense militarily to hit an enemy hard, force the survivors into a confined and difficult position, and then simply place a minor watch and pick them off as necessary while the main army moves on."

"Yeah, but the gilded riders don't appear to be picking anyone off. They surely must know about the evacuation boats given they've established a number of watch platforms along the Black Glass Mountains and the island, and would have to see the boats come and go even if the daylight restrictions keep them from doing anything."

"Presuming the restrictions are a truth rather than a deception," Mom said. "Given how little we know about them, anything is possible."

"Then maybe we need to capture one of the riders alive and interrogate them."

Rion's eyebrow's rose. "I'm thinking the drakkons would not be fond of such a quest."

Wouldn't, came Kaia's thought. *But do if helps.*

Are you always going to be in my thoughts like this?

Thoughts and talk interesting.

What on earth did you do before I came along to amuse you?

Got bored.

"She's talking to Kaia," Mom was saying. "The queen likes to know what is happening at all times."

Not when mating, came her response. *That boring.*

I grinned. *Sex is a participation sport rather than a spectator one. For most, anyway.*

What sport?

A game. Like when you chase longhorns but don't capture or kill.

Is fun.

I returned my full attention to my parents. "Kaia says she's willing to help us capture a rider alive if it would help uncover who they truly are."

"And if you *are* successful, then we can employ Fergus's skills."

Fergus was a witch whose mind-speaking specialty was humans rather than animals, and he generally worked in the healing wards helping those with various forms of memory loss to remap and recover them.

"He'll definitely be needed," I commented. "The few times I've heard them talk, it's not been in any recognizable language. Have you sent messages to all our allies?"

Rion nodded. "None so far have had much to say in regard to who we might be dealing with."

"So far?" I said. "Who hasn't replied?"

"Kaligorn and the Green Islands."

Both were smaller nations situated at the far edges of the known world, and getting to them involved many months at sea—at least two for Kaligorn and three to reach the first of the Green Islands—even with the help of air mages. Many traders thought the risk of so much time at sea worth it, though, because the two nations were rich in spices, silks, and raw cotton, and there was money to be made if they returned safely to Arleeon.

"I've heard the ambassadors from both places speak, and the gilded riders use a completely different dialect." I paused to sip my shamoke. "Is it possible the reason we haven't had a reply from one or both of them is because they've also been attacked?"

My father wrinkled his nose. "Unlikely—Ithica stands between us and them, and they've seen no sign of our raiders."

"Of course," Mom said wryly, "even the Mareritt tread lightly around the Ithican. They are... formidable... despite their declarations of being a peaceful race."

They were so peaceful, in fact, that they made indestructible weapons and also, apparently, armor, though few outside Ithica itself had ever seen it. "Which leaves whatever lands lie beyond Mareritten."

The riders weren't likely to have come from those continents in the seas beyond Zephrine's shores—not if they were attacking us first.

"I'd suggest *that* is the most likely answer. The Mareritt may not be seafarers, but they must have trading partners," Mom said. "Their weapons are evidence enough of that."

"Most especially their recent ones." I quickly told them about the cylinders and the liquid they'd sprayed at Kaia and me. "Perhaps we also need to capture a damn Mareritt to see what they know."

"Given their tendency to take their own lives if the likelihood of capture is imminent, that could possibly be harder than capturing a rider."

"Not if we sedate them," Mom said thoughtfully. "An arrow dipped in papaver might do the trick."

Papaver was a drug derived from a small, somewhat innocuous red flower that dotted the banks of the Grand Alkan River, the largest of the rivers to run through Eastern Arleeon. While it didn't actually knock the recipient out, it quickly and efficiently inhibited motor functions while providing a euphoric rush and utter relaxation. It was sometimes used in our hospitals to calm patients down, but it was very easy to overmedicate, which could lead to death.

Not that anyone would consider *that* a problem when it came to the Mareritt.

"Worth a try," I said, then glanced around as someone knocked on my door. "Who is it?"

"I've a message for Commander Silva. I was told he was here."

"Enter," my father said.

The door opened; a black-clad soldier took three steps inside, then stopped and crisply saluted. "Commander, the captain's scout team has returned to the military quarter. Second Kerryn Vertale and Prince Velez ride on to the palace."

"Thank you, Martin. Tell Jarin I will meet him in the war room shortly."

Martin nodded, saluted, and left. Rion's gaze came to mine. "If you're going to accompany me to hear their report —and we all know that *is* your intention, no matter what your mother and I might suggest—then you had best get dressed, and quickly."

With a laugh, I bounced to my feet, dropped a kiss on his cheek, then half ran, half limped into my dressing room. After pulling on fresh leathers and a silky undershirt, I shoved my boots on and grabbed a thick coat made from the wooly hide of a capra, putting it on and buttoning it up as I went back out.

"Don't keep Damon overly long, Rion," Mom said. "I dare say our two newlyweds are planning appropriate welcome home celebrations this evening."

I grinned. "Said celebrations that depend entirely on how tired the man is."

"*No* man is ever too tired for sex," my father said. "Trust me on that. Come along."

I laughed again, blew my mother a kiss, then followed him out the door. With long, easy strides, he moved through the hall and down the stairs to the main foyer. The guards saluted and opened the doors as we approached. We both returned the gesture and headed out.

The night was clear but so bitterly cold that our breath frosted on the air. I shoved my hands into my pockets in an effort to keep them warm and followed my father down the steps. The walls and courtyard lay in darkness, the large light cylinders having been turned off to avoid providing location guidance to the gilded riders. I had no doubt the main wall would also lie in darkness, though in truth, the lights from the various military and residential zones that made up a good part of Esan would likely provide a good enough line of sight to anyone viewing us from on high.

We were halfway across when the sharp clatter of hooves on stone echoed across the stillness.

"That'll be them," I said, stating the obvious.

He stopped. "And we might as well wait for them here."

As the gates were slowly cranked open, three stable lads appeared, ready to collect the coursers for cooling down and stabling. They lightly saluted us both, then rubbed their hands together, shuffling from one foot to the other in an effort to keep warm even though they, like me, wore thick wooly coats. Three coursers clattered through the now open gates, Desta being led alongside Damon's mount, Red. All of them steamed with sweat but, despite this, Desta was being all kinds of difficult, dancing sideways and tossing her head in agitation, her thoughts on the rubdown and the carrots she knew would be waiting.

I glanced at Mik. "Give Desta her usual extra ration of carrots, but all of them can have additional grain, and mix in some molasses. They deserve it."

"Aye, Captain," he said.

As they drew closer, it became very evident that Kerryn's "no major battles" had been something of an understatement. Their leathers were torn and bloody in numerous places, and Kerryn had a large gash across his cheek. Damon's left eye had almost closed over, the bruising seeping down his cheek. Weariness rode both, but in Damon's case, it was so damn deep I could physically taste it. He'd used his blood magic to defend the squad, and more than once.

My gaze rose to his and, just for an instant, everything—everyone—else faded away. It was just him and me and this big wave of emotions that threatened to pick me up and wash me away. But as easy as it would have been to allow that, I had to stand firm. Until there was complete and utter honesty between us, I dared do nothing else. I was already losing just about everything I loved. I dared not lose my heart as well.

Something flickered through his one good eye; recognition of my unspoken determination, perhaps? If this wasn't *Dhrukita*, then what in Vahree's name was it? It *had* to be more than a bleed over from my strega ability to hear the thoughts of animals, if only because it was something that had never happened before.

He pulled Red to a halt, kicked his feet free of the stirrups, and dismounted. As Desta danced away from his movement, Mik and Yannos hurried past to grab her and Red's reins, while Jace grabbed Kerryn's mount. Desta was still dancing in anticipation as they were led away.

"Second Vertale," my father said, briskly acknowledging the salutes of both men, "accompany me to the war room— it'll be far easier on us both if you make your report in warmer surrounds. Prince Velez, I'll talk to you in the morning, when you look less inclined to collapse with exhaustion."

"Thank you, Commander."

Rion nodded and walked away. Kerryn hesitated, then gripped Damon's arm and said quickly, "Thank you, my lord, for your efforts out there. We might not have made it home otherwise."

"There's no need to thank me for doing what duty requires," Damon said dryly. "Besides, your captain would have been displeased had I returned home with anything less than a full complement of men and women."

"Indeed, she would have," I agreed wryly.

Kerryn chuckled softly, then casually saluted and ran after Rion.

As the two men clattered up the steps, I returned my attention to Damon. He stank of sweat and blood, but at least the latter seemed to be mostly confined to the cuffs of his jacket and was a result of him cutting his arms to raise the blood magic.

"Good to see you alive and well, husband." Though it was lightly said, it was taking every ounce of control I had not to throw myself into the man's arms. He looked like he was about to collapse, for Vahree's sake. The last thing he needed was my weight on top of him.

Although, given the wicked heat so visible in his good eye, maybe that was a false belief on my part.

"Good to see you awake and walking, wife," he said in the same light manner. "I am somewhat disappointed though."

The heat in his eye was increasing, and a smile twitched at my lips. "Over what?"

"Well, I was rather expecting a welcome befitting the manner of our triumphant return. Or, at the very least, hugs and—"

The rest of *that* ended in a slight oomph as I threw myself into his arms and claimed his lips, kissing him with all the relief and the passion that surged through me. His arms tightened around my waist, pressing me so close to his wonderfully hard length that I could feel every breath, every tremor, be they exhaustion or desire. For too many minutes, this kiss, this man, and the unacknowledged emotions that swirled between us were the only things that mattered, the only thing I wanted. Now and possibly forever, though *that* was a thought I quickly dismissed. I really didn't want to contemplate such a thing as yet, even if, in practical terms, we were already forever bound.

Eventually, even the heat that surged between us was not enough to erase the bitterness of the night. He pulled back fractionally and said, his lips so close to mine I could almost taste them, "Shall we take this inside?"

"We should." I turned, hooked an arm through his, and made an effort not to limp as we made our way back to the palace. "Although you will be bathing, not bedding. No man who smells as foul as you do will ever grace my bed."

"Welcome home sex in the bath is perfectly appropriate."

"There will be no sex until you have bathed *and* eaten."

"You're a hard woman, Bryn Silva."

"No, I'm simply a woman determined to ensure her man has the appropriate strength to satisfy her. You, my dear husband, do not."

The glance he sent my way was so damn heated my insides just about melted. "Care to test the validity of that statement?"

"Not until you smell less odorous."

His laugh danced warmly across my skin, stirring my already needy hormones into an even greater frenzy. We hurried up the steps and walked through the doors, quickly making our way up to the next floor. But he didn't stop—or allow me to stop—at the door into our room, instead continuing on to the thermae at the far end of the hall.

"And what are we doing here?" I asked, even though the answer to *that* question was patently obvious. He intended to satisfy two very pressing needs in a more comfortable environment.

"I intend to bathe, as you ordered."

"Hmmm" was all I said to that.

He chuckled softly but didn't reply as a young bathing attendant appeared and placed two towels on a nearby bench. "May I get you anything else?"

"A scented soapweed for the prince—the greenwood, I think—and two robes. We'll toss his clothes in the chute for cleaning and repair, so there's no need to remain on call, Deedra."

A small smile tugged at her lips. Couples all but requesting privacy was a scenario she'd no doubt encountered on more than one occasion. "Thank you, ma'am."

She quickly retrieved the requested soapweed and robes, then left, discreetly closing the internal door behind her. I stepped away from Damon and motioned to the water. "In you go."

"Not without my wife."

And, moving with surprising speed for a man whose exhaustion echoed through me, he scooped me up and threw me in. I went under and came up spluttering and cursing. He laughed, hastily stripped off, then strode into the steaming bubbly water. Every inch of him was honed to muscular perfection, his cock rigid and ready for action.

But he'd thrown me in fully clothed, and I intended to stay that way—at least for the next few minutes.

I grabbed the greenwood soapweed from the platform next to the pool then held out a hand in warning. "You can keep those salacious intentions to yourself until you smell a whole lot fresher and I'm sure none of your wounds need immediate treatment."

Lazy amusement played about his lips. "May I propose a more exciting arrangement?"

My eyebrows rose, even as my already racing pulse ratcheted up several notches. "And what might that be?"

"One part washed for one piece of clothing removed."

"Would it not be better—and quicker—to just let me wash you?"

"Undoubtedly, but where is the fun in that?"

"Did you play these sorts of games with all your lovers?"

"No, but then, there were actually very few that I wanted to play such games with."

"Huh" was all I said to that.

"You don't believe me? I'm mortally wounded."

It was mockingly said, and yet, just for a second, irritation and perhaps a bit of anger flickered through his one good eye. But what other response did he expect, given his reputation—one he'd never denied?

I motioned him to turn around. "Let's start with the back."

"No, let's start with the front—yours, not mine."

I rolled my eyes, handed him the soapweed, then stripped off my coat and tossed it onto the thermae's coping. The silk undershirt was plastered to my skin, revealing my breasts and painfully hardened nipples.

He sucked in a breath and reached out, gently brushing his thumb across them—and causing all sorts of inner havoc —before I lightly slapped his hand away. "There was no mention of touching, my dear prince. Now turn around so I can wash your back."

"You, as I noted before, are a hard woman to deny a man in need the sight of your glorious body."

"Aside from the fact you've only one good eye at the moment and are obviously delusional, you can distract yourself by telling me what happened out there."

"Nothing more than what was to be expected, given our attack on their encampment." He handed me the soapweed, then turned. "They gave chase. We rode hard. There was the occasional battle."

I gently washed away the blood from multiple minor wounds. "There's enough evidence on your back to suggest there was more than one close call."

"They're not wounds from weapons. The ghost tree

fronds are as sharp as any whip when you go through them at speed, and they seemed to have an almost unnatural affinity for human flesh rather than courser."

"Hate to say this, but I'm not overly saddened by that development. Better you than them. At least you understand what is happening. They would simply think it's the riders whipping them."

"While that is true, I cannot help but think it also indicates your affection for me lies below the drakkons and the coursers."

"Well, I have known them longer, and they have proven their worth. You, my dear Damon, have not."

"Oh, you wound me." He turned and took the soapweed from me. "Next item of clothing—I suggest the boots."

"Is that not two items?" I countered, amused.

"Yes, but I wouldn't want you to be standing there lopsided or anything." Devilment danced through his expression. "Besides, I can hardly prove my worth to you if you insist on remaining fully clothed."

"Perhaps not, but if you're going to remove two items, then I need wash two items. Fair is fair."

"If you're going to be pedantic—"

"And I am."

"Then feel free."

He returned the soapweed, and I got down to the business of washing, starting with his glorious chest and shoulders and working my way down his washboard abs before following the happy trail of hair down to his crotch.

"You're flirting with danger there, my dear Bryn," he warned as I lightly swept the soapweed over his cock. "That thing is primed and ready to go off."

"Well, if it's intending to go off in me, it had better be clean then."

He laughed, a warm sound that ran across my senses as sweetly as any caress. I continued, every gentle sweep down his shaft and across his balls drawing a near incomprehensible sound from his throat.

Eventually, he caught the soapweed and tossed it well away from me. "Enough torture, woman. The boots need to come off."

My gaze jumped to his, and my laugh died in my throat. I lightly pressed a hand to his cheek, skimming my thumb just under the swollen flesh under his left eye. "This did not come from a frond."

"No, it did not."

"Then why are you brushing aside the seriousness of the situation? Why say there was only the occasional battle, when evidence—your bone weariness and Kerryn's statement that they wouldn't have made it back without your help—states otherwise?"

"I am doing nothing more than what you always do."

"I don't—" I stopped. I actually did, and we both knew it. "Okay, lesson learned. I will try to do better in future, as long as you promise the same."

"Oh, I do believe we can both promise that, but I also think we'll both find the implementation a fraction harder."

I couldn't help but chuckle. "Oh, I do believe you might be right."

"Well, at least we agree on something." He caught my waist and lifted me onto the coping. "Let me assist you with those boots."

Amusement tugged at my lips. "Just the boots?"

"Well, it's a tad harder to remove your leathers when your delicious butt is sitting on them."

"Said butt can be lifted."

"I thought you said there will be no sex until I have been fully scrubbed?"

"And the important bits now have been. Besides, a woman is entitled to change her mind, and that rod you have happening is looking desperate for attention."

"Oh, it is, Princess, it is."

He tugged off my boots, dumped them beside my jacket, then grabbed the bottom of my undershirt and tore it open, straight up the middle.

"And what," I said, with mock crossness, "if that was a favorite shirt?"

"I'll have another one made for you."

"*That* is not the point."

"No, sex is, so do be quiet and let me concentrate on getting these clothes off you."

"I'm not one to be silent or do what I'm told."

"I have noticed that, and I will admit, I find it quite arousing."

"I'm thinking you'd find *any* woman arousing when you've a hard-on like *that*."

"Not any woman. They do have to be conscious and willing, at the very least."

"So glad to hear you have standards, even if the rumors would suggest otherwise."

"I suggest you ignore the rumors and concentrate on this—on *us*. This thing between us is the only thing that means anything, no matter what happens in the future."

I suspected he was talking about far more than the looming battles we faced on two fronts now, and I really, *really* wanted to question him about it. But Mom's warning rang lightly in the back of my mind, so I kept quiet.

For now.

He undid the lacings on my pants, his fingers lightly

brushing my skin; every touch, however brief, however inconsequential, had heat and desire stabbing through me. The sexy, almost arrogant smile tugging at his lips suggested he was well aware of it, too.

I rested my weight on my arms and lifted my butt, allowing him to tug the wet leathers from my hips and down my legs. He tossed them beside the rest of my clothes, then briefly—critically—examined the fresh scar on my leg before stepping close again and placing his big hands either side of me, all but boxing me in. I could slip back and get away if I wanted, but who in their right mind would ever want that when this man was so damn sexy?

"It may be just me," I drawled, "but our current positioning isn't going to allow any... meaningful... interaction."

He nodded thoughtfully. "I do believe you are right. Perhaps we should fix that."

He shifted his hands to my butt, then slid me closer to the edge, a position that put my breasts at his mouth level. "Ah," he said softly. "A meal in the waiting."

"Hardly a meal," I retorted. "More a nib—"

The rest of that sentence was lost in a gasp as his mouth encased my right breast and he sucked hard. A shudder of sheer delight ran through me, and he chuckled, the low rough sound of a man who knew exactly what he was doing and how to please his partner. Which he certainly did over the next heady few minutes as he alternated between my breasts, walking me to the edge of gentle pain first with his teeth before using mouth and tongue to soothe and delight.

Then he journeyed upwards, dropping languid kisses on my collarbone, my neck, my chin, before claiming my lips. Our tongues tangled and teased, testing and tasting each other to the fullest as the kiss went on and on. As desire and hunger surged to heady heights, I slid a hand from around his neck, trailed it down his body, and lightly brushed my fingers across his cock.

He groaned softly, caught my hand and pulled it away, then rested his forehead against mine for several seconds, his body quivering and every breath a harsh, rapid gasp that tore across my lips. Then, still keeping hold of my fingers, he slid his free hand up my thigh and lightly brushed his fingers across my mound. I groaned and pressed against his touch, wanting, needing, a whole lot more. His clever fingers slipped down, finding and teasing my clitoris until I was a shuddering and shaking mess, and so damn wet with need it was almost painful.

"Damn it," I said fiercely, "if you don't sheathe yourself in me this minute, I will be forced to take matters into my own hands."

With a hearty laugh, he slid his hands under my butt and pulled me onto him. I wrapped my legs around his waist and thrust down on him hard, sheathing him so very deeply inside. A low moan of utter pleasure escaped my lips, but I didn't immediately move. I simply closed my eyes and enjoyed the utter perfection of this most basic human interaction.

Then he made a low, almost desperate sound in the back of his throat and began to thrust, every movement fierce and urgent. I wrapped my arms around his neck again and moved with him, matching his desperation, riding him hard, needing the ultimate release.

When it came, it was glorious. He followed me over that edge a heartbeat later, his body rigid against mine, his seed exploding into me. For several minutes afterward, neither of us moved, our foreheads touching and our rapid breaths mingling.

When I actually felt capable of movement *and* speech, I

pulled back a fraction and said, "It's just as well I'm protected against pregnancy, because it felt like you were aiming for the ultimate prize at the end there."

He chuckled softly. "I can assure you, I was simply intent on making every glorious inch of you mine."

"Well, you've certainly done that. Should we leave the thermae and return to our room? You do need to eat."

"The only thing I need to eat right now is you. In case you haven't noticed, I have not had my fill of you yet."

I'd have been hard pressed *not* to notice, given he remained partially erect inside. No wonder the men of the Velez line had so many offspring—they were nigh on insatiable. "You can't survive without food, you know."

"Perhaps I cannot survive without you." He walked us across the pool, up the steps, and then placed me on my feet. The partial erection was definitely moving into fullness.

"You say the nicest things, even if you don't mean it."

He raised an eyebrow. Though amusement teased his lips, there was an odd fierceness in his expression. "I do not often say things I do not mean."

"You're heir to the Zephrine throne," I said dryly, doing my best to ignore the uncertainty that light was causing. "Saying and doing things you do not mean comes with the territory."

"Perhaps for my father, but I am not he or my brother." He grabbed the robes and tossed me the smallest. This particular conversation was now over, I suspected—a fact he confirmed when he added, "And given you'll no doubt be ordering a breakfast at an unforgivable hour so you can go fly with your drakkon, I will rise and eat then."

"I need to introduce Kele and Hannity to their drakkons and get them used to flying as one—which is going to be harder than it was for me and Kaia, because neither woman can mind speak." I tightened the sash on my robe. "But you don't have to get up."

"Have you forgotten that Hannity won't get into the aerie without me expanding the spell?"

"I actually had." I wrinkled my nose. "That reminds me, have you had time yet to scribe home and ask about that combining spell?"

"No, but I'll send a message once I get back from the cavern. I noticed the other day that your father had a quill connected to Angola."

"He has them linked to Kriton and other western cities, too, but they're not often used. Your father does *not* approve of us approaching his seaport or regional cities directly."

"My father doesn't approve of many things at all." Damon did up his robe, then gathered his clothes and tossed them into the chute before walking around to collect mine. "But the quills do still work, don't they?"

"Yes." I opened the door and waved him through. "Wouldn't it be easier to simply use the one Gayl is holding?"

"Easier, yes. Safer, no. Besides, it's not paired to Angola."

"No, but it would be easy enough to send a message and ask for it to be scribed there from Zephrine."

"I would not trust my aunt nor indeed Zephrine to relay such a message."

"Why wouldn't Zephrine pass it on? Is it because they have no drakkons and don't want us gaining any sort of military advantage? Surely your father wouldn't be so petty."

His smile was mirthless. "You have met my father, haven't you? There is absolutely nothing he wouldn't do to gain the upper hand and overall control."

I frowned, wanting to question him further about their relationship but knowing well enough he would not elaborate. So instead, I said, "What is the problem between you and your aunt? You clearly don't like each other, so why is she staying here with you?"

"You're astute enough to guess the reason, Bryn."

"She's spying on you."

"She's my father's guarantee that everything I report about your father *and* the developments here is the truth."

"How, when the only time she leaves her room is when she's getting her 'daily exercise' by walking the wall?"

"She's a powerful reader and a minor seeress. She cannot read my thoughts or indeed those of anyone from her bloodline, but she can skim the thoughts of many others and sometimes divine their future actions through their thoughts. Her targets here have been all those within the war room." He glanced at me, amusement lifting his grim expression. "Perhaps I fill you with my seed in the vague hope it can offer you some protection."

I nudged him; he laughed and staggered sideways in an overly exaggerated movement.

"What's her range?" I could read or command the minds of animals from a good distance, but from what Fergus had said over the years, his range was nowhere near that.

"Fifty or so feet, but she doesn't have to be in sight of the person to read their thoughts."

Which was one up on Fergus—he did have to see the person he was reading. "That's why her daily exercise walks along the wall happen at random times, and she often takes a break close to the war room section underneath."

"Indeed."

There was a part of me wanting to ask why he'd never

said anything, but the answer would undoubtedly be the same damn one he'd countered all my other recent questions with. I guess I had to be thankful he was even answering these ones.

"Is there any means of preventing her from reading us? Or divining our future actions?" Túxn only knew, if she'd been listening in to my conversation with my parents this afternoon, that could be disastrous.

"I did bribe a guard a few days ago to let me know if she came to our side of the palace—"

"And has she?" I cut in, alarmed by both him resorting to bribery and the fact that one of our guards actually accepted it.

"She did yesterday, although the guard said she only used the thermae."

"Yesterday, but not last night?"

"Yes." He glanced at me. "I daresay she was getting a discreet update on your condition and what we found in Mareritten."

At least that meant she hadn't overheard our conversation about Damon, her, and the spies we had in Zephrine trying to uncover what was going on. "Is there any way to stop her skimming our thoughts when we're in our rooms?"

"I did warn her that if she came over to 'our' side of the palace, even to use the thermae, I would shield our rooms from her. I now have a legit reason for doing that."

"Which leads to the question—why wasn't it the first thing you did? And why not also protect the war room?"

"Given how little personal information is discussed there, her skimming the war room will lead to nothing more than a confirmation of what I report." A smile tugged at his lips, though it held little in the way of humor. "Remember what I said about lives being in danger? I dare not make any move without reason and me shielding the war room without such a reason could lead to consequences I do not want to consider."

"Damon, you cannot keep making statements like that without providing full context."

"And that is something I cannot do just yet. You have to trust me, Bryn. Please."

I drew in a deep breath and released it slowly. "Fine. But I will not leave for Zephrine until I get those answers."

"If there's one thing I can promise, it's that. I would not expect you to upend your entire existence without knowing the truth of my father's machinations. What happens after that depends entirely on you."

"And what the fuck does that mean, Damon?"

"Nothing more than it implies. And yes, I am well aware that these cryptic comments are not helping the situation, but in truth, I have already said too much." He opened the bedroom door, ushered me in, then locked it behind us. There was a fresh pot of shamoke sitting on a heating pad and a platter of breads, cheese, and cooked meats. Mom, ever thoughtful.

He drew in a deeper breath then sighed. "Would you be horribly put out if I decided to partake in some food before I consume you?"

It was tempting to tell him to forget the very idea of sex until the truth was forthcoming, but that would be punishing me as much as him. And if that made me shallow, then so be it. "It's not going to take you the entire evening to do said partaking, is it?"

"Certainly not."

"Then partake away, my dear man, and pour me a shamoke while you're at it."

He laughed, poured us both a drink, then sat down and made serious inroads on the platter.

He was as good as his word, though. He didn't take long, and he certainly did consume me. To say I fell asleep a very boneless but contented woman would be the understatement of the year.

———

Dawn's rosy fingers were creeping across the still-dark sky as we made our way up the mountain. I would have preferred to wait until the sun had fully risen before making the journey, but, according to Kaia, both Yara and Rua were keen to get their "flamers" and start hunting the gilded riders.

Am too, Kaia said. *Hate hiding.*

You're not hiding. You're being appropriately cautious.

Feels like hiding.

I couldn't help grinning. *Have you warned the aerie's newest residents that they are not, under any circumstances, to attack any human who enters the aerie, be they female or male?*

Have.

And will they listen?

Am queen. Will attack if don't.

Yara is a queen.

Younger. Must obey.

I hoped she did, because I definitely did not want to see Damon or anyone else I cared about end up as drakkon food.

Humans who come here too lean. No extra meat. Not good food, Kaia commented.

I chuckled softly and continued on. It took a little under

an hour more to reach the vent, which was a three-foot-wide jagged slit in the otherwise smooth rock face. Though it had never been a lava vent, the air rolling out of it warned of the heat and danger that still bubbled deep under the mountain's dark heart.

I slung off one of my packs—I was carrying two, along with my sword, bow, and quiver—and dragged out my water flask, taking a drink as I scanned skies filled with clouds and the heavy threat of rain. There was nothing aloft, aside from a smattering of longwings and the black hawks that hunted in this area, and no indication of movement across the distant Mareritten plains far below us.

And yet, I couldn't escape the sudden notion that something was wrong.

"Problem?" Damon said, as he stopped beside me.

"No. Just grabbing a drink."

His raised eyebrows suggested he wasn't believing that statement, but he didn't say anything.

"How much farther have we got to go?" Hannity asked, stopping behind Damon.

She was young—barely nineteen, in fact, though she'd been in military school since she was fourteen, had been sent on her first scouting mission when she was sixteen, and had her first major encounter with the Mareritt when she was eighteen—and was practically dancing from one foot to the other in her excitement. In many ways, she reminded me of Desta. She had the same sort of build and coloring too —long of limb, with black skin and hair. Her eyes were green rather than Desta's velvet brown, and the mote in her right eye gleamed a bloody hue in the hazy morning light.

"Probably another hour," I replied. "You might want to grab a drink while you can."

"I'm fine. I just want to meet my drakkon, you know?"

I not only knew, but I also totally understood the nervous excitement that practically oozed from her skin. "I also need to send back a quick report, so—"

"So, there *is* a problem," Kele cut in, amusement evident. She, like most fire witches, was long and lean in build, but her hair was a closely shaven blonde and her features made even fiercer by a puckered scar that ran from temple to chin on the left side of her face.

"My father asked me to report when we safely reached the vent," I said dryly, "and it never pays to disobey your king and commander."

"A truth I shall not deny, even though we both know you do have a proclivity for doing both."

I grinned. "Not recently. And if you're not going to drink, you can take the lead and head in. I'm not sure Hannity is going to survive if we delay too much longer."

Hannity laughed but didn't deny it. She stepped to one side of the path to let Kele through, coming so dangerously close to the edge that I half reached out to grab her.

As the two women moved into the vent, Damon said, "You want me to wait for you?"

I shook my head. "It'll only take a couple of seconds, unless my father is busy with something else. I can catch up easily enough."

His expression suggested he wasn't buying my "update my father" excuse, but after a moment, he turned and followed the two women. I dropped my other, heavier pack down beside the first. While Kele and Hannity were both carrying all the gear they'd likely need, I was carrying extra harnesses, ropes, girths, and D-rings. I figured it'd be easier to store an additional supply in the aerie, so we had them to hand if needed.

I dug out the small scribe quill and screen from the side

pocket of the first pack then sent, *Have reached the vent. Wanted to warn you that Gayl is a reader, and she's regularly positioned on the section of the wall above the war room, listening to plans and reporting them back to Aric.*

The little cursor blinked for several seconds before the reply came through. *Damon told you this?*

Yes. He said he'll place a barrier around our room and yours to give us some privacy, but dare not do any more. I hesitated. *You can't let him know I told you, and you can't confront her.*

His pause was longer. Knowing my father, he was probably swearing right now. *Whatever threat Aric holds over his son must be dire indeed.*

Lives are at stake, he said, remember. The sooner your spies can find out what that means, the better.

I'll do what I can, but to date, there has been little in the way of information forthcoming. Whatever is happening there, few know about it. I'll talk to Fergus about Gayl. Perhaps he can come up with a solution to the problem she presents.

Worth a try, I said. *But talk to him at the hospital not in the war room. That should be well out of her range.*

There was no immediate response, but the little cursor was still blinking, an indication the quill remained active on his end.

Eventually he sent, *Have you decided on a direction for your flight today?*

Why? I sent back, even as trepidation surged. *Has something happened to the Islands? Has there been another attack?*

He didn't reply, not for several, incredibly long seconds.

The Islands remain secure, as far as we're aware. But we've just lost contact with Hopetown.

CHAPTER 6

"AH FUCK," I muttered. This was *not* the news anyone wanted to hear, even if it was also not unexpected. *Even if we could fly out immediately, we wouldn't get there in time to protect the city.*

And with only three fire witches on drakkons, was that even possible?

Can call more, came Kaia's comment. *They will come.*

But they have no defenses against the weapons of the gilded riders.

Are faster. Can distract.

It's too dangerous, Kaia. I don't want to be responsible for their deaths. Not when their numbers were finally in the healthy range after all our years of hunting them.

If mate give fire, we have weapon.

Magic isn't always that easy. Nor is it always that successful.

You trust mate?

Yes. Because I instinctively did, no matter what his secrets or how dangerous they might be to me and mine. And it wasn't just because Mom's second sight said he meant us no harm. It was that deeper, an unspoken, connection, perhaps, or even a promise that had been silently made, and one that held trust hard to my heart.

I hoped he didn't break it. I really did.

Get more flamers, magic give us fire, we kill gilded ones.

I couldn't help but smile at her optimism, even if I didn't share it. *All of which we can't do yet, so please don't call in the cavalry until absolutely necessary.*

What cavalry?

A large force of mounted warriors who ride to the rescue.

We fly to rescue.

We do indeed, I replied with a mental laugh and returned my attention to the scribe screen.

No, my father was replying, *but you can give a sitrep. Hopefully, they have at least evacuated all citizens and relocated the remainder of the fishing fleet.*

And, hopefully, the fiery, acidic spray the gilded riders used hadn't caused carnage in the underground shelters Hopetown's council had been creating for its citizens.

It'll be afternoon before we get there. Which would mean it was going to be a very long day for our new drakkon riders.

I'll be here.

And no doubt Gayl would be on the wall above, feverishly remembering all that was being said so she could tattle to Aric. I hesitated, then added, *Can we send out a wider call for more fire witches? The more witches we can mount, the greater our chances of success against the riders.*

Sent out messages yesterday, when you were still unconscious. Apparently your drakkon was nagging your mother.

What nagging? came said drakkon's question.

Constantly asking the same question over and over.

Nag you, not mother.

I snorted and signed off, then tucked the quill and screen back into the pack and retrieved a light cylinder. After squeezing through the vent's opening, I slung my packs over my shoulders and turned on the light before moving deeper. I made quick progress through the roughly hewn tunnel, reaching the first of the old lava tubes in good time. This particular one was spectacular, thanks to the forest of lava stalactites that hung from the roof and the thick black "high lava" lines that ran its length. The air was warm and still, smelling faintly of sulfur and damp earth. The latter came from the main tube, which was the oldest and biggest of all the tunnels and had long ago been reclaimed by mosses and string ferns.

Though there was no sign of the others yet, I could now hear the soft echo of their chatter and knew, through that nebulous connection between me and Damon, that they were only a few minutes ahead of me now.

I continued on until I reached the side tunnel that snaked up toward the old aeries. The heat gradually increased as I drew closer to the aerie, and sweat trickled down my spine. Though no one truly understood the reason why this section of the range was so much warmer than the rest, it was thought to sit above a deep but still active lava tube, and that this area, with its multiple fissures, allowed the overheated air to rise more easily. Which was no doubt why the drakkons had hatched their eggs and raised their young here for eons—that and the soft bed of sand covering the rock, a relic from the time when much of this area had been an ancient seafloor.

I caught up with everyone just as we neared the entrance into the aerie. Damon must have caught a wisp of my trepidation, because he stopped abruptly and turned around. "What's happened?"

"Hopetown was attacked this morning. We've been ordered to fly over there and investigate." I glanced at Kele and Hannity. "It's going to be a long day, I'm afraid."

Kele shrugged. Hannity looked even more excited by the prospect.

"No word of casualties?" Damon asked.

I shook my head. "The scribe quills went down, but hopefully most made it to the underground shelters they built." Or even the damn caves that littered the Black Glass Mountains, although that range was a long way out of Hopetown itself and probably not viable in this sort of situation. I had no idea if the "leg" portion of the Black Glass was similarly pocked with caves, but surely if it had been an option, they would have used it rather than building new shelters.

"Hopefully."

His tone suggested he held no more hope than I did that there wouldn't be massive casualties and death. I motioned him on, and it only took us another five minutes to reach the barrier. As it flickered briefly in warning, Damon called a halt, then motioned Hannity forward.

"We've placed a magical barrier across the entrance to prevent unwanted intrusions into the aerie, so I'll need several drops of your blood to broaden the spell and include you in the entry parameters."

Hannity was shoving her hand at him even before he'd finished. Damon's gaze met mine, and we both chuckled.

"What?" the younger woman said, her gaze darting between us.

"I believe our captain and her prince are laughing over the fact that I *wasn't* so eager to have my life's blood drained away," Kele said dryly. "But I do assure you, it doesn't hurt, and it is only a few drops."

"Wouldn't care anyway—there be drakkons ahead!"

Kele grinned and patted her shoulder. "There are indeed, and they are awesome."

Damon retrieved a small container from his pack, then unsheathed his knife, whispered a few words, and lightly cut Hannity's finger before turning it upside down to drip into the container. After half a dozen drops had gone in, he righted the finger. The wound was already healing.

"This shouldn't take too much longer, but best you all step back, just in case something goes wrong with the adjustment."

"Does that happen often?" Hannity asked curiously.

He smiled at her. "No, but it is always better to play it safe around magic."

She immediately took several steps back, but her expression remained fascinated. I couldn't wait to see how she reacted to her first close-up with a drakkon.

I leaned a shoulder against the wall and crossed my arms. Damon began to spell, his words rich and melodious, the language not one I knew but a sound I could listen to all day. Unlike the time he'd first raised the barriers here, he didn't use his own blood, probably because this time it was simply an adjustment to the spell's already existing rules. As the force of his spell rose and the small hairs at the back of my neck prickled in response, Damon thrust a hand into the wall none of us could see, then tipped the blood out of the small container. The softest of shimmers ran across the opening, then disappeared. Damon nodded, withdrew his hand, and finished the spell.

"Done." He tucked the used contained into a side pocket of his pack, then slung it over his shoulder. "I shall leave you ladies to the business of drakkon riding."

"You're not coming with us?" Kele asked, surprised.

"No, I've business I need to attend to." His gaze came to mine. "Fly safe."

Come back to me. He might not have said that last bit out loud, but it nevertheless echoed through me.

I hesitated, then responded the same way. *I will, for as long as you don't betray me.*

Something flickered in his expression. He'd heard me. This connection, whatever it truly was, definitely went both ways.

He nodded, though whether that was in acknowledgment of my statement or a simple goodbye, I couldn't say, then walked away.

I watched him for several seconds then pushed away from the wall. "Shall we go meet some drakkons?"

"I think Hannity will bust if we don't," Kele drawled.

She grinned and once again didn't deny it.

"Be prepared to be awed," I murmured, then led the way in.

The barrier responded, its magic briefly pressing against us, then we were through and walking down the rest of the tunnel to the large main aerie cavern. The musky scent of drakkons filled every breath and the scrape of claws against stone echoed lightly as big beasts shifted in anticipation of our arrival. They were all here, all watching us, their eyes gleaming like jewels in the ruddy glow of the sands. Even though I'd now been here multiple times, joy still danced through me at the sight.

I turned to watch Hannity's reaction. A mix of wonder, respect, and perhaps a little fear washed through her expression.

"They're *huge*," she whispered eventually. "I wasn't expecting—"

She stopped abruptly, her eyes as round as plates as

Gria hurried toward us—she was in desperate need of an eye scratch, apparently—then took a hasty, perhaps instinctive, step back.

"This," Kele said, reaching up to scratch the young drakkon's eye ridge, "is Gria, Kaia's daughter. She loves a good eye scratch, and you'll immediately win her heart if you comply."

Hannity hesitated, then said, "May I?"

I motioned her to approach and sent to Gria, *Go gently with this one. She's young and not used to drakkons.*

Gria lowered her head to the sand and eyed the young woman with interest. Hannity tentatively reached out and scratched the drakkling's eye ridge; delight ran across the younger woman's features while happiness rumbled through the young drakkon's thoughts.

She flamer like you?

Yes.

I want.

That sounded so very much like her mother that I couldn't help but laugh. *When you're much older, Gria.*

Can fly now.

Grow first, came Kaia's very amused response.

Gria grumbled something I couldn't quite catch and stomped a foot. Sand flew lightly as Hannity jumped back. "What did I do?"

"Nothing. Gria's just having a teenage tantrum over being told no." I chucked the backpack containing the spare gear onto a homemade hook, then grabbed all the harnesses. "Follow me, and I'll introduce you both to your drakkons."

We moved deeper into the cave. Drakkons watched us from various positions near the wall, with Kaia and Yara taking the prime positions either side of the exit. Rua had tucked her butt close to one of the larger hatching caverns, her tail curled up around her rear legs. She didn't move as we approached but she did lower her head. I reached up and scratched her eye ridge. "Hannity, meet Rua."

"She's gorgeous," Hannity said, awe evident.

Am, came Rua's reply. *She smart.*

I grinned. It wasn't only the queens who loved a compliment, it seemed. "I'll let you two get acquainted while I officially introduce Kele and Yara."

"Can she understand what I say?" Hannity asked.

"When I'm here, yes, because they're listening to you through my connection with them."

"Does that mean you have to be here for us to even approach them?"

"No. They won't attack; they just won't have a clue what you're saying to them."

"But," Kele added, "an eye ridge scratch is always understood and appreciated."

"Good to know," Hannity said and immediately began to scratch.

I smiled and walked on. Our younger queen watched our approach with interest, her thoughts filled more with the need to get flying and hunting the gilded riders than any real need to get acquainted with the woman who would be her rider. That might well change once the two had had more time together. After all, I'd haunted Kaia's hunting ground for fifteen years, and that had given us time to build up trust. I couldn't expect our other drakkons to so easily give to Kele or Hannity what Kaia and I had earned over long years.

Once the formal introductions were over, I reminded the two drakkons that neither woman could mind speak, only flame, and that orders would come through either me or Kaia. Then I moved over to Kaia.

"Right," I said to the two women. "This is how we assemble the gear and mount up."

I went through the entire process, showing not only how to harness up their drakkons but also how to mount and then attach themselves securely so that they didn't fall to their death if either drakkon shifted directly suddenly.

"What happens if we *do* fall off?" Hannity asked, worry creasing her forehead. "I mean, we'd still be attached by the rope but how will our drakkons react to the sudden shift in weight?"

"They'll no doubt grumble to Kaia and me about your lack of balance and how damn difficult you've now made things."

Truth, came Rua's thought. *Better not to fall.*

I repeated this out loud for their sakes, and they both grinned.

"Now, gear up, both of you."

I watched as both carefully "saddled" their drakkons, providing guidance where needed before asking each drakkon to extend a front leg so that the two women could clamber up.

Kele sucked in a breath when she was finally seated behind Yara's last neck spine. "Damn if the ground isn't a long way down."

"Wait until you're in the clouds before you complain about *that*." I glanced at Hannity. "You good?"

She nodded, her expression a mix of awe, determination, and fear. The latter was certainly natural, given how very new all this was to her. At least Kele had spent enough time around the drakkons now not to be overawed by them.

"I'll use the usual hand signals to communicate directions when we're in the air. Until you're used to flying, it's better we not risk losing the scribe quills. Kaia will, as I said, relay all directions to your drakkons." I paused. "If we do come across the gilded riders, be aware that the stuff they spray is acidic, and they will aim for the wings of the drakkons in an effort to bring them down."

"And if we get hit?" Hannity asked, frowning. "I've only a basic field medical kit with me and nothing in there will counter an acid-like substance."

"Water will stop the damage, so if either you or your drakkons get hit, you'll be ordered to a shoreline to soak in the sea. You'll need to be in the water for at least ten minutes."

"The sea water will sting like a bitch on any wounds," Kele commented.

"Yep, it certainly will, but better that than the liquid shit eating through flesh, muscle, and bone."

"Put like that, I'd have to agree."

I grinned. "The launch out of the aerie can be some- what... daunting. Just hang on and you'll be fine. Oh, and if the wind gets too fierce, hunker behind her spine—it'll deflect the worst of it."

Both women nodded. I spun and strode over to Kaia, scrambling up her extended leg and onto her neck. After clipping my pack and quiver onto their D-rings, I attached my harness then glanced around. "Right, let's do this."

We test? she asked.

I grinned. *We should. It's not right that I'm the only one to experience the terror that is that drop.*

She chuckled and headed out of the cavern, her body rolling from side to side. When we reached the edge of the landing platform, she spread her wings and bellowed. Behind us, Yara joined in, and the sound reverberated sharply across the peaks. The queens were ready to fight, and they didn't care who knew.

Then she leapt off the edge and flew—or more precisely, dropped—down the side of the steep, dark mountain, arrowing toward the barely visible valley floor far, *far* below. The speed of our descent shoved me back hard, snapping taut the rope holding me on, but a grin nevertheless stretched my lips. I'd been through this more than once now, and the initial terror had very definitely given way to exhilaration.

As the foothills started looming way too fast, Kaia spread her wings to halt our plunge and soared upward at a gentler pace. I twisted around to check the others. Yara and Rua were still plummeting, and Kele was grinning fiercely. Hannity was screaming, though it was definitely a mix of exhilaration and fear rather than sheer and utter terror.

They do, came Kaia's comment.

Will, Yara agreed. *Like this one. Fierce.*

Rua didn't say anything, and I had a feeling she was reserving judgment. That was fair enough given how little interaction the two had had.

We flew high along the spine of the Black Glass Mountains, cutting through wispy clouds that encased its various peaks, the darkly turbulent seas to our left and the foothills and plains to our right. Hours slipped by without sign of the gilded riders, and while that wasn't unexpected given our belief that they avoided the daylight hours, tension nevertheless rode me. The riders would no doubt expect us—well, me and Kaia, given they'd not yet seen any other drakkon riders—and might well have set a trap for us.

As we neared the aerie in which Yara and her younger drakkons had almost been trapped, we got the first sighting of destruction. It was little more than a layer of ruddy-brown smoke darkening the low-lying clouds ahead, but the color suggested the fires feeding it had not yet dissipated.

Better tell Yara and Rua to keep alert, I told Kaia. *The gilded riders might have set up sentry positions in the foothills sweeping down to Hopetown. Tell them not to react if we do see them until you or I say so.*

I could have passed the message on myself, but it would hold more weight coming from Kaia.

Yara not happy.

Remind her just how easily their acid shit can burn a drakkon's wing.

She did so. *Still not happy.*

She has an anger problem, doesn't she?

She young. Not as controlled.

Tell her she must remain in control if we want any chance of beating these bastards.

Have. She considering.

Tell her if her actions damage my friend, I won't be happy.

There was another pause while Kaia passed on the message. *Won't damage.*

At least that was something. We continued to follow the mountains' spine, then swept along the long left leg of the Sinopa Pass, remaining above the streams of cloud and smoke in an effort to ensure any ground sentries wouldn't easily spot us.

The closer we got to Hopetown, the more that smoke seemed to smell of destruction and death. I had no doubt it was, at this stage, more imagination than reality. Even if the fishing port had been wiped out as thoroughly as Eastmead, the scent of death surely wouldn't be evident this high up or this far away. I really hadn't smelled it at Eastmead until I'd gotten much closer.

And even then only in the marketplace, where the

bodies had been piled up on top of each other and semi burned.

Once we were near Sinopa's toes, I ordered the drakkons to begin a sweeping descent to the right so that we could approach Hopetown low and fast from the sea. While there didn't appear to be that much wind about—if there had been, the thick layer of smoke wouldn't be hanging so stubbornly over the seaport—the fact it also wasn't drifting out to sea suggested we'd be flying with what little there was at our backs. Coming in underneath it should also allow a clear view of what was happening in the port—if there actually was anything *left* of it, that was—and whether the gilded riders remained in the area, as they had at Jakarra.

We slowly angled down through the clouds and the haze, then hit clear air. As the drakkons swept around, it quickly became evident that the destruction, while bad, had been contained to the port, administration, and market areas, as well as the military encampment near the port. The main military section situated again the curtain wall had also been destroyed, but I couldn't see any bodies, either human or courser, to indicate any sort of fight had occurred there. In fact, there was very little evidence of *any* sort of resistance *anywhere* in the main sector. There didn't even appear to be a pile of burning bodies, as there had been in Eastmead.

Had the whole town simply walked away and let the enemy do as they willed? Had the arrival of the refugees from Kinara convinced the council that there was no winning against this foe? At least not with the weapons we currently had at hand?

If they *had* managed a total evacuation, that might well explain why the outlying living, schooling, and trade areas had basically escaped unscathed, although there were several fires burning that, if left unchecked, would soon change that. It didn't explain the lack of any immediate sign of the gilded riders, although perhaps we were simply too far out to see them.

Not, came Kaia's thought. *Magic ahead.*

My gut twisted. *Is it the same magic that we came across in the blue vein tunnel?*

Feel same.

I scanned the seaport we were fast approaching but couldn't see anything that twinged my instincts, magic wise. But the certainty we were walking—flying—into a trap was definitely on the increase.

Where is the magic located?

Above grass.

Meaning the grass that lay behind the ruins of the administration buildings and accommodation wings. All I could actually see was a strange haze covering the area and a sea of building wreckage and glittering glass before it.

If that haze was the magic Kaia could sense, did that mean it was concealing something? Something like a regiment of tube-armed riders, ready to attack a drakkon intent on killing, perhaps?

We couldn't discount the possibility. But, by the same token, we needed to know what had happened here and had no choice except fly on and see what eventuated.

Are you seeing or smelling anything to suggest those birds are near?

No. Wind at tail.

A statement that did not help ease the increasing tension within at *all*.

I flexed my fingers, trying to ease the tension. Sparks flew lightly, but were quickly whisked behind me. I twisted around, signaled to Kele and Hannity to stay alert, then returned my attention to the port itself. Three of the five docks had been destroyed, but there were currently two boats tied up at the remaining two and at least a dozen brown-clad men unloading boxes, sacks, and goodness knows what from the boats and carrying them down the pier to one of the few intact buildings in the immediate area. Hope rose that these boats had been tasked by the council with procuring vital supplies, but it almost immediately faded. Aside from the fact that all the men visible on the dock had green hair, Kriton—the only other major shipping hub in Arleeon, and the one most likely to have all the supplies Hopetown would need—was at *least* a good day's sailing away, even with the aid of an air witch and good winds, and both these boats bore flags that featured a long-clawed golden bird flying over crossed spears that sat on a blood-red background.

The flag of the nation that had spawned the gilded riders.

We burn? Kaia asked.

We burn, I replied grimly. *Tell Yara to sweep over the one on the left; we'll take the one on the right. Order Rua to remain back and keep watch for gilded riders.*

Kaia relayed the orders then said, *Rua not happy. Want fight.*

Tell her if the riders attack, she and Hannity will get more than enough chances to fight and burn.

You want to capture rider?

I hesitated. *Let's burn those boats first and see if that brings the gilded riders out of the woodwork. We can decide what to do then.*

What woodwork?

I smiled. *Woodwork is making things out of wood, but the term itself means something or someone appearing suddenly*. Or, as the case may be here, flying out from the cover of magic.

Your sayings strange.

Yes, indeed.

I signaled to Kele and then Hannity to let them know what we were doing. Both raised their fists in acknowledgement. Rua immediately circled away while Yara arced left to begin her run at the second boat.

On the pier ahead, the green-haired men were now pointing and probably shouting, though with the speed we were flying, it was impossible to hear anything. Most dropped whatever they were holding and ran—some toward the port, others back to the boat—though there were a few who aimed metal crossbows our way. Arrows wouldn't pierce Kaia's scales, but I nevertheless warned her to be cautious.

Her response was a deep roar that echoed loud and long, then she dropped hard toward the first boat, banking briefly, then folding her left wing close to her body so that I had a clear path of destruction. I unleashed a thick and deadly spray of fire, sweeping it across the deck from stern to bow, cindering anyone who got in the way and setting the entire boat alight. Crates similar to the ones we'd seen in the cave near the Beak exploded, spewing flames and burning liquid into the air, along with the remnants of several men who'd been standing close.

Kaia roared again as we swept over the bow and smashed her tail across the boat's mast, snapping it in two. As it crashed down, she extended her claws and dropped a little lower, scouring the pier, ripping up the ancient wooden planks as easily as she scooped up the still-running men. She crushed both in her murderous claws, then dropped them into the sea.

More explosions, this time to our left. As the mast on the second boat fell, a destructive rain of wood speared the air, forcing Kaia to bank away sharply. As she did, I caught a glimmer of gold in the blackened and burned remains behind the administration building. A heartbeat later, Rua's warning swept through my mind.

The gilded birds were rising.

I'd been right about the magic Kaia had sensed being a concealment spell, but *very* wrong about the ability of the birds to fly during the day.

Not, came Kaia's comment. *They hooded. Look.*

She briefly deepened our connection, allowing me to see through her eyes. The five birds appearing above from the ashes of the administration section were all wearing the same sort of hoods as the one we'd spotted tied up at the watch station near the Beak, which completely covered their heads, leaving only their sharp beaks exposed.

How in Vahree's name could they fly when they couldn't see?

Bands on leg, Kaia said. *You said use to talk.*

I'd certainly theorized that the metal bands worn by both the "lead" bird of any attacking flight and its rider allowed the two to communicate directly. Obviously, that connection also allowed the birds to see through the eyes of their rider when necessary.

And the fact that it was *only* the birds and riders wearing the bands who'd risen in response to our attack did seem to confirm that they actually *couldn't* fly in daylight *unless* they had the advantage of a connected rider.

So why not fit all birds and riders with those bands? Was it simply a matter of not all birds and riders being compatible?

That was a question we could ask when we caught one of the bastards alive.

See other birds now, Kaia growled. *We need kill.*

I squinted past her lowered head. I wasn't yet seeing them, but the haze that had covered that area was definitely fading. Perhaps the birds, in rising, had shattered the protective spell. *Aside from the fact we need to get past these five birds first, the other riders will be well aware of our presence now, and they will protect their mounts.*

We in air. They on ground. Have advantage.

Not when their weapons can burn wing and flesh.

They fire, you burn.

Let's just concentrate on the five first.

She grumbled in response but nevertheless turned and swept back toward the burning boats and the shoreline. The riders had formed a wide reverse V, the largest of the five birds holding the anchor position at the rear, distinctly behind the others. Perhaps he needed to do so in order to view our movements and direct the response of the other riders.

Tell Rua to fly up and come in from behind, I said, then twisted around and signaled the same information to Hannity, just to be sure she knew what was happening. I had no idea how well she could see me given the distance between us, and we really did need to find a better means of communication between riders, but for now, we just had to use what worked on patrols.

I'd barely finished signaling when Rua soared up sharply, her red scales gleaming bloody fire in the hazy light. As she disappeared into the haze of cloud, I ordered Yara to attack the left "arm" of their flight, which not only gave them another drakkon to worry about but also a lesser mass of drakkon flesh to target.

The riders didn't split. They didn't go after Yara, or even send a rider to investigate Rua's disappearance.

They just kept coming toward Kaia and me.

Because they knew us, I thought. Because they knew the threat we represented.

May not see Rua and Yara have flamers, Kaia said. *My sight sharper than yours. Perhaps gilded riders same.*

Possibly. Especially when all four riders were wearing helmets. They surely had to restrict their peripheral vision, even if only a little bit.

Am high, came Yara's thought. *Dive now?*

Yes. And don't bellow and warn them you're coming.

You no fun.

Apparently not, I replied wryly, then said to Kaia, *Let's cover her descent. Roll sideways and I'll flame the bastards.*

She immediately did so, the movement so fast she almost unseated me. The minute her belly was partially exposed, the four riders in the "arms" raised their tube weapons and fired. I unleashed a fire steam and swept it across the sprays, setting them alight in an effort to take some of the momentum away. As they began to fizz and burn, I directed my flames on, pushing them straight down the middle of their V before looping them around the lead bird's foot, just above the metal band. Metal might resist my flames, if only for a few seconds, but flesh could not.

As the bird's clawed foot fell away, the poor creature screeched and briefly fought its rider's control. Then Yara dropped out of the haze, a red streak of fury intent on murder. She hit the lead bird hard, forcing it down and away from its companions, her talons snaring and then piercing the body of the rider, slicing him in two. Then she rolled away, and Kele unleashed her flames, sweeping them across the length of the bird's body, melting feather, flesh, and then bone. As blood and metal dripped like rain to the ground, the poor creature screeched again—a sound that ended abruptly as Yara snapped her tail across the bird's head and broke its neck.

As it spiraled lifelessly to the ground, two of the remaining four came straight at Kaia and me while the third rolled around and chased after Yara. The fourth retreated, flying back toward the ruins of the administration building, perhaps to find reinforcements.

It didn't make it.

Rua appeared out of the gloom and dropped down hard onto the bird and the rider, her teeth tearing into the bird's neck. Hannity unleashed her flames a heartbeat later, looping them around the creature's body and attacking the tender flesh underneath. It was dead well before Rua ripped away and then spat out the bird's head.

Then my whole body lurched sideways, the ropes snapping taut as Kaia flung herself down and left. I'd been so damn busy watching the other drakkons that I'd forgotten our own situation and the fact we remained under threat.

Two thick streams of brown shot past Kaia's shoulder; the majority missed but the tail end caught me, splattering fine droplets across my clothes and my unprotected face. I swore and twisted around, spraying fire at the oncoming gilded riders. One bird immediately dropped away while the second flew on. I let the first go and dealt with the immediate threat, flicking my flames under its belly, attacking the unprotected flesh there, punching a hole deep into its flesh and burning it from the inside out.

It rolled away from us and dropped upside down toward the sea, a movement that blocked its rider's line of sight, preventing him from firing at us a second time. I spotted him a heartbeat later, leaping from his mount, diving feet first into the sea. Flames flickered around my hand, but I didn't unleash, waiting for the rider to come up. He didn't, so maybe the sheer weight of his armor had dragged him down before he could remove it all.

Hold, Kaia said, barely giving me the time to do so before she did a belly roll and somehow came up upside down under the retreating second bird. With one quick but deadly slash of her claws, she gutted the thing. As its blood and innards splattered across the two of us, the rider twisted and fired his tube, the brown liquid skimming the very edge of Kaia's right wing. She bellowed and snapped her tail sideways, smashing bird and rider away. Then she rolled sideways again, trailing her burned wingtip through the sea as she flew toward the shoreline.

There was murder on her mind, but her target wasn't the remaining bird—Yara and Rua were already dealing with that.

She was going after the ones who remained grounded.

Kaia—

Do this. Kill them. Crunch them.

The riders—

First fly, you burn, second fly, I kill.

There was, apparently, no arguing with our queen when she had her mind set on a definitive course of action. And while it did make strategic sense to attack an enemy while they were in disarray, my inner alarm of incoming trouble had suddenly ratcheted up several notches.

When you crunch, try not to bite into the intestines. Remember, these birds produce acidic shit, so you may just burn your mouth if you bite too deep. And please, stay wary, as I really think they've something else planned.

I have plan. They die.

Which was a good plan, as far as it went, but a little

lacking when it came to dealing with all the finer details an attack entailed.

We flew over the remnants of the port buildings and deeper into the heart of Hopetown. The riders had indeed set up on the grassy strip. As they'd done on Illistin, they'd erected two lines of metal tents—fifteen in all this time—but only ten of those had the birds tethered in front. All were hooded, and I couldn't immediately see any indication of sentries. Maybe that was because the senses of their birds were sharp enough to alert their riders of any approach, but tension nevertheless ratcheted up several more degrees.

As we swept closer, the birds raised hooded heads and squawked loudly. I tensed immediately, flames pressing at my fingertips to counter whatever response their still absent riders might send our way, but nothing happened. No one ran out of the metal tents. No guns were raised our way.

Kaia— I stopped, finally spotting movement.

Four men had moved out from under the remains of a building and were rolling what looked to be a fat mead barrel on wheels toward open ground near the first tent in the left line. More movement, this time to the right. Another four men with another fat barrel. That nubilous sense of danger crystalized. *Kaia, this is definitely a trap. We have to retreat.*

No retreat. Her mental tone was determined. Unswayable. *I kill them. Now.*

Which meant she no longer intended to fly past and allow me to flame them first. I silently cursed her but nevertheless sucked in a deep breath and called to every ounce of fire strength I had left. As she swooped down to begin her murderous fly over, I cast flames to the left and right, aiming for the men and the fat barrels. I cindered three of the men on the left and set that barrel alight, but the fire was quickly extinguished by the survivor. I hit him again, this time sweeping my fire up the barrel and onto his flesh, ensuring he was too busy trying to douse the fire consuming *him* to worry about the damn barrel. My aim on the right hadn't been as successful; the barrel was barely singed, and the four men were emerging from the ruins of a wall they must have ducked behind. I flung another stream of fire at them, but my flames were rapidly losing intensity. I pushed more strength into them and set the barrel alight, but the mote in my eye popped, a warning I was fast reaching my limits.

Then Kaia thrust her claws forward, jarring me backwards. As the rope snapped taut, she flew down the line of tethered birds, her claws spearing the first couple then scooping up the next few. She threw them all into the air, then bit through their bodies, crunching through metal and bone. Blood and metal feathers flew everywhere—but not the innards—and still no alarm rang out.

The sense of threat was so damn fierce now I could barely breathe.

Then, from behind us, came a soft *whoomp*.

I twisted around again and saw smoke drifting from the mouth of the fat barrel on the right. Glanced up, and saw a metal net spreading out, briefly resembling the extended wings of a bird as it flew high above us. Saw the multiple metal cables attached to its tail, leading back to the right barrel and what looked to be a well anchored winch now sitting behind it.

The bastards were intending to net us and then bring us to the ground.

"Kaia," I yelled, physically and mentally, "we're about to tangled in a net. You need to go sideways *now!*"

Me *physically* yelling at her finally broke through the haze of her murderous fury, and with a snap of her wings, she veered sharply away. But not fast enough. The falling net snared her left wing and immediately tightened. It brought us to an abrupt halt, and she screeched, a sound of fury and pain combined. How it didn't break phalanges or wrench her scapula from her shoulder joint, I'll never know.

She banked her free wing and tried to pull free from the net. When that didn't work, she snapped at the cables leashing the net to the winch, trying to bite through them, with little effect. Every single move she made had the netting around her wing grow tighter—bite ever deeper— drawing blood and tearing membrane. If it continued, she would not be flight capable. Which, obviously, was the whole point.

I streamed fire at the ropes, but it no longer contained any real heat and had little hope of melting the metal. Kele and Hannity might have more flame strength left than me, but the last thing I wanted was to call in more drakkons and risk them being ensnared. Especially when the cables had started biting into Kaia's wing even *before* they'd started to reel us in, suggesting there might well be magic entwined through the metal to either strengthen it or make it more "sticky."

Luckily, I did have one other trick up my sleeve. Or rather, in the scabbard hooked onto the rope in front of me.

Another *whoomp*, this time from up ahead. I glanced up, saw another metal net flying toward us. Kaia somehow twisted out of its path, but her left wing remained entangled, her right wing was barely keeping us aloft, and the cables were now being retracted at a faster rate, dragging us closer and closer to the winch and the ground. There were no riders or soldiers down there as yet. No one was attempting to attack us with acidic or flaming shit. Maybe they wanted us contained before they killed us. Or maybe they wanted to examine her and question me.

I'd die before I allowed either to happen.

I needed help. We were doomed if we didn't get it. It would take some time for the second barrel to be reloaded, so it was now or never when it came to getting free. I contacted Yara and ordered her to sweep down the line of remaining birds and cause chaos. As much as I wanted her to attack the cables attached to the netting or even the winch itself, the men there had weapons at the ready now and would no doubt fire if she came near them. Kele might be able to crisp them before that happened, but that was presuming she did have fire strength left and hadn't burned out like me. She was the stronger fire witch of the two of us, but it remained a gamble.

As Yara bugled and dropped down to finish what Kaia had started, I ordered Rua to sweep in behind the men up ahead who were attempting to reload their fat barrel. Then I unsheathed my sword, took a deep breath, and disconnected myself from the restraints keeping me on.

What do? Kaia said.

I'm going to cut you free. Extend your leg.

Dangerous to ground.

And we'll be captured and/or dead if I don't do it

Not happy.

Neither am I, trust me on that. At her for getting us into this situation, and at me for not being more forceful about my objections.

She extended her front leg. I wasted a second or two watching the desperate sweep of her still-free wing in an effort to get my timing right and avoid being skewered by her wing thumb, then scrambled down her leg and leapt off her claws.

It was a fucking long way down.

I managed to keep my knees slightly bent when I hit to protect my body against the shock of landing, then followed the natural momentum of the fall and rolled forward, keeping my sword arm extended to avoid skewering myself. The ground was awash with stone, broken bits of building, and glass, and even my leathers couldn't protect me from all of it. A dozen different hotspots of agony flared across my back and buttocks, and warmth trickled wetly down my spine. I ignored it all. I had no time—*we* had no time—left. The riders manning the winch were shouting, and though I had no idea what they were saying, I very much suspected they were finally calling in reinforcements.

I rolled back onto my feet and charged underneath Kaia and the cables anchoring the net tangled around her wing. If I could slice through the three of them, she could fly free, out of the way of danger. The netting encompassing her wing we could deal with later, once the riders and whatever regular soldiers were headed our way were dealt with.

A whisper of wind stirred across the back of my neck, and I instinctively went sideways. Metal gleamed as it shot past me and thudded into the ground several yards ahead, fletching quivering with the impact.

The bastards might want Kaia captured alive, but they obviously weren't so fussed about me. I flung my free hand back and swept a stream of fire behind me, trying to create a protective wall more than aiming at anything or anyone in particular. Blood began to pour over my lashes and, deep in my brain, the ache began. I continued to ignore it. Right now, there was nothing else I could do.

As Yara swept up from her first murderous run along the squawking, agitated birds, Rua appeared and swept in, claws first, at the other barrel and the men readying it for use. The latter wisely ran, but Hannity's fire chased them, turning them to ashes between one long step and another. A heartbeat later, the barrel itself was also ash.

Men, running toward you, came Rua's thought. *Are gold, like riders.*

Not Hopetown's military forces, then. *Attack them.*

Kill them, she amended and swept away.

Be careful of the metal tubes—remember they spray the acid, I yelled mentally after her. I had no idea if she heard me. She certainly didn't acknowledge me.

Another arrow, glinting with deadly intent. I batted it away with my sword, then ran between Kaia's claws and underneath her captured wing. Blood dripped like rain, staining the ground and filling the air with its dark metallic scent.

Yara dropped like a stone from the sky once more and flew down the remaining line of birds, gathering them in her claws and soaring upward again. Once again, she squeezed them until they popped, then dropped them to the ground, their bloody, broken bodies landing wetly all around us. Kaia's wing at least sheltered me from all that, but the dark rain of her blood was increasing as the ropes bit deeper. Too much more, and she wouldn't be able to fly.

I reached the first of the three blood-drenched ropes attached to the netting, gripped the sword with both hands, then swung it with all the force I could muster. The blade bit through it with ease, sparks flew—the sort that came with magic rather than fire—and the two severed ends of the rope snapped away, one barely missing my face.

More arrows shot past me, but either the gilded riders were deliberately shooting wide because I was under Kaia, and they didn't want to risk hitting her—not that these arrows were any likelier to hit anything vital than the others at the port had been—or her wing sweeps were creating enough of a windstorm to alter the trajectory of the arrows.

I ran to the next rope, this time standing slightly to one side as I swung the sword. As it snapped away, Kaia bellowed and thrust back against the remaining one. As it vibrated sharply, I swung the sword a final time and severed the thing, then hunkered down low to avoid the maelstrom caused by Kaia's wings as she rose.

The net still trailed from the ends of her phalanges, still cutting into bone and membrane. I couldn't deal with it. Not yet. Not until the threat of another attack had been removed.

Grab you, she said, even as tried to position her claws above me.

No, go, before they snare you again. I'll take out the bastards reloading the last barrel.

Not safe on ground.

You're not safe in the air if I don't get rid of that net caster.

Will be high. Call if want, she grumbled, then rose and swept away, her movements unsteady thanks to the weight of the net still entangled around her wing.

I thrust up and ran through the field of building remains and bloody body parts, heading for the men and the winch. A storm of arrows now flew around me, though I had no idea where the damn archers were hiding. I couldn't see them, and they obviously couldn't really see me given the inaccuracy of their attack.

But I knew without a doubt that my luck would run out sooner than later.

Rua, I yelled mentally, even as I desperately signaled to Hannity, *find and kill the archers.*

What archer?

I sent her a mental image of an arrow and one of a bow I'd seen the rider use.

Do, she said. *See.*

As she swept away, movement dragged my attention back to the barrel ahead. A lone, helmetless rider had raised a larger than usual tube weapon, stepping out in front of his two companions who were now reloading the barrel. I needed it destroyed. Needed *them* destroyed.

There was definitely more than a little of our queen's viciousness residing within me.

I roared in fury, raising my sword, and charged at the rider, even as I cast a sneaky snake of fire toward him, keeping it low to the ground until the very last moment. A wide anticipatory grin stretched the rider's thick, pale lips, but as his fingers curled around the firing mechanism, I directed my flames into the tube's barrel, then dropped hard to the ground and threw my hands over my head. The tube exploded, spraying metal and flaming liquid into the air with violent force. Remnants shot all around me but none hit my exposed hands or body. Luck, it seemed, was finally falling my way.

I jumped to my feet and strode toward the man who'd tried to kill me. Half his shoulder and neck had been blown apart by the explosion, and I had no idea how he was even alive, let alone screaming, and though the inner viciousness definitely wanted to drag out his suffering, I resisted and gifted him with death.

I moved on. The barrel had large chunks of metal imbedded into its fat body, one of them spearing all the way through. It was likely enough to render it unusable, but to be sure, I raised the sword and brought it down hard. The force of the impact shuddered up my arms, but the blade easily bit through the wood, and the front end dropped heavily to the ground. I repeated the process at the rear end, cutting away the firing mechanism, then checked his two companions, both of whom were lying in a tangled mess of limbs, bloodied and unmoving. One, at the very least, seemed to be breathing.

I moved closer, my sword held at the ready, but before I could check either man, something sliced into my calf, and red-hot agony exploded through me.

An arrow. It was a fucking arrow....

I stumbled, coming down hard on hands and knees, sucking in deep breaths to battle pain and nausea. From high above came a bellow of utter fury. I immediately reached out to Kaia. *I'm fine.*

Not. You hurt. Men come.

Of *course* they fucking did. I sucked in a breath and tried to remain calm. To give in to panic, to act without thinking, would more than likely result in Vahree calling my soul to his kingdom. *How many?*

Two hands.

Twelve men. Fuck.

I twisted around and saw them, running through the ruins, coming straight at me. They were carrying regular swords and knives rather than the tubes, but given the number of them, it was a pretty good guess the end result would be the same.

Me.

Dead.

CHAPTER 7

I COME. *I kill.*

No, I growled. *Remain high.*

No, Kaia retorted. *Run. I kill them.*

You can't—

Net throwers destroyed. No archers. I kill these, you safe.

Safe being a relative term given the situation, but there was little point in arguing with her. She wasn't listening anyway.

I forced my body upright, using the sword to help me balance. But the movement had another wave of agony pulsing through me, and sweat broke out across my brow. I had to do something about the arrow, otherwise movement was going to be impossible. I sucked in a deeper breath, then caught the end of the arrow to stop it moving and drew a knife. Then, before I could really think about it, I swept the blade down hard, slicing the shaft away from either side of my calf, leaving the bulk of it embedded inside. I had no idea what it might have hit—whether it was just flesh and muscle or something more serious like an artery—so it was better left in rather than pull it out and cause Vahree only knew what other damage.

And without the inner section sticking out and hitting my other leg, I could at least move around a bit easier.

But my attackers had passed the shattered remains of the metal tents now. I was out of time. I streamed fire at them, briefly scattering them, then turned and hobbled away through the wreckage of buildings and bodies, using my sword to steady myself over the rougher patches of ground. The back of my neck twitched, and the knowledge of impending doom rose, but I ignored them both and hurried on.

Then a fierce wind hit my back, sending me staggering forward. It wasn't a storm of air caused by one incoming drakkon, but multiple. The men didn't scream. They likely didn't have time, because Kaia and Yara swept through them with deadly precision and killed them all.

A few seconds later, Yara appeared above, blood dripping from her claws and fierce waves of bloody satisfaction running through her thoughts. Kele was little more than a small knot of humanity sitting behind the young queen's wing spine. *What do now?*

Join Rua and do a thorough sweep around of the entire area to see if there are any other pockets of riders or gold-clad ground soldiers. Destroy them if you find them.

As I said all that, I signaled to Kele, letting her know what was happening. She acknowledged, then asked if I was okay. I punched up a yes. She didn't say anything—and I probably wouldn't have heard it over the wind noise anyway—but tossed something down. As Yara banked away, I hobbled over to see what it was. A medikit. Thank Túxn for that.

I join, Kaia said.

If you move that wing about too much, you could permanently damage it.

Won't.

I didn't argue. It was still pretty obvious she wouldn't listen. I hobbled over to the wall remnant to sit, then opened the kit. It not only contained all the usual pain tonics, numbing and antiseptic salves, and bandages needed to treat wounds in the field or keep them stabilized until proper medical help could be reached, but also additional bone straps, wound sealers, and some silk webbing. Even though there wasn't much of the latter, the combination of the three should be enough to make Kaia's wing strong enough for the flight home.

I carefully sliced open the side of my boot—I didn't want to risk taking it off entirely in case my foot swelled, and the last thing I needed was to be walking around shoeless in a place like this—then did the same to the leg of my pants. The entry and exit points were small and neat, and very little blood oozed from either side of the wound. Hopefully, that meant nothing major had been damaged. I grabbed the antiseptic salve and carefully applied it. Pain surged, and I had to grit my teeth against the scream that rose up my throat. After several deep breaths that did absolutely nothing, I repeated the process with the numbing lotion. Unfortunately, relief was *not* instantaneous; I knew from past experience it would take a good ten minutes to fully kick in.

It was the longest fucking ten minutes in my life.

Once the numbing salve had done its stuff, I tugged out the bandages and securely wrapped the entire bottom half of my leg, not only to stop the swelling but also to ensure the remaining bit of arrow didn't move around too much.

As I uncapped and drank one of the pain tonics, Kaia appeared overhead, the force of each wing sweep stirring the ashen splinters of buildings, beasts, and men that littered the ground, sending them rolling away from me.

No more gilded ones.

I nodded, not really surprised. When they'd all but erased Jakarra, they'd done so with a force of twelve riders. They'd increased that to fifteen here, but the main change was the fact they'd apparently sent in their boats—and their ground forces—at the same time, perhaps in response to a perceived greater threat. If they'd scouted before they attacked, they would have been aware of the military presence here, even if they had no knowledge of the numbers they'd be facing.

In truth, while Hopetown's forces were well trained, they didn't have the battle experience of those who protected Esan, simply because, up until now, it hadn't been necessary. And given the utter destruction of the port and admin quarters, I couldn't help but wonder if the military had simply abandoned those areas in order to protect its evacuating citizens. After all, a town and its buildings could all be replaced. It's people could not.

So why had the gilded riders left the outer reaches of Hopetown untouched? Was it because they planned to use the port as their base in Arleeon? It made military sense to do so, giving them a foothold on our continent from which they could reach the rest of Arleeon. It wouldn't help their attack on Esan, however, as we'd see them coming from Hopetown far more easily than we would from Jakarra. Unless, of course, they took the course we had coming here and flew along the sea side of the Black Glass Mountains.

How bad hurt? came Kaia's soft question.

She was well aware how bad it hurt, because she'd feel it in my mind. *I'll survive.*

No want die.

I half smiled, despite my annoyance. *Not something I want either.*

Next time will listen.

Which was probably as close to an apology as I was likely to get from our queen. *I'd appreciate that. If it's safe to land, do so, and I'll remove the net.*

She carefully obeyed, raising another storm of dust and debris and forcing me to tug up the neck of my undershirt in an effort to stop breathing in the muck. Once she was down, I carefully pushed upright. My leg twinged, but the expected tidal wave of pain didn't eventuate; the potion and the salve had both kicked in. Which, of course, meant I needed to be extra careful, because I likely wouldn't feel anything if I somehow damaged the leg further, and that could be deadly.

I picked up the medikit, then hobbled over to her. She hunkered as close to the ground as she could, then spread out her wing. I thanked her and began the odious task of cutting away all the damn rope. In some areas, it had bitten so deep there was nothing but bare bone. Left any longer, and there might not have been even that.

By the time I'd removed the last of it, I was drenched in sweat and shaking with fatigue, the latter not helped by the multitude of cuts littering my back that continued to ooze blood. Still, Kaia was bleeding a whole lot more than me, so she had priority.

I sealed the worst of her wounds and patched the torn section of membrane as best I could, then stepped back. "That's the best I can do for now."

Is good. I heal fast.

"That is certainly a gift I wish I had." I rubbed my head wearily. "Could you ask Yara to land so Kele can dismount, then tell Rua to fly over the ocean and see if there's any boats approaching the port. But ask her to fly over us first so I can signal Hannity and let her know what is happening."

She immediately did so. Rua, who was closer, swept in and hovered low, creating yet another mini storm of soot and debris. Once Hannity had acknowledged my message, she slapped Rua's shoulder, and the drakkon immediately swept away. The two might not share mind communications, but they'd obviously worked out a crude means of communication. That definitely gave me hope that this whole crazy scheme of ours to pair fire witches with drakkons might just work.

But would it be enough to stop the riders? That was a question none of us could answer just yet.

With the younger drakkon gone, Yara landed with a harrumph and a quick, *Am hungry, go hunt.*

Night comes. Hunt not safe, Kaia said.

Find roost. Will be.

I hesitated, not wanting either to go too far or get too close to the Black Glass Mountains. As Kaia had noted, the approaching night brought with it the danger of more riders. Those who'd been sent here undoubtedly had some means of direct communication back to their main encampment, wherever *that* might be located, so it was logical to presume they'd managed to send a missive off before we'd wiped them out. Even if they hadn't, the lack of subsequent communications would be warning enough of a calamity having befallen them, and would no doubt elicit a response. I didn't want the drakkons in the way of that.

There's a small island off the coast that would provide a perfect roost for the night, I said, sending Kaia an image so she knew what to look for. *It's about fifty wing sweeps from here if you head in the direction of the sunrise—*

What sun? Yara immediately cut in.

Light in sky that gives day, Kaia said for me.

It's not inhabited by humans, I continued, *and the cliffs are a popular roosting grounds for birds. But there's large herds of wild, fat capras inland, and the riders aren't likely to attack you there, even if they hit us overnight.*

What you do? Kaia asked.

Look for survivors, and see if we can contact those who rule here.

And Rua?

I'll send her over once she returns. To Kele I shouted, "The drakkons are going to hunt. You need to dismount."

She immediately grabbed all her gear, then quickly slid down Yara's extended leg. After scratching the offered eye ridge, she slung her stuff over her shoulder and walked across to me. "You want me to grab your gear before Kaia takes off?"

"That would be great, thanks."

I glanced up at Kaia, and she immediately extended her leg. Kele dumped her packs beside me, then climbed up, unhooked all my stuff, and slid back down. As Yara took off, Kaia ambled away so the wind of her rising wouldn't knock us over, then leapt skyward and followed the younger drakkon into the clouds.

"That," Kele murmured, her gaze still on the spot where they'd disappeared, "was possibly the most exhilarating experience I've had in my entire life. Of course, it was possibly also the most *dangerous* thing I've ever done in my entire life."

I grinned. "That feeling of exhilaration and danger never goes away. At least, it hasn't for me yet."

And I truly hoped it wouldn't. Truly hoped that riding Kaia continued to remain as magical and as special as our very first flight together.

"I don't think it'll fade for me, either." Her gaze came to mine. "What's the plan now?"

I reached for the pack containing my quill pen. "I'll message Esan and let them know what's happened. Hopefully they'll have reestablished contact with the council by now and can pass them a message that we're here."

"And if they can't?"

"Then we find a safe place to wait out the night."

"We can't stay here indefinitely. Aside from the fact we've little in the way of supplies, it's not safe for the drakkons—too exposed." She paused, her gaze dropping down my length. "And I'm thinking that leg of yours will need attention before too long."

"If the arrow had hit anything vital, I probably would have bled to death by now."

"No doubt, but Vahree only knows what nasties they might have laced their arrowheads with. I mean, we're talking about a people who use *shit* as a weapon."

"I did put some salve on it."

"Salve doesn't help the internal festering though."

"True." I motioned toward the two riders who'd been taken out when my flame had exploded the tube. "Can you check the condition of those two over there? I think at least one of them might be alive."

"You want me to kill them if they are?"

I shook my head. "The only chance we might have of finding out who the hell these people are—and what their full intentions are when it comes to Arleeon—is to interrogate a prisoner or two."

"I think it's pretty clear what their damn intentions are,"

she said, but nevertheless headed over, picking her way cautiously through the rubble.

I dug the quill and tablet out, then messaged my father, giving him what amounted to an itemized list of what had happened.

The cursor blinked for several seconds then he came back with a simple, *Any injuries on your side?*

An arrow through the calf and a damaged wing, but neither is life threatening.

Right. I could almost hear the dry disbelief in that short reply. But then, I did have a habit of understating things when it came to personal injuries, and he was well aware of that. *Any gilded riders left alive?*

Kele's just checking that now. Were you able to reestablish contact with Hopetown's council?

Yes, a couple of hours ago. They're underground, and safe.

Let them know we're here and need some help.

With those injuries that aren't life threatening, you mean?

I smiled. *In part, but also in setting up sentry positions. I fear the riders will be back, as Hopetown provides a good jumping-off point into the rest of Arleeon.*

We've been discussing defensive priorities. They're intending to temporarily restrict access into the harbor.

That won't stop the riders. Or indeed, the boats. They could just sail farther down the coast or even anchor offshore and use rowboats to access the shoreline.

The air mages are also working on a wind cell around the city, with the hope it'll stop the riders.

We'd used wind cells in the past, with varying degrees of success. They were basically an envelope of fierce winds placed around a city—or fortress, in Esan's case—that prevented anyone or anything from entering. If humans, beasts, or indeed weaponry *did* enter the wind zone, they were swept up then around, until they reached the very top of the funnel storm and were spat out. Usually with enough force that they broke—or in the case of the Mareritt, died on impact.

The trouble was, the cells were also easily dismantled by magic. The Mareritt had certainly become successful in doing so over recent decades, which was why we rarely used them now.

You're forgetting they've mages of their own, I said, *and I don't think something as simple as a windstorm is going to stop them.*

We're aware of that, but they'll likely not be expecting the move, so that alone makes it worth the effort. Plus, it gives us a little additional time to find a means of combating their weapons and their riders.

I personally doubted that the little additional time we gained was going to be of much help, simply because I had a growing conviction that a shitstorm was coming straight at us. Which, considering what their riders used as a weapon, happened to be quite a factual statement.

We're going to remain here overnight, just in case the riders hit the port before the council has time to raise the defenses.

Good idea. We've just messaged them, letting them know you're on the ground. They're sending in a team, and I asked for a medic to be included.

Who had no doubt been ordered to report back on my condition. He was my commander and would never hesitate to send me into a dangerous situation if he deemed it prudent, but he was still my father, and he would never *not* worry about my safety. *Could you please update Damon on the situation?*

Yes. The cursor blinked for several moments, then the message scrolled on. *He has taken possession of the quill and tablet linked to Angola and has been sequestered in your room all day.*

And is no doubt directing the search of the Angolan spell library with the help of their masters. He believes there might be one that would allow the drakkons to gain the ability to flame from us.

Yes, that is what he has said.

You don't believe him?

I do. But there is much more going on than that. And I do not think it a coincidence that he protected our rooms from his aunt's intrusions only after *he'd discovered we had the Angolan scribe quill.*

And his reasons for doing so might be nothing more than the fact that his father—and his aunt—disdain magic.

Yes, but I fear the secrets he keeps. Fear that they will end badly for us all.

Trepidation stepped through me. *Does Mom share your fears?*

No, but she has far more faith in the overall goodness of people than I do. The cursor blinked a second or so. *Though it has to be said that* that *belief does not extend to Aric.*

It certainly did *not.* *Well, whatever else he might be up to, let's hope he can get that damn spell. We were lucky today, but that luck can't hold.*

I agree, and we are working on contingency plans. Be careful out there, Bryn.

Always, I replied with a smile, and signed off.

I replaced the quill pen and tablet, then grabbed my sword sheath and strapped it on. I kept the sword free, however. Aside from the fact it was a handy brace, it was also better—given my calf did restrict my speed and movement—if I kept it to hand. The drakkons had assured us there were no more riders or even magic here, but that didn't mean this place was empty. And given the untouched nature of Hopetown's outer edges, there could be a whole battalion of them hiding out there for all we knew.

I doubted it, but still...

"We got one live one," came Kele's comment. "He's not in a great state though."

"Conscious or unconscious?"

"In between."

"I'll grab my kit and wander over."

"Should you be moving around with that leg of yours?"

"Probably not," I said cheerfully and, after retrieving the kit, hobbled over to her.

The rider was on his side, partially propped up by the chunk of building rubble sitting against his stomach. He was in pretty bad shape, with finger-width chunks of flesh taken out of his exposed face and hands. The feather armor he wore had protected his torso and the front part of his legs from the bulk of the explosion, but the back of his legs had no such protection. Perhaps they figured there was little point, given that area was not exposed to normal attack when flying. When the tube had exploded, something large and obviously very sharp had sliced through his leg just above the back of his knee and had all but severed it. He'd been conscious enough at some point to put a tourniquet around his upper thigh, but he'd very obviously lost a lot of blood before he'd managed to do that. The odds of him surviving weren't great, even if we could get medical help here soon enough. It would be very inconvenient if he died before we'd had a chance to question him.

I handed Kele the kit. "Give him the bloomweed. We need him awake and aware."

Bloomweed was a small herb bush that had wiry stems and small, hairy white flowers. It was used mainly to reduce fevers, but it had two rather odd side effects. One was the adrenaline kick it provided, and two, it was something of a truth serum. While it was usually used in the field for the former, there had been occasions when we'd needed to keep a captive conscious *and* talking, and the bloomweed had certainly helped achieve both aims. Hopefully, it would work on this rider as well as it had the Mareritt.

"Might be wise to leash him first," she said. "We have no idea what these bastards are capable of."

"Good idea. There's a length of rope in my smaller pack."

Once she'd retrieved it, she bound his hands to his good foot to prevent any sudden attempt to lash out at either of us, then tied the rope to a nearby chunk of building. I moved his weapons beyond his reach with my foot— balancing a little precarious on my sore leg—then gave Kele the go ahead. She unstopped the small vial from the kit, forced several drops into his mouth, and then stepped back.

The good thing about bloomweed was its effects kicked in within a matter of minutes.

The rider growled deep in his throat, then muttered something that, while I couldn't actually understand his words, very much sounded like a curse. Then his eyes snapped open, and he immediately began to struggle.

I pressed my blade against his exposed throat and said, "Stop."

I wasn't sure if he actually understood me, but the point of a sword against an exposed bit of flesh was a pretty universal language. He stilled, but his expression was murderous and his yellow—almost bird-like—eyes promised death. It was something I'd seen more than once in the eyes of Mareritten captives, but there was something about this man's glare that sent a chill through my soul.

"You name and country of origin, soldier."

He growled something unintelligible—at least to me—and sent a globule of spittle my way. I sidestepped it, then repeated the question.

He fought the order and bared his teeth, but eventually reeled off a short sharp sentence in which the only word I understood was *Grie-i-ton*.

"Is Grie-i-ton the name of your country?"

He bared his teeth but eventually ground out, "Grie-i-ton."

Amusement twitched Kele's lips. "Either Grie-i-ton is his country's version of 'fuck off' or it is indeed the name of his country."

"There's no such place marked on any of our maps."

"Then maybe he's simply not understanding the questions."

"Oh, I think he *can* understand us, even if only partially. He wouldn't be fighting the urge to reply otherwise. We're the problem here when it comes to communication, not him."

"I take it he's not using a language common to any of our trading partners?"

"No." While I wasn't fluent in all the different languages our trading partners used, I'd heard a good range of them over the years, thanks to the ambassadors and advisors who'd been sent our way to renew or renegotiate trade deals. But there was also a common language used by most of our trading partners, so I tried that. "Your name and place of birth, soldier."

Kivlighan was added to *Grie-i-ton* this time.

"Well, that did elicit a different response. Not sure it helps us all that much more though." Kele frowned. "There's a rumor running around the barracks that the Mareritt are constructing larger versions of the tubes the riders use—is that true?"

"It seems the military grapevine remains a force to be reckoned with, but yes. Why?"

"Well, it means there must have been at least some trade contact between the two, and that, by default, suggests they found a way to communicate. So, it's worth trying Mareritten."

"The problem being I only know a few words. Besides, any interaction would have been between the commanding forces of each party, not the grunts."

"Grunts or no, they'd pick up a word here or there. As you said, we have."

"Yeah, but we've had more than a decade of interaction with them."

"For all we know, Mareritten and this man's people have been trading partners for decades."

"True." I hesitated, then added in Mareritten, "Why you here?"

It, and the phrase, "Stop or I'll kill," were the only two I really knew, and the latter definitely wasn't appropriate right now.

He reeled off another answer, his voice more guttural this time, almost echoing the tonality of many Mareritt.

"Most of his reply went straight over my head," Kele said grimly, "but I did recognize the words 'conquer' and 'resettle.'"

Most of us were familiar with those two words, mainly because many a captured Mareritt had uttered them over the years. Conquering Arleeon and resettling their people in our richer lands had been their goal for almost as long as our two people had settled on the continent.

"Where is your homeland?" I tried again, switching back to common tongue.

His reply remained all but unintelligible, though the word *Grie-i-ton* featured once more. It *had* to be his homeland. There was no other reason for him to be repeating the word every time I asked the question. Unless, of course, it *was* his version of "fuck off."

"Where is Grie-i-ton located?"

I didn't understand his response. I swore and wearily rubbed my head. The pain wasn't getting worse, but it wasn't easing, either. I needed sleep, I needed food, and more than anything, I needed to go home so I could talk to my husband.... And *that* was an alarming development, given the murky wall of secrets that might yet destroy us.

I returned my attention to our captive. "Point to where Grie-i-ton is located."

He cast a hand to the northeast. The bastard *was* understanding me.

"At least they're not coming from Mareritten," Kele said. "That has to be something, right?"

"Just because Grie-i-ton lies northeast doesn't mean their main invading force is also there." I studied him for a second, then added, "Where are your boats, soldier? Where do your birds roost?"

Another unintelligible reply, this time far fainter. The bloomweed's adrenaline effect was fading fast.

"Point in their direction," I said.

He growled something but nevertheless obeyed, pointing first to the east, and then to the north. Mareritten lay to the latter.

"Do the boats lie that way?" I asked, pointing to the north. "Or the birds?"

He said something that sounded like *barques*, which I knew from a couple of meetings my father had had with ambassadors from both Kaligorn and the Green Islands was their term for three-masted galleons. And if he was using the term, it suggested his people might be from the same area. They might also be the reason those two islands had not replied.

"How many barques that way?" I said, pointing north. "Use your fingers to show us."

He thrust up three, the gesture obviously a rude one even if it did answer my question. Then his eyes fluttered closed and he coughed; blood-colored spittle dribbled past his lips.

"Internal injuries," Kele commented.

"Looks like it." I kicked his good foot lightly, and he jerked briefly, his yellow eyes opening to glare at me. I pointed to the east. "How many ships that way? Show on your fingers."

He muttered something, then thrust up both hands. I sucked in a breath. If there were ten boats the size of the ones we'd burned here today, we were in deep trouble. While the galleons docked here had appeared to hold little more than supplies, the men to move them, and at least one ground regiment, they were similar in size to ours, which meant they were capable of holding more than one hundred and fifty men plus whatever livestock and supplies they might need for the journey.

"How many flights of birds?"

He coughed, spraying more bloody spittle. Then he grinned and growled, in a rough form of common language,

"The Stymphalian will cover your skies with gold. All will die."

And on that charming proclamation, he did so.

"So the bastard *did* understand us," Kele muttered. "But at least he had the decency to die and thereby save us the decision of whether or not we should get him medical help —although we both know I would have fallen on the side of 'not.'"

"Had it not been for the need of information, I would have too." The fact they'd killed Kaia's drakkling made it an easy enough choice, let alone everything else they'd done since then.

"Captain Silva?" someone called from the ruins of the administration building. "It's Commander Iker Green, of the Hopetown Brigade. We're told you're needing some help."

"Over here, in the field," I replied.

"The drakkons?"

"Well clear, and there's no indication that enemy ground forces remain in the vicinity."

"They don't," came the response. "We had our earth mages checking before we resurfaced."

A tall, broad, middle-aged man with a thick thatch of silver hair and a rather impressive moustache strode through the ruins of two pillars. With him were six fully armed men and a tall thin woman with a nest of red hair tied back at the nape of her neck. She wore the brown robe and loose pants of a field healer and had a sizeable medical kit on her back. After ordering the soldiers to form a defensive circle, the commander added, "I'm told there's been an injury?"

"I took an arrow through the calf," I said. "You've come up through one of the tunnels?"

He nodded. "This whole area is littered with them—it's how we were able to evacuate so quickly. Once Teagin stabilizes your wound, we'll take you both underground to our field hosp—"

"We've a drakkon still out on patrol," I cut in, "so I can't go anywhere until she returns."

"And how long is that likely to be?" the commander said. "Night approaches, and it's not likely to be safe above ground until we can get our protections up and running."

How long is a piece of string? I wanted to retort, but kept it to myself. The commander had the look of a no-nonsense sort of fellow who wouldn't take kindly to that sort of backchat. "She'll be here before nightfall."

The commander didn't look particularly happy at the delay, but motioned the healer forward rather than reply.

She hurried toward me, her movements sharp and quick, reminding me somewhat of the fragile spur wings that played around the peaks in spring.

"Please sit on the half wall behind you," she ordered.

Once I had, Teagin dropped to her knees and began unwinding the bandage. The numbing effects of the salve and the painkiller I'd taken remained in force, so even though I could feel the small movements of the arrow in my flesh, I wasn't in any sort of pain.

"I have to say," she said, "there is a rather odious smell emanating from both you and your companion."

"That would be the scent of drakkons," Kele said cheerfully. "You get used to it after a while."

"If they smell that bad, then perhaps it is a good thing they do not enter populated areas too often. It could wipe out entire towns."

"If drakkon scent *did* have that effect," Kele replied, "we'd already be using it as a deterrent against the riders."

"Given how bad *their* birds smell, I'm thinking it won't be an effective ploy." I twitched in pain as she tugged the final bit of bloody bandage off my leg.

Teagin tossed the bandage to one side, then swung the field kit from her back. "Glad to see you've sense enough to immobilize the foreign body rather than try to pull it out like most do."

"It's something we're all taught in basic field medicine," I said.

"Yeah, but you'd be surprised how many fools don't actually remember their training in the heat of battle."

"Teagin," the commander snapped, "please do remember who you're talking to."

She glanced up sharply. "No offense meant, Captain."

As far as apologies went, *that* was as insincere as they came. I returned my attention to the commander. "What are the plans for sentry positions? I'm aware an air cell will be created, but it won't be enough."

"They're working on extending the Sinopa's toes to create a temporary barrier into the port as we speak. We've four earth witches, and they're working in rotation to ensure no one burns out completely. It should be done within a day."

"And sentry positions?"

"Will be placed either side of the new barrier. Even if they drop anchor in deeper waters, we will see them."

Seeing them wasn't the problem. Fighting them—beating them—was. "If you don't mind a suggestion, it would be prudent to have additional sentry positions farther down the coast. A fit army could march back to Hopetown within a day from either Lowcliffe Beach or Gore Bay."

And while neither had docks, both were naturally deep-water harbors that had often provided shelter for trade boats in fierce storms. Lowcliffe also had a sweeping sandy beach that made it very easy for rowboats heavily laden with men to land.

"I will approach the council with your recommendation."

"It is a recommendation that would be wise to accept," Kele muttered. "Our captain is one of the few who has witnessed the multiple levels of destruction these bastards are capable of."

"And you are...?" the commander said, tone cool.

Kele snapped a little straighter, obviously remembering she was not facing one of *our* commanders, who tended to be a little more lenient when it came to backchat, and saluted. "Kele MacCaa, drakkon rider, and second-in-command, Brown Recon Team."

Curiosity briefly flashed across the commander's otherwise stern features. He returned his gaze to mine. "How many drakkon riders do we now have? I was under the impression you were the sole rider."

"We now have three, but it won't be enough."

"You stopped them today."

"We were lucky, because they weren't prepared for the additional drakkons. Next time, they will be."

"The drakkons are larger—"

"And have no innate means of attack other than tooth and claw, and both of those involve getting far too close to riders armed with weapons that can tear through flesh and stone with equal ease."

"But you have fire—we saw it in action today."

I half smiled. "We are also human, Commander, with all the limitations that come with that—something you should be aware of, given you've no doubt been dealing with air and earth witches on a regular basis of late."

Annoyance flashed through his eyes, but he gave it no voice. I suspected the only reason he *didn't* reprimand me as he had Kele was because of who I was—the only daughter of Esan's king.

"Fine. I'll update the council while we await the arrival of your drakkon."

"Thank you, Commander."

He nodded, then turned sharply on his heel and walked back through the half-destroyed pillars and down the hill. I'd expected him to use a quill and tablet, but either he wasn't carrying one—which would be unusual for any field commander—or he simply wanted to remove himself from the stink of drakkon that permeated our clothes.

Teagin continued her examination of my leg, muttering softly to herself as she gently probed the wound with fingers that were overly warm. It was then that I realized she was more a "diviner" than a healer. Diviners were able to "read" what was happening within the body, providing a clearer picture for those who healed or repaired with magic or knife. Most of them were very skilled herbalists, able to work medical "magic" with many of their potions and salves, but you didn't often find them working as field medics. That was usually a position taken by "true" healers.

"I'm not sensing any major damage." She sat back on her heels and studied me. "You were lucky, young woman. A wound like that could have easily sliced through any of the major muscles or arteries in your calf and bled you out. Good job on stabilizing the shaft, too, because that bastard is barbed."

I frowned. "I can't remember seeing notches on the other arrows they aimed my way."

"You probably were too busy fighting or avoiding them to do that," she said, somewhat dryly. "And the notches aren't big, but they'll rip your leg apart if removed the wrong way."

"Your healers can remove it, though, right?"

"Sure can. I'll not touch it—the numbing salve you applied will remain active for another four or so hours, but holler if it does start hurting, and I'll give you a stronger potion."

"Thank you."

She nodded. "I'll just head down the hill and order a stretcher, because you're not walking on that leg until that arrow is out, I'm afraid."

Amusement tugged at my lips. "And downhill just happens to be upwind of us. No coincidence, I'm thinking."

She laughed and patted my knee. "Indeed not."

Once she'd collected all her gear and the discarded bandage, she rose and moved away.

"The drakkon scent must be pretty odious, given the distance everyone is keeping," Kele commented, "so why can't I smell it?"

"Used to it, I suspect."

"I suspect *not*. If that were the case, the odious scent of unwashed bodies during a five-day scouting mission wouldn't worry me at all."

I laughed and dragged some trail rations out of my pack. "I can't disagree with that statement, though I will say that after five days of riding Desta through Mareritten scrub, my nose has generally desensitized itself."

"Wish mine did," she grumbled, sitting down beside me. "But maybe the men and women from the Brown Recon Team are more... ambrosial."

I laughed again and, with a grin, she pulled the rations out of her pack and began to eat. By the time an hour had ticked by, the commander had disappeared into whatever hole he'd appeared from, Teagin had perched halfway down the hill on a freakishly undamaged chair she'd found from goodness knows where, and the soldiers guarding us had widened the circle by several yards.

Rua and Hannity appeared on the horizon just as the first stain of sunset was creeping across the sky, her scales gleaming with red fire in the day's dying light. There were audible gasps from several men encircling us, and one reached for his sword. I barked at him to stand down, and the soldier instinctively obeyed, even though I was not his captain.

As they drew closer, I reached out to Rua and said, *Sweep over us and land in the upper area close to the wall so Hannity can dismount. Did you find any boats?*

Some. Not like ones we destroyed.

Good. I paused, checking the images she sent. *How did Hannity go?*

She good. I approve.

I smiled. *Hannity will be pleased to hear that.*

Rua swept over us, low enough that her claws were only yards above the soldiers' heads, which had most of them instinctively ducking. I glanced at Kele. "Can you go tell Hannity she needs to grab all her gear and dismount?"

She nodded, thrust upright, and jogged up the hill to the landing drakkon.

Where queens? came Rua's thought.

I sent them to a safe place to feed and roost for the night. I gave her the mental directions then added, *Tell Kaia I said not to come back until I contact her.*

I still hear, came her immediate comment. *Hunting good here. Will come more often once gilded ones killed.*

There's other islands in the area with a similar abundance.

Must stop gilded fast, then.

I laughed. *Wish it was that easy.*

Is. I trust.

And the weight of that was getting heavier.

As Rua took off, heading west to join her queens, Teagin reappeared with two men carrying a stretcher between them. By the time I was lashed on, Kele and Hannity were beside me, the latter grinning fiercely.

"I take it the experience was an awesome one?" I said with a wry smile.

"You have no idea." She paused. "Well, actually, you do. Wish I could talk to them like you, though. It would make things far easier."

"It seemed to me you did work out a means of communication."

"A very crude one, and not ideal under most circumstances." She wrinkled her nose. "It's a shame the drakkons can't flame."

"We're working on that." My grip tightened briefly as the stretcher was lifted and we headed down the hill. "Did you see anything unusual out there?"

"We spotted a number of trading vessels, but they were heading away from Hopetown rather than toward. No galleons resembling those we destroyed here, though."

"Any sign of gilded riders?"

"No, but there's not many places for birds like them to perch in deeper seas."

"Captain," Teagin said, "we're about to head down steep stairs, and, in a stretcher, it's going to be unpleasant. I'll knock you out—"

"That's not necessary—"

"I believe it is, and in medical matters, my opinion is

law. When we wake you, you'll be in the hospital, all patched up, which is far better for all concerned."

I glanced at Kele. "Grab the quill and tablet from my pack and make a quick report to the commander once we're underground and safe. Hannity, add your report."

They both nodded. Teagin barked a command for the stretcher bearers to halt, then gave me a few drops of some sweet-tasting and rather thick liquid. Within minutes, the world went black, and I knew no more.

———

The soft sound of steps woke me. I instinctively reached under the pillow for my knife, but it was gone. Alarm stirred briefly, then I smelled the sharpness of soap and antiseptic, and felt the cool impersonal touch of fingers against my wrist, and realized where I was. In the hospital. *Hopetown's* hospital, situated Vahree only knew where underground.

I didn't immediately open my eyes or acknowledge whoever was taking my pulse, instead reaching for Kaia. *Everything okay on that island?*

Feeding good here. Capra fat and lazy, came her thought.

Yara and Rua still there?

Want to fight. Can't without flamers. We fly today?

If I have any say in it, yes.

Good. Need go.

Yeah, so do I, I replied, and finally opened my eyes.

The woman pressing two fingers against my wrist smiled. "Welcome back to the world, Captain. You'll be pleased to know the operation was a success and there is no lasting damage."

"The 'no lasting' portion of that statement suggests there was indeed some."

"The arrow was a nasty beast of a thing, and several of its thorns broke off as we tried to remove it. That meant cutting open your calf more than we might have wished. You have yet another scar on that leg, I'm afraid, and it will remain tender for a few days, but you were extremely lucky, considering."

"Sounds like it." I briefly glanced around. The room—though it was more a cave carved out of black rock than anything resembling a regular hospital room—was small and sparsely furnished. Aside from the bed in which I lay, there was a square table to my right, barely big enough to hold a plate and a glass, and which had been placed on wheels so it could be pushed out of the way easily. A somewhat spartan-looking chair lay to my left, and a simple curtain covered the doorway directly ahead. "Where are we, exactly? Besides a makeshift hospital underground, that is."

"We're in the hills to the east of Hopetown, close to what many call Sinopa's right knee."

I blinked. "That's a good distance from the port—how in Vahree's name did your earth witches manage to dig tunnels out to here so quickly, let alone create a viable hospital shelter?"

"This shelter was created eons ago—it's the remote emergency administration center—so all they really had to do was extend what already existed to include a hospital."

"And the bulk of the population? Where are they?"

"In various older caves littered under Sinopa."

"I thought they were creating new caverns closer to Hopetown?"

"I believe that was the initial intent, but given the urgency of the situation, the council considered it prudent to use what already existed, even if many areas are less than ideal by today's standards."

"Better to be housed in less than ideal than dead."

"That is indeed my feeling also, but a surprising number of people disagreed and left."

"What? Where did they go? Because we certainly didn't see any indication they'd returned to Hopetown."

"They headed inland, from all reports." She released my wrist with a nod, then flipped the plain sheet away from my body, exposing my skin to the cool air. She ran her fingers lightly along my calf, concentration evident in her slight frown. Pain shivered up my leg. It was a distant thing, suggesting I still had plenty of painkillers onboard.

"And what about the two soldiers who were with me?" I asked. "Where are they?"

"They've been housed in the military quarters, but your second currently stands guard in the corridor, waiting until I give clearance for her to come in. I believe she's in an agitated state and anxious to get going."

"Too damn right she's agitated and anxious," came Kele's comment. "We've been here too long already."

I frowned at the doctor. "How long have I been unconscious?"

"Two days."

"*Two* days?" I repeated, a little shocked. "Why so long?"

"We needed to keep your leg immobilized for a period of time after the operation. After conferring with your healers back in Esan—we had to consult them to ensure you had no allergies to the strong potions we were about to give you, and also to check what had been done during your other recent surgery—it was decided the best way to achieve that was to keep you knocked out. Apparently, you have something of a history when it comes to not obeying medical orders." She raised an eyebrow, as if daring me to disagree. I couldn't, of course, so after several beats of silence, she added, "The benefit of doing that, of course, is that you're now free to leave."

"As in, right now?"

"Yes, although I do suggest you get dressed first. Your clothes have been washed and repaired, and hang on the hooks to your right. Your impatient second has your weapons and packs."

"Thank you, Doctor."

She nodded. "Good luck with your drakkon riding. I'll be praying for Túxn to gift you good fortune ridding the skies of this scourge."

"We certainly need all the prayers and good fortune we could get right now." Especially if Damon's transference spell wasn't workable.

As the doctor left the room, Kele strode in. She looked fresh and no longer smelled of drakkon, and I had no doubt that was due to the military folk insisting both she and Hannity take a long soak in a scented bath before they inhabited their area. Military personnel generally had a good tolerance for odious scents—bathing facilities on long recons weren't exactly plentiful—but the reactions of the commander and his people definitely suggested the musk of our drakkons was a little too strong for their tastes.

"What news from Esan?" I swung my legs off the bed and warily stood. My damaged calf muscles twinged, and pain swirled yet again, a distant warning that I still needed to be careful. And one, no doubt, that I'd forget soon enough. I hobbled over to my clothes and began to dress.

"There's been a couple of minor skirmishes with the Mareritt, but no further signs of the riders."

"Were the Mareritt using the gilded riders' tube weapons?"

"No, but the commander said they are building numbers up in the wastelands."

"They're readying for an attack."

"It would appear so." She placed our gear on the bed, then sat down beside it, her nose wrinkling. "We should be doing a preemptive strike now, while their numbers remain low."

"Except for the fact that if the Mareritt are working with the riders, however peripherally, then the build-up might be nothing more than a means of drawing our strongest forces and our drakkons away from our fortress, thereby ensuring Esan isn't fully equipped to counter an attack by the riders."

"I'm not entirely sure we're equipped now," she replied, somewhat gloomily. "Three drakkons, however mighty the combination of them and us might be, will never defeat the sheer number of people they can put in the air. Presuming, of course, that rider wasn't talking shit and they do intend to fill our skies with gold."

"They haven't done so yet, so there's still time to figure out a solution. Even if it is simply getting more fire witches onto drakkons. Where's Hannity?"

"She found a friend to play with last night. She'll meet us in the mess."

"Good, because I am starved."

Not just for food, came Kaia's comment. *Mating heat high.*

I just about choked. *Kaia!*

True.

"And it's moments like this I wish I could hear the drakkons," Kele said dryly. "Kaia obviously said something very... interesting, because your face is a picture right now."

"Trust me when I say you really *don't* want to hear

them. They stick their noses into your personal affairs and make all sorts of comments, whether you want them to or not."

She raised her eyebrows, amusement lurking around her lips. "I take it Kaia made one such comment?"

"Involving mating heat and how bad it rides me."

"Well, she's not exactly wrong. You are just married, and you do have a lusciously virile man waiting for you at home."

He was certainly home, and he was certainly virile. Whether he was actually *waiting* for me was another matter entirely. I strapped on my sword and knives, then picked up my packs. "Enough of this rubbish. Let's go eat."

She chuckled, but grabbed her packs and followed me through the curtain. Once in the hall, I motioned her to the lead and followed her through the myriad of wide tunnels that connected the various hospital areas, and then on into the not-so-wide tunnels that were obviously a part of the older emergency administrative system.

The mess hall was narrow but long, containing two rows of stone tables and wooden bench seats. Smallish serveries sat at either end, and the delicious scent of roasting meats filled the air, as did a slight haze of smoke. Obviously the vents weren't working to full capacity right now.

There were at least two dozen other soldiers dotted about, some in groups, some singular. Hannity sat alone at a table to our right and rose as we approached, saluting casually.

"Good to see you up and about, Captain. Commander Green was here a few minutes ago, looking for you, and said he'd be back in half an hour to escort us to the surface."

I nodded, a little surprised he hadn't relegated the task to a junior officer. But perhaps he was paying deference to my position at the palace rather than my military one. "Then we had best eat."

I dumped my packs, then hobbled over to the servery. A big sweaty man in brown plated me up a meal consisting of roasted meat, four potatoes, a few rather sad-looking vegetables, and several slices of thick bread, then motioned me toward the end of the servery where there were several pots of steaming shamoke. I poured myself a drink in the largest mug I could find and then headed back to the table to eat. I was damnably hungry and would probably have gone back for seconds had not Green arrived with two other soldiers.

I stood up and saluted. "Morning, Commander. Any news regarding Hopetown?"

"There's been no additional attacks, but riders have been sighted on high. We suspect they're looking for any indication of additional fortifications before they send a new invading party in."

"Or they're looking for the drakkons," I said.

"Indeed. Shame we do not have more of them."

"If we can work out a means of nullifying the acidic weapons of the riders," I replied, "then the need for drakkons would be lessened."

"I can't help but think an army of drakkons would be of benefit to Arleeon, especially when the Mareritt remain a problem."

"Given how close we came to causing the extinction of the drakkons," I couldn't help but bite back, "it's a miracle they're willing to help us at all."

He looked a little startled at that. "You don't control them?"

"No, Commander, we do not."

"Then perhaps *that* should be a prior—"

"Commander, I would *not* finish that sentence. The

drakkons are every bit as intelligent as we humans, and they are not ours to rule or force into obedience and servitude."

"Captain, they are nothing more than a large animal—"

"All large animals can either eat or kill you if they're hungry or angry enough," I cut in. "And the drakkons have very long memories."

"Which doesn't matter given she is *not* here—"

"Except," Kele drawled, "for the fact that our captain and her drakkon have an open line of communication, and our queen drakkon is no doubt listening to every word we are saying. I wouldn't be roaming the streets alone anytime soon, Commander, because she does have something of a temper."

Truth, Kaia said. *Would crunch his bones and spit him out.*

And I would definitely let you. I flexed my fingers lightly against the flames burning against my fingertips. "Slavers once considered the people of Arleeon and other nearby continents to be no more than wild creatures to be tamed and used. Do you approve of that, Commander?"

"That is a very different—"

"No, Commander, it is not. Now, if you don't mind, we need to get to Esan. Please provide us with a guide back to Hopetown."

Annoyance flickered through his eyes, no doubt thanks to the inference I didn't want *him* leading us, but he turned and snapped his fingers at the two soldiers behind him. "Greta, Marc, escort the captain and her people back to Hopetown."

"Thank you, Commander."

He nodded, spun on his heel, and stalked out. I couldn't help but wonder what my father thought of the man. Maybe it was nothing more than his opinion on the drakkons rubbing me the wrong way, but I definitely would *not* have placed him in overall control of Hopetown's fighting forces.

I collected my packs, threw them over my shoulder, then motioned to the two soldiers to lead the way. They did so at a good clip, and over the course of the next hour we passed numerous guard stations and several unmarked but extremely strong-looking metal doors. By the time we neared the steep steps I only vaguely remembered, my calf was beginning to ache. Obviously, the painkillers were wearing off.

Greta motioned us to halt, then quickly ran up and activated a vertical long viewer with an L-attachment at the eye end. It allowed her to use the viewer without the inconvenience of needing to squat underneath.

"All clear," she said, after a few minutes.

Her companion ran up the steps, slid the hatch open, and quickly jumped up. After a few more seconds, he echoed, "All clear."

Greta motioned us on. I went first and climbed out into the remains of what had obviously once been a grand building. It had no roof and only two walls remained, neither of which looked particularly stable, but the plaster that clung to the stone was brightly painted, and the windows were ornate in style even if no glass remained.

After Hannity had climbed out, I thanked the two soldiers, then waited until they'd retreated and closed the hatch. The thing all but disappeared. If I squinted hard enough, I could see the faint outline of one edge, but other than that, there was absolutely no indication it existed, and no sign of soil disturbance, meaning there was some form of earth magic happening here. Which made sense. I dared say there were multiple protections—aside from the guard stations—inside the tunnels that we hadn't even noticed.

Near, came Kaia's thought. *Where land?*

I glanced around and realized we were halfway between the green strip behind the admin buildings and the remnants of the older port buildings. *Land on the undestroyed pier. It should fit two of you easily enough—you keep watch and land last.*

Am biggest, need more room.

That too, I said with a smile.

The three drakkons appeared on the horizon as we made our way through streets littered with destruction and the vague scent of decay—the latter no doubt coming from the birds and the riders we'd killed and whose bodies remained scattered about.

"I will never get over the awe of seeing them," Hannity said, her gaze on the distant specks that were the drakkons rather than where she was placing her feet. "Nor will I ever forget the fact I was lucky enough to ride one."

"Me neither," Kele agreed softly.

Or me, I echoed, though I didn't say it out loud. "They're going to land on the remaining pier. You two mount up first and then rise to keep watch while Kaia lands."

"We heading straight home or on through Mareritten?" Kele asked.

"Why would we go through Mareritten?" Hannity asked.

Kele glanced at her. "Apparently the riders have three boats docked there in need of destruction."

"I'm up for that."

"We may or may not investigate that report tomorrow once I've discussed tactics with the commander, but for now, we're going home. Kaia has a drakkling she needs to see."

Miss, came Kaia's comment.

I know.

"Not to mention," Kele was saying, amusement playing through her expression, "that need she mentioned earlier in regard to you."

"*That* has nothing to do with my decision. You two harness up and head down, but on your way, can you collect some of the armor scattered about? Our mages and smiths can use it to design weapons able to pierce it. I'll contact Esan to let them know we're on our way."

Kele gave me a sketchy salute and, once she and Hannity had their harnesses on and ropes at the ready to clip on, they moved out. I pulled out the scribe quill and its tablet and quickly sent a message to my father.

Be wary coming over Dante's Peak, came his response. *We've spotted riders flying there.*

Dante's Peak lay midway between the part of the Black Glass Mountains Kaia hunted over and the Beak, and it was just over an hour's riding—not flying—away from Esan. He must have reinstated the old watch towers there.

I doubt they'd want to risk the destruction of any more of their "control" birds and riders just yet, I replied, *and we should be well home by dusk and the time the rest of them rise.*

Hope you're right, but remain on guard.

We will. See you soon.

I tucked the tablet and quill away, pulled on my harness, and clipped on the various ropes, ready to connect, then slung my packs over my shoulder and moved down to the dock, collecting various bits of rider armor and stuffing them in my packs along the way. Yara and Rua swept in, the force of air coming off their wing sweeps had the whole pier swaying in an alarming fashion.

"I would suggest we don't linger," Hannity said, her expression dubious as she studied the pier. "Because that thing doesn't look like it'll hold too much more."

"Then move fast but light." I paused as the two drakkons landed, then added, "Go."

They ran onto the dock and mounted their respective drakkons. Once they were both tied on, I ordered the two drakkons to rise. Kaia swept in under them; though she landed lightly, her larger bulk had the old pier groaning alarmingly.

I ran down to her, the old wooden planking swaying under my feet, and chunks of wood splashed loudly into the sea underneath. She offered her leg, and I scrambled up fast, wanting to get off the pier before the whole thing collapsed. She was rising before I fully strapped on; several large gaps appeared in the pier as wood disintegrated, but the bulk of it remained doggedly upright.

Kaia turned lazily and flew toward Esan, Yara and Rua taking up position on the left and the right behind her. We flew in that formation through the long hours that followed, stopping twice for privy breaks—which caused much amused discussion among the drakkons, who couldn't understand why we simply didn't defecate or urinate on the wing like them. Trying to explain caused even more hilarity, and their joint decision was that drakkons were definitely "better" designed.

I couldn't actually disagree with that.

It was just after three by the time we finally reached the aerie. Rua and Yara preceded us, then Kaia trumpeted her return and swept in, landing on the strip then striding gracefully inside. Gria waddled over and twined necks with her mother, happiness radiating through her thoughts. Guilt twinged through me, even though I was well aware that Kaia could have returned home any time she wished. I detached everything then slid down her leg and removed the neck girth.

Fly tomorrow? Kaia asked, presenting her eye for a scratch.

I need to speak to my father first, so rest up tonight and fly with Gria in the morning to feed. I'll update you when I can.

Gria appeared under her mother's neck. *Must scratch.*

I grinned and obeyed.

Harder, she demanded.

She's going to be a queen one day, isn't she? I asked Kaia. *She definitely has the attitude.*

My line always queens.

Except when they're males, I said wryly.

My males always worthy of queens. Fact.

I chuckled softly and left her and Gria to their snuggling, carrying her gear over to the hooks. Once Kele and Hannity joined me, we retreated, walking through the shield and making our way at a reasonable clip through the myriad of tunnels.

Even so, dusk was settling in by the time we reached Esan.

Once we were through the gates, I collected the packs that contained the armor from them and said, "Go home and rest, both of you. If we do fly out tomorrow, it won't be until after dawn. I'll have word sent."

They both saluted, then Kele touched my arm. "Make sure you take your own advice and get some food and rest tonight."

"And ignore the mating heat?" I replied with a grin. "Unlikely."

She laughed, squeezed my arm, and followed Hannity. I took a deep breath, then headed for the war room to make my report.

My father, mother, and Jarin were leaning over the main continental map, their expressions grim. Alarm slipped through me. "What has happened now?"

"A report just came in via Hopetown's council. A trading boat who'd been hoping to restock supplies at the port scribed them an update on sea conditions." My father glanced at me. "According to them, Ezu has been overrun by hundreds of strange golden birds."

CHAPTER 8

"HUNDREDS?" I repeated, horrified. "Surely not."

Though it would certainly fit with what that rider had said before he'd died.

Ezu was the most distant of the Jakarran Islands, and a good day's sailing away from the other four. It was also relatively small, being only a fraction larger than Halcraft or Zergon. Unlike those two, or indeed any of the other islands, it wasn't blessed with volcanic caverns, having been formed from a deep undersea eruption. It was instead half covered by thick forests, but that would offer Ezu's people little protection from the riders or their ground forces—especially given what had almost happened to the escapees from Kinara.

"The weather was apparently foul," Jarin said. "And the captain was running without lights because of the recent reports of pirates in the area—"

"The pirates likely being ships belonging to the riders," I cut in.

Jarin nodded. "It was luck that they even saw the birds

—it was a combination of a flash of lightning and a barrelman with a long viewer pointed the right way."

"Hard to be a good judge of numbers from such a distance and in the dark," I said.

"Indeed," my father said. "But I think his 'the entire island seemed washed in gold' comment is evidence enough that there is a sizable force building there."

"But why? Ezu doesn't give their riders a good base from which to attack," I said. "It'd have to be a good day's flight from there, and that wouldn't give them the necessary time to inflict true damage on us before daylight sweeps in."

"They hold Jakarra, remember," Mom said softly. "And that *is* close enough."

"Has Jakarra reported any such build-up?"

"Not as yet."

"This is another possibility." I swept a finger along the northern shores of Mareritten. "These two ports are within flight range of both Esan and Ezu. Our captive might have said there were only three docked there, but that doesn't mean there can't be more by now."

"True, which is why I have approved your request to fly across Mareritten tomorrow." My father's gaze fell on me. "It is a scouting mission, nothing more, unless attacked. Understood?"

"Understood, Commander." Whether the drakkons would was another matter entirely. I dropped the packs containing the armor on the floor. "We collected some rider armor from Hopetown; thought our mages and smiths can use for weapon development."

"They definitely can." My father motioned a soldier forward and added, "Take these to Franklyn immediately."

"And you, commander, should go bathe and rest," my

mother said. "It will be another long flight over Mareritten tomorrow."

The amused gleam in her eyes that accompanied her light emphasis on the word "rest" suggested she was well aware that wasn't likely to happen. Not for a few hours, anyway.

"Can you arrange for Kele and Hannity to be informed that we fly out two hours after dawn? That should give our drakkons plenty of time to hunt."

My father nodded. I saluted them both then spun on my heels and headed out. No light tubes gleamed along the walls, and the guards were little more than well-armed shadows. The palace had been locked down for the night, but the guards once again opened the side door for me. I half ran, half limped up the stairs and headed toward my rooms. As I neared, I felt the soft caress of Damon's magic. He had indeed shielded this area against his aunt's intrusions.

I opened the door and quietly stepped inside, my gaze sweeping the room. A large pot of shamoke steamed away on the table, which also held several platters of bread, cheese, and meats. Or, at least, the remnants of them.

He was asleep on the sofa, head resting back on the cushions, a quill on the cushion underneath his hand and its tablet resting on his lap. He was wearing breeches, but his feet and his chest were bare, and all I wanted to do was walk over and run my fingers over all the magnificence on display.

But given how badly I no doubt smelled, it was probably better if I bathed first.

I stripped off, tossed my clothes into the laundry chute, then ran the bath. His soft snores filled the room, evidence of how deeply he slept. Disappointment lightly stirred, and

I couldn't help but smile. Who knew that one could fall so deeply in lust in such a short amount of time?

I grabbed the soapweed—a stronger, gingery-vanilla one this time to counter the heavy drakkon scent—and set to scrubbing my body and hair clean. He barely even stirred. Once I'd dried off and brushed my hair out, I padded barefoot and naked over to where he lay. The tablet's cursor was blinking, meaning whoever held the quill's matching pair remained active. On the screen were the words, *it will be extremely dangerous.*

Had they been talking about the spell, or something else?

I had no idea, and as much as I wanted to send back a message and ask, I didn't. Not only would that be a breach of trust, but possibly dangerous given the little he'd said about his home situation. I carefully lifted the tablet from this lap, placed it on the table, then grabbed a blanket and lightly spread it over him.

Then I went to bed and slept, just as Mom had ordered —something neither she nor I had expected.

———

I woke the next morning with Damon's naked length pressed against mine, his arm lightly resting over my left hip, and his breath whispering past my ear. I'd obviously been so soundly asleep that I hadn't stirred when he'd joined me in bed. Which wasn't really surprising—riding, whether courser or drakkon, was surprisingly strenuous, especially when you were doing it for more than six hours at a time.

At least, that was when I always hit the wall, weariness wise.

I didn't immediately move. I simply enjoyed this moment of quiet closeness while I still could... and really, *really* didn't want to examine that particular thought, and I *definitely* didn't want to acknowledge the growing suspicion that this might be the only moment we got for quite a while.

From the courtyard outside came the everyday noises that accompanied the palace and its people waking for the day, and, far more distant but still surprisingly clear, came the sharp call of a blackhawk on the wing. If they were out hunting, then day had well and truly risen.

Has, came Kaia's thought. *We hunt.*

Eat up big, because we've another long day's flight ahead of us, I'm afraid.

Kill more gilded ones?

It's just a scouting mission right now.

Better kill.

I agree, but I have orders.

Me not.

I half smiled. *No, but we are working together to get rid of this threat, are we not?*

Still should kill.

We'll see what happens when we get there.

She didn't reply, but only because she'd spotted a fat capra and had swooped to claim it.

As my stomach rumbled a loud reminder that it hadn't eaten anything for an indecently long amount of time, I carefully edged away from Damon.

His grip almost instantly tightened, and in a warm, almost languid voice he said, "And where do you think you're going, my dear wife?"

"I need to pee, and I need to eat, and I have a flight out over Mareritten I need to get ready for."

"How urgent is the need to pee on a scale of one to ten?

Ten being 'if you don't release me now I'm going to wet this bed.'"

"About a three," I replied, amused. "Why?"

"Because it is unseeming for a wife—or indeed a husband, because this relationship is all about equality—to leave a bed without kissing their partner good morning."

"Is kissing going to lead to sexing?"

"That would be my preference, yes."

I laughed, turned in his arms, and kissed him, long and lingering. He slid his hand down my spine to my butt, then lightly pulled me closer. His erection pressed against my belly, hard and heated, and the deep down well of wanting that I'd been successfully ignoring up until then exploded.

From that moment on, there was little talk, but there was a whole lot of exploration and a mind-blowing culmination. How the hell it was possible for sex with this man to get better each and every time, I had no idea, but long may it continue.

While he ordered breakfast, I took a quick bath, then got dressed. Our meal arrived just as I was tugging on my boots, and the sharp smell of shamoke had me hurrying over. I thanked the servant as she left the room, then sat down and poured us both a drink. The quill pen and its tablet, I noted, were nowhere to be seen.

"Did you have any luck talking to your people back on Angola?"

"Some." He handed me a bowl of the creamy pottage, then spooned out a second for himself. "There's definitely a spell that could work, but everything we've uncovered so far says it comes with some rather life-altering consequences."

Did that explain the warning I'd seen on the tablet last night? Maybe. Probably. The problem was instinct, which was saying no.

"Consequences are to be expected, given we're not only dealing with magic but trying to transfer an innate psychic talent from one being to another."

"Except it's *not* as simple as transferring a talent."

I didn't think it would be, but I nevertheless asked, "Why not?"

"The writings we've uncovered imply that it's a more universal *and* equal transfer—that for every ability you give to her, one of hers will be transferred to you."

I contemplated that for several seconds as I ate my pottage. "Does that mean I will become more drakkon-like?"

"It won't alter flesh—you will physically remain as you are—but it could well leave you with drakkon-like attributes such as quick healing and a longer lifespan."

I smiled. "I can't see a downside in that."

"What it gives it may well take. Her lifespan may well be shortened to compensate."

"Then that is something we need to tell her. Only she can decide whether gaining fire is worth losing life years over."

"Of course, and in truth, there is no certainty about any of this. The spell, as far as we have been able to uncover, was only performed once, and the results were... unsatisfactory."

"In what way?"

He grimaced. "It didn't really explain, though there was a note in another book that suggested the spell invalidated both parties."

"Invalidated? What the hell does that mean? That they both died or what?"

"I have no idea." He picked up his shamoke and took a drink. "Though I would think that, in this context, it might mean cancelled."

"Meaning their native abilities were cancelled?"

"Again, no idea, which is why I asked for them to look deeper before we attempt the spell. The last thing I want right now is you being dead or cancelled."

I half smiled. "The last thing I want right now is to be dead or cancelled."

"At least we agree on that." He finished his pottage and put the bowl on the table. "There's also the physical consequences to consider. A deeply invasive spell such as this could easily drain most of your strength and leave you unconscious for at least a day, if not more."

"And Kaia? How will it affect her?"

Amusement twisted his lips. "You're always more concerned for her safety than your own."

"Gria's already lost her brother—I don't want to take her mother away as well."

"I suspect that if there was no Gria to take into consideration, your concern would still fall on Kaia's side."

"I suspect you might be right," I replied with a smile.

He picked up his shamoke and leaned back. "What's on the agenda today?"

I raised an eyebrow. "I take it, given you didn't answer the question, that you have no idea how it'll affect Kaia?"

"I daresay it'll affect her in the same way as you, but again, nothing is certain in any of this. If it were my choice—"

"But it's not," I cut in softly. "It's hers and mine."

"And the other drakkons' and their riders'."

"Indeed, but do you honestly think any of them would refuse?"

His lips twisted. "No, because they are as crazy as you."

"And you're stuck with that crazy, I'm afraid."

"I can't be sad about that," he said, echoing my earlier comment.

I smiled. "To answer your question, we're flying over Mareritten to see if our gilded riders have ships docked at Mareritten ports."

"They have several, so that is likely to be another long day."

Did he sound a little relieved, or was that my imagination? "What's on your agenda?"

"More back and forth about the spell." He shrugged. "As I've said, while we have the basics, I want to be absolutely sure we've done everything we can to stop anything going awry."

"Because it will be extremely dangerous?" I said, echoing what I'd seen on the screen last night.

Something flickered through his eyes—an awareness that I'd seen what had been written. But all he said was, "Indeed it will be."

And once again that nagging feeling he wasn't talking about the spell rose.

I really, *really* wanted to ask for an explanation, but what was the point? He'd only deny anything else was going on, for reasons he'd already explained. Besides, he was no doubt also thinking that the less I knew, the less his aunt could steal from me.

And I couldn't argue against that, even if I wanted to.

I drained my shamoke, then put the cup on the table and rose. "I'd better get going."

He nodded. "Be careful up there."

"Be careful plotting," I said.

Again, that flicker. Again, no explanation was forthcoming.

Frustration surged anew, but I pushed it away, collected my weapons and my packs, and headed out.

The halls were abuzz with movement and sound, and the scent of freshly baked breads combined with the faintest touch of ginger and spice was so strong in the air that, despite the fact I'd already eaten, my stomach rumbled. I couldn't resist the temptation and followed my nose down to the kitchen. Trail rations were all well and good, but nothing—*nothing*—ever beat fresh-out-of-the-oven bread. Especially when it was Hutzelbrot, a thick and heavy loaf that was jam-packed with dried fruits and had a delicate gingery-cinnamon flavor. Candra—our chief baker—generally only made it when ginger had come into season.

She turned as I entered the overpoweringly hot room and gave me a wide smile. "Wondered how long it would take you to follow your nose down here, Princess. You never used to miss baking day when you were younger."

I grinned. "I think it fair to say I practically lived for Hutzelbrot season when younger, and I definitely consumed more than my fair share."

She laughed. "Aye, I think you did. How many do you need today?"

"Three, please. We're off on a day-long scout."

She slapped her hands together to get rid of the excess flour covering them, then walked over to where the racks of various breads stood. "Had another visitor in here earlier."

There was something in the way she said that that had my instincts twitching. "Not one of the usual Hutzelbrot thieves, I'm taking it?"

"No, this one was sneaking around, looking for the entrance into the servants' tunnels. Rude woman; Zephrine origins, I'm thinking."

There was only one fitting that description staying here

right now, and that was Gayl. "Did you ask her why she was looking for it?"

The why was pretty obvious—she was trying to find a way around Damon's protection barriers—but it had to be asked, or Candra would think it odd. Of course, none of the tunnels to the upper floors ran into our suites—for security reasons—instead opening into the hall, close to our rooms but in full sight of the guards stationed there. But there *was* a network of tunnels between the walls throughout the ground floor that catered to the banquet and various smaller dining rooms, and a number of them ran right underneath both my suite and my parents'.

If Damon's spell only encompassed the walls, and not the ceiling and floor, then it was very possible she could still listen in to our conversations

"Of course I did," Candra was replying. "Got no time for sneaks obviously up to no good. She claimed she heard rodents in the walls and wanted to check the tunnels. The affront of the woman, thinking I'd allow those dirty animals to run about."

"Hard to believe indeed." I paused. "Can the door into the tunnels be locked?"

She hesitated. "Please excuse the bluntness, Princess, but it'd be fucking inconvenient, given we're never sure when your family or your guests will scribe down for food."

"Then I'll have a guard placed here in case she appears again."

"I thought she was a guest?" Candra wrapped the three loaves separately in oil-treated cotton to give them additional protection if it rained, then placed them all in hessian sacks for easier carrying and handed them to me.

"She is, but that doesn't give her the right to be going wherever she wants." I raised the sacks. "Thanks for these."

"Welcome, Princess. You want a loaf sent up with breakfast tomorrow?"

"If you could, I would love it."

She laughed. "Done. Enjoy your day, Princess."

"Thanks, Candra." I turned and headed back out, but hesitated once I'd reached the foyer. I really had to get going, because the later we left, the closer it would be to night when we returned. But if I didn't warn Damon about his aunt, and his machinations reached his father's ears, subsequently placing people in danger, I wouldn't forgive myself. I swore softly and ran back up the stairs to our room.

Damon was squatting in the middle of the floor, examining the tablet he held in one hand while chalking various symbols onto the stone with the other. I stopped in the doorway and frowned. "What are you doing?"

"Practicing." If he was at all put out by my sudden reappearance, it didn't show. But maybe that nebulous connection neither of us were verbally acknowledging had already warned him. "What did you forget? And what is that gorgeous smell?"

"Got some Hutzelbrot from the kitchen, which is where I learned your aunt was trying to get into the servant tunnels. If your protection spell doesn't cover the floors and ceilings, you need to extend it—today."

"I will but—"

"Sorry, I have no time for buts." I paused. "What are you practicing?"

"Spell craft. I thought you were in a hurry?"

"I am." And I had vague suspicion *he* was in a hurry to get rid of me. Or maybe that was just my paranoia showing. "Talk later."

I left, slamming the door behind me. The noise echoed, and the door to my parents' suite opened. My father stepped out and strode toward me, a long cup of what smelled like shamoke in one hand.

"Lovers' tiff?" he said as we headed down the stairs together.

"No. I'm just running late."

"Considering you're supposed to meet your fellow scouts in five minutes, I would say late is an understatement."

"I know." I waited until we were out in the courtyard and hopefully beyond Gayl's range, and quickly told him what I'd discovered.

Annoyance flickered across his features. "I'll order the dust covers to be placed over all furniture in the pertinent rooms and have them locked. We won't be using them anytime in the foreseeable future anyway, as most of our trading partners have been warned of the danger and are keeping clear until we give the go-ahead again."

Which meant that if these attacks did develop into a war, certain commodities were going to become scarce. East Arleeon's rich farmlands could provide the basics, and the west had plenty of woods and mines to supply the smiths and fletchers with all the raw materials necessary for making weapons, but there was plenty we didn't make—like shamoke.

A shortage of *that* was nightmare material in itself.

"Oh," he added, "please do remember what I said about not attacking. We don't need to be prompting a retaliatory attack until we have some means of combating their weapons."

"I understand, but if we *are* attacked, we will respond."

"If you're attacked, I expect you to destroy them."

I couldn't help smiling. "You do know that, in theory, I

could just claim we were attacked and destroy the bastards anyway."

"Yes, but you're generally a bad liar, and guilt would soon have you confessing the truth anyway."

I laughed, rose on my toes, and kissed his cheek. "That is a statement I can't argue with. I'll see you tonight."

"Aye," he said, lightly touching my cheek. "Keep safe."

I nodded, saluted, then ran down to the gates that led to the mountain path. Kele and Hannity were already waiting.

Kele eyed the sacks I was carrying with something close to avarice in her expression. "Are they what I think they are?"

"It is indeed."

"I think I love you."

Hannity's gaze flicked between us. "Why? What's in the sacks?"

"Hutzelbrot," Kele replied, with a dreamy expression. "Once eaten, never forgotten."

"I've never heard of it." She took a deeper breath. "It smells like bread."

"It is an affront to call Hutzelbrot mere bread." I handed them each a sack. "You'll have to eat on the wing, because we can't risk landing in Mareritten for any longer than it takes to pee."

Hannity raised her loaf and sniffed. "*Oh.* I think I get it now."

I smiled. "Wait until you taste it. Let's go."

We moved as fast as my still-healing leg would allow up the mountain path. Though the morning had started out fine, by the time we reached the halfway point, the wind had whipped up and dark clouds were gathering. Thankfully, the storm held off until we reached the tunnel, but if it didn't clear as quickly as it arrived, it was going to be a miserable day's flying.

As it turned out, it was *worse* than miserable.

By the time we reached the first of Mareritten's ports on the far side of the continent, my jacket had given up any pretense of being waterproof, and moisture leaked steadily down my spine and between my breasts. My boots remained dry, but only because I was pushing heat to my extremities in an effort to avoid frostbite. I could have flamed hot enough to keep the worst of the moisture off my skin, of course, but I had no idea what lay ahead and no desire to risk burning myself out.

The drakkons were not in a better mind space. On days like this, they would normally have been hunkered down in their warm aeries to wait out the weather; the only thing that kept them flying on now was the possibility of hunting gilded birds.

Thankfully, the rain eased off by the time we reached the far side of Mareritten. Though the low blanket of gray remained, it at least provided us with some cover while not totally blocking our ability to see the ground.

The first port—L'Gon, which apparently meant *back-water* according to a trader familiar with the place—lived up to its name. There were neither birds nor ships visible through the long viewer, and the three piers were definitely in a state of disrepair, with large slabs of wooden planking missing from two while the third had a rather calamitous lean. Either this port was no longer in use or the Mareritt didn't care about it enough to keep it in top condition.

After a brief scout around the surrounding area, we flew east, following the wild and rugged coastline to K'Anor, the second but by far the largest Mareritten port.

Unlike the first port, it teemed with life. There were six

boats docked, and on the masts of five the gilded riders' flag fluttered. The flag on the sixth boat was blue and white, with a yellow sun in the middle. I had no idea what nation it belonged to, but Harris, our master of the fleet, probably would.

The gilded riders—or rather, their land-based counter-parts, as their leather clothing was the same strange green as their hair—moved with ease through the seaport, ferrying crates and packages to the various holding buildings. The Mareritt were also here in numbers, but what caught my eye were the two squat towers that sat at either side of the harbor's entrance, and the third located atop the two-story storage building situated in the middle of the main port area.

Those towers had large metal tubes attached to them.

The same sort of tubes the Mareritt had been constructing near the Barrain Ghost Forest. These were larger and undoubtedly more dangerous, not only because of the greater volume of acidic shit—or whatever the Mareritten equivalent actually was—they could spray at one time but because they appeared to be mounted on a base that could swivel, enabling them to track a fleeing target.

This was *not* a good development.

We no attack, came Kaia's thought. *Too dangerous.*

Surprise flitted through me. I hadn't expected her to be so reasonable.

Not foolish. She paused. *Yara might be.*

Tell her if she attacks, she loses her flamer.

There was a pause. *She want flamer. No attack.*

Good. Tell her and Rua we'll sweep around and see if there's any gilded birds in the area.

We did a slow turn right and flew beyond the edges of

the port, but there was nothing to suggest the birds, or their riders, had ever landed here. We continued on, out over the semi-barren countryside. There were plenty of long hill-sides with flat tops that would have been perfect for a squad —a swoop?—of gilded birds but again, there was nothing to be seen but brown soil, dying summer plants, and the prickly yellow trees that grew so abundantly in this area.

It didn't make sense.

K'Anor provided the perfect launching place for a flighted attack. It was within a night's flight of Esan, it would allow them to hit us in the pre-dawn hours, and it would still give them time to retreat back to whatever roosts they'd set up near the Beak or their other watch stations.

Of course, it was possible that, given the Mareritt were building up their presence in the wasteland, they intended to use *that* area as a staging point. But if that *were* the case, we would have had reports of it. Our scout teams were still going out, despite the growing danger.

But perhaps the answer was simpler than that. The Mareritt were a warrior race, and as a result had few allies—even those who traded with them on a regular basis did so cautiously. While there was undoubtedly good money to be made—or so the traders who also dealt with us claimed—it came with the risk of the Mareritt randomly deciding to take and kill rather than trade. They didn't often, of course. The Mareritt might be arrogantly sure of their superiority over all other races, but their part of the continent could not supply all that they needed to survive, just as ours couldn't —though we did have the advantage of more fertile soils.

All of which meant that perhaps the riders didn't trust the Mareritt enough to reside in their lands, or maybe—just maybe—the Mareritt were wary of them.

But if the riders weren't here, where in Vahree's name

were they? They might be building their presence on Ezu, but that really *couldn't* be their main base. It was just too far away from Esan to be practical. And while Jakarra was a definite possibility, Mom had already said there'd been no report of an increase there.

What do now? came Kaia's thought as the drakkons continued to widen their circles.

I hesitated. *Let's follow the coastline home and see what's happening along the Black Glass peaks.*

Take longer.

Yes, but we need to know where those birds are roosting.

If know where, we attack?

When we have an idea of their numbers, and better weapons than just the three of us, yes.

We need fire.

Damon's working on it.

Needs hurry.

He's worried about the danger.

Gilded ones danger. We need weapon.

The spell that gives you fire could bind our life forces.

What life force?

I hesitated again. *It's the spirit, the energy, that gives us both life. By combining our energies to give you flame, it might also pass on to me your resistance to magic and a longer life. But in doing that, it could shorten yours.*

No want shorten.

Which is why we can't proceed until we understand more about the risks for us both. Let's fly home.

She passed on the new flight directions to Yara and Hannity, and we flew west, keeping in the lower streams of clouds so that I could still see the ground through the long viewer, but we weren't as immediately obvious to a casual glance around. As the barren countryside gave way to long beaches lined by cliffs, the weather closed in again. We banked and headed south. The distant, rugged outline of the Black Glass Mountains was a barely visible blot in the rain, but gradually grew ever larger as the hours passed with unbearable slowness. Not even eating the few remaining chunks of now damp Hutzelbrot lifted my mood.

Dusk was closing in—though the only reason I could tell was thanks to the rain easing, allowing the faintest glimmer of warmth to stain the underbellies of the clouds—when I caught a soft flicker of light. It wasn't coming from the formidable mountains to our right but from the deeper seas to our left. There were no major islands out there, and no reason for boats to be out. Not in this area, and definitely not this late in the afternoon, anyway. The Throat of Huskain might still be a good distance away, but the seas underneath us remained treacherous.

The pale light swept across the gathering darkness, then disappeared again.

Was it a signal? Or something else?

I had no idea, but we definitely needed to investigate. I asked Kaia to pass on our change of course to the other drakkons, then signaled to Kele and Hannity.

We swung right and flew toward the intermittent light, remaining high so there was less chance of anyone seeing us if that light was some kind of watch station. As the darkness grew deeper, the sweeping light grew brighter, and the closer we got to it, the more evident it became that there were shapes clustered around it. Not boats, more... barges? They were extremely long, but wide, and flat, and... my stomach sank. At least one was crowded with shadows that gleamed gold in each turn of that light.

As we drew closer, the barges became visible; only one was filled with gilded birds, while a second held the longer versions of the metal tents I'd seen before and obviously housed the riders. The other two barges were currently empty.

There were probably a good thirty to forty birds roosting on that one barge, though, and that many could certainly decimate Esan's mighty walls. When the others arrived... perhaps from Ezu... well, they really could fill our skies with gold.

I wearily scrubbed a gloved hand across my wet face. There was nothing we could do right now. Not against so many birds. Not when the four barges had long tubes mounted at either end of them and guards at the ready. For our flames to be effective, we'd have to fly far too close to either of the barges, and even at full speed, would provide easy targets for those fucking tubes. The drakkons were just too big to miss at close range.

Why we need flames, Kaia commented. *Could burn from height.*

Damn it, Kaia, we're fucking working on it! I sucked in a breath and released it slowly. *Sorry, I'm not angry at you.*

Just the situation, our impotency, and the escalation of a threat for which we seemed to have no answer.

Know, she said. *Understand.*

Thank you. Let's go home before this lot gets wind of us and rise.

Would not be good.

No. We might have bested five of them, but we would never win against nearly tenfold that number. *Tell the others we're leaving.*

I once again signaled as Kaia passed the order on. Kele, who was closer, sent an affirmative, but Hannity didn't. Maybe, with the gathering darkness, she was simply too far away to see.

We really, *really* needed to work on a better means of communication, though I was not entirely sure there was anything better than scribe quills and tablets at the moment, and at the speed the drakkons were often going, they were simply impractical.

Maybe Damon could work something into his spell. If all riders could talk to their drakkons, it would be a whole lot easier to pass messages around.

Yara rumbled unhappily as we looped around and flew once again toward the peaks we couldn't see. There was no response from Rua.

I twisted around, caught the glint of red scales caught in the light as she swooped toward the barge holding the riders. The birds looked up and squawked sharply, the noise deafening in the stillness of the gathering night. Men scrambled out of metal tents in various stages of undress, most running across the various planks linking the barges while a few aimed smaller tubes at the descending drakkon.

Rua banked sideways, and Hannity unleashed her flames, sweeping them across the barge, setting alight several of the men. But they were too far away for Hannity's fire to melt the tents, and not precise enough to explode the tubes. And Rua was too low, too close to the barges, and far too close to the larger tubes now aiming her way.

Kaia roared an order to retreat even as I screamed mentally at her. Rua shook her head, as if in denial, then cut to the left, smashing her tail against the end of the boat and the tube built there. As metal cracked and men scrambled out of the way, the bolts holding the thing onto the barge lifted from the decking, and the whole tube toppled, almost in slow motion, into the sea. Hannity unleashed more fire at the dark liquid spilling across the deck and set it alight, but as the fire chased the liquid along the length of the barge, the guards stationed on the other barges unleashed their deadly weapons.

Help her, came Yara's metal scream. *Must.*

Go no closer, I yelled back, physically and verbally. *They'll just hit us—and we're no good to either of them if we can't fly out of here. Kaia, bank left.*

She immediately did, and I unleashed a stream of fire so hot it shone blue and white in the night. I whipped it around the bobbing light onto which the barges were tied and destroyed it. As the surrounding area dropped into darkness, I spread my fingers and sprayed the flames across the other three boats, trying to get at least a couple of the tubes—big and small—that were firing the liquid shit at Rua and Hannity.

I hit several, exploding them, but I didn't hit them all. Five larger ones remained.

Two of those five unleashed a second round of liquid. Rua banked away from them, rising hard and fast, her wings a blur. My heart lodged somewhere in my throat, hoping against hope she would make it.

She didn't.

CHAPTER 9

MULTIPLE SPRAYS HIT HER BODY, wings, and Hannity. Both screamed, but Hannity nevertheless twisted, unleashing fire at the acidic streams that still chased them.

I swore and said to Yara, *Rua's wings are going to disintegrate pretty quickly, even in this rain, so fly underneath her and help hold her weight. Just don't squash Kele.*

Won't, Yara said, and immediately chased after the younger drakkon.

Us? Kaia asked.

Fly high, swoop down fast, then bank so I can flame the barge holding the birds.

A fast sweeping pass wasn't likely to kill any birds, but that wasn't the aim. Causing chaos and buying us a little time was.

Kaia swooped upward, the air practically screaming in response to her speed. But that was nothing to the noise she made as we came down. She was furious and she was letting them know.

The riders scrambled for weapons, and several of the larger tubes swung our way. I rained fire down upon them, setting the men ablaze, then pushed my flames on, sweeping them through the two lines of agitated birds. I did little more than scorch the tail feathers of the first few half dozen or so, but that was enough to cause the others to panic. Hooded as they were, they'd have no idea what was happening, but they would feel the heat, smell the smoke, and hear the sharp squawks of those I'd hit.

It would take time to calm them down, time to get them harnessed and mounted. Even so, I doubted we had more than twenty minutes, at best, in which to disappear.

Kaia swung up and around and flew hard after the others. Rua was still in the air, though her movements were becoming increasingly unstable and her pain radiated through our link. The drizzly rain was no doubt helping to slow the speed of disintegration, but she still needed to be fully immersed in the water—as did Hannity, though I had no idea how badly she'd been hit—to fully wash the acidic shit from her wings. Otherwise, it would continue to eat through everything and perhaps even take both their lives.

We were never going to make it home. Not like this. Yara and Kaia could help keep Rua in the air if she maintained some flight capability, but if they had to carry her—though how in Vahree's name they were going to do that, I couldn't say—the gilded riders *would* catch us.

I hesitated, trying to remember the maps I'd seen of this area, then told the drakkons to bank left and head east, away from the Black Glass Mountains and home.

Why? came Kaia's question, even as she and the others obeyed.

They'll expect us to fly home. They won't be expecting us to fly in the other direction.

Nothing out here.

There's a chain of tiny islands. I had no idea how much

cover they'd provide or whether anything actually lived there aside from seabirds, because I'd only ever seen them on a map. But they did have two important location advantages—one, they were nowhere near any of the Jakarran Islands, and two, they should be well away from the path any riders might take flying between Ezu and those barges. *We need to get Rua and Hannity somewhere safe so that they can soak their bodies in the water.*

Hope close. Rua bad.

Perhaps next time she'll not ignore her queen.

She young. She will learn.

If she survived this lesson, that was. *You're a damn sight more understanding than I am. Drop lower. We won't see the islands through the rain from this height.*

She passed the message on, and all three dropped, Yara remaining underneath Rua, and Kaia flying beside them both, the very tips of her wings caressing the foamy crests of the bigger waves.

It took us another ten minutes to find the chain of islands. The gilded riders had to be in the air by now; I just hoped we'd been far enough away when we'd changed direction. If they had long viewers, we'd be in deep trouble.

We flew past the first two islands—they looked too small, little more than wide, flat specks of stone—but the third was much larger and shaped like a fisherman's hook, with a high craggy range dominating the central area and a deep bay wide enough for a drakkon to bathe in.

As we swooped in through the heads, I asked Kaia to fly closer to Rua so I could signal Hannity. She glanced at me as we flew up beside her, and even in the gloom of mist and darkness, I could see the paleness of her face. Her leg was a raw and bloody mess. Diving into the sea was going to fucking hurt... but if she didn't, she could possibly lose the limb.

Still might, depending on how much muscle and bone had been eaten away.

There was no signal designed for what I was about to order her to do, so I did a mix of shouting and over-the-top arm movements. She seemed to understand, because as Rua began to skim the water and her claws kicked up a fierce wave of spray, she clipped her backpacks and sword onto the ropes, then detached herself. The minute Rua plunged in, she rolled off over the back of her wing and dropped hard into the water. I twisted around to ensure she came up and saw her bobbing safely in the water.

Kaia ordered Rua to spread her wings to allow the sea to wash over the membrane, then swooped around and landed on sands that were as dark as the mountains that loomed above us. Yara did a circuit around the inner part of the hook, then landed beside us.

No beasts to eat, she said. *But long fins in water. Flesh sweet.*

Hunt in morning, Kaia said, in a voice that suggested she would take no arguments.

Once the sun is up, you two can hunt for us all. I unclipped myself, my packs, and my weapons, then slid down Kaia's extended leg.

Rua healed by then, Kaia commented. *Will be able to hunt own.*

"She was hit pretty hard, Kaia, and I'm not sure if we've enough webbing and bone straps to hold her wings together enough to reach the aerie."

She young. Heal fast.

I hoped she was right, because I did not want to spend any more time on this isolated island than necessary.

Kele walked up and dumped her packs beside mine. "You want me to scout the area and see if there's anywhere decent to hunker down for the night?"

I nodded. "You go left; I'll go right. Just remember, we need to keep within easy reach of the drakkons, just in case the riders sweep past and spot us."

"Let's hope not, because the drakkons are easy targets when they're on the ground."

"So are we, and their acid tubes have greater range than our fire."

"Yeah, but they're also flammable, so we do have that advantage."

True—and perhaps it was one we could use on the wall. Flaming arrows directed at the streams of liquid shit, perhaps? Though that might just result in a rain of fiery shit falling down on everyone, so maybe not.

Kele strapped on her sword, then spun and walked away, whistling softly. I did the same without the whistling, the sand crunching lightly under my boots as I walked up the beach and entered the thick vegetation. The majority of the trees here were cloud trees, which were often found on volcanic islands alongside blackwoods, their more prized cousin. They were a needle-straight and extremely tall soft-wood that used their cup-shaped leaves to collect all the water they needed to survive rather than drinking it through their roots.

I risked turning on the light tube—it was either that or use my flames, because the darkness under the trees was absolute—and quickly found several small creeks. I warily tasted each one, because if we were going to be on this island for any length of time, we would need fresh water—and was surprised to discover they were all free of the gritty, often acidic taste found in the runoff from newer volcanic islands. There was little else here—no volcanic caves, and no decent-sized rocky outcrop under which we could shelter. Túxn had given us all the luck we were going to get tonight; if we wanted shelter, then we were going to have to make it.

At least there were plenty of trees about to cut down and use.

I returned to the beach and walked down to the edge of the sand, my toes barely touching the gently lapping waves. "How's it going, Hannity?"

She no longer bobbed about, so she'd obviously found ground on which to stand.

"It's fucking icy in this water, and my leg is burning like nobody's business, but other than that, I'm fine. Perfectly fine."

Sarcasm dripped from her voice, and I couldn't help the smile that twitched my lips. Though to be honest, I would have reacted a whole lot worse had someone asked me the same stupid question.

"It's been close to twenty minutes, so the acid should have been nullified by now."

Me leave? came Rua's thought.

No, the acid caught far more of you than Hannity, so it's better if you remain a bit longer.

Hates water.

Well, perhaps next time you'll listen to Kaia and not get sprayed by the acid.

Her head dipped, and the faintest trace of regret ran through her thoughts. *Wanted kill.*

We all wanted to kill them, Rua, but it does no one any good if you and Hannity die.

Understand.

Which was not an indication of regret. Indeed, I

suspected that, given half the chance, she'd do the same thing over again.

Do you really? I snapped. *Because you risked not only your own life, but Hannity's. If you ever do that again, you will not get flame. If you can't obey your queen's orders, we can't risk giving you fire.*

Understand, she repeated, and this time, I believed her.

Is young, Kaia commented again. *Young foolish.*

That does not excuse her actions, Kaia.

Know.

But?

You make good queen. Is why you my kin.

I snorted and glanced at Yara. Both she and Kaia had created large hollows in the sand and were now hunkered down within them, their tails curled around their bodies and something close to a contented rumble rising from their throats.

Me not ignore queen or kin, she said, then added, *Sands warm.*

Meaning the volcanic activity that had created this island was still ongoing underneath it. Perhaps Kele and I should dig a similar hole and just drag some wood from the forest to create a crude lean-to. Normally we would have constructed something within the forest, but with two big drakkons curled up on the beach and a third currently dominating the bay, there was little point.

As Hannity limped out of the water, I ran back to the tree line to grab a thickish branch. The beach wasn't exactly a great place to be treating a bad wound, but if we could at least keep it raised and the sand out, that was half the battle.

I dragged the log down the beach and then motioned for her to sit. Once her leg was raised, I drew my knife and carefully sliced away her pants leg. The wound underneath no longer bubbled, but large chunks of the flesh on her thigh had been eaten away, and in one section, I could see bone. But given she could still use the leg and she hadn't bled out, it had obviously missed major muscles and blood vessels, and that in itself was a miracle.

I rose to retrieve my medical kit from my pack, then gave her both a pain potion and one to fight any infection that might brew from being hit by what was basically shit. Once the pain potion had kicked in and I was able to start cleaning, sealing, and bandaging the wounds, I said, "Tell me, Hannity, did you see my signal to retreat?"

She hesitated. "Yes."

"Then why didn't you respond?"

"Because Rua wanted to attack, and it wasn't like I could stop her."

"And in truth, you weren't opposed to the idea anyway?"

A longer hesitation, then, "No."

Annoyance surged. "Damn it, Hannity, do you understand the problems it would have caused if you and Rua had died? Not everyone in Esan thinks it's a great idea to be using the drakkons, nor does every drakkon think they should be helping us after nigh on being hunted to death. Your death, and hers, could have been held up as an example by both sides."

Confusion flitted across her expression. "But I'm a soldier, and death is part of life—why should being on drakkon back be any different to courser?"

"Because fucking coursers don't eat humans when they get mad." I took a deep breath to calm down, and then frowned. "How did you know Rua wanted to attack?"

"I felt it. I can't talk to her, but I can sense her emotions, and she was feeling murderous."

"You should have signaled there was a problem. We would have dealt with it."

"I know. I'm sorry."

"If you do it again, you'll return to regular scout duty —understood?"

She gulped and lightly saluted. I didn't respond. I didn't like chastising people and didn't do it often, but both she and Rua had to be made aware that there would be severe consequences if they ever disobeyed direct orders again.

By the time I'd finished, Kele had returned, the ends of her coat bunched up in front of her stomach to form a basket. "Nothing in the way of caves, but I did find a couple of butternut trees. They're a little off full ripeness but will still be edible."

I nodded. The butternut nuts were slightly oily but lovely and sweet, though the shells could be bastards to crack, especially if still a little green. They were also extremely good at filling an empty belly, though eating too many of them could have you running to the bathroom. "Good find."

She dropped onto her knees and poured the nuts onto the top of my pack. "There's no sign of life other than a bunch of birds roosting on an outcrop of rock just off the shore. Unless the gilded riders do a sweep this way, I think we're pretty safe."

I nodded. "Let's create a rough shelter, then I'll contact Esan and let them know what is happening."

"Four-hour rotating watch shifts, as usual?"

I nodded again. The drakkons would undoubtedly sense and see anything long before we did, but it never hurt to be cautious.

By the time we'd constructed our lean-to, tiredness was riding me, and my stomach rumbled with hunger. As much as I would have loved to do nothing more than simply eat the last of my rations, then curl up on the warm sands like the drakkons and go to sleep, I couldn't. Not yet. As Kele began cracking nuts open with her sword hilt, I dragged out the quill and tablet and scribed home.

That, came my father's reply, *suggests they plan to hit us on two fronts.*

Yes, but hopefully the riders will move their barges to another location to prevent a second attack and give us more time. Though we were definitely running out of it. *Are we any closer to finding a means of neutralizing their acidic spray?*

The engineers have worked out a system that can spray water across the outer wall and neutralize the acid, and the earth mages believe they can alter the stone's molecules to better enable them to withstand acidic attacks.

The latter was going to take time—probably more than what we had—but it was pointless saying what everyone already knew. *Has Damon said anything about the fire transfer spell?*

The cursor pulsed for several seconds before the answer came through. *Damon here. I've asked Angola to send additional witches. That way, we can do all three drakkons at the same time.*

It took a couple of seconds for his words to actually register, because my silly mind had zeroed in on the fact that he'd been in the war room, very likely waiting for word from me. Maybe I was reading too much into such a small action, but it nevertheless had my heart singing.

It'll take them too long to get here from Angola, though. In fact, given the build-up of both the Mareritt and the riders, there was a very good chance we'd be under siege before they even got close to Esan.

No. They will be here within the day.

I frowned. Even with the strongest wind at their back, it was, at best, a two-day sea journey from Angola to Hopetown—not that they could dock there now—and from there, on the fastest, strongest coursers traveling non-stop day and night, it would take a further two to three days to reach us. All of which meant it was logistically impossible for them to arrive here that quickly *unless* he'd called for their help almost immediately after our marriage, and at that point, we hadn't even discussed the possibility of giving the drakkons fire.

How?

Explain later.

Frustration stirred through me, but I did my best to ignore it. His aunt no doubt lurked on the wall above them, mind snooping to gather all pertinent details to report back to Aric. While I had no idea why he'd want to keep this sort of information from his parent, maybe it was tied up with the whole "lives on the line" concerns that seemed to be the basis of all he was doing.

Including our marriage.

I take it this means you've sorted out the spell?

Not entirely. Risks remain.

All magic has risks. And I suspected neither Yara nor Rua would be happy to wait until we knew whether the spell was successful or not. They wanted fire... *now.*

Yes, but it's theoretically possible that by giving the drakkons fire, you'll lose yours. And, as I mentioned earlier, it remains possible that it will kill you both.

I would hate to lose my fire—I'd long depended on it as a means of protection, whether personal or when I was with my squad on scouting missions—but strangely, I wasn't so worried about the possibility of this spell killing me. I trusted Damon. Trusted that, no matter how dangerous it might be to me, the drakkons, or—given the amount of personal strength it would take to perform a blood spell like this—himself, he wouldn't do it unless there was a very good chance of success. No matter what his secrets, he was on our side when it came to the riders and protecting Esan. I was sure of that, even if everything else about he and I remained uncertain.

It's a risk we'll have to take. I paused. *Not that I can speak for Kaia, or the drakkons as a whole.*

There are some here who believe that by giving the drakkons fire, we are giving them the means to destroy us.

Who are these "some"? Not my parents.

No. Vaya, to name at least one. She believes we should be more cautious.

We haven't got time to be cautious. Besides, the drakkons don't do revenge. At least, not in the same way.

Vahree only knew, they could easily have hunted us out of existence from the plains and farmlands had they really wanted to—ballistas might successfully bring them down, but they were not the easiest of weapons to move around the countryside—but they'd simply retreated to more distant locations instead.

I agree, but you have to remember, people have feared them for a very long time, and that will not change overnight, regardless of how many drakkons help us through the current crisis.

Maybe not, but once the riders descend on us and their farms and livelihoods are destroyed, they'll rather quickly change their minds.

You have far more faith in people than I do. The cursor blinked for a few seconds, and I had the strongest feeling that he wanted to add something else, something more personal, like "I miss you, I want you"... but maybe that was nothing more than a projection of my own emotions. *Talk when you get back.*

The tablet disconnected on their end, surprising me a little. I'd expected my father to get back online to offer a final few comments or to at least bid me to be careful, and I really hoped that the fact he hadn't didn't signal something had happened. Something like the riders who'd chased after us deciding to do a retaliatory run against Esan's walls and people.

"Everything all right back home?" Kele asked, as I tucked the quill and tablet away.

I nodded. "They're working on measures to protect the walls from the acid—"

"I hope it also protects *us* from the fucking acid," Hannity commented, "because that will wipe *us* out faster than it'll wipe out the walls."

I glanced at her. Her leg was still propped up on the log, but she'd created a hollow in the sand and looked as comfortable as she was likely to get with half a good chunk of her thigh eaten away. "I think they consider the walls the priority right now."

She snorted. "No use protecting the walls if there is no one left to stand and fight on them."

That was a truth I couldn't argue with. I pushed to my feet. "I've got a drakkon to repair. Kele, can you grab your first-aid kit? It's going to take the rest of the sealer and webbing we have left to repair her wing."

Kele nodded, handed Hannity the nuts she'd cracked open, then walked over to her packs. I climbed out of our shelter and called Rua out of the water.

She grumbled something along the lines of "about time" and rather awkwardly walked out, tucking her good wing up close to her body but letting the other trail behind her. Perhaps with all the loose membrane, she simply wasn't able to draw it any closer.

With Kaia and Yara watching on—more to keep Rua in check from any instinctive, snappish reactions than any real interest in what we were doing—we stretched out Rua's wing and started the repairs. The wing wasn't as damaged as I'd feared—no major bones had been hit, even if a good percentage of her wing membrane either hung loose or had been completely eaten away—so there was a good possibility she would be able to fly tomorrow if we had enough webbing and sealer to rejoin the majority of it.

It took several hours to do that, though, and we used everything we had. I asked Rua to keep the wing extended for a couple of hours just to give the webbing additional time to set across the wider holes, then grabbed Hannity's packs and walked back to the shelter. After a quick meal, I took first watch. The rain eased, and a pale half-moon sat low in the sky, no doubt providing just enough light for any passing riders to spot us.

They didn't pass. Nothing did, not even pipistrelles—small, winged creatures whose fuzzy black bodies were no bigger than my fist and whose leathery wings were a glorious blue-black in color—despite the fact they were readily found on most islands situated in warmer climes.

I woke Kele once my four hours were over, then lay down on the warm sand, wrapped my coat around me, and went to sleep... only for it to be haunted by images of Vahree reaching with greedy hands to claim the souls of my family.

I hoped it was nothing more than the natural tension that rose from facing an unknown situation and foe. Hoped that it wasn't an indication that Mom's seeress ability was finally rising with greater strength in me.

Feared that hope would soon give way to reality, and all that I loved would soon disappear in a cloud of acid dust.

———

It was close to midday when we decided to risk the flight home. I scribed my father before we left, requesting not only a stretcher for Hannity—there was no sign of infection as far as I could see, but she was barely able to put weight on her leg, and the potions weren't doing a whole lot to cut the level of her pain—but also additional webbing, sealer, and numbing salve. If Damon's plan to do all three of us at the same time eventuated, then we needed both Hannity *and* Rua to be at peak fitness—especially given the danger of the spell and the physical toll it would take on us all.

We started off slowly, keeping low to the sea and our speed down, until we were sure Rua's wings weren't going to shred, then gradually raised our pace and height. The hours ticked by slowly, and by the time we neared the aerie, I was shaking with fatigue and so damn hungry I could have eaten a whole damn capra—raw if necessary.

Me eat three, came Kaia's thought.

You've enough time to hunt before dusk, but don't dillydally.

What dillydally?

Take too long to hunt or eat.

Hunt fast, bring back to aerie. Gria hungry.

Gria is always hungry.

Truth.

We swooped toward the aerie's landing tongue, the younger drakkons preceding Kaia. Gria once again greeted us enthusiastically, rubbing necks with her mother and demanding they go hunt.

The interaction between the two, the obvious love, hit me hard. What I was asking Kaia to do, what I was asking her to risk, was just too much....

Me chose, she said softly, *not you.*

But—

Am queen, she cut in. *I must protect. I fail Ebrus. Will not happen again.*

But Gria—

Will die, like Ebrus die, if gilded ones not stopped.

I drew in a deep breath and released it slowly. I could not deny the truth of the words, but I still worried about the risks.

You risk.

I don't have a child.

Would not stop you. You queen too.

It was the second time she had said something like that, and I couldn't help but laugh. *I will never be queen. Not in the same way as you are.*

But even as I said the words, the dreams rose anew to haunt the outskirts of my mind, and the bitter taste of bile rose up my throat. I clenched my fists against the heat that instinctively pressed against my fingertips; I would *not* lose my family. No matter what it took, I would protect them, even at the cost of my own life.

That queen thinking, Kaia commented.

I laughed again, unclipped my packs and all the harness bits and pieces, and then slid down her leg. After giving Gria the demanded eye scratch, I stepped out of the way as the two of them ambled toward the exit. Yara followed, but Rua remained, her mate leaving instead to hunt for them both. Her pain was a distant song that ran through the back of my thoughts; the long flight had taken its toll and torn more membrane. Thank Vahree I'd ordered more supplies to be brought up—I really didn't have the energy to walk all the way down there and back.

"I'm hearing voices outside," Kele said. "Sounds like the stretcher you ordered is here."

"Let's help Hannity out there—"

"Hannity *is* capable of walking," she cut in somewhat crossly.

I glanced at her. "No doubt, but why risk further damage and the possibility of not being able to ride Rua again?"

Her eyes widened briefly, then she glanced at Rua. "I swear, I won't—"

"You need two good legs to ride her, same as she needs two good wings to fly," I cut in. "So, stop arguing, soldier, and let us help you out of here so I can get back and finish the repairs on your drakkon's wings."

"Oh! Sorry, I didn't know." She paused. "Is she in much pain?"

"Some."

"But she'll be okay?"

"Yes."

"Good."

We carried her out, the shield shimmering softly as we went through. There were six soldiers waiting outside—four for the stretcher and two relief—and a number of packs sitting to one side. I was a little disappointed—more than a little, if I was being at all honest—that Damon wasn't also here, but it wasn't like he didn't have other problems to deal with. I might be his wife, but I was not a priority right now —and maybe never would be.

I did not like the ache that accompanied that thought.

Did not like the implications.

"You want me to stay and help with Rua's wing?" Kele asked.

I shook my head. "Go get some rest. You deserve it."

Kele snorted. "So do you, Captain, but I'm not seeing you rushing to do so."

I smiled. "With the title comes responsibility. Go. I won't be that far behind you."

She hesitated then lightly saluted and ran off after the stretcher bearers. I grabbed the three packs and carried them back through the shield into the aerie. The other drakkons who'd come here with Yara watched with wary interest as I patched the newly torn sections of Rua's wing. While that was not unexpected, given how little interaction they'd had with humans until Kaia and I had intervened in the attack on their aerie, if we were truly going to build an army of fire-breathing dragons and riders, we needed them to trust us. Right now, while they would obey Kaia, they remained wary of us.

Of course, if we couldn't find more strega witches willing to ride drakkons then it wouldn't really matter.

Once I'd rubbed on the last of the numbing salve, I rinsed my hands with the last of my water, then scratched Rua's eye ridge. "Keep that wing as still as you can for the next few hours."

Will. Appreciate.

I smiled. "You're welcome, Rua. Just don't do something that stupid again."

Won't.

I gave her eye a final scratch, then picked up all the empty wrapping and salve tubes, shoving them in the pack and tossing all three into a corner, out of the way. I had my own to carry down and no desire to add additional weight. Not when I was feeling bone weary.

Once I'd strapped on my sword and slung my bow and quiver over my shoulder, I grabbed my packs and headed home. Night had well and truly settled in by the time I reached the gate, where I discovered that, for the first time in ages, the portcullis had been lowered into place. Obviously security measures had been increased, even for minor gateways that were never likely to be a point of entry for either the Mareritt or the gilded riders.

I hailed the guards, and, after a visual check, the portcullis was raised enough for me to slip under. One of the guards stepped forward and, with a crisp salute, said, "Captain, I've a message from Commander Silva for you."

"And that message is?"

"Head immediately to your quarters and report in the morning."

Relief spun through me. I needed food, I needed a bath, and I needed to see my husband—and not necessarily in that order. "Thank you, soldier."

I returned his salute and continued on, making my way through the short tunnel, then across the courtyard and into the palace. The foyer was dark and still, and if not for the presence of various guards, it would have been very easy to believe the entire building was empty. I ran lightly up the stairs, my stupid heart racing at the thought of seeing Damon again. His magic shimmered over me as I approached the door, a familiar caress that felt as strong and real as the man himself. I nodded at the guard positioned at the midpoint between my room and the thermae—a new assignment, and perhaps one to prevent Damon's aunt getting to come to family apartments—then stepped into my room. It was as quiet and as still as the rest of the building and utterly empty. Once again, disappointment shot through me.

That's what I get for falling for a man for whom I would never be a first priority... except I didn't fall. I was given. Big difference.

Even if my heart was suggesting the end result was the same—me, foolishly tripping along the path to caring. To loving...

Nope, I was *not* going there. Wasn't even going to think about it.

I dumped my packs into the holding bin, then stripped off my weapons and hung them over the hooks. Once I'd taken off my boots and my jacket, I padded over to the scribe tablet and ordered a meal and shamoke, half smiling as Candra's comment about never knowing when the family was going to scribe down for food echoed through my mind.

As I turned and headed for the bathroom, I noticed the symbols Damon had written on the floor now glowed with an odd, bloody luminance. I paused briefly, wondering if it was wise to approach a possibly active spell, but, rather unsurprisingly, curiosity got the better of me. Three steps away from the symbols, I hit a shield and was stopped. Light flared across its surface, its hue yellowish rather than the red of the letters—a warning, I suspected, rather than a threat. I raised a hand and pressed a finger against the magic continuing to tingle across my body. Light gathered where my fingertip met the spell, buzzing around it like tiny moon flies, even if their color was yellow rather than silvery. Frowning, I circled the symbols, keeping my finger against the shield as a guide; the moon flies trailed after my touch, reminding me a little of a falling star's tail.

The symbols were completely encased. I rose on my toes and ran my finger up its surface to see how high it was;

there was a slight curvature, suggesting it wasn't so much a wall as a complete bubble.

Was this a mini version of the spell he would use to share my strega abilities with Kaia? Or was it something else?

The suspicious part of me said it was the latter, and the instinctive part of my soul loudly agreed. It was frustrating that Damon wouldn't confide in me, but in truth, why would he? We might be married, we might be fire in bed and out, but it took more than sexual compatibility to build trust, let alone a relationship.

I dropped my finger and continued on to the bathroom, running water into the bath before stripping off and tossing my clothes into the laundry chute. A long soak in the hot water made me feel fresher, if no less tired. The food arrived just as I was tugging on a gown, one woman carrying a tray while her companion carried a large pot of shamoke. I thanked them both and helped myself to the latter, savoring the smell for several seconds before taking a drink. But as I sat down to eat, I spotted a sealed piece of paper with my name on it.

The writing was Damon's.

Heart hammering unreasonably, I slid a fingernail under the seal and opened the letter.

My dear wife, it said, and I could almost hear his dry tone as I read that, *I have gone to meet—and escort—the Angolan witches here. They had some trouble with their mode of transport, but we should be back by the morning. I've left a leather bracelet on our bed—please wear it. It will stop my aunt stealing your thoughts when beyond our room. I have also given one to both your parents. As stakes rise, it will be more important than ever that our secrets are kept.*

It was simply signed, *D*.

I immediately rose and walked over to the bed. In the middle lay a plaited bracelet of brown and black leather with threads of red and gold—the colors of his house and mine—interwoven through it. Even without picking it up, I could feel the familiar caress of power emanating from it, and wondered if the darker leather had been soaked in his blood in order to hold his magic.

I warily picked it up; it seemed overly large for my wrist, but I nevertheless slipped it on. The pulse of energy running through the darker thread sharpened briefly, and the bracelet contracted until it sat snugly but comfortably against my wrist. I lightly pulled on it; the leather gave fractionally but didn't move. It appeared that, at least for the moment, there was no taking it off. Which, given Gayl remained a threat to whatever Damon was truly up to, was not a bad thing.

I returned to the seating area, eating my meal and consuming the entire pot of shamoke, then stripped off the gown, climbed into bed, and went to sleep. This time, it wasn't dreams of deception and betrayal that haunted me, but rather a sullen warning that our time was up.

Vahree was coming for us, and this time, he wouldn't take no for an answer.

———

I woke to the faintest brush of warmth against my lips. I stirred, caught the scent of warm spices and man, and opened my eyes. Damon lay beside me, his head on my pillow, his face inches from mine.

Almost instantly, the urge to wrap myself around him, to beg him to kiss me, caress me, lose himself within me, rose, but I held still. I'd already given too much of myself to this man and, until he opened up, I needed to slow things down.

"When did you get back?"

"About two hours ago. Had to report to your father, then make myself presentable for my wife."

"The wife appreciates the cleaner presentation."

His lips quirked. "But would not have rejected the dirtier?"

"Depends on the type of dirt we're discussing."

His soft amusement fell away. He knew I wasn't talking about *actual* dirt but made no reply to it. Instead, he touched my cheek, then ran his finger down to my lips, leaving a tingly, burning trail in its wake. When his finger brushed my bottom lip, I closed my mouth around it and lightly sucked. Heat and hunger stirred in his eyes and echoed deep within me. My brain might be wanting me to slow down but my body definitely had other ideas. I released his finger, and it moved on, down my chin and neck, still trailing heated chaos behind it.

"What of the Angolan witches?" I asked softly, a slight catch in my voice. He might be doing nothing more than lightly touching me, yet it felt like I was being branded.

"They await our arrival in the caverns."

His slow journey continued to my collarbone, sweeping from one side to the other, encompassing the shoulder I wasn't lying on. I had the odd feeling he was determined to refamiliarize himself with all the parts of my body he could reach, and while I was not against such slow exploration, I also wasn't sure I could stand the torture. I wanted this man with a fierceness that almost felt like desperation. And maybe it was, because if the dreams that had plagued me over the last couple of nights were to be believed, this moment, this perfect bubble of peace and desire, was all that we had left; life, war, and treachery were about to sweep it all away.

I licked my lips, saw the hunger in his gaze deepen, and once again felt its deeper echo within. "Why the caverns? Why not perform it here, given you've already marked all the symbols on the floor? Or do you need the drakkons' presence rather than just their blood?"

"The latter, I'm afraid. There has to be a physical connection between the two elements we're trying to combine for the spell to work."

"Then if you're not using the spell here, why does it still glow?"

"Because I'm still refining the process."

"That may not be a lie, but it's not entirely the truth now either, is it?"

He grimaced. "No, but I cannot say anything more just yet—"

"That response is getting so fucking tedious, Damon."

"I know, and I'm sorry." He paused. "Do you want me to stop?"

"No, I fucking don't."

He chuckled softly and, with one lone finger, continued to circle my left breast's areola. It pebbled in response, and my breath caught in my throat. Vahree only knew, I wanted the man so badly... but I needed to ask my questions even more, no matter how fruitless that particular endeavor might be.

"And what of your aunt?" I somehow said, a quiver that spoke of the desire building within so very evident in my voice. "Won't she be—"

"I do not wish to talk about my aunt or indeed my father right now."

"Then what do you wish, Damon?" I snapped back.

"What part will I play in your future once the machinations that currently rule your life end?"

His fingers stilled again, and his gaze came to mine. For the briefest of moments, it felt like I was falling into a sea of blue. A sea that was warm, caring, and dangerously beautiful, filled with ghostly promises that couldn't possibly be.

"What part do you play?" he echoed softly, somehow so much closer than he had been only a heartbeat before. "You are a light that shone brightly at the darkest point of my night, a promise of what might yet be. If you believe nothing else, then believe this; I will *never* relinquish you. You are mine, and only mine."

Before I could question the oddness of that statement and the intensity with which it was spoken, his lips claimed mine. While the kiss was neither fierce nor hungry, it held an odd intensity. It felt like both a beginning and a message, one filled with a determination to assert his claim over body and soul.

Over the course of the next hour, it was a message he delivered to every part of my body, and it left me in little doubt that, no matter what the origin of the darkness haunting his every move, he was utterly serious about his vow.

I could only hope that Aric allowed him to keep it.

———

My mother sent a message for me to join them in their suite before we headed out to the aerie. I left Damon working on final preparations of the spell that continued to glow eerily on the floor and strode down to the other end of the hall to my parents' suite.

Lenny, their longtime door guard, watched me

approach, a smile touching his lips. He was a bull of a man, with a thick mane of brown hair tied up in a tail at the back of his head—following the newer fashion in hair styling rather than the more traditional plaited—and dark green eyes.

"Good afternoon, Lady Bryn," he said, reaching for the door.

"Afternoon, Lenny. How's the family?"

"Good, thanks. Rodkin is heading into military training next week."

My eyebrows rose. "He can't be old enough, surely."

Lenny laughed, a warm rich sound. "Nearing sixteen he is, now."

"Time flies." I shook my head. "Do you know the name of his training officer?"

"Gert Hankin, I believe."

"Then Rodkin is in good hands. Please send him my best wishes, won't you?"

"I will, Lady Bryn. Thanks."

He stepped back to let me enter, then closed the door behind me. The suite's layout was a larger version of mine, though my parents also had an additional dining and a living room beyond the family ones so they could entertain guests less formally.

Mom stood near the window slit that looked out over the courtyard, the pale afternoon sun filtering through barely warming her skin. She turned as I entered, her face drawn. Which, given so many of her kin on Jakarra remained missing and the long hours she'd spent organizing relief supplies and evacuations, was not surprising.

What *did* surprise me was the anger. It blazed from her blue eyes and practically radiated from the pores of her skin.

I stopped cold, my heart lodging somewhere in my throat. "What's happened?"

"Nothing." She waved a hand. "Everything."

"As statements go, that's definitely not one of your clearer ones."

Amusement briefly tugged at her lips but did little to ease the fiery fury in her eyes. "Sorry, between my fears and my seeress abilities deciding to light up, I'm a bit all over the place."

"What are your visions telling you?" I asked, even though it wasn't hard to guess given the dark threads running through my own dreams.

"Death comes to Esan," she replied. "And so too does Aric."

CHAPTER 10

IT WAS another statement that left me more than a little confused. "Didn't Aric return home because he couldn't stand Esan's bleakness?"

"Yes, but his ship was scuttled by raiders en route to Zephrine."

Raiders sailing off our southern shores was the last thing we needed right now. "Given the bastard survived, Túxn obviously wasn't feeling favorable toward us that day."

Mom's lips twitched again. "I will admit to thinking along those very same lines, although it is not seemly for the queen consort."

I dared say it wasn't seemly for a princess either, even one soldier trained. "Then why isn't he making his way to Zephrine? Why return here?"

She rubbed her fingers across her forehead and sighed. "I don't know."

"Your visions aren't supplying any information?"

"Just that he will take advantage of a situation that comes." Her gaze met mine, a touch of bleakness running through the fury now. "And that situation revolves around Damon and the secrets he keeps."

I swore and stalked over to the table where a shamoke pot steamed lightly. I'd already had a good number of cups today, but a situation like this definitely required more. A big jug of honey mead would have been even better, but that wasn't practical—or wise—given what still lay ahead. "Damon remains closed mouth about *that* whole situation."

I poured two cups, then picked them up and walked over to her. She nodded her thanks and took a sip. "My visions suggest it involves his sisters."

"He hasn't got any sisters..." I trailed off. "Or do you mean half-sisters? By all accounts, he has plenty of those."

"No, full sisters, and don't ask me to explain impossibility because I can't—and my visions won't."

I downed my shamoke in several gulps, then went back for another. At this rate, I'd be waddling, not walking, up the mountain to the aerie. Or even worse, needing to pee halfway up. "Is Aric's looming presence the reason my father isn't here?"

"No. The mages are running their first test of altering the wall stone, and he wished to be there."

"I hope they're not experimenting on the main wall, because if things don't go as planned, that could lead to it being more easily breached."

"Indeed, which is why they're testing the alterations on the storeroom section between the war room and the admin block. If the experiment fails, it isn't likely to cause a major problem."

Mainly because the Mareritt didn't have a weapon powerful enough to strike our second wall, let alone the war room. Even the mounted tubes we'd seen at K'Anor weren't large enough to have the reach needed to do any real damage. Which didn't mean they couldn't still cause unimaginable chaos in the areas between the outer wall and the inner.

Of course, the gilded riders didn't need long-range weapons. Not when they had birds almost impervious to anything we could currently throw at them. Air turbulence might work extremely well, as did the blood barrier Damon had raised, but neither were practical long-term fixes. Witches tired, blood ran out. We needed something else. Something proven.

Like fire wielded by drakkons rather than strega witches.

But even if the exchange spell was a success and the drakkons gained the ability to flame, there was no guarantee the riders and their mages weren't already working on a means of countering our fires—especially after the chaos we'd caused on the barges.

I downed the second cup but resisted the temptation of a third, grabbing one of the sweet pastries instead. "And Aric? Do we know where he's currently located?"

"No. He and several others made it onto rowboats and were able to reach Lowcliffe Beach. From the information we received from Hopetown's forces stationed there, a Zephrine boat was already anchored. It remains, as does most of the seamen, but Aric and his guard left."

"On foot?"

"No. They confiscated the guards' mounts and told them to scribe back for more."

"Such a charming man," I muttered. And wondered, once again, why father and son were so very different, especially given Damon had been raised in an environment that was all about the importance and superiority of the Velez line of kings. "His actions make no sense, though, not if there was already a boat waiting for them in the bay. Why come here rather than go home? Especially when he hates this place?"

"Again, I do not know, and *that* is what makes me furious."

I finished my pastry and reached for another. "Maybe it has something to do with Gayl."

Mom frowned. "She is nothing more than a reader—"

"Who apparently also has minor seeress abilities that enable her to divine the future using the thoughts and actions of the present," I replied. "What if she's seen something? Something that makes Aric run the risk of returning?"

"The only thing that could do that is Rion's death."

"Aside from the fact he *isn't* dead, why would that make any difference to Aric?"

"Aric has long hungered to claim Esan's throne and unite Arleeon entirely under his rule. That is why he was mighty angry when Tayte failed to do his duty and marry you. Aric wanted Damon, as firstborn, on Zephrine's throne, not ours."

First born, second born, what did it really matter? They were both his sons. "The problem with that line of thinking is twofold; one, Garran is heir, not me, and even if his death is confirmed, his son will take the throne when he's old enough. And two, any son I bear will be backup for Zephrine's throne, not ours."

"Did you not read the finer details in the marriage contract?"

"Why would I when I was in denial about the whole event?"

She chuckled softly and touched my shoulder sympathetically. "Aric insisted on a clause that states the first son born to you and Damon will, should anything happen to the currently nominated heir, take the throne once he reaches his majority rather than Garran's heir. Until said son reaches his majority, you and Damon would act as joint regents."

My breath caught in my throat. "You don't think Aric is working with the gilded riders, do you?"

She shook her head. "He truly believes that his bloodline is far superior to anything we can produce, and therefore both East and West Arleeon should be united under his sole rule. He would not do anything to endanger that ambition or indeed his own rule in Zephrine."

"But you do believe he would have taken out Garran if Damon and I produced a son?"

"Yes, I do, and we had been discussing means to prevent that happening. Túxn saved us—and Aric—the effort, however." Mom looked away briefly, but not before I caught the sheen of tears. After a moment, she added, "I will, however, attempt another scrying; perhaps this time I will see what Túxn has planned for us."

I touched her arm comfortingly. "At the very least, we know Rion is safe in the war room. Even if the riders' acid does breach it, they will never be able to destroy the whole building, let alone the wall on which it rests. Not without days and days of endless attacks—and even then, only a limited number of the gilded birds wear the bands that allow them to fly during the day."

Of course, a limited number could still cause terrible destruction, both on the wall and within the fortress itself.

Mom rubbed her arms. "I hope you're right."

But feared I wasn't, if her troubled expression was

anything to go by. And there was nothing I could say to that, because I felt the very same way.

I finished my pastry and licked the sticky syrup from my fingers. "I'd better go. Damon wants to attempt the spell as the moon rises. Apparently, it's a blood moon that will add potency to the spell."

"So he said last night, when he was here updating us on the process and the dangers." She hesitated. "There are many pushing back against this decision—and in some respects you can't blame them. Fear of drakkons is deeply ingrained into much of the population; it's going to take a long time for that to dissipate."

"But it will dissipate? You saw this?"

She nodded. "Though it will not be weeks in the making, but rather years; decades, even."

"Did your intuition also step in while Damon was here?"

"No, but the bracelets he gave us to protect against Gayl's mental intrusions might also ward off any seeress intuition I might have when in his presence."

"Given his aunt apparently has similar abilities, it no doubt does."

She smiled, walked over, and hugged me tight. "Be careful, my darling girl. I've already lost enough family—I do not need to lose you as well."

"You won't." And silently prayed, even as I said that, that I hadn't just tempted Túxn. I dropped a kiss on her cheek then pulled free. "I'll see you once I wake from the spell."

She nodded. "You can be sure I will not sleep until I know you have."

"Damon will no doubt scribe—"

"Oh, your father threatened violence if he *didn't*."

I laughed, hugged her one more time, then turned around and walked out. Damon had the packs ready at the door and handed me the three smaller ones. The scents that rose from them were a thick and tangy mix that made my nose twitch.

"What in Túxn's name have you put in these?"

He smiled, though it failed to ease the worry crowding the corners of his eyes. "Yours carry various herbs to help increase the potency of the spell and ease the physical cost on us all. The rest hold spell anchors and the like."

I slung two of the packs over my shoulders, strapped on my knife and my sword, then clasped the third pack by its straps as I walked back out into the hall.

As Damon fell in step beside me, I said, "I take it both Kele and Hannity have been apprised of the risks involved in the spell?"

His packs clinked with every step, the sound metallic. Probably the various bowls and cups they needed to collect blood. "I talked to them both this morning, while you slept. I believe you could guess their joint responses."

"Something along the lines of 'who the fuck cares? I'll be one with a drakkon.'"

He laughed, the sound echoing warmly across the everyday noises that filled the palace. "That's exactly what they both said. In unison, I might add."

I grinned and clattered down the stairs. The two guards saluted as we headed out the main doors, and I returned them absently, my gaze on the skies. Though dusk remained a good hour away, shadows were already haunting the deeper corners around the stables and other nearby buildings. The sky was clear and though the moon hadn't yet risen, its bloody hue stained the very edges of the visible horizon.

Kele and Hannity were waiting near the gate, both carrying a number of packs.

"Treats for our drakkons," Kele said when she saw my raised eyebrow. "I got some for Kaia, too."

Kele thoughtful, Kaia commented. *Perhaps should have chosen her.*

I snorted. *Still time to change.*

Not change. You stronger.

No, I'm not.

Not talking flame.

Huh. I returned my attention to Kele. "And what might the treat be? Because the closer I get, the more odious the scent coming from those packs becomes."

Hannity grinned. "Smoked white fin. Gave some to Rua, and she appeared to love it. Figured if she did, the others would."

"I do hope you've brought enough to share with Gria, otherwise she will be cross."

"We have one entire pack for her," Kele said dryly.

I laughed and followed Damon up the path. It was night by the time we reached the crooked entrance into the mountain, and the moon sat like a fat croaker on the horizon, lending the few stars currently visible a bloody hue.

One that seemed to echo in Damon's eyes.

The power was rising in him, a cloak so visible that it felt like I could reach out and touch it. Neither Kele nor Hannity commented, which suggested they weren't seeing it. Maybe the fact I could was a natural result of our deepening connection. Or maybe it was due to my connection to Kaia, allowing her ability to see magic seep through to me even if we weren't as deeply linked as we had been in the past. Either way, it was a somewhat eerie sight.

We continued on, the ache in my leg increasing as we made our way through the various tunnels until we reached the barrier into the aerie. I really had done some serious damage if healed muscles continued to complain this far out.

Four witches—all women, ranging in age from early twenties to late sixties, if I was any judge—rose as we approached, their gazes unerringly coming to me.

I guess that was natural, given my marriage to Damon, but it was nevertheless unnerving, if only because it felt like they were looking past my outer shell—past all physical attributes like clothes and body shape—and instead searching the "inner" me, weighing my thoughts, my heart, and my soul. Which was ridiculous, because these were blood witches, not readers or seeresses, but I couldn't help but wonder what their judgement was, and whether I'd been found wanting.

If I had, then their expressions certainly didn't give it away.

The oldest of the four—a somewhat grizzled-looking woman with short silvery hair and green eyes that glimmered with bloody starlight—stepped forward and held out her hand. "You'd be Bryn Silva, then. Heard a lot about you."

Her grip was as fierce as the power radiating from her skin, but there was something in its feel that reminded me of Damon.

"And I," I replied, resisting the urge to flex my fingers once she released them, "have heard nothing about you."

"That is as it should be." Her gaze went past me. "This'll be Kele and Hannity, then?"

"Pretty easy guess, given we're the only other women here," Kele said dryly.

The old woman's gaze narrowed dangerously. While Kele simply raised an eyebrow in response, Hannity took a half step back, her eyes wide and fire flicking faintly around her fingertips. I couldn't say I blamed her—the old woman's gaze was *fierce*. She obviously wasn't someone who suffered fools—or indeed backchat—lightly.

"I would suggest politeness when dealing with your elders, young woman, especially when they'll soon be magically messing about with your being." She paused, and the fierceness faded a little. "Now, you've all been informed about the risks, haven't you?"

"Yes," we echoed.

"And you understand them?"

Another "yes" echoed in unison.

"And what of the drakkons?"

"The drakkons want fire, above all else," I replied.

She grunted. "Can't say I think it's wise, but desperate times and all that. Damon, you're lead."

He glanced at me again, the bloody light in his eyes growing, then strode through the barrier. The witches followed, meaning he'd already added them to the spell that guarded this entrance, with us three bringing up the rear. The drakkons were already aware of our presence, and their curiosity stung the air.

The older woman stopped at the tunnel's end and, with her hands on her hips, she surveyed the aerie critically. After a moment, she wrinkled her nose and shook her head. "This isn't suitable—is there another, larger cavern we could use? The spell will leave all of you comatose for at least a couple of hours, and it would be better if there was no danger of an accidental stomping by random drakkon movement."

"There's the upper cavern," I said. "It's much bigger and not currently in use."

"Perfect." She clapped her hands, drawing multiple jewellike gazes. "The three drakkons involved in this transference, off you go."

It was said in the manner of an old schoolmarm who expected instant obedience from her charges. Trouble was, if it wasn't for my presence, most of the drakkons here wouldn't have understood a word she was saying. It was only my connection to them all—even though I wasn't actively talking to them—that allowed comprehension.

Kaia's amusement rumbled through me. *She strange.*

She is indeed. But you'd better obey before she gets annoyed.

Kaia ordered Rua and Yara to precede her, then called Gria close and wrapped her neck around her drakkling. Gria obviously knew that what was about to happen was dangerous, but she, like the rest of the drakkons here, trusted me. And she, like the rest of them, wanted fire—even if she wasn't large enough to hold a rider aloft yet.

As Kaia finally ambled after the other two, Gria wandered over for the requisite eye scratch and eagerly accepted Hannity's offering of dried fish.

Give mine, Kaia said. *I good.*

We did, then followed the drakkons to the very back of the cavern and up the steep, rocky ramp that led to the upper cavern. The sand here was darker and didn't radiate the same sort of heat as the lower cavern, which was no doubt the reason why the only hatching caves up here were situated near natural heat vents. The aerie exit here faced west, and in daylight would have given an unending view of

Esan and the lands beyond her. Right now, though, it showed a sky dominated by the bleeding moon.

Yara and Rua had each hunkered down in one of the half-moon caves that dotted the perimeter, while Kaia stood near the exit, her scales set aflame by the moon's light.

The older woman stopped in the triangular "middle" of all three, then glanced at me. "Tell your drakkons everything I say."

I resisted the urge to say it wasn't necessary and simply nodded.

She continued, "I'm aware you all claim to understand the dangers, but just to be clear—there is no guarantee that this will work, and it could very well kill you. All of you, drakkon and strega. It could share your powers or remove them. It may give the drakkons fire but may also take years off their lives. It may completely remove fire from you stregas or gift you with whatever elemental powers the drakkons have. But most of all, it will bind you—and likely that of any offspring you might have from this moment on—together, forever."

"I can't see that as a problem," Hannity murmured.

The older woman's gaze darted toward her. "A life force shared is a life force endangered. If one is hurt, it will be felt by the other. If one is killed, it is likely the other will die."

You and I no die, Kaia rumbled. *Problem solved.*

That is definitely a plan I can get behind. All we had to do was hope the riders and the Mareritt allowed us to implement it.

"I do have one question." Kele stepped forward slightly. "If this spell is successful—if the drakkons do get fire and we retain ours—will they still need us to ride them?"

"That," the old woman said, "is very much a question for the drakkons. But if this spell works as we believe, then the binding might make it necessary for drakkon and rider to act as one fighting unit to be at their most powerful."

We be kin, Kaia said. *Should fight together.*

She said it to the other drakkons rather than just me, and it sounded more like an order than a comment.

Like flamer, Yara said. *Gives more protection.*

The old woman's gaze came to mine. "And you? Any questions?"

I hesitated. "If we're transferring abilities, will we also transfer knowledge? Will the drakkons have to learn from scratch how to flame, or will our experiences and memories transfer across to them?"

"The complete entwining you will all undergo means knowledge should be shared. However, given the vast biological differences, they will likely have to learn how to employ *your* knowledge to their beings."

I nodded. Given how long it had taken *me* to learn control, and how many things I'd burned in the process, it was damnably good to know they didn't have to learn from scratch. The last thing we needed was drakkons unintentionally flaming each other or us.

"Nothing else?" she asked, leaving me with the odd feeling that perhaps I should be asking more questions.

"Nothing I can immediately think of, so can we stop talking and just do? Time is running out real fast."

Her eyebrows rose. "You got seer abilities?"

"Mom has."

"Ah." She eyed me speculatively for a second, then switched her gaze to Damon. "You brought the items?"

He nodded and shucked off his four packs, handing one to each of the younger witches before giving the third to the older woman. He then took my three, handing out two and keeping the third.

"I'll work the circle around Bryn and Kaia," he said. "Carrie can work around Kele and Yara, and Sue, Hannity and Rua."

The older woman nodded. "Leaving me as guide and step-in spare if your strength fails—"

"Hang on," I cut in. "Why would Damon's strength fail and not the other ladies'?"

"Because," she snapped, annoyance evident as she stabbed a finger toward Kaia, "that drakkon is huge—almost a third larger again than the other two."

Am queen, Kaia said. *Should be larger.*

I resisted the urge to smile and motioned the older woman to continue. She did so, though her voice remained somewhat cross. "Now, our preparations may take some time, so you ladies will sit your butts down next to your drakkons and wait patiently—without talking."

Is she old queen? Yara commented. *She bossy.*

I couldn't help smiling. *With age comes bossiness and wisdom.*

Depends on queen. Some not wise. She paused for a long moment, probably realizing what she'd implied. *Not mean Kaia.*

Not old, came Kaia's unconcerned response.

As Kele and Hannity walked over to their respective drakkons and gave them the smoked fish, I stopped next to Kaia and leaned a shoulder against her neck as I stared out over lands lit by the moon's bloody hue. A shiver stole through me, and I lightly rubbed my left arm. *In Túxn's name, let it not be an omen of what lies ahead.*

Footsteps approached, and even before I looked around, I knew it was Damon. The power surrounding him was so intense, it felt like lightning across my skin. "You wear your magic like a cloak."

"It's a cloak you should not be able to see," came the old woman's response before Damon had any chance to reply. "And did I not advise silence?"

"I'm not one to remain silent unless absolutely necessary," I retorted. "Do you actually have a name? And do you always listen in on other people's conversations?"

"Yes, and yes," she replied with a cackle.

I waited several seconds, but she went no further. I raised an eyebrow and met Damon's gaze questioningly.

Amusement briefly lurked in his red-hued eyes. "She's known to the outside world as simply the Prioress."

"Why? Angola is a place of teaching, not priories."

He shrugged. "In times past, there were many who did not understand—or indeed condone—a woman's need to study, but most respected a religious priory."

"Has Zephrine really moved beyond that belief? Because I'm hearing echoes of it every time your father opens his mouth."

"My father is not Zephrine, no matter what he believes. Now, I need to set up the circle around the two of you." He glanced up at the drakkon. "Kaia, you need to remain still—no tail swishing."

No swish tail, she acknowledged. *No move.*

I repeated what she said, then added, "And me? Should I strip off yet?"

Heat stirred briefly in his eyes. "As much as I would enjoy that, I need to concentrate, and you, my dear wife, are too much of a distraction."

"And yet, here you remain, chatting and being all distracted."

"She makes a point," the Prioress said crossly. "Get a move on, Damon—I have no desire to be in this wretched place longer than absolutely necessary."

Damon cast an amused look her way, then moved closer to the side wall and emptied out his pack, placing the various jars of herbs, knives, jewel-like stones, a metal cup, and a pouring jug in a neat row. Then he picked up the herbs and returned, briefly pausing a few yards away. "We begin. You both ready?"

I nodded. He turned to the side and began to circle us, murmuring in that gorgeous old language again and slowly pouring the herbs onto the sand. As the moon rose higher in the night sky, the jewels joined the herbs on the ground, and his voice grew stronger. His magic pulsed around us now, a curtain of power that rose in harmony with the spells being cast around Kele and Yara, Hannity and Rua.

I hoped, *really* hoped, that Túxn was in a generous mood and we all made it through this successfully.

Once Damon had finished the jewel circle, he picked up the first of his knives and a cup, then approached us, carefully stepping over the jewels and the herbs. "I now need blood from you both. Kaia, I'll take it from your claw pad, but the blade is blessed to ensure it does not hurt."

Trust, came Kaia's comment.

I repeated that, my gaze on the rather large-looking cup. "It's going to take a lot of my blood to fill that thing."

"It won't drain you to the point of danger." His gaze held mine. "I made a promise. I intend to keep it."

My heart did an odd sort of twist. One that suggested I'd fallen faster, and deeper, than I'd feared when it came to this man. I continued to hold his gaze and, just for a second, felt the unsteady beating of my heart echoing through his.

Or was that merely wishful thinking?

Because despite everything he'd said last night, for all the promises he'd made, never once had love been mentioned.

He didn't say anything, though the faintest flicker in his eyes suggested he was well enough aware of my thoughts *and* my fears.

"We need to talk, Damon."

He didn't ask what about. He didn't need to. "We will. When there's time."

Time, I suspected, was the one thing we didn't have. I held out my right hand, wrist up. "Best drain me first then, just in case the sight of Kaia losing all that blood makes me faint."

"Though I suspect fainting isn't in your nature at *all*, if there's one thing that *could* cause it, it would be the sight of your drakkon losing blood."

"You misjudge me," I replied lightly. "The sight of you losing a lot of blood is no good for my equilibrium, either."

Before he could reply, the Prioress snapped, "Will you two stop flirting and just get on with it?"

He smiled, gently caught my hand, then placed the blade against my skin and glanced at me, eyebrow raised in question. I nodded and, with a quick sharp motion, he cut my wrist. As blood welled from the wound, he turned my hand sideways so that the rich red liquid flowed steadily into the cup. When it was close to full, he righted my wrist, then placed the knife's blade on the wound. It instantly began to heal.

"Feel okay?" he asked softly, his gaze searching mine.

"Of course—though it's not in my nature to say otherwise."

Amusement briefly twisted his lips, and just as quickly fell away. He stepped over the herbs and the jewels, placed my blood carefully beside a large metal jug, then picked up the second cup and returned.

"Kaia, can you please move your foot so I can reach the pad."

She immediately did so. Drakkons, like many much —*much*—smaller reptiles, had four claws and a dew claw, with a pad of tissue between the two to cushion and protect their feet when walking. Damon placed the bloody knife on the pad's thick edge, then drove the point in. It went deeper than I expected, but Kaia didn't flinch, and no pain washed through her thoughts. Damon withdrew the knife, and dark blood followed, flowing easily into the cup. As it neared fullness, he once again placed the flat of the blade against the wound, this time murmuring in old Angolan. Her wound, like mine, sealed almost instantly.

His magic heal faster than mine, she commented.

But yours is part of your being and instinctive, which is far better.

I returned my attention to Damon. He was murmuring again, waving a hand over each of the cups before picking them both up and pouring them into the jug. At the point where the two flows combined, a luminous, bloody mist arose.

It was the same sort of mist that now surrounded the moon.

I shivered and rubbed my arms again, but it didn't help. The sheer amount of power now filling this cavern was a heated river that flowed across my senses and danced through my veins, a fire so intense it made my whole body vibrate.

And the most dangerous part of the spell hadn't even started yet.

Am here, Kaia said. *We do this, be one.*

Kin, I replied, though with far less confidence than she had.

I trusted Damon. I was just... afraid.

He turned to face us, the bowl in his hand. There was no blue, no white, left in his eyes; their color was now the same red as the mist that surrounded him—a mist born of combining our blood with the moon's power.

For the very first time, I wondered what this spell would cost *him*.

"You may strip off your clothes now, Bryn." Though his voice was gossamer soft and impersonal, it echoed loudly through and around me. "Toss your clothes and your weapons beyond the circle, ensuring none of them touch it. Then you must lie prone on Kaia so that your entire length is in contact with her."

"That is going to be uncomfortable naked," I commented, nevertheless pushing to my feet.

He didn't answer. Perhaps he couldn't, given the power he now exuded.

I stripped off, shivering a little as cold fingers of air curled around my torso, then stepped closer to the stone circle and tossed my clothes beyond it. Once my boots had followed, I turned and studied Kaia. Where did I lie? Her neck and back were out of the question because of all her spines....

Leg, she said, stretching her nearest front leg out just enough that it touched her snout.

I scrambled up onto her claws, then sat down, leaning back against the front of her leg and stretching my legs out to her claws. Her scales were cold and rough against my skin, but I didn't raise the inner fire to keep myself warm, as I had no idea how that would affect the spell.

Perhaps *that* was one of the questions I should have asked.

"Comfortable?" Damon asked in that same soft but distant voice.

"As I'll ever be."

"Then the true spell begins."

He picked up the second knife and sliced his left arm open, then lowered it, allowing the blood to trickle down his palm and fingers onto the ground. Then he raised the jug and began to spell; with every step, he dribbled our combined blood onto the jewels and the herbs. A vortex of power began to rise, and lightning flashed, fierce and bright. Not across the night sky or its bloody moon, but rather inside me. It burned through muscle, veins, and bone, stretching me, expanding me, making me a being that was more than flesh, a being that was ethereal and translucent, here and yet not.

Pain followed, pain unlike anything I'd felt before. I tried to scream, but in this place of blood and power, fire and fury, I had no voice. There was just the vortex, tearing at me, pulling me apart, drawing the past and the future, my hopes and my fears, my strengths and weakness, accomplishments and failures—all that I was, and all that I could be—from my being and spinning them away, tiny specks of ash lost in a maelstrom of blood and magic.

But I was not the only soul caught in this madness.

Kaia curled around me, a gossamer being made of starlight. *Red* starlight that burned like fire.

The vortex's intensity increased, and the world seemed to scream. Or maybe that was me. It was hard to tell in this place of bloody power.

Starlight began to pull away from my incorporeal being and spun toward Kaia's, the flow gentle at first but quickly increasing, until it seemed like a flood of light was pouring from me to her. It danced briefly amongst her starlit form, then gradually combined—merged—with the red, becoming one.

Then the vortex shifted direction, and a smaller stream flowed from her incorporeal form into mine. Each star hit like a club, then ran amok through me, burning, destroying, rebuilding.

I screamed, endlessly screamed, into that fiery darkness, but I wasn't alone. Kaia was here, and she too screamed.

Then the spell reached its pinnacle and exploded, taking me, Kaia, and consciousness with it.

CHAPTER 11

AWARENESS RETURNED SLOWLY, piece by agonizing piece. Every bit of me felt bruised and bloody, like I'd been taken apart piece by piece then haphazardly put back together.

So haphazardly, in fact, that it felt like there were still parts missing.

I instinctively twitched my fingers and toes, and though it hurt like blazes, they all responded. And yet, the notion that things had changed, that things were missing, grew.

I opened my eyes, only to be met with utter darkness. For an instant, panic surged, then the darkness gave way to silver glistening in a sea of black.

Stars, no longer stained by the bloody hue of the moon.

I wearily—carefully—rubbed my forehead, though it didn't ease the pounding ache, and looked around. I was still lying on Kaia's leg, my feet touching the end of her nostrils, her warm breath washing up my legs. She remained asleep, and though her thoughts were still and distant, I could still hear them.

What I couldn't hear was the other drakkons.

I sat so abruptly, pain hit in a wave and doubled me over. I clasped my arms over my stomach and rocked back and forth, breathing deeply in an effort to control not only the agony but also the soft "What the fuck have I done?" litany running through my mind.

Footsteps approached, and I forced myself to look up. My vision swam, briefly blurring the figure, but it was very clearly female, not male.

The Prioress, not Damon.

Disappointment—and perhaps a touch of anger—washed much of the pain away. "Where is he?"

She stopped just shy of the circle we remained encased in and raised an eyebrow, her expression tolerantly amused. "I'm so pleased to see you, too."

"I haven't the energy for word play right now—where is he?"

"The scribes weren't working in this place, so he returned to Esan in order to report to your parents."

It wasn't a lie... but it wasn't the entire truth, either. "Why didn't you go?"

"Your appreciation of my presence and my efforts truly makes my heart swell."

I sucked in another breath and tried to calm the anxious anger rising within. "Sorry, I didn't mean to sound so—"

"Rude? Ungrateful? Curt?"

I waved a hand, the movement weak. "All of the above."

She sniffed and crossed her arms. "How do you feel?"

"Weirdly incomplete... and I can't hear the other drakkons. Are they okay?"

"They're all alive, if that's what you're asking. Whether they are all okay is something we will only know when they wake."

"Kele and Hannity?"

"Also alive. They, like their drakkons, stir, but have not as yet woken. I expect they will soon."

"If the drakkons stir, why can't I hear them?"

"Because, dear child, you bound your being—your essence—to *your* drakkon. Any ability to hear the others has now likely gone. We did warn there would be a cost, remember, and if that is the only loss you face, then you will have escaped lightly. Can you flame?"

I reached for my inner flames, but pain rose instead, clubbing me so hard that tears sprang to my eyes. I gasped and bent over, once again clutching my stomach even though the pain was absolutely everywhere.

"That would be a no, then," the witch replied, somewhat dryly. "Though I do suspect it's too soon to be testing the range and limitations of the merging. You will need more time for flesh and essence to heal."

"We haven't got time," I ground out, rocking back and forth again in an effort to control the waves of agony still rolling through me.

"The spells performed here tonight are the most powerful spells Angolan witches have ever done, and the fact all survived is a miracle. The bigger miracle will be them working as designed. Remember, while the base spell was listed in our archives, the framework we built it upon was never tested, hence our harping on the dangers involved."

I nodded. There was nothing I could say, nothing I could do now, except hope. "Is Damon okay? I'm aware blood magic takes a serious toll on the body—"

"Indeed, it does, which is why I stepped in to finish the spell. We could not afford to have him drained to the point of utter exhaustion. Not now."

I frowned. "Why not now?"

She waved the question away. "He will tell you when he is able."

"A reply he's made multiple times and, let me tell you, one I'm getting mighty tired of hearing."

"There are many sorts of evil in this world, young woman, and sometimes it takes the form of a king who believes there is nothing more divine in these lands than his right to rule."

Which was basic confirmation that Aric *was* behind whatever was going on with Damon. "My mother's visions suggest it involves Damon's sisters as much as his father—do you deny that?"

"I neither deny nor confirm. It is not my place."

"But what harm can there be in at least joining the dots—"

"There will be no dots connected on *my* watch. As I have said, it is for Damon to tell you, and he is not likely to do so until the problem has been sorted, one way or another. Now, you should close your eyes and get more rest, while you still can. Darkness comes, and you must be prepared to fight."

"I can't fight without fire."

"You are more than your flame, young woman, and you jump to conclusions that are far from reality just yet. As I said, the spell appears to be successful, but it will take time for body and soul to heal. Only then will you and the drakkons be able to access old skills and new. Now, go to sleep."

Though I was desperate to question her further, her magic obviously still lingered within the circle, because my eyes closed, and I was soon fast asleep.

When I next awoke, Kaia's thoughts were alive in mine. Even though I'd sensed her the first time I woke, the relief that swept me was so fierce tears stung my eyes. I'd lost the other drakkons—and likely my ability to talk to any other animal, including Desta and my grey hawk, Veri—but at least I still had Kaia.

No feel fire, she said.

"Nor I. The witches believe it will take a little time for our bodies to recover."

Feel no heat within.

"I can't either, but it'll come." I had to believe that. Had to believe the risks we'd all taken were not for nothing. "Can you still talk to the other drakkons?"

Yes. They not happy. No fire.

I laughed softly but didn't reply as the Prioress returned. She didn't say anything, nor did she look at us. She stopped inches away from the circle, a knife held loosely in one hand and her other raised. After sprinkling what looked to be more herbs onto the ground, she began to spell. As the power lingering within the circle pulsed in time to the rhythm of her words, she raised the knife and sliced open the tip of her finger. Once the steel had been bloodied, she bent and dragged the point through the line of herbs and jewels. The power remaining within the circle bled through the fine gap she'd created, and the air seemed suddenly colder.

She straightened and wiped her blade clean on a cloth. "You may both leave the circle now, but try not to do anything too strenuous for the next twenty-four hours. As I have said, your essences need time to embrace the abilities we have cross-pollinated."

I climbed from Kaia's claws and walked a little unsteadily toward her. "Do we have to stay here? Or can we return to Esan?"

"I do not think any of us want to remain here longer

than necessary. Besides, we will need your guidance back through the tunnels."

I stepped past her, heading for my clothes. Behind me, Kaia rose and stretched. *Am hungry.*

So was I. Famished, in fact. *She said not to hunt.*

Am queen. Others hunt for me.

Can you order them to hunt for Yara and Rua too? They need to rest as well.

Will. They want flame. Won't risk losing.

I shivered my way into my clothes, then tugged on my boots, an exercise that left me exhausted and panting. Walking down the mountain would likely be a nightmare. As I laced up my coat, I met the Prioress's gaze and said, "I got the distinct impression from Damon that coming into Esan was not something you'd planned."

"You have more riders and drakkons to magic, do you not?"

"Well, yes, but—"

"Young lady, I am old. I need my comforts—bath, hot food, good conversation. There is none of those things to be found here."

For drakkons, perfect, Kaia commented. *Go now, see Gria.*

She rose and, moving at a far more cautious pace than normal, left the upper aerie. As Yara and Rua followed, I spotted Kele and Hannity getting dressed.

I slowly headed over, nodding at the two younger witches as they walked past to join the Prioress. Both looked pale and drawn, their faces almost skeletal. It suggested the Prioress hadn't stepped in for them, and I couldn't help but wonder again why she'd done so for Damon. There was something other than Kaia's size behind it; of that, I was sure.

I stopped in front of Kele and Hannity. They looked as crappy as I felt, which in some ways was comforting.

"Before you ask, I feel like I've been trampled by a herd of capra," Kele said. "Who fucking knew the mere act of breathing could hurt so much?"

"You've obviously never broken ribs." I glanced at Hannity. "And you?"

She grinned. "I can hear Rua. I can *talk* to her. Who cares if every bit of me is screaming in pain?"

"I care," Kele said. "Especially when I can't reach my fire. I hit a wall of pain every time I try."

"Apparently our 'essences' have to heal before we'll know if the transference really worked or not, and that may take twenty-four hours or more," I said. "In the meantime, we should get back to Esan and see what has happened while we've been gone."

"If they'd been attacked, we would have seen the smoke, at the very least." Hannity's gaze was on the aerie's entry. "But dawn rises, and the sky is clear."

I glanced over my shoulder. She was right, but that didn't help the deep-down uneasiness. "Kele, you lead. Hannity, keep close to our witches. I'll take rear guard."

Kele frowned. "Why the cautiousness? No one is going to attack us in the aerie, and the drakkons are no danger."

"I know. I just—" I stopped and shrugged.

Kele grimaced and glanced at Hannity. "Meaning, her gut is telling her trouble is closing in."

Hannity's eyebrows rose, amusement lurking. "And is her gut generally right?"

"Sadly, yes." She saluted me lightly, then gathered the now empty packs that had held the smoked white fin and headed across the vast, still-shadowed emptiness, making her way toward the ramp. Hannity walked over to the witches and asked them to follow her, then followed Kele across the aerie. I watched for a second, then walked to the very edge of the aerie's entrance, one hand on the wall to steady myself as the wind tugged at my hair and limbs. Esan glistened like a black jewel far below me, but in Mareritten, dust rose. They were on the move—and Esan would not see them. Not even the war room, lined as it was with long viewing tubes, could see that far into their lands.

The death I'd dreamed of was coming.

I needed to get home and warn my father.

I spun on my heel and headed for the exit ramp. The ruddy glow of the sands in the bottom cavern lent the air a deep warmth, but there was a chill growing inside of me now, and it was all I could do not to push into a run. The Prioress had warned me not to do anything strenuous, and the last thing I needed was to endanger the healing and perhaps destroy the bonding.

Could it be destroyed, without destroying us both?

I didn't know, and I certainly didn't want to find out.

But not knowing how well it had—or hadn't—worked was so damn *frustrating*.

I flexed my fingers, but no fire warmed their tips. I yet again reached for my flames, and yet again hit that wall of pain. I swore and closed my eyes, breathing slow and deep until the pain fractured and slipped away. Maybe it was my imagination, but that seemed to happen a whole lot faster this time than it had only minutes ago.

We reached the breeding cavern, and Gria ambled over for her ridge scratch. I complied but could see the confusion flicker through her eyes. Once again, a deep sense of loss swept me. I didn't regret the decision I'd made, because it was necessary and needed, and yet... I gulped and glanced at Kaia. *Have you told her the spell that shared my fire took my ability to speak to her?*

Have. Said she wants fire, but also wants to speak. Should still understand your talk because we kin.

And there was only one way to test that…. "You'll be able to speak to your own rider, Gria, if that's what you want when you're older."

Wants, came Kaia's amused reply.

I glanced at her again. *Will the other drakkons?*

Five more come.

Which would give us eight fire-breathing drakkons *if* we could find more stregas willing to become kin. Presuming, of course, the spell did work as it was intended. I scratched Gria's eye ridge a final time, then hurried after the other women. But as I neared the tunnel, I spotted the harness hanging on the wall, and instinct twitched.

I stopped. "Kaia, would you mind terribly if I put the harness on you?"

Why necessary?

"The Mareritt are coming—I saw the dust of their movement rising from the upper cavern—and we may not have time to get back up here. If you're wearing the harness, you can come to us."

We still fight if no flame?

"Yes. I have arrows and I can get spears. Both will kill the Mareritt, as will your claws."

Like this plan. Do.

I glanced at the younger drakkons. "Yara and Rua? Can I harness you?"

Both say yes.

"Thank you," I said to them both.

I grabbed the harnesses from the hooks and carried them over. I started with Rua and worked my way around.

By the time I'd finished Kaia, I was shaking with exhaustion and dripping with sweat.

So much for not doing anything too strenuous.

I gave all three drakkons an eye scratch, then finally left. I'd expected to be well behind the others but found them waiting for me near the exit onto the mountain path.

The Prioress looked me up and down, then sniffed. "You look like shit. Take this."

She thrust a brown bottle at me. I accepted it somewhat dubiously. "What is it?"

"Strength potion, and you'll be needing it. Trust me on that."

I raised an eyebrow and gulped it down. It tasted like mud. *Sour* mud. I blanched, and the Prioress chuckled. "Has that effect on some, but it's always a good sign. Means it's likely to be more potent in your system."

"Meaning it's likely to be less so in mine because I didn't react that way?" Hannity asked.

"Maybe. And maybe it just means your system needs less boosting." The Prioress accepted the bottle back from me, then glanced at Kele. "Off your butt, young woman. We need to get moving again. I feel breakfast a-calling me."

With a slight groan, Kele obeyed. The two younger witches followed her through the crooked exit, with Hannity behind them.

The Prioress didn't follow, instead drawing a scribe quill and tablet from her pack and shoving them toward me. "Damon will have made arrangements with your father to have rooms ready for us all, but it would be best if you warn him we're on our way and will brook no delay in reaching our accommodation. If he wants a report, we shall provide one once rested."

And that was an order, not a suggestion. I raised my

eyebrows but, as she followed the others, nevertheless obeyed.

Damon did say the Prioress would likely demand rest on arrival, came the response. *Was the spell successful?*

Unknown. I'll explain when I get there.

No, you'll explain once you've rested. Rion can wait.

Meaning it was Mom manning the scribe, not my father. *Tell him the Mareritt are on the move, and if the dust was any indication, there's a lot of them.*

I will. I'll also arrange for a meal and shamoke to be waiting for you in your room.

Thanks, Mom. I paused briefly. *Is Damon there?*

He went to rest after reporting to us last night. Haven't seen him so far today.

Which, given it was still relatively early, wasn't really surprising. And yet, that annoying spark of suspicion rose within me again. I just couldn't shake the feeling that something else was happening. That the witches, while they were definitely here to help us, were very much involved in whatever else Damon was doing.

If you do see him, tell him I'm on my way home.

But even as I wrote that, I knew she wouldn't be seeing him.

And Vahree only knew how damn frustrating it was to be getting these snippets of suspicion without getting anything in the way of answers.

The cursor blinked out. I tucked the quill and tablet into a pocket and started after the others. It was a long and tiring journey down the mountain, made worse by the torrential rain that swept in when we were halfway down. By the time we reached the gates, I was soaking wet, freezing cold, and barely able to remain upright.

I wasn't the only one. Kele looked bone weary, Hannity

was shivering so badly her teeth chattered, and the two younger witches looked like death warmed up. Even the Prioress looked pale and gaunt.

Two guards met us on the other side of the gate and immediately escorted the Angolans away. I told Kele and Hannity to rest until I contacted them, then forced my feet on, crossing the courtyard to the palace. Men and women scurried about, preparing for the upcoming attack and the possible evac of noncombatants. I had no doubt there would be the same hive of activity happening across Esan's many levels.

I made it up the palace's outside and inside steps without collapsing, but I was barely moving by the time I reached my suite. It was only the desperate need to see my husband that kept me going.

I stumbled through the door, then closed it behind me and just stood there, my gaze sweeping the suite, searching for the man whose scent lingered. He wasn't here but the supposed "test" circle was, and it was clearly pulsing and active.

It also looked nothing like the circle he'd encased Kaia and me in.

I forced my feet on, stumbling across the room until I hit the spell's protective barrier. Energy rippled across its surface and stung my skin. I stepped back, shivering, wondering what in Vahree's name this thing did.

I didn't know, but I'd wager the Prioress did. If I'd had the energy, I would have stormed over to her guest room and demanded answers, even knowing the futility of doing so.

But I didn't, so I stumbled over to the seating area, where Mom's promised meal and shamoke awaited. After consuming enough of both to feed a drakkling, I stripped off, then stepped onto the bed platform and fell into bed, where I slept like the dead, undisturbed by dreams of doom.

And yet the awareness of its fast approach continued to pulse through me when I finally awoke.

For several minutes, I didn't move. I didn't even open my eyes. I just listened to the external noises of a palace going about its business. Nothing in those sounds suggested a problem, let alone an attack—and we were prepared for the latter—so why did the certainty of death keep growing?

Had the spells done something strange to my other strega skills? In taking away my ability to speak to all other animals, had it somehow strengthened by hereto unheralded seer skills? I wasn't—and never would be—as powerful as Mom, even when her skills were playing hard to get, but it would at least explain the deep knot of wrongness growing in my gut.

What I didn't hear, of course, was the background chatter of birds, coursers, and all the other animals that inhabited the palace and the skies. I hadn't always acknowledged that chatter—hadn't even been aware of it most of the time—but now that it was gone, it had left a huge well of silence that could not be ignored.

I pushed back the brief welling of... not regret, but certainly grief... for all that I'd lost and reached again for my flames. Once again, I hit that wall of pain. This time, though, I did at least feel some warmth behind it.

Whether the wall dividing me from it would ever fall was a question yet to be answered.

I also feel heat, came Kaia's response. *It deep in gut. Can't reach.*

The fact you can feel its presence has to be a good sign. I flicked off the bedcovers and swung my feet onto the floor. Damon remained nothing more than a spicy scent in the air, and the symbols he'd etched onto the floor continued to send warm shadows pulsing through the room. *Did the knowledge on how to use it come through to you?*

It strange. Your memories in mine. I see what you did, how you use.

All my memories?

Flame related.

Which made sense. By transferring that particular set, they were giving Kaia and the other drakkons a base on which they could more quickly learn the best way for them to deploy flame. How the witches had plucked those specific memories free, I had no idea, but it did at least explain why my brain still felt on fire, even if the overall body ache had drastically decreased.

How are Yara and Rua?

Yara feels heat, frustrated can't use.

I frowned. *And Rua? Is she okay?*

Mind heated. Not sure.

Mind heated? I had no idea what that meant, but maybe the Prioress would. *Is she lucid?*

What lucid?

Talking clear in her mind.

Is young. Young not always lucid.

I smiled, even though concern flickered through me. If Rua wasn't entirely lucid, did that mean Hannity wasn't? She'd probably looked the worst of all of us last night. *Warn them that when the fire does come through, they'll need to practice somewhere where they can't hurt anyone else. Either on wing or in the upper cavern.*

Already up in cavern, waiting.

And you?

On wing, hunting with Gria. She hungry, I hungrier.

May the capra be fat and lazy for you both, then.

Are. Had two already. Need more.

My stomach rumbled as she said that, despite the fact I'd eaten more than I normally did last night. I climbed down from the platform and walked over to the scribe quill, ordering a pottage, breads, and cheese as well as shamoke, then headed into the bathroom for a much-needed bath. The food arrived as I was getting dressed, and my father was right behind it.

I sat on the bench to pull on my boots. "You didn't have to come here—I was going to report once I'd had breakfast."

"I may be king, but not even I dare disobey the queen. She ordered me to check on your condition, and check I will." His gaze scanned me as I approached. "You look... different."

I frowned and poured us both a shamoke. "Different how?"

"More alive." He accepted his cup with a nod, his brows creased. "There's this odd air of strength about you now that wasn't there before."

I raised my eyebrows, amusement lurking. "Are you saying I previously exuded an air of weakness?"

He laughed. "Of course not. It's just different —stronger."

"More drakkon-y?" I picked up a bowl and motioned to the pottage.

He shook his head. "Perhaps. Was the spell successful?"

"Well, we're all alive, so that's something." I paused. "Have you had any report from the barracks? Kaia told me Rua is feeling off, and if she is, maybe Hannity is."

"No, but I can order a check done, if you wish."

I waved the suggestion away. "It's probably best if I take the Prioress down there, given it might have something to do with the spell."

He nodded. "Do the drakkons now have fire?"

"Not yet. The Prioress said our 'essences' need to heal before we know whether the transfer was successful or not."

"Do you still have fire?"

"No."

"That is not a good development."

"As the Prioress said to me, I am more than my flames." I shrugged, a movement that belied the inner uncertainty. "I'm still a captain, and I have no intention of giving the position up until I absolutely have to."

A smile tugged at his lips. "Given it seems Aric is about to hit our doorstep again, that may not be anytime soon."

"Then you know where he is?"

"Not specifically."

"And Gayl? She's not been able to enlighten you?"

"Gayl has disappeared."

I just about choked on my pottage. "How is that even possible?"

"I don't know. Perhaps we should ask Damon. Where is he, by the way?"

"That is a great unknown. I take it you've received no reports of either of them leaving?"

His frown deepened. "No, and I would have."

"Then perhaps it has something to do with the active spell over there."

I pointed toward it with my chin, and he glanced over his shoulder. "What spell?"

I frowned. "You can't see the markings on the floor?"

"No." He glanced at me. "If there's a spell, perhaps it was a deliberate choice of his to make it visible to only you."

"Possible, though I was seeing it before he completed it. I guess we can question him about it when he gets back."

If he got back.

"Is it worth questioning the Prioress?"

"You can certainly try. I got absolutely nowhere. What room is she in, by the way?"

"The Blacknut suite."

Blacknut being a tree that emitted a spicy, citrus scent that seemed to linger even when the tree was harvested and made into furniture. I finished my pottage, then scooped up some more. It seemed Kaia wasn't the only one who couldn't fill her stomach. "What's Mom doing?"

"Waiting on news from Katter. Their scouts reported ship remains and bodies being washed up on Green Bay, and they've sent a small team to investigate." He grimaced. "She won't leave until she hears back from him."

My breath caught. "You don't think Garron is amongst them, do you?"

"I can't see why he would be, given he was land defense, not ship."

"Maybe they managed to get a few ships out of the harbor before the riders destroyed it."

"If that *is* true, then this wreckage suggests they didn't get far." He drained his shamoke and rose. "I had best get back."

I rose with him. "How much closer have the Mareritt gotten?"

"A couple of miles out by all accounts, and their numbers are vast according to the scouts who've managed to get close." He paused. "We've lost contact with Marcon's team, though."

"Marcon is too canny a soldier to be caught unawares by the Mareritt." Though it was also true that even the canniest of soldiers could be overwhelmed by sheer force of numbers. I really hoped that wasn't the case. "If they're so fucking close, we should be able to see—"

"They're using a wide sheet of fog to cover their precise location and numbers," he cut in.

I swore softly. "Does the fog roll up to the wall?"

"Not yet."

"Meaning they'll have to break cover to attack us, and even if they do have more of those large mobile tubes with them, we should have ample warning."

"That is the hope." He dropped a kiss on my cheek. "You're to remain off duty for the rest of the day—your mother's order, but one I entirely agree with, even if I'm also aware you will discard it the moment you deem it necessary to do so."

I laughed and impulsively hugged him. "I do love you both; I hope you know that."

"Of course we do. Now, you'd best be letting this old man leave while you settle down and eat that mountain of food you have happening there. Anyone would think you've been given your drakkon's appetite."

"It'd just be my luck to get that and nothing else."

He laughed. "Túxn has smiled on you your entire life, Bryn. I'm thinking she's not about to abandon you now."

"And I hope she's listening to that comment and taking it as a compliment, not a challenge."

He left. I sat down and made my way through said mountain of food and finally felt the pangs of hunger subside. Once I finished the shamoke, I rose, grabbed my coat, then strapped on my sword and my knife. My gaze fell on my bow and quiver—abandoned up until now in favor of Mom's—and instinct twitched. I wasn't sure why, but given the continuing sense of doom pulsing through the background of my thoughts and the nearness of the Mareritt, I wasn't about to ignore it. I slung the quiver and bow across my back, then opened the door and walked around to the guest quarters, my footsteps echoing softly. My leg, I couldn't help but notice, no longer ached. Perhaps the transference had gifted me with some of Kaia's fast healing and it had finally settled those grumbling muscles.

The guard near the Blacknut suite saluted as I approached. "Is the Prioress in?"

"Yes, Lady Bryn."

"Thanks." I stopped in front of her door and knocked loudly. The sound echoed and, after a few seconds, steps approached. The door opened to reveal the Prioress in a loose brown gown, eating a slab of cheese on bread, looking much fuller in the face than the last time I'd seen her.

"Bryn," she said, seeming surprised to see me. "You're awake. Obviously. Do you wish to come in?"

"No, thanks. I've reports that both Rua and Hannity are overheating. I was wondering if you could come down to the military section and check Hannity for me."

She wrinkled her nose. "I'm not sure what I could do, given I'm a blood witch, not a healer—"

"What if her natural ability to control her inner flame has been disrupted by the spell?" I cut in. "What if the spell didn't fully transfer?"

"If it didn't, she will die. There is no spell that can prevent that. If she *is* running hot, then perhaps your best option would be to get a healer to her and get her core temperature down until her body and mind have had time to adjust."

I swore and thrust a hand through my still-wet hair, snaring several strands from the plait. "Where did Damon go? Did he take Gayl with him?"

"You know I will not—"

I raised my wrist and shoved up the coat's sleeve, showing her the bracelet he'd given me. "He said this was designed to protect me from Gayl's thoughts, but does it also prevent Aric from reading them? Because he's on his way here, and he's the only reason you could be so afraid of sharing Damon's current location."

"The gift runs through her mother's line, not Aric's. He cannot read minds, for which we are eternally grateful." She bit into her bread and contemplated me while she chewed. "Now, young woman, you had best go see to your friend. You will need their help with what comes."

"For Vahree's sake, will you lot stop speaking in riddles and just tell me the—"

I stopped, because the witch stepped back and slammed the door in my face. It was tempting, so damn tempting, to order the guard to batter it down, or, better yet, slice through the thing with my sword, but I resisted the urge to do either.

Mainly because her words had deepened the sense of doom gathering within.

I swore again, then spun on my heel and raced down the hall, taking the steps two at a time and racing out the doors. The wind clubbed me sideways, forcing me to slow to catch my balance. The air felt thick and heavy, and overhead, lightning flashed. I softly counted and barely reached three before thunder rumbled.

The storm was close, and it was big.

And that doom I sensed... it was as close as that storm. So close I could almost taste it.

I started toward the hospital, then stopped. Harnesses... I might have geared up the drakkons, but ours were still hanging on the hooks in the cavern. I swore yet again and ran for the store, quickly searching the shelves for the older-style climbing harnesses and eventually finding them stashed at the very back. I grabbed three, then continued on to the hospital, my heart beating so fast my chest ached. The day nurse looked up as I all but slammed into the reception area, her expression alarmed. "Is there a problem, Captain?"

"I need the services of a healer who can deal with a deep fever whose source may or may not be strega based."

She hesitated. "I think Riki might be the—"

"Summon him, now."

"*Her*," the nurse snapped, but nevertheless made the call.

I paced the floor as I waited, my body cold, still empty of the flames that generally kept me warm. The barrier remained in place, though at least pain no longer accompanied it.

"Captain Silva?" a cool voice behind me said. "There's a problem?"

I swung around. The woman was tall and blonde, with pale skin that suggested either she or her parents were not Arleeon born. "Yes, I have a soldier with a deep fever—"

"Was she caught in the recent downpour by chance?" Riki cut in. "Because we've a number of infantry personnel come down with hectic fevers over the last twenty-four hours, but the military hospital is far from overrun and more than capable of dealing with it."

Hectic fever was an unpleasant ague that came with wild swings in temperature along with chills and sweats. I'd had it once, and that was more than enough. "Yes, but what afflicts Hannity is likely linked to her strega fire ability. I need you to gather your kit and come with me."

It was an order, not a request, and she acknowledged it with a nod. "I'll be two minutes."

She disappeared back through the door, and I resumed my pacing. Riki returned on time, and, without a word, I spun and led the way out. It was a long journey down through the various tiers, one made longer by the growing depth of my inner anxiety. The guards at the entry point into the military section opened the gates as we neared; a third soldier waited on the other side and saluted as we entered.

"Commander Vaya has ordered me to escort you to Scout Gordan's bunkhouse."

Meaning my father had ordered it and Vaya had passed it on. There was no other way Vaya could have known I was coming down here.

"Thank you, soldier."

He saluted again, spun round, and marched off at a good clip. We hurried after him. The military section was basic in layout—four squarish quarters around a central rectangular core. The latter contained the mess, hospital, administration, and the commanders' and captains' accommodation. The closest two quarters contained the barracks for the regular soldiers, and the far one, those for scouts. The coursers were stabled behind them. I knew where Kele was quartered but had no idea where Hannity was, so it was lucky I didn't have to waste more time checking with admin.

We followed the wide path straight through to the core, then around to the left of the main admin building, and all around me, the preparations for attack were ongoing. The barracks, like everything else in Esan, were made of black stone, but many of their exteriors had been painted with various images and symbols representing the various squads housed within them. My squad—housed to the right—bore depictions of a gray hawk with flame coming from its claws. Kele's squad—housed in the section behind my squad's—were represented by a fiery courser. Hannity's group was in the rear left section, and the barracks' front wall bore a fiery fist.

There were several soldiers lounging out the front when we turned the corner, but they were all kitted up ready for action. They all snapped to attention as we approached.

"At ease," I said. "Is Hannity Gordan inside?"

"Aye, Captain," a lean man with a heavy red plait said. "We had the medics out to her early this morning, but I don't think she's any better."

"Do you know what they gave her, if anything?" Riki asked.

"Some sort of tea to bring her temperature down—"

"Meaning she was lucid at that point in time?" Riki cut in.

The lean man nodded. "She was also given a painkiller to take at four-hourly intervals. They said it was likely hectic fever, as it's going round, and she was soaked when she came."

"A natural assumption under normal conditions," Riki said. Her comment was aimed my way, even if she didn't look at me. "May we go inside?"

"Yes, ma'am." He opened the door, then stepped aside so we could enter.

I thanked and dismissed our guide, then followed Riki in. Like most of the barracks, this one held six beds, and five were empty. The sixth had privacy curtains drawn around, and even from here I could hear the restless stirring and occasional soft moan.

Hannity really wasn't in a good state.

Riki tsked and hurried over, sweeping aside the curtain, then knelt beside the bed and touched her fingers either side of Hannity's forehead. She didn't say anything, but energy flickered from her to Hannity via her touch, meaning she was one of our mind healers.

After a few moments, she sat back on her heels and looked at me, her expression alarmed. "What on earth happened to her? Her biometry is all over the place, and partially filled with an essence not her own."

"The three of us underwent a spell to share our strega fires with the drakkons."

"With the—" She stopped and shook her head. "Why on earth would anyone in their right mind want to do that?"

"Because it might be the only way to defeat what comes."

She snorted. "We've been defeating the Mareritt—"

"I'm not talking about the Mareritt, but rather the gilded riders."

"Those people on metal birds? There's not enough of them to be a threat to us, surely?"

"On that, you would be wrong." I waved a hand toward Hannity. "Can you help her?"

Her gaze returned to the younger woman, and she wrinkled her nose. "Her body fights what has been done to it, so I can't give any guarantees. But if I can force her into a coma and get her core temperature down, it should help her body's natural healing ability."

An ability that had, hopefully, been enhanced with Rua's innate fast healing. "Do that then, please, and if you could stay here and keep an eye on her—"

"Indeed, because the next couple of hours will tell the tale of survival or not. But I'd be checking on the third member of this group if I were you."

"I'm about to, but thank you."

She nodded and swung her kit from her back. I hung a climbing harness on the nearby clothes hook, then left Riki to it, providing a quick update to Hannity's bunkmates before hurrying over to the next quadrant and Kele's quarters. There was no one sitting outside and little noise coming from within.

Thankfully, she was not only awake but sitting on her bunk reading. She glanced up as I entered and, to my relief, looked her normal self aside from the few wisps of pain still haunting her gaze. "Bryn, what on earth are you doing here?"

"I came to see how you were faring."

"Why? What's happened?"

I sat down on the edge of the bed and grimaced. "Hannity's not doing well."

"Ah fuck, that explains Yara's comments about Rua."

"What affects one affects the other," I said grimly. "If nothing else, this confirms that the spells did bind us to our drakkons."

"Won't do either race much good if for every two we bind we lose one." She put her book down. "Is there anything the medics can do?"

"There's a specialist healer with her now."

"Then there is nothing either of us can do except pray. While we wait, you want to grab some grub? I know the mess is not up to palace standards but—"

I laughed and slapped her leg. "I lived here for more than ten years, remember. It was only after the marriage declaration that I went back."

And reluctantly at that.

She grinned and bounced to her feet. "Let's go eat... why are you clutching climbing harnesses?"

"Because we left ours in the cavern, and I think it best we keep them close in case we have to call in the drakkons and mount in a hurry."

Her eyebrows rose. "Is that instinct speaking or mere caution?"

"Hopefully the latter, but the Mareritt are moving toward us in numbers, and we need to be prepared for anything."

"Huh." She stepped into the harness and hauled it on. "When my roommates mock me for wearing it, I shall remind them that I ride a drakkon and they never will."

I laughed and, after slipping on my own harness, turned around and walked out, Kele close on my heels. I couldn't help noticing that the air felt thicker, more dangerous, and overhead, the dark skies were ominous and heavy.

"Looks like we're about to get a drenching," Kele commented. "Might want to pick up the pace a little, boss."

"We were told not to strain ourselves, remember," I said, almost absently, my gaze searching the skies, looking for... I had no idea what. But something was coming. Something bad.

As thunder boomed overhead with enough force to rattle nearby windows, something thick and round trailing fire behind it arced across the sky and exploded in the tier beyond the military zone.

A heartbeat later, the sirens sounded—and it wasn't just the normal alarm. It was the one that signaled *all* fighters to the wall.

Esan was under attack... and it was *big*.

CHAPTER 12

"GRAB YOUR WEAPONS," I said to Kele, and then ran toward the nearest steps leading up to the top of the battlements.

Another fireball flew overhead, exploding deeper in Esan. Screams now filled the air, almost smothering the broadcasting orders that all noncombatants should retreat to the underground caverns.

I raced up the steps two at a time, one of dozens doing the same. Organized chaos reigned on the wall; orders were being shouted, soldiers lined the wall while others hurried to their stations, and weapon runners raided stores to ready restocks. All the while, arrows and spears sang through the air, hitting stone and flesh with equal force. Soldiers screamed and went down, and medics scurried around, dragging the injured and the dead out of the way of the living.

I pushed toward my station; Sora, Jax, and Kerryn were already there, but there was no sign of the others as yet. I stopped beside Kerryn, leaned over the wall, and gasped.

The valley below was full of Mareritt.

There were at least five hosts of the bastards holding position at the far end of the valley, and they filled the air with arrows and spears, the latter flung using atlatls—a spear-throwing lever that gave greater velocity and distance.

But it was the Mareritt charging the wall that had my heart leaping into my throat. Not because of their numbers, though that was daunting enough, and not because of the multiple siege ladders being carried. We'd dealt with them before and would do so again.

No, it was the number of short metallic tubes they carried.

I could see at least thirty of them, and I dared say there were far more I couldn't see.

"Shoot at those carrying the tubes," I yelled, pointing. "They fire acid that eats through stone. We can't let them get near the wall."

I drew my bow, nocked an arrow, and released in one smooth motion, quickly losing sight of it in the forest of arrows coming back at us. Far below, Mareritt soldiers fell, their bodies trampled by those behind them; their weapons, however, were scooped up and carried forward.

Several more flaming orbs tumbled clear of the deep fog still covering the bulk of the lands beyond the valley and arced toward Esan. The air around us swept upward with enough force to snatch our plaits upright; fists of wind caught the fireballs and flung them down into the surging mass of Mareritt below, killing dozens.

But dozens made little difference when there was a sea of them.

A sea of them armed with tubes that were now being raised.

We needed fire. *I* needed fire.

And it still wasn't fucking there.

I swore, slapped a hand on Kerryn's shoulder to catch his attention, then said, "Go find Falconie—tell him to issue incendiary arrows and fire pots, because hitting those tubes with fire will destroy them."

"Your flames?"

"Currently absent. Go."

He turned and disappeared into the controlled chaos. We continued firing our arrows, hitting target after target but making little difference. On the wall around us, soldiers fell, some dead, some not, their positions immediately filled. Overhead, the skies cracked open and unleashed their full fury, the rain torrential, cutting visibility down to mere yards.

I wiped my sleeve over my face in a useless attempt to clear the water and kept on firing arrows until my quiver was empty. I tore it off, swung around, and yelled for a replacement. A soldier hurried forward with a fresh quiver and handed it to me, but as I swung back to face the wall, an arrow clipped my cheek, biting deep.

I swore, and deep inside, fury echoed. Not mine. Kaia's.

I come. I help.

NO, I yelled back mentally. *It's too dangerous, and we can't risk undoing the spell.*

You risk life.

I'm not going to die, Kaia.

Can't promise.

There is revenge to be had. I'm going nowhere until that is done.

Go nowhere after.

I certainly don't plan to. Stay. Please.

Her response was an unhappy grumble. I dropped the quiver at my feet, drew and nocked an arrow, and unleashed it into the wildness, aiming for the foe I could no longer see.

Orders were shouted across the wall for the beacons to be lit. It was pointless, us remaining in the dark, and it wasn't like the Mareritt didn't know where we were. All they had to do was push forward until they hit the damn... I stopped as a shudder ran through the stone under my feet.

The sense of doom sharpened.

"They're attacking the wall's base," came Falconie's shout from farther down the line. "Soldiers, aim down. Earth mages, repair. Air mages, attack."

As the air abruptly shifted direction and plunged downward, Kerryn returned, two men carrying a fire pot and another a large cache of arrows wrapped with oil-soaked cloth. We weren't the only ones receiving them—it was happening along the length of the wall.

Another shudder ran through the stone. I grabbed an arrow, plunged the head and the soaked cloth just below it into the pot, then nocked it, leaned over the wall, and fired. As it shot down, I saw the shadows. Mareritt on ladders.

"They're scaling," I shouted, plunging another arrow into the fire and shooting it down. Again and again, I repeated the process, until my arms and shoulders ached, and my fingers burned. Not from my fire, but rather the flames dripping from the arrows.

And still the Mareritt climbed.

The wind battered the ladders, sending some toppling while ripping multiple other Mareritt free, smashing them into the steep sides of the mountains on either side of us.

It didn't stop them.

The stone under our feet pulsed harder, the power so strong it burned through the soles of my boots. Our witches, fighting the acid that ate into the base of the wall.

Lightning cracked down, hitting a tower to my right. It exploded, spearing deadly shards of stone into the air. Men and women went down screaming, some dead, others crawling away; soldiers stepped into their positions and kept on firing.

Oil pots were levered onto the wall, the boiling liquid poured over the edge. Screams rose as Mareritt flesh was burned and melted.

And still they came, uncaring and determined.

Another shudder ran through the stone, this time more violent. The earth mages were not winning the war against the acid....

"Zara, get your teams up to the water—" The rest of Falconie's order was lost to the chaos that surrounded us.

Dead, I thought, though I never saw him fall.

More fiery orbs erupted from the distant blanket still covering much of the wasteland. Not one, not two, but at least a dozen, burning through the weeping, turbulent air so fast they were little more than streaks of ruddy light. Their speed wasn't natural—it was mage enhanced. Had to be. Even the most powerful ballista or catapult ever built wasn't capable of casting items through the air that fast.

The wind rose to meet them; it stopped some, but at least five were pushed through by the magic that surrounded them. They tumbled over our heads and continued with unnatural speed past the military and tiered living sections.

I spun, grabbed an arrow and lit it, then drew back and released. It cut through the air, hit an orb, and exploded on contact. The orb wobbled briefly, then the magic propelling it surged, and it flew on.

Air chased after them, three thick fingers that caught one orb and tossed it back into the valley and the Mareritt. The rest flew on, sweeping upward, their target clearly the second wall. Which made no sense. Why destroy that when they had to first get through this first one—and it was far from falling, even if the shudders running through it were growing.... A stream of heat sizzled past my cheek and splashed onto the stone several feet away. Acidic shit—or at least, the Mareritten version of it.

The rain was slowing but not stopping it eating into the stone.

I swore, doused another arrow, then leaned over the wall and fired down. And saw, in the few seconds before it disappeared into the storm-clad darkness, the tube the Mareritt on the ladder was holding.

They weren't using the ladders to breach us. They were simply a means of getting the deadliest of their weapons closer.

I shouted a warning to everyone and ordered more oil to be poured over the wall. Pots were tipped over along its length and arrows fired into its flow, igniting the liquid and everything in its path. The stench of burning flesh filled the air despite the wind and the rain, and burning humanoid figures lit the ground far below, some moving, some not.

Then the alarm sounded again, this time one long wail of noise that echoed through my brain and had my heart racing. Evacuation. They were ordering an evacuation....

Not of this wall. Of the other.

I swung around and watched, helpless, as the four remaining fiery orbs smashed into the war room and the attached administration building.

For several heartbeats, nothing happened.

Then the entire building exploded, jettisoning deadly shards of black stone into the air.

For too many seconds, I could only stare in horror as destruction rained around us.

Then I screamed. Screamed like I never had before. Screamed in horror and pain and loss.

Something within me broke, and fire erupted from every pore, turning me from a being of flesh into something far more dangerous and incorporeal, if only for the briefest of moments. Deep inside me, another roar echoed, and the heat that burned my mind said Kaia had found her flame.

We come, she said. *We burn.*

Hit the ones on ladders first. My mind voice was calm, controlled—everything my heart and soul wasn't. *They have acid tubes, so be fast.*

Flames explode tubes.

And explode they fucking would. Fire erupted from every pore, and curses echoed either side of me. I paid them no heed, trying to concentrate on control, on remembering *how* to control, as I leaned far over the wall and directed all the fury burning through directly down its side. It was a blanket of fire that lit the rain-soaked air and shone brightly off the multiple tubes carried by the Mareritt on ladders below. I hit them, hit the tubes, furiously, gleefully, cindering flesh and exploding the cylinders.

Then the drakkons swept in; two, not three.

They opened their mouths and roared, but the sound was chased by fire, a thick, deadly stream that cindered everything in their path. The Mareritt on their ladders desperately shifted position and tried to re-aim, but drakkon flame caught them in midmovement and cindered them.

It cindered combatants on the wall, as well.

I pushed upright and ordered an evac. The shout went up and down the line, and soldiers began to run for the various steps. The deadly rain of arrows and spears continued, but none touched me. None could. My flames were a wall of heat that surrounded me, cindering anything that close.

Control, where the fuck was control? Why the hell had I—

The Prioress's words rose like ghosts: *the binding might make it necessary for drakkon and rider to act as one fighting unit to be at their most powerful.*

Perhaps what she'd been talking about was *control.*

Kaia, I shouted, *land so I can mount you. It'll help control our joint flames. Tell Yara.*

She did so, then swooped overhead, thrusting her claws forward as she landed, scouring the black stone. I ducked under her wing and scrambled up her leg, quickly seating and clipping on. She crouched, then launched, her wings pumping hard as she fought for height. The rain of arrows and spears continued, thudding into her leathery wings and bouncing from her scales. Her spines protected me from the torrent of wood, which was a good thing, given the moment I'd mounted, my shield of fire evaporated.

I was once again in control.

Right, I said grimly. *Let's send these fucking bastards to Vahree's realm.*

Kaia roared in agreement and swooped down, the sharp movement throwing me back hard. The Mareritt on the ground below raised their weapons but never had the chance to unleash the acid; drakkon flame caught them, erased them, before their fingers ever touched the release.

Move on? she asked.

Move on, I confirmed.

Yara flew in and, wing tip to wing tip, they scoured the valley with their flames, ashing everything and everyone in their path. It wasn't in the Mareritten nature to run, and they fought until the flames hit them, sending a continuous deluge of arrows and spears and even acid into the air. I flung fire at anything that approached us, cindering again and again, until the mote in my eye popped, my brain ached, and only ashes lay on the valley floor far below. Until the utter fury that had consumed me bled away, leaving only grief.

I pushed it aside. I couldn't acknowledge it. *Wouldn't* acknowledge it. Not until I was sure, absolutely sure, that everyone I cared about, everyone I loved, had been in the war room.

Fog? came Kaia's question, her weariness a pulse I felt deep inside. *We search?*

I hesitated. The two of us—and no doubt Yara and Kele —were approaching our limits, and while I knew we shouldn't risk pushing beyond them when we were still healing from the aftereffects of the spell, we also couldn't leave without pressing into that fog, if only to see what had launched those flaming orbs and destroy it if we could.

Fly in, but don't go too low until we know what's there. And don't flame.

I signaled Kele what we were doing, though in truth it was no longer necessary, given her connection to Yara, then hung on as Kaia swooped down into the fog. Thankfully, it was just fog, and not the acidic stuff raised by the gilded riders' mages.

The air became cold and tacky, clinging to already soaked skin and clothes. Visibility was zero for too many seconds, then gradually, it lifted.

There were hundreds of Mareritt on the ground below. We flew over them, unseen, unheard, partially covered by their mages' unnatural fog. They appeared to be readying for retreat, perhaps to regroup and refortify. I couldn't see any of those mounted tubes we'd destroyed in the Barrain

Ghost Forest, suggesting that maybe they hadn't had time to rebuild. What I did see was a good dozen enormous catapults.

Have you and Yara enough flame to destroy them? I asked Kaia.

Can. Will. Then go home?

Then go home. And discover if I had anything to go home to.

Grief surged. I swallowed heavily, fighting it even as I knew it was a battle I would lose. Vahree had come to Esan and even now danced with the souls of our dead. Not even Túxn could forever stop his skeletal fingers reaching deep into the heart of my family.

Kaia swooped around, into the full force of the rain, and began her fire run, Yara behind and to one side. Their flames lacked power and heat now, but still set the catapults alight. I flamed down, spraying what fire I had left at those running or raising weapons. Then we were done and flying up through the foggy muck, into open air again.

I swiped at the blood pouring over my lashes, smearing its warmth through the torrent of rain streaming down my face, then sighed. *Kaia, could you tell Yara to land on the wall so Kele can dismount? Tell her to get some food and rest.*

And we?

I'll dismount in the palace courtyard.

Amongst the rubble. Amongst the dead.

Another sob rose. I pressed my fingers against my lips and refused to let it go.

Yara peeled away to land on a relatively empty section of wall, but we continued on, over the various levels. I didn't look down. I looked up. The wall still stood, relatively untouched, as did, rather incongruously, a small middle section of the building between the admin section and the war room. The section where our earth mages had run their tests and refashioned the stone, perhaps?

But the rest... I sucked in a breath that ended in a sob. The destruction was vast.

The war room and a good section of the administration building was simply gone. The few remnants of wall that remained were little more than black fingers reaching forlornly toward rumbling skies. Huge chunks of rubble scattered the ground on this side of the wall—and no doubt the inner courtyard—some so large they'd crushed the buildings they'd landed on. Smoke rose along the length of the wall, encasing the few sections that remained. But the wall remained manned, the injured were being removed, and the dead covered. Life might have been taken, but life continued on.

I sucked in another quivering breath and, as Kaia soared over the wall and readied to land, I detached my harness, then leaned forward and undid hers, letting it drop to the ground as she landed amongst the remnants of building and bodies.

I didn't look at the bodies.

I wasn't ready yet.

I slid down her leg, hitting the ground hard and staggering a little before I caught my balance. Then I scratched her eye ridge and bid her to go rest.

Will, she said wearily. *Burning take strength.*

It does, but it's worth it.

Is. We hunt riders now?

My lips twitched, despite the gathering wall of grief. *Maybe not today.*

But soon?

Yes.

I go. You eat. Must get strong. Revenge to be had.

I swallowed heavily and stepped out of her way. She crouched low, then leapt high, her wings pumping hard, stirring dust, ash, and humanity into the air.

Then I turned and resolutely walked back into the destruction. A familiar figure emerged from the gloom, and for a second, my heart leapt. Then reality stepped in and sent hope crashing.

It wasn't either of my parents. It was Jarin, our night shift commander. If he was here rather than down on the wall... I crossed my arms and refused to follow that thought through to the end.

I stopped and saluted, but the question I needed to ask was stuck in my throat, and I just stared at him.

For several long seconds, he didn't say anything. He just stood there, grief and sympathy in his eyes. Then he dropped his gaze and said, in a voice as broken as my heart, "I'm sorry, but it is my duty to inform you that you now bear the mantle of grand commander and—"

I didn't hear the rest of it. I didn't need to. Grief surged, and I screamed. Screamed in heartbreak and despair, and dropped hard to my knees, hugging my body and rocking back and forth as I sobbed. Deep, heartbreaking, all-encompassing sobs.

They were gone.

They were *all* gone.

Everyone that had meant anything to me, leaving me broken and alone.

Not alone, came Kaia's soft comment. *I here. Gria here. We kin.*

And *I* was now Queen. Grief could wait.

I sucked in a deep breath, then swiped grubby hands

across bloody tears and climbed to my feet. "Right, Commander, what needs to be done?"

He hesitated. "Are you—"

"I'm fine," I said flatly, even though I wasn't and maybe never would be. "We've people to look after and a war room to rebuild, and the sooner the better."

He nodded and turned, filling me in as we walked back across the courtyard.

We would rebuild.

And we would have our revenge.

I would have my revenge.

Even if it was the very last thing I ever did.

Wraith's Revenge (Feb 2023)

Killer's Kiss (Oct 2023)

Shadow's End (July 2024)

The Witch King's Crown Trilogy

Blackbird Rising (Feb 2020)

Blackbird Broken (Oct 2020)

Blackbird Crowned (June 2021)

Kingdoms of Earth & Air

Unlit (May 2018)

Cursed (Nov 2018)

Burn (June 2019)

The Outcast series

City of Light (Jan 2016)

Winter Halo (Nov 2016)

The Black Tide (Dec 2017)

Souls of Fire series

Fireborn (July 2014)

Wicked Embers (July 2015)

Flameout (July 2016)

Ashes Reborn (Sept 2017)

Dark Angels series

Darkness Unbound (Sept 27th 2011)

Darkness Rising (Oct 26th 2011)

Darkness Devours (July 5th 2012)

Darkness Hunts (Nov 6th 2012)

Darkness Unmasked (June 4 2013)

Darkness Splintered (Nov 2013)

Darkness Falls (Dec 2014)

<u>Riley Jenson Guardian Series</u>

Full Moon Rising (Dec 2006)

Kissing Sin (Jan 2007)

Tempting Evil (Feb 2007)

Dangerous Games (March 2007)

Embraced by Darkness (July 2007)

The Darkest Kiss (April 2008)

Deadly Desire (March 2009)

Bound to Shadows (Oct 2009)

Moon Sworn (May 2010)

<u>Myth and Magic series</u>

Destiny Kills (Oct 2008)

Mercy Burns (March 2011)

<u>Nikki & Micheal series</u>

Dancing with the Devil (March 2001 / Aug 2013)

Hearts in Darkness Dec (2001/ Sept 2013)

Chasing the Shadows Nov (2002/Oct 2013)

Kiss the Night Goodbye (March 2004/Nov 2013)

<u>Damask Circle series</u>

Circle of Fire (Aug 2010 / Feb 2014)

Circle of Death (July 2002/March 2014)
Circle of Desire (July 2003/April 2014)

Ripple Creek series
Beneath a Rising Moon (June 2003/July 2012)
Beneath a Darkening Moon (Dec 2004/Oct 2012)

Spook Squad series
Memory Zero (June 2004/26 Aug 2014)
Generation 18 (Sept 2004/30 Sept 2014)
Penumbra (Nov 2005/29 Oct 2014)

Stand Alone Novels
Who Needs Enemies (E-book only, Sept 1 2013)

Novella
Lifemate Connections (March 2007)

Anthology Short Stories

The Mammoth Book of Vampire Romance (2008)
Wolfbane and Mistletoe--2008
Hotter than Hell--2008

ABOUT THE AUTHOR

Keri Arthur, the author of the New York Times bestselling ***Riley Jenson Guardian series***, has written sixty novels–35 of them with traditional publishers Random House/Penguin/Piatkus—and is now fully self-published. She's won seven Australian Romance Readers Awards for Favourite Sci-Fi, Fantasy, or Futuristic Romance & the Romance Writers of Australia RBY Award for Speculative Fiction. Her Lizzie Grace series won ARRA's Fav Continuing Romance Series in 2022 and she has in the past won The Romantic Times Career Achievement Award for Urban Fantasy. When she's not at her computer writing the next book, she can be found somewhere in the Australian countryside taking photos.

for more information:
www.keriarthur.com
keriarthurauthor@gmail.com
Buy eBooks & Audiobooks directly from Keri & save:
www.payhip.com/KeriArthur

facebook.com/AuthorKeriArthur
x.com/kezarthur
instagram.com/kezarthur

www.ingramcontent.com/pod-product-compliance
Ingram Content Group UK Ltd.
Pitfield, Milton Keynes, MK11 3LW, UK
UKHW012101020625
6199UKWH00001B/20

9 781923 169319